從英文文法句型到短文寫作

零基礎 也能一步步攻克 大考英檢作文

作者 ● 黃瑜汎 / 孫雅玲
審訂 ● Dennis Le Boeuf / 景黎明

英文寫作不燒腦
跟著本書 STEP BY STEP
圖解文法與句型 **練句寫文更EASY！**

字詞 → 句子 → 段落 → 文章

從英文文法句型到短文寫作

零基礎 也能一步步攻克
大考英檢作文

作　　者	黃瑜汎／孫雅玲
審　　訂	Dennis Le Boeuf／景黎明
編　　輯	李盈瑩／Gina Wang
內文排版	葳豐企業有限公司／林書玉（解答）
插　　畫	高嘉玟／譚宇翔
封面設計	林書玉
製程管理	洪巧玲
發 行 人	黃朝萍
出 版 者	寂天文化事業股份有限公司
電　　話	+886-(0)2-2365-9739
傳　　真	+886-(0)2-2365-9835
網　　址	www.icosmos.com.tw
讀者服務	onlineservice@icosmos.com.tw
出版日期	2025 年 2 月 初版一刷

本書原書名《英文寫作高分班 Just Write It!》

版權所有 請勿翻印
郵撥帳號 1998620-0 寂天文化事業股份有限公司
訂書金額未滿 1000 元，請外加運費 100 元。
〔若有破損，請寄回更換，謝謝〕

國家圖書館出版品預行編目 (CIP) 資料

從英文文法句型到短文寫作：零基礎也能一步步攻克大考英檢作文 / 黃瑜汎, 孫雅玲作. -- 初版. -- [臺北市] : 寂天文化, 2025.02
　面；　公分
ISBN 978-626-300-293-7 (16K 平裝)

1.CST: 英語 2.CST: 作文 3.CST: 寫作法

805.17　　　　　　　　　　　　　　113018299

PART 1 英語句子的基本概念

前言   10

Unit 1　字彙：單位元素

1. 名詞   17
2. 冠詞   23
3. 動詞   24
4. 形容詞   33
5. 連接副詞   39
6. 數量限定詞   44
7. 一字多重詞性   46

Unit 2　句型架構

1. 基本結構   49
2. 五大基本句型   51
3. 七大常用句型   54
4. 多種句型混合套用   59
   - Quiz 1   60
   - Quiz 2   61

Unit 3　常見片語與連接詞

1. 動詞片語   65
2. 常見的關係連接詞組   71
   - Quiz 3   74

Unit 4　時態變化

1. 現在式的時態變化   77
2. 過去式的時態變化   79
3. 未來式的時態變化   81
4. 被動與時態搭配   83
   - Quiz 4   84
   - Quiz 5   85

PART 2 英文句子的種類與結構

Unit 5 直述句與疑問句

1. 直述句的肯定與否定用法 　89
   Quiz 6 　91
2. 疑問句的肯定與否定用法 　92
   Quiz 7 　96
3. 直述句改為疑問句 　97
   Quiz 8 　101

Unit 6 直接問句與間接問句

1. 何謂間接問句？ 　103
2. 直接問句與間接問句的結構差異 　104
   Quiz 9 　106
3. 如何將直接問句改為間接問句 　107
   Quiz 10 　109

Unit 7 主動與被動

1. 將主動句改為被動句 　111
   Quiz 11 　116
2. 被動句要注意的事項 　117
   Quiz 12 　121

Unit 8 祈使句

1. 何謂祈使句？ 　123
   Quiz 13 　127
2. 祈使句的附加問句 　128
   Quiz 14 　129
3. 如何將直述句改為祈使句 　130
   Quiz 15 　133

Unit 9 比較句型

1. 何謂比較句型？ … 135
2. 形容詞的比較級和最高級 … 137
3. 副詞的比較級和最高級 … 140
   Quiz 16 … 142
4. 比較句中的常見詞組與句型 … 143
   Quiz 17 … 147

Unit 10 對等連接詞

1. 常見的對等連接詞 … 149
2. 對等連接詞的重要性 … 153
   Quiz 18 … 154

Unit 11 從屬連接詞與副詞子句

1. 從屬連接詞 … 157
2. 副詞子句的功能 … 159
3. 副詞子句的用法 … 161
   Quiz 19 … 167

Unit 12 名詞子句

1. 名詞子句的特性與功能 … 169
   Quiz 20 … 171
2. 名詞子句的種類 … 172
   Quiz 21 … 177

Unit 13 形容詞子句

1. 如何形成形容詞子句（關係子句） … 179
   Quiz 22 … 182
2. 形容詞子句的功用和種類 … 183
   Quiz 23 … 191

Unit 14 分詞片語／分詞構句

1. 認識分詞構句 … 193
   Quiz 24 … 198
2. 分詞片語的用法 … 199
   Quiz 25 … 203

PART 3 英語段落寫作

Unit 15 段落結構的安排
1. 文體：敘述文和描寫文 — 207
2. 短文的架構 — 210
   Quiz 26 — 215

Unit 16 短文的開頭（起）：主題句
1. 撰寫主題句的技巧與注意事項 — 217
   Quiz 27 — 223

Unit 17 短文的中間（承、轉）：支持句
1. 撰寫支持句的技巧與注意事項 — 225

Unit 18 短文的結尾（合）：結論
1. 撰寫結論的技巧與注意事項 — 231
   Quiz 28 — 235

PART 4 中譯英的步驟與技巧

Unit 19 中譯英類型破解
1. 譯法的技巧轉換 — 239

Unit 20 中譯英的翻譯步驟
1. 步驟❶：句子的分割與組成 — 241
2. 步驟❷：決定主詞與動詞 — 243
3. 步驟❸：決定時態 — 248
4. 步驟❹：選擇句型 — 251
5. 步驟❺：文章修飾 — 257

Unit 21 中譯英的翻譯技巧
1. 直譯 — 259
2. 意譯 — 260
3. 直譯與意譯的交互運用 — 261
4. 不同譯法的轉換練習 — 263

Unit 22 中譯英的特殊用法與常犯錯誤
1. 與 to 有關的特殊用法 — 273
2. 「形容詞」與「副詞」的運用 — 275
3. 以 -ly 結尾的形容詞（副詞）— 276
4. 動詞變化 — 278
5. 時態混用 — 281
6. 語氣連接詞 — 282
7. 中英對應的易犯錯誤 — 283
- Quiz 29 — 284
- Quiz 30 — 285

PART 5 英文作文題型破解

Unit 23 英文作文的寫作步驟
1. 圖片申論 — 289
2. 短文銜接 — 294
3. 書信寫作 — 299
4. 書信寫作範例 — 306

Unit 24 英文作文的寫作技巧
1. 前後句的邏輯銜接 — 309
2. 轉換主旨的語氣轉折詞 — 313
3. 以關鍵字發展句型 — 316
4. 英文字詞的慣用搭配 — 319

Unit 25 英文寫作的常犯錯誤與對策
1. 完整的英文句子結構 — 325
2. 英文句的文法檢查 — 327
3. 易混淆的字詞 — 334
   Quiz 31 — 336
   Quiz 32 — 337

PART 6

十篇寫作練習與實例解析

1	我的嗜好	340
2	難忘的經驗	348
3	寫Email	357
4	昨天是情人節	366
5	母親節要到了	375
6	電腦	383
7	座右銘	392
8	給讀者的信	401
9	導盲犬	409
10	流浪狗	416

前言

英文寫作的基本概念

字詞 ➔ 句子 ➔ 段落 ➔ 文章

　　英文文法可以協助學習者有系統地縮短語言學習的過程，是一套有規則可循，並且符合邏輯思考的語言學習技巧。也因此，英文寫作不能憑一己之好或隨性地組合字詞，連接句子，或是隨意地使用逗號、句點，甚或加入語氣轉折詞。

　　英文句的結構嚴謹，**句子開頭第一個字母一定大寫，句尾結束一定加句點、問號或驚嘆號**等，才是完整的英文句。在句子的開頭與結尾句點之間，要以適當的文法做連接，字與字之間的關係按照詞性有一定的組合方式。

　　要將兩句以上的英文句子做連接，也有一定的方法。若選擇區分主句與子句，須先決定主句與子句的邏輯關係，是對比關係（雖然……但是……）？因果關係（因為……所以……）？還是假設關係（如果……那麼……）？接著再選擇句子連接方式，是對等連接？還是附屬連接？不同的連接方式需搭配不同的文法規則。

　　相信讀者過去都曾經學過這些文法，但是若沒有事先在腦中建立一套完整的文法概念，可能只能隨機零散地使用。因此，本書希望讀者在閱讀以下章節前，能在腦中建立這樣的架構：英文寫作是從**字詞**發展成為**句子**，再發展成為**段落**，進而形成一篇**文章**（字詞 ➔ 句子 ➔ 段落 ➔ 文章）。

　　對英文句的基本結構和英文單字的詞性不熟悉，不但不容易寫出正確又有變化的英文句，閱讀時也無法理解文法難度稍高的句子。下面的例子可以說明文法如何幫助我們從一句話發展成一個段落。讀者應該在初級文法學過英文簡單句的結構：「主詞＋動詞」，讓我們一起來看看如何利用詞性幫助我們進行英文寫作。

STEP 1：簡單句

1　英文簡單句

主詞 ＋ 動詞

1. Birds sing.　　　　　　　　　　　　鳥兒唱歌。
2. The wind blows.　　　　　　　　　　風在吹。

2　加入副詞修飾動詞

主詞 ＋ 動詞 ＋ 副詞
（修飾動詞）

1. Birds sing beautifully.　　　　　　　鳥兒優美地唱歌。
2. The wind blows gently.　　　　　　　風輕輕地吹拂。

3　加入形容詞修飾主詞

形容詞 ＋ 主詞 ＋ 動詞 ＋ 副詞
（修飾名詞）

1. Blue birds sing beautifully.　　　　　藍鳥們優美地唱歌。
2. The south wind blows gently.　　　　南風輕輕地吹拂。

STEP 2：連接句子

1　連接句子：加入對等連接詞 and 將兩句合為一句

子句 ＋ and ＋ 子句

① Blue birds sing beautifully, and the south wind blows gently.

> 藍鳥優美地唱歌，南風也輕輕地吹拂。

2　連接句子：加入附屬連接詞 when 將兩句合為一句

子句 ＋ when ＋ 子句

① Blue birds sing beautifully when the south wind blows gently.

> 當南風輕輕地吹拂，藍鳥優美地唱歌。

3　連接詞與副詞的加入

主句 ＋ 副詞 ＋ 附屬子句

1. 可另外加入一個主句，再將對等連接詞與附屬連接詞並用，可以表達更多不同的內容。
2. 還可以加入副詞 especially 修飾由 when 所帶出的兩個子句；這兩個子句以 and 作連接。

① I enjoy the spring especially when blue birds sing beautifully and the south wind blows gently.

主句　　　　　　　修飾 when 帶出來的子句　　　附屬子句

> 我很喜歡春天，特別是當藍鳥優美地唱歌，而南風也輕輕吹拂時。

STEP 3：段落完成

1　加入轉折副詞 however

主句 ＋ however . . .

在句子後面加入轉折副詞 however，將想表達的意念繼續延伸，成為兩句或三句話，甚至可成為一小段落的文章。

① I enjoy the spring especially when blue birds sing beautifully and the south wind blows gently. However, I am very sad.

> 我很喜歡春天，特別是當藍鳥優美地唱歌，南風也輕輕吹拂時。但是，我卻感到非常悲傷。

2　再加入附屬連接詞和轉折副詞

主句 ＋ because / moreover . . .

加入附屬連接詞 because 及轉折副詞 moreover，又可將文章段落往下發展，表達更多想法。

① I enjoy the spring especially when blue birds sing beautifully and the south wind blows gently. However, I am very sad because I just broke up with my boyfriend. Moreover, I can't get him out of my mind.

> 我很喜歡春天，特別是當藍鳥優美地唱歌，南風也輕輕吹拂時。但是，我卻感到非常悲傷，因為我剛跟男友分手，而且我無法忘記他。

上述八個概念示範了如何加入不同詞性，將短句組合成段落。不知讀者是否注意到，不同的連接方式，有不同的寫作方法，標點符號與句型結構也不相同。本書接下來的章節，將按照上述步驟的邏輯，逐步介紹讀者如何進行「字詞 ➔ 句子 ➔ 段落 ➔ 文章」的寫作步驟。

PART 1

英語句子的基本概念

Unit 1　字彙：單位元素

Unit 2　句型架構

Unit 3　常見片語與連接詞

Unit 4　時態變化

Unit 1 字彙：單位元素

Warm-up 暖身

閱讀以下段落，找出所有的主詞和動詞。

One night when Miranda was watching TV, a burglar broke into her house. The threatening burglar shouted loudly, "Don't move or I will hurt you." Miranda was so scared that she was shaking all the time.

暖身題解答

One night when <u>Miranda</u> <u>was watching</u>
　　　　　　　　主詞　　　動詞
TV, <u>a burglar</u> <u>broke into</u> her house.
　　主詞　　　　動詞
The threatening <u>burglar</u> <u>shouted</u> loudly,
　　　　　　　　主詞　　　動詞
"Don't <u>move</u> or <u>I</u> <u>will hurt</u> <u>you</u>."
　　　　動詞　　主詞　動詞　　受詞
<u>Miranda</u> <u>was</u> so scared that <u>she</u>
主詞　　　動詞　　　　　　　　主詞
<u>was shaking</u> all the time.
動詞

1 名詞（noun）

本單元要介紹構成句子的基本元素：單字。依在句中的功用，單字可分為**八大詞類**（parts of speech）。唯有認識英文單字的詞類及其特性，寫作時才能正確地使用字彙。八種詞類為：

名詞　代名詞　動詞　形容詞　副詞　介系詞　連接詞　感嘆詞

名詞用來表達人、事、物等名稱的詞，可作句子的主詞、受詞或補語。依名詞的各種屬性和用法，介紹如下。

1 單數名詞與複數名詞

單數名詞 → 前面要加——
1. **冠詞**（a, an 或 the）
2. **所有格**（my, your, his, her 等）
3. **指示形容詞**（this, that, each 等）

✗ We bought present for Linda's birthday.
✓ We bought a present for Linda's birthday.

> 我們買了一個禮物送給琳達當生日禮物。

→ present（禮物）為單數名詞，前面要加不定冠詞 a。

✗ Present was necklace.
✓ The present was a necklace.

> 這個禮物是條項鍊。

→ 指上句中的禮物，因此 present 前面要加定冠詞 the。
→ necklace（項鍊）是可數的單數名詞，前面要加 a。

複數名詞 → ① 字尾通常加 -s 或 -es
② 不可加不定冠詞（a 或 an）
③ 如果指特定的人或事物，則可加定冠詞（the）。

✗ There are many necklace and ring in the store.
✓ There are many necklaces and rings in the store. 商店裡有很多項鍊和戒指。
→ many 形容複數名詞，necklace 和 ring 要用複數形（字尾加 -s）。

✓ The necklaces and rings are beautiful. 那些項鍊和戒指很漂亮。
→ 指上一句中的「很多項鍊和戒指」，所以要加 the，並用複數形。

2 名詞複數形的規則變化與不規則變化

1 規則變化

❶ 字尾 + -s

- girl → girls（女孩）
- book → books（書）
- chair → chairs（椅子）

❷ 字尾 + -es

ⓐ 字尾為 -s, -sh, -ch, -x, -z 時：

- bus → buses（公車）
- class → classes（班級）
- dish → dishes（盤子）
- watch → watches（手錶）
- box → boxes（箱子）
- quiz → quizzes（測驗） → quiz 要先重複字尾 z，再加 -es。

ⓑ 字尾為「子音 + o」時，加 -es。

- tomato → tomatoes（番茄）
- hero → heroes（英雄）
- potato → potatoes（馬鈴薯）
- 例外 piano → pianos（鋼琴）

ⓒ 字尾為「母音 + o」時，只加 -s。

- radio → radios（收音機）
- zoo → zoos（動物園）

❸ 字尾 + -ies

ⓐ 字尾為「子音 + y」時，去 y 加 -ies。

- country → countries（國家）
- cherry → cherries（櫻桃）
- baby → babies（嬰孩）
- city → cities（城市）

ⓑ 字尾為「母音 + y」，只加 -s。

- boy → boys（男孩）
- day → days（日子）
- monkey → monkeys（猴子）
- key → keys（鑰匙；解答）

④ 字尾 ＋ ves：字尾為 -f 或 -fe 時，去 f 或 fe，加 -ves。

- wife → wives（妻子）
- leaf → leaves（葉子）
- thief → thieves（小偷）
- knife → knives（小刀）

例外
- roof → roofs（屋頂）
- belief → beliefs（信仰）
- chief → chiefs（首領）

2 不規則變化

① 改變母音，或字尾加 -en 或 –ren

- man → men（男人）
- woman → women（女人）
- tooth → teeth（牙齒）
- foot → feet（腳）
- mouse → mice（老鼠）
- goose → geese（鵝）
- child → children（小孩）
- ox → oxen（牛）

② 單複數同形

- sheep → sheep（羊）
- Taiwanese → Taiwanese（台灣人）
- deer → deer（鹿）
- Japanese → Japanese（日本人）

3 可數名詞與不可數名詞

可數名詞 →
① 具有複數形式
② 作單數時，和不定冠詞 a 或 an 連用。

不可數名詞 →
① 被視為單數。
② 通常不加冠詞，也沒有複數形。
③ 指特定的事物時，要加定冠詞 the。

❶ **That family keeps several pets.**
→ pet 為可數名詞，複數型態為 pets。

那家人養了很多隻寵物。

❷ **The little boy lost a lot of blood in the accident.**
→ blood 為不可數名詞，前面用 a lot of 修飾，指流了很多血。

小男孩在意外事故中流了很多血。

4 名詞的種類：專有名詞、抽象名詞、物質名詞、集合名詞

1 專有名詞

專有名詞指特定人、地、物所專用的名稱。通常第一個字母要**大寫**，且**不加冠詞**，也**沒有複數形**。例如：

- 人名 Bill James
- 地名 New York（紐約）
- 山名 Mt. Ali（阿里山）
- 國名 Canada（加拿大）
- 節名 Christmas（聖誕節）
- 月分 September（九月）
- 星期 Monday（星期一）

1. **Christmas** is coming. 聖誕節快到了。
2. After leaving school, I spent a month traveling in **Canada**. 離開學校後，我到加拿大旅行了一個月。

> **NOTE**
>
> ① **人名的複數**：和一般複數名詞的規則變化一樣
> * There are two **Marys**, three **Vivians**, and two **Jameses** in our class.
>   我們班上有兩個瑪莉，三個薇薇安，還有兩個詹姆斯。
>
> ② **星期名的複數**
> * Erica goes to church on **Sundays**. 艾瑞卡每星期日都去做禮拜。
>   → on Sundays = every Sunday 每個星期天

2 抽象名詞

沒有形體、不能用手去觸摸的名詞，稱為抽象名詞，例如**想法**、**感覺**、**觀念**，或事物的**性質**、**狀態**等。

- happiness（幸福）
- truth（真實）
- friendship（友誼）
- beauty（美）
- love（愛）
- honesty（誠實）

1. Our **friendship** has lasted for many years. 我們已有多年的友誼。
2. I appreciate your **honesty**. 我欣賞你的誠實。

3 物質名詞

物質材料、食物、液體、金屬等，稱之為物質名詞。例如：

- air（空氣）
- water（水）
- sugar（糖）
- tea（茶）
- coffee（咖啡）
- bread（麵包）
- meat（肉）
- pork（豬肉）
- beef（牛肉）
- chicken（雞肉）
- luggage（行李）
- silver（銀）

❶ **I need to drink coffee to wake me up every morning.**
我每天早上得喝咖啡來讓自己清醒。

❷ **The coffee I make is tasty.**
我泡的咖啡味道很棒。

→ 專指「我泡的咖啡」，所以要在 coffee 前加定冠詞 the。

4 集合名詞

生物或事物的集合體名稱，有**單數名詞**和**複數名詞**的不同使用方式，例如：

- family（家庭）
- class（班級）
- company（公司）
- audience（觀眾；聽眾）
- team（團隊）
- committee（委員會）

當單數名詞時 → 集合名詞當作**單數**名詞使用時，是把所指的集合體視為**一個整體**。

my family
指整體的一家人

當複數名詞時 → 集合名詞當作**複數**名詞使用時，則是將組成集合體中的成員視為**個別個體**。

my families
指個別的家庭成員

❶ **I have a big family.**
我有一個大家庭。

❷ **Our class is going to have a field trip this Friday.**
本班將於週五舉行戶外教學。

③ **My family is** having dinner at a buffet restaurant. 我們全家正在自助餐廳用餐。
  → 這裡的 My family 指的是「全家」，視為一個整體。

④ **My family are** having dinner at a buffet restaurant. 我們一家人正在自助餐廳用餐。
  → 這裡的 My family 指的是「家裡每一個人」，視為個別成員。

有些集合名詞前要加**定冠詞 the**，而不是在字尾加 -s 或 -es。
這類集合名詞通常被視為**複數**，要用複數動詞。例如：

* The police are chasing the thief now.
  警察正在追捕小偷。
  → the police（警察）

* The French are romantic. 法國人很浪漫。
  → the French（法國人）

* The German are practical. 德國人很實際。
  → the German（德國人）

2 冠詞（article）

1 不定冠詞 a、an

冠詞分為不定冠詞和定冠詞，不定冠詞有 a 和 an，用在**非特指單數可數名詞**前。

冠詞 ─┬─ 不定冠詞 ─┬─ a
　　　│　　　　　　└─ an
　　　└─ 定冠詞 ──── the

a **an 用在首字母為母音的字**，如：

- an apple（一個蘋果）
- an egg（一顆蛋）
- an elephant（一隻大象）

b **a 用在首字母為子音的字**，如：

- a dog（一隻狗）
- a cat（一隻貓）
- a book（一本書）

an apple　　*a banana*

① I eat an apple and a banana every day.　　我每天吃一顆蘋果和一根香蕉。

2 定冠詞 the

定冠詞只有 一個，那就是 the，用於**特定的名詞**前，作用是**限定**此名詞。

the apple　　*the table*

① The apple on the table looks good.　　桌上的那顆蘋果看起來很不錯。

→ 限定是放在桌上的那顆蘋果，所以用定冠詞 the。

3 動詞（verb）

動詞用來表示動作、存在或狀態。依時態和動詞性質，有以下用法的差異：

1. 動詞三態（現在式、過去式、過去分詞）
2. be 動詞（現在式、過去式、未來式）
3. 連綴動詞（be 動詞、感官動詞、狀態動詞等）
4. 使役動詞（let, make, have, get）
5. 不定詞形式（to ＋原形動詞）
6. 動名詞形式（V-ing）
7. 接「不定詞」或接「動名詞」時，意義有所不同的動詞
8. 助動詞

1 動詞三態：現在式、過去式、過去分詞

❶ **Peter plays the piano very well.** 彼得的鋼琴彈得很好。
　　　　現在式
→ 陳述一件事實時，用現在式敘述。主詞為第三人稱單數，動詞加 s。

❷ **Peter and Sue were my students.** 彼得和蘇以前是我的學生。
　　　　　　　　過去式
→ 表示過去的狀態時，使用過去式。主詞為複數（Peter and Sue），be 動詞用 were。

❸ **They have studied English for three years.** 他們學英文已經學三年了。
　　　　　　完成式
→ 表示「已經……」，要使用完成式「have/has ＋過去分詞」。
→ 複數主詞（They）後面的動詞，要使用複數形 have。

> **NOTE**
> ❶ 動詞的三態變化，有規則和不規則的變化。
> ❷ 動詞的**人稱**和**數目**，要和主詞一致。

2　be 動詞：現在式、過去式、未來式

1 be 動詞的現在式（am, is, are）

be 動詞的三態變化，依人稱而有所不同。現在式的變化為：

- I → am
- he, she, it → is
- we, you, they → are

（否定用法加 not）

1. I am a senior high school student. 　我是高中生。
2. My younger sister is a junior high school student. 　我妹妹是中學生。
3. We are both students. 　我們兩個人都是學生。
4. He is not the person you are looking for. 　他不是你要找的人。

2 be 動詞的過去式（was, were）

- I → was
- he, she, it → was
- we, you, they → were

（否定用法加 not）

1. I was at home all day yesterday. 　我昨天一整天待在家。
2. Where were you when the movie began? 　電影開演的時候，你們在哪裡？
3. Nick wasn't with my brother last night. 　昨天晚上尼克沒有和我哥哥在一起。

3 be 動詞的未來式（will be）

各個人稱皆可加 will be，來形成 be 動詞的未來式：

- I, he, she, it, we, you, they → will be

（通常使用縮寫形式：I'll, you'll, he'll, she'll 等）（否定用法加 not）

1. My younger brother will be eight years old next Monday. 　我弟弟下星期一就八歲了。
2. It won't be easy to find a job during the period of economic recession. 　經濟不景氣時，工作很難找。

3 連綴動詞：be 動詞、感官動詞、狀態動詞

連綴動詞（linking verb）包括 **be 動詞**、**感官動詞**、**狀態動詞**等，用來描述或確認句中的主詞狀態，以完成句子。連綴動詞連接句子的主詞和**補語**，補語可以是名詞、代名詞或形容詞，但不接副詞（常接**形容詞**作**主詞補語**）。

1 be 動詞

① George is handsome in that suit.
　　　　　　主詞補語
喬治穿那件西裝很帥。

② Mary has been busy with her wedding.
　　　　　　　　主詞補語
瑪莉一直忙著準備她的婚禮。

③ Everything will be fine.
　　　　　　　　主詞補語
一切都會沒事的。

2 感官動詞

- feel（感覺起來）
- look（看起來）
- taste（嚐起來）
- smell（聞起來）
- sound（聽起來）

① I feel comfortable when being around with my family.
　　主詞補語
跟家人在一起我感到很自在。

② The food tastes delicious.
　　　　　　　主詞補語
這食物嚐起來很好吃。

③ Your job sounds very challenging.
　　　　　　　　　主詞補語
你的工作聽起來很具挑戰性。

NOTE 感官動詞後面如果接其他動詞，就要由**主動**語態或**被動**語態，來決定是要接原形動詞、現在分詞還是過去分詞。

主動句 感官動詞後面接的**動詞**是**主動語態**時，要接**原形動詞**或**現在分詞**。

主詞 ＋ 感官動詞 ＋ 受詞 ＋ 原形動詞 或 現在分詞

* I saw many birds **fly**. 我看到很多鳥兒在飛翔。
  原形動詞
* I saw many birds **flying**. 我看到很多鳥兒正在飛翔。
  現在分詞

被動句 感官動詞後面接的**動詞**是**被動語態**時，要接**過去分詞**。

主詞 ＋ 感官動詞 ＋ 受詞 ＋ 過去分詞

* I saw an airplane **shot** down. 我看到一架飛機被擊落。
  過去分詞

感官動詞被動語態 感官動詞本身為**被動語態**時，要使用「to ＋原形動詞」。

主詞 ＋ be 動詞 ＋ 感官動詞的過去分詞 ＋ to ＋ 原形動詞
                                              to＋原形動詞
* The dog **was seen to run** away. 那隻狗被看到逃跑了。
       過去分詞

3 狀態動詞

狀態動詞表示「過程」，指「**從一種狀態變成另一種狀態**」。例如：

- seem 似乎
- turn 變得
- appear 看來好像
- become 變成
- remain 保持
- stay 保持
- keep 繼續
- go 變成
- continue 繼續

1. Ben **seems** (to be) a friendly person.
                    主詞補語
   班似乎是個友善的人。

2. Students **stay** quiet because they don't
              主詞補語
   know how to answer the question.
   學生們保持沉默，因為他們不知道要如何回答這個問題。

3. The girls **went** crazy at this sight.
                     主詞補語
   女孩們看到這樣的景象都瘋狂了。

4. Our English class **becomes** more and more interesting.
                              主詞補語
   我們的英文課變得越來越有趣。

4 使役動詞：let, make, have, get

1 使役動詞 ➕ 另一個動詞

使役動詞用來引發另一個行為的動詞，常見用法如下。

Ⓐ 使某人，做某事

[let / make / have] ➕ [人] ➕ [原形動詞] ➡ My mother **let** me **wash** her car.
　　　　　　　　　　　　　　　　　　　使役動詞　人　原形動詞

我媽讓我洗她的車子。

Ⓑ 使某物，被……

[let / make / have] ➕ [物] ➕ [過去分詞] ➡ I **had** my car **repaired**.
　　　　　　　　　　　　　　　　　　　使役動詞　　物　　過去分詞

我把車子送修了。

Ⓒ 使某人，做某事

[get] ➕ [人] ➕ [to] ➕ [原形動詞] ➡ I **got** the mechanic **to repair** my car.
　　　　　　　　　　　　　　　　　使役動詞　　人　　　to＋原形動詞

我請技工修理車子。

Ⓓ 使某物，被……

[get] ➕ [過去分詞] ➡ My car **got repaired**. 我的車子修好了。
　　　　　　　　　　使役動詞　過去分詞

2 使役動詞本身為被動語態時，要使用「to ＋原形動詞」

[主詞] ➕ [be 動詞] ➕ [使役動詞的過去分詞] ➕ [to] ➕ [原形動詞]

🍀① Roy **was made to do** his homework again by his teacher.
　　　　被動語態　to＋原形動詞

羅伊被老師要求重寫作業。

5　不定詞形式：to ＋原形動詞

在基本句型中，一個句子只有一個主要動詞，如果有兩個以上的動詞時，則可以使用**不定詞**。

1. He **decides** **to study** harder.　他決定更努力讀書。
   　　動詞　　to＋原形動詞
2. Mitch **begins** **to study** at 7:00 every morning.　米奇每天早上七點開始讀書。
   　　　動詞　　to＋原形動詞
3. He **expects** **to pass** the college entrance exam.　他期望通過大學入學考試。
   　　動詞　　to＋原形動詞

> **NOTE**
>
> ❶ 某些動詞後面，習慣使用**不定詞**，如：
>
> - begin（開始）
> - wish（希望）
> - try（嘗試）
> - expect（預期）
> - like（喜歡）
> - desire（想要）
> - prepare（準備）
> - help（幫助）
> - decide（決定）
> - love（愛）
> - want（要）
> - start（開始）
> - hope（希望）
> - mean（意圖）
> - hate（恨）
>
> ❷ 在 help 之後，可接「to ＋原形動詞」（英式），也可以省略 to，只接原形動詞（美式）。
>
> ❸ 和愛、恨、喜好相關的動詞，像 like, love, hate，以及 begin, start 等動詞，後面可以用**不定詞**或**動名詞**形式。
>
> ＊ Michael **likes** **to play** basketball.
> 　＝ Michael **likes** **playing** basketball.　麥克喜歡打籃球。

6 動名詞形式（V-ing）

　　在基本句型中，如果有兩個以上的動詞時，除了使用不定詞，還可以使用**動名詞**（V-ing）。一定要接動名詞的動詞或動詞片語，例如：

- avoid（避免）
- admit（承認）
- appreciate（感謝）
- consider（考慮）
- deny（否認）
- enjoy（喜愛；享受）
- finish（完成）
- give up（放棄）
- keep（繼續）
- imagine（想像）
- mind（介意）
- miss（錯過）
- practice（練習）
- suggest（建議）
- be used to（習慣於）

1. He is considering learning German. 　　他正在考慮學德文。
2. My mom is used to brushing her teeth after she finishes eating her breakfast. 　　我媽媽習慣在吃完早餐後刷牙。
3. John practices speaking English as much as possible. 　　約翰盡量練習說英文。

7 接不定詞與動名詞時，意義會有所不同的動詞

A remember

| remember | ＋ | 不定詞 | → 接不定詞表示動作尚未發生 |
| remember | ＋ | 動名詞 | → 接動名詞表示動作已經發生 |

（不定詞：to ＋原形動詞；動名詞：V-ing）

1. I will remember to buy that book. 　　我會記得去買那本書。
2. I remember buying that book. 　　我記得已經買那本書了。

B forget

| forget | ＋ | 不定詞 | → 接不定詞表示動作尚未發生 |
| forget | ＋ | 動名詞 | → 接動名詞表示動作已經發生 |

（不定詞：to ＋原形動詞；動名詞：V-ing）

1. I forget to buy the newspaper. 　　我忘記去買報紙。
2. I forget buying the newspaper. 　　我忘記已經買報紙了。

C stop

| stop | + | 不定詞 | → 接不定詞表示停止某個動作，去做另一個動作 |
| stop | + | 動名詞 (V-ing) | → 接動名詞表示停止某動作 |

（to + 原形動詞）

1. When the telephone rang, I **stopped writing** my composition.
   當電話響起時，我就停止寫作文。

2. I **stopped to answer** the telephone.
   我停下（工作）去接電話。

D go on

| go on | + | 不定詞 | → 接不定詞表示正在做某事之外，再繼續另一件事 |
| go on | + | 動名詞 (V-ing) | → 接動名詞表示繼續做這件事 |

（to + 原形動詞）

1. We discussed the plan, and then we **went on to discuss** the transportation problem.
   我們先討論這個計畫，再繼續討論交通問題。

2. We **went on discussing** the plan.
   我們繼續討論這個計畫。

E try

| try | + | 不定詞 | → 接不定詞表示動作已經發生 |
| try | + | 動名詞 (V-ing) | → 接動名詞表示動作尚未發生 |

（to + 原形動詞）

1. I **tried to reach** her, but I couldn't find her telephone number.
   我試著聯絡她，可是我找不到她的電話號碼。

2. Why not **try writing** her an email?
   何不試著寫電子郵件給她呢？

31

8 助動詞

1. **助動詞**用來幫助主要動詞本身無法表達的各種意思，可表示：
   ① 動詞的時態；② 構成疑問句、否定句、被動式；③ 加強語氣。
2. 常見助動詞：can（可以；能），should（應該），must（必定），will（將），may（可能）
3. 助動詞後的內容，不論時態為何，都要接**原形動詞**。
4. 助動詞的過去式，除了表達發生在過去的事以外，也會用在現在式或未來式中，表示**可能性較小**，或**語氣較為客氣**。

❶ Irene **can** speak Hakka. 　　艾琳會說客家話。
　　　　會（表示能力）

❷ She **should** study harder. 　　她應該要努力讀書。
　　　應該（表示怎麼做會更好）

❸ She **may** pass the exam this time. 　　她這次可能通過考試。
　　　可能（表示可能性）

4 形容詞

1 形容詞在句中的位置

1 置於名詞前：用來修飾名詞，提供更多名詞相關的訊息

- Linda has a very **beautiful** **smile**.　　琳達的笑容很美。
  　　　　　　　　形容詞　名詞
  　　　　　　　　　　修飾

2 接在連綴動詞後：作為主詞補語

- **Linda's smile** is very **beautiful**.　　琳達的笑容很美。
  　主詞　　　　　　　　形容詞
  　　　　　　補語

2 一般形容詞

這是大家最熟悉的形容詞，通常用來描述人或物的特性。

1 形容人動作、外表、狀態	• aged 年老的　• athletic 運動的　• attractive 吸引人的 • awkward 不靈巧的　• bald 禿頭的　• charming 迷人的 • clumsy 笨拙的　• brilliant 傑出的　• drowsy 困倦的
2 形容事物特性	• acid 酸的　• automatic 自動的　• awful 可怕的 • elegant 優美的　• extensive 廣泛的　• casual 非正式的
3 形容顏色	• colored 有顏色的　• white 白的　• red 紅的 • purple 紫的　• copper 紅銅色的
4 形容方位	• east 東方的　• west 西方的　• south 南方的　• north 北方的
5 形容天氣	• chilly 寒冷的　• cold 冷的　• hot 熱的　• humid 潮濕的
6 強調	• complete 完全的　• absolute 絕對的　• total 總計的

3 分詞形容詞

有些形容詞借用了動詞變化中的現在分詞（動詞加 -ing）及過去分詞（動詞加 -ed）來作為形容詞，因此這類形容詞在意義上就帶有主動（-ing）與被動（-ed）的意味。

分詞形容詞 { 主動意味：現在分詞（V-ing）
　　　　　　被動意味：過去分詞（V-ed）

1 主動意味 **That teacher is boring.** 　　那個老師令人覺得無聊。
→ 老師教課很無趣，學生覺得無聊，老師是引起無聊的主因

被動意味 **That teacher is bored.** 　　那個老師感到無聊。
→ 可能是老師教課時，學生沒什麼反應，老師被學生影響，因此老師自己覺得很無聊

2 主動意味 **This movie is interesting.** 　　這部電影很有趣。

被動意味 **Many children are interested in this movie.** 　　許多小孩子對這部電影感興趣。

3 主動意味 **Traveling is very tiring but exciting.** 　　旅遊令人很疲累，但也很刺激。

被動意味 **People usually become very tired after an exciting trip.** 　　人們在刺激的旅行後，通常非常累。
→ 人因旅遊感到疲累，但旅行本身很刺激

34

4 複合形容詞

兩個單獨的字要形成一個形容詞時，通常會使用連字號（-）連接，或直接將兩個字合併為一個字，稱為複合形容詞。複合形容詞的組成方法有很多種，常用組合如下：

名詞 +

- 現在分詞
  - **attention-getting** 引人注意的
  - **heartbreaking** 令人心碎的

- 過去分詞
  - **left-handed** 左撇子的
  - **air-conditioned** 裝有空氣調節設備的
  - **home-made (homemade)** 自製的

- 形容詞
  - **age-old** 古老的
  - **trouble-free** 輕鬆自在的
  - **accident-prone** 容易發生事故的

- 名詞-ed
  - **baby-faced** 娃娃臉的
  - **bald-headed** 禿頭的
  - **dark-haired** 深色頭髮的

形容詞 +

- 名詞
  - **after-hours** 營業後的
  - **part-time** 兼職的
  - **all-purpose** 多用途的

- 現在分詞
  - **good-looking** 美貌的
  - **easygoing** 隨和的
  - **long-lasting** 持久的

- 過去分詞
  - **kind-hearted** 仁慈的
  - **old-fashioned** 過時的
  - **short-tempered** 脾氣壞的
  - **open-minded** 心胸寬廣的
  - **short-sighted** 近視的；目光短淺的
  - **middle-aged** 中年的
  - **high-heeled** 高跟的

副詞 +
- 現在分詞
  - hardworking 努力工作的
  - never-ending 永不結束的
- 過去分詞
  - above-mentioned 上述的
  - well-dressed 穿得體面的

數字 +
- 過去分詞
  - one-sided 偏於一方的；片面的
  - two-faced 表裡不一的；雙面的
- 名詞
  - four-way 四面通達的

三個字的複合形容詞
- five-year-old 五歲的
- around-the-clock 日夜不斷的
- around-the-world 全球的

5 補語形容詞

這類形容詞只能用來作為補語，必須接在連綴動詞之後，不可以置於名詞前。

- alike 相像的
- alive 活躍的
- alone 孤獨的
- afraid 害怕的
- asleep 睡著的
- aware 知道的
- apart 分開的
- unable 不能的

1 That little girl is afraid of being home alone.

那位小女孩害怕單獨在家。

→ afraid 是補語形容詞，不可以直接形容名詞 the afraid girl

✓ The frightened girl doesn't want to be at home alone.

害怕的小女孩不想要單獨在家。

→ 用 frightened 修飾名詞 girl

2 He was unable to cope with this difficult situation.

他無法處理這個困難的局面。

→ unable 不可放在名詞前修飾

✓ That incapable worker couldn't handle this difficult situation.

那位能力不足的員工無法處理這困難的局面。

6 形容詞的比較級和最高級

在英文中，表示「比較」的形容詞片語皆有固定的片語來搭配，因為屬於制式片語，所以句子結構必須遵循既有的文法結構。

1 比較級「形容詞比較級 ＋ than」

1. 正式用法 Jake is taller than I (am). 傑克比我高。
   口語用法 = Jake is taller than me.
2. Susan is a better teacher than Sam. 蘇珊是一位比山姆更好的老師。
3. This customer wants to try on a bigger dress (than this one).
   這位顧客想試（比這一件）大一點的洋裝。

2 比較級「more / less ＋ 形容詞原級 ＋ (than)」

1. We feel more comfortable in an RV than in a hotel.
   我們覺得住在休旅車裡比在飯店更舒服。
2. The red coat is less expensive than the green one.
   紅色的外套比綠色的便宜。
3. The marketing department is more flexible on this matter.
   more flexible 是補語　行銷部對這件事情的處理是較有彈性的。
4. We need to be less anxious, for anxiety can make you sick.
   我們不要太焦慮，因為焦慮會使你生病。

3 最高級「the ＋ most / least ＋ 形容詞最高級」

1. Bob is the tallest student in the class. 鮑伯是班上最高的學生。
2. Sally is the most intelligent of all the girls at the party.
   莎莉是派對中最聰明的女生。
3. This vacuum cleaner is the least expensive one in the store.
   這台吸塵器是店裡最便宜（最不昂貴）的機型。
4. I need to find the cheapest machine in the market.
   我要找到市場中最便宜的機器。

4 「The ＋ 比較級 ＋ 對等結構, the ＋ 比較級 ＋ 對等結構」

1. **The** harder you work, **the** more you earn.
   你工作得愈努力，你賺到的錢就愈多。

2. **The** more you earn, **the** bigger house you want.
   你賺到的錢愈多，你就想要愈大的房子。

3. **The** bigger house you have, **the** higher mortgage you need to pay off.
   你擁有愈大的房子，你就要付愈高額的貸款。

5 「too ＋ 形容詞原級 ＋ to ＋ 動詞原形」太……以至於不……

1. The wedding ceremony was too long for our children to sit straight.
   婚禮進行得太久，小孩子們無法乖乖地坐著。

2. There were too few guests to start the ceremony.
   到場的客人太少，所以典禮無法開始。

6 「形容詞 ＋ (not) enough ... to」（不）夠……，所以……
「(not) enough ＋ 名詞 ＋ to」……（不）夠，所以……

1. The wedding ceremony was interesting enough for our children to sit straight.
   婚禮夠有趣，所以小孩子們都乖乖坐著。

2. There were enough guests to start the ceremony.
   到場客人夠多，典禮可以開始了。

3. There were not enough guests to start the ceremony.
   客人到得不夠多，所以典禮還無法開始。

7 「as ＋ 形容詞原級 ＋ as ...」和……一樣……

1. Kevin is as handsome as his father.
   凱文和他爸爸一樣帥。

2. As a politician, Kevin is as successful as his father.
   凱文和他爸爸一樣是成功的政治家。

3. His father is not as ambitious as Kevin.　凱文的爸爸不像凱文那麼有野心。
   ＝ His father is less ambitious than Kevin.

5 連接副詞

在英文寫作及翻譯中，與語氣變化關係密切的還有連接副詞，或稱轉折詞。此處要介紹的連接副詞可以表達出更多樣化的語氣轉折，有些連接副詞與連接詞意思類似，讀者可以互相代換來表達同一概念，只是寫法上稍有不同。連接副詞只能表達語氣轉折，不能將兩句連接成為一句，因此在兩個句子之間使用連接副詞時，前句需以句點結束，連接副詞置於後句句首，並以逗點區隔，帶出後句。

1 解釋原因或說明結果的連接副詞

- therefore 所以；因此
- hence 因此
- thus 如此；因此
- for this (that) reason 因為如此
- consequently 結果；因此
- as a result 結果

1 Samantha loves her puppy Rover very much. **Therefore**, she will never get angry at him.
　　　└─ 連接副詞

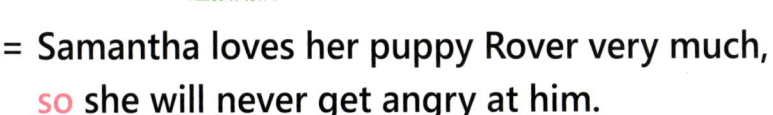

= Samantha loves her puppy Rover very much. **For this reason**, she will never get angry at him.
　　　└─ 連接副詞

= Samantha loves her puppy Rover very much, **so** she will never get angry at him.
　　　└─ 對等連接詞 so

莎蔓珊很愛她的小狗羅弗，因此，她絕不會對他生氣。

❷ Samantha will never get angry at her puppy Rover, for she loves him very much. 　　對等連接詞 for

= Samantha will never get angry at her puppy Rover because she loves him very much. 　　連接詞 because 的附屬連接

莎蔓珊絕不會對她的小狗羅弗生氣，因為她很愛他。

❸ Samantha loves her puppy Rover so much that she will never get angry at him. 　　片語 so that 的附屬連接

莎蔓珊太愛她的小狗羅弗，她才不會對他生氣。

2　說明時間或表達先後順序的連接副詞

- then 然後
- next 接下來；然後
- afterward(s) 之後
- later (on) 後來
- after that 之後
- meanwhile 同時
- in the meantime 就在這段時間裡

❶ Martin got off the airplane. After that, he called his mother.

馬丁下了飛機，之後他打電話給媽媽。

= Martin called his mother after he got off the airplane. 　　連接詞 after 的附屬連接

馬丁下了飛機之後，打電話給媽媽。

❷ Mother went to answer the phone. Meanwhile, the water on the stove was boiling.

媽媽去接電話，同時爐子上的水正在滾。

= Mother went to answer the phone while the water on the stove was boiling. 　　連接詞 while 的附屬連接

媽媽去接電話時，爐子上的水正在滾。

❸ Mother turned off the stove before she went to answer the phone. 　　連接詞 before 的附屬連接

媽媽去接電話之前把爐火關掉了。

= Mother turned off the stove. Then she went to answer the phone. 　　then 後面可以不加逗號

媽媽把爐火關掉，然後去接電話。

3 表示讓步的連接副詞

- however 然而
- still 儘管如此；如此
- nevertheless 然而

① Diana likes David very much. **However**, she won't marry him.
戴安娜很喜歡大衛，但是她不會嫁給他。

② Diana likes David very much. **Still**, she won't marry him.
戴安娜很喜歡大衛，儘管如此，她不會嫁給他。

③ Diana likes David very much. **Nevertheless**, she won't marry him.
戴安娜很喜歡大衛，然而，她不會嫁給他。

④ Diana likes David very much, **but** she won't marry him.
　　　　　　　　　　　對等連接詞 but
戴安娜很喜歡大衛，但她不會嫁給他。

⑤ **Although** Diana likes David very much, she won't marry him.
　　連接詞 although 的附屬連接
雖然戴安娜很喜歡大衛，但是她不會嫁給他。

4 呈現對比的連接副詞

- on the contrary 正好相反
- in contrast 相對地
- on (the) one hand 一方面
- on the other hand 另一方面

① I was upset about my test score. **On the contrary**, my parents thought I had done my best.
我對自己的考試成績感到很沮喪，相反地，我父母覺得我已經盡力了。

② My parents accepted the fact that I had not done well on the test. **In contrast**, I blamed myself for not studying harder.
我父母接受了我沒考好的事實，相反地，我責怪自己沒有更用功。

5 補充說明訊息的連接副詞

- moreover 此外；並且
- besides 此外
- in fact 事實上
- furthermore 而且；再者
- in addition 另外

🍀 I will never go to that restaurant again. Moreover, I will tell all my friends about its terrible food and lousy service.

= I will never go to that restaurant again. Besides, I will tell all my friends about its terrible food and lousy service.

= I will never go to that restaurant again. In fact, I will tell all my friends about its terrible food and lousy service.

= I will never go to that restaurant again, and I will tell all my friends about its terrible food and lousy service.
　　　　　　　　　　　　　　　　　↑ 對等連接詞 and

我再也不要去那家餐廳了，還有，我要告訴我所有的朋友那裡的食物很糟，服務也很差。

6 假設情況的連接副詞

- otherwise 否則

🍀 We have to complete this project by tomorrow. Otherwise, we may get into serious trouble.

= If we fail to complete this project by tomorrow,
　　↑ 連接詞 if 的附屬連接
we may get into serious trouble.

= We may get into serious trouble unless we complete this project by tomorrow.
　　　　　　　　　　　　　　　　　↑ 連接詞 unless 的附屬連接

我們必須在明天完成這個案子，否則我們就會有大麻煩。

7　舉例說明的連接副詞

- for example 舉例來說
- for instance 例如

1 Taiwan is an island of diversity. **For example**, people in Taiwan can speak two or three dialects.

台灣是座充滿多樣性的島嶼。舉例來說，台灣人民會說兩到三種方言。

8　陳述一般情況的連接副詞

- generally speaking 一般來說
- in general 一般的
- generally 通常

1 **Generally speaking**, teachers do not like students who are intelligent but lazy.

一般來說，老師不喜歡聰明但懶惰的學生。

9　歸納結論的連接副詞

- in conclusion 總而言之
- in short 總之
- in summary 簡而言之

1 **In conclusion**, listening to loud music will do harm to your hearing.

總而言之，聽大聲的音樂會損害你的聽力。

6 數量限定詞

名詞搭配多或少等與數量有關的表達時，也有其相對應的數量限定詞，其作用類似形容詞，置於名詞前用來修飾名詞。

1 some（一些）
　　a lot of（很多）　＋ 複數可數／不可數名詞
　　lots of（很多）

① There is some food left in the refrigerator.　冰箱裡留了一些食物。
　　　　　　　↳ food 不可數，指食物的量。
② There is lots of food left in the refrigerator.　冰箱裡有很多種食物。
　　　　　　　↳ 用 lots of foods 不符合英文習慣，至少美式英文不這樣用。

2 any（任何）＋可數／不可數名詞
　　（常用於否定及疑問句）

① Is there any food left in the kitchen?　有任何食物留在廚房嗎？
　　　　↳ any 用於疑問句
② There isn't any food left.　沒有任何剩下的食物。
　　　　　↳ any 用於否定句

3. {
   many（許多）
   a few = some（一些）
   few = not many（很少）
} + 複數可數名詞

❶ There are **many** people waiting to get on the bus.
有許多人在等著上公車。

❷ I like to have **a few** eggs for breakfast.
我早餐想吃些蛋。

❸ There are very **few** people in the theater.
戲院裡的人很少。

4. {
   much（許多）
   a little = some（一些）
   little = not much（很少）
} + 不可數名詞

❶ There isn't **much** coffee left.
└─ 不可數名詞
咖啡剩下的不多。

❷ We need **a little** bread for the party tomorrow.
└─ 不可數名詞
我們明天的派對需要一些麵包。

❸ We have very **little** butter left.
└─ 不可數名詞
我們只剩下一點點奶油。

7 一字多重詞性

　　同一字可具有不同的詞性，呈現多種用法。例如單字「up」，通常 up 是當作介系詞使用，但其實 up 也有其他不同詞性的用法。

1. Louis and Lucy walked up the hill.

   路易士和露西走上山。

   up 在此作介系詞用，有「向……上」之意。

2. Brian follows the ups and downs of the market.

   布萊恩追蹤市場的起起落落。

   up 在此作名詞用，有「繁榮」之意。

3. University tuition has been upped by 2% this year.

   今年大學的學費上漲了百分之二。

   up 在此作動詞用，有「增加」之意。

4. Emily needs to look up this word in the dictionary.

   艾蜜莉需要用字典查這個字。

   up 在此作動詞片語用。

❺ The up escalator is broken again. 往上的電扶梯又壞了。

　　　　up 在此作形容詞用，有「向上的」之意。

❻ Brad looked up at the sky. 布萊德仰頭看著天空。

　　　　up 在此作副詞用，有「向上」之意。

Unit 2 句型架構

Warm-up 暖身

將下面的段落，用正確的標點符號，分為數句，並做適當的修改。

my family and I took a trip to canada last winter the weather was very cold so we put on thick coats when we went skiing we also bought many souvenirs for our friends it was a wonderful trip

暖身題解答

My family and I took a trip to Canada last winter. The weather was very cold, so we put on thick coats when we went skiing. We also bought many souvenirs for our friends. It was a wonderful trip.

1 基本結構

主詞（S） 動詞（V） 受詞（O） 補語（C）

1 主詞（S）：說明句子的主體，多為名詞或代名詞。

① Jack is a manager in a high-tech company.　傑克是一家高科技公司的經理。
　主詞

2 動詞（V）：表現有關主詞的一切。

句型 1 及物動詞：一定要接受詞

① Jack loves his daughter.　傑克愛他的女兒。
　　及物動詞　　受詞

句型 2 不及物動詞：不需要接受詞

① Jack works very hard.　傑克很努力工作。
　　不及物動詞 works 不需要接受詞

句型 3 連綴動詞：連接主詞與主詞補語（如 be 動詞、appear、become、seem）

① Jack seems very happy today.　傑克今天似乎很高興。
　　連綴動詞

49

3 受詞（O）

句型 1 直接受詞：受到動詞動作影響的人、事、物，搭配及物動詞

🍀 Jack bought a house.
　　　　　　　　直接受詞

傑克買了一棟房子。

句型 2 間接受詞：通常指人，為間接受到動詞動作影響的人
　　　　　可直接放在動詞或介系詞之後，需搭配及物動詞

🍀 Jack bought his daughter a house.
　= Jack bought a house for his daughter.
　　　　　　　直接受詞　介系詞　　　間接受詞

傑克買給他女兒一棟房子。

4 補語（C）

句型 1 受詞補語：補充說明有關受詞的一切

🍀 Jack wants his daughter to be happy.
　　　　　　　　　　　　　　　　受詞補語
　　　　　　　　補充說明 his daughter

傑克希望他女兒開心。

句型 2 主詞補語：用在連綴動詞之後，補充說明有關主詞的一切

🍀 Jack's goal is to buy a house.
　　　　　　　　　主詞補語
　　補充說明 Jack's goal

傑克的目標是要買一棟房子。

2 五大基本句型

句型一	主詞 + （不及物）動詞
句型二	主詞 + （及物）動詞 + 受詞
句型三	主詞 + 動詞 + 間接受詞 + 直接受詞
句型四	主詞 + 連綴動詞 + 主詞補語
句型五	主詞 + 動詞 + 直接受詞 + 受詞補語

1 主詞＋（不及物）動詞

1. 這是英文句型中最基本的句型。因為動詞為不及物，所以不需接受詞，即可表達完整概念。
2. 本句型常常使用副詞來修飾動詞。

① **Marco runs**. 　　　　　　　　　馬可跑步。
　　主詞　不及物動詞

② **He runs fast**. 　　　　　　　　　他跑得快。
　　　　　　副詞

③ **It snows heavily in Alaska**. 　　阿拉斯加雪下得很大。

④ **The robber ran away**. 　　　　　搶劫犯逃跑了。

⑤ **This bus pass has run out**. 　　公車票已經到期了。

　　有時，只有一個動詞單字不足以表達的意義，可藉由兩個字以上的動詞片語，來表達與單一動詞不同的意義。

2 主詞＋（及物）動詞＋受詞

句子中的動詞或動詞片語為及物，所以後面一定要接受詞。

① **Lois loves her parents**. 　　　　露易絲愛她的父母。
　　主詞　及物動詞　受詞

② **She won a gold medal**. 　　　　她贏得了一面金牌。

③ **I found the book**. 　　　　　　　我找到了這本書。

④ **Pitt ran into his friend**. 　　　　彼特巧遇他的朋友。

⑤ **He has run out of money**. 　　他把錢用完了。

> **NOTE**
>
> **1** 動詞的受詞除了名詞之外，包括不定詞、動名詞片語、子句等，也都可以當作受詞。
> * George and Sarah intend <u>to marry</u>.　喬治和莎拉打算要結婚。
>   　　　　　　　　　　　不定詞
> * Julia should avoid <u>having an argument</u> with customers.　茱莉亞應該避免和顧客爭辯。
>   　　　　　　　　　　動名詞片語
> * My father hopes <u>that James will take over</u> the business.　我爸爸希望讓詹姆斯接管生意。
>   　　　　　　　　　　　子句
>
> **2** 英文中有許多動詞同時兼具及物與不及物的特性。
> * Maria <u>eats</u> fast.　瑪莉亞吃得很快。
>   　　　不及物動詞
> * Maria <u>eats</u> breakfast fast.　瑪莉亞吃早餐吃得很快。
>   　　　及物動詞

3　主詞＋動詞＋間接受詞＋直接受詞

間接受詞通常指**人**，直接受詞通常指**物**。有時也可以在間接受詞前加介系詞（for），置於直接受詞之後。

1. Tom bought his girlfriend a diamond ring.　湯姆買鑽戒給他女朋友。
   ＝ Tom bought <u>a diamond ring</u> for <u>his girlfriend</u>.
   　　　　　　　　直接受詞　　　　　　間接受詞

2. Our math teacher gives <u>us</u> <u>assignments</u> every day.　數學老師每天分配作業給我們。
   　　　　　　　　　　　　直接受詞　間接受詞

4　主詞＋連綴動詞＋主詞補語

1 主詞補語是補充說明有關主詞的一切，可以是名詞、形容詞、副詞、不定詞或動名詞等。

2 運用在本句型的連綴動詞可分為：

A	B	C
	五類感官動詞	其他動詞
be 動詞	look　smell sound　feel taste	appear、become、come、fall、get、go、grow、keep、make、prove、remain、seem、stay、turn 等

3 這類句型的主詞，除了名詞或代名詞之外，也可以代換成不定詞、動名詞、名詞子句等。

1 Susan <u>is</u> generous. 　　蘇珊很慷慨。
   　be 動詞

2 The dog <u>is</u> in the garden. 　　小狗在庭院裡。

3 You <u>look</u> tired. 　　你看起來很累。
   　五類感官動詞

4 This pizza <u>tastes</u> good. 　　這披薩真好吃。

5 Linda has <u>become</u> my best friend. 　　琳達成為我最好的朋友。
   　　　　　其他動詞

6 Mark often <u>falls</u> asleep in the classroom. 　　馬克經常在教室裡睡著。

7 <u>To become a reporter</u> is my goal. 　　我的目標是成為記者。
   　不定詞當主詞

　= My goal is to become a reporter.

8 <u>Traveling around the world</u> is what I always want to do. 　　環遊世界是我一直想要做的事情。
   　動名詞當主詞

9 <u>What you do</u> is none of my business. 　　你做什麼都不關我的事。
   　名詞子句

5 主詞＋動詞＋直接受詞＋受詞補語

受詞補語是補充說明有關受詞的一切，可以是名詞、形容詞、不定詞等。此類句型中的動詞通常包括 call、elect、make、name、paint、find、declare 等。

1 <u>Making new friends</u> always <u>makes</u> <u>me</u> <u>happy</u>. 　　結交新朋友總是讓我覺得快樂。
　　　主詞　　　　　　　　動詞　直接受詞　受詞補語（形容詞）

2 He <u>named</u> his son Jeffrey. 　　他把兒子取名為傑佛瑞。

3 We <u>painted</u> the door blue. 　　我們把門漆成藍色。

4 He <u>declared</u> his intention <u>to travel around the world within 80 days</u>. 　　他宣告要在80天之內環遊世界。

　　不定詞片語「to travel around the world within 80 days」可有兩種文法解釋：
　　(1) 作受詞補語，修飾直接受詞 his intention。
　　(2) 作形容詞，修飾名詞 his intention。

3 七大常用句型

以下的常用句型是從基本的英文句型所衍生出來，可視之為半成品，因為這些句型已經幫你完成了一半的句子。只要熟悉這些句型，再加入其他元素，便可輕鬆成句。

1 以**不定詞**或**動名詞**為主詞的句型

句型 以不定詞（To V）或動名詞（V-ing）作主詞時（一般視為單數，用單數動詞）。

不定詞（To V）
動名詞（V-ing）
＋ 單數動詞

不定詞和動名詞可以互相替換

❶ **Keeping** an English diary
　　動名詞作主詞
= **To keep** an English diary
　　不定詞作主詞
} **improves** your writing ability.
　　單數動詞

寫英文日記可以增進寫作能力。

不定詞和動名詞可以互相替換

❷ **Reading** English novels
　　動名詞作主詞
= **To read** English novels
　　不定詞作主詞
} **is** helpful to improve your reading ability.
　　單數be動詞

閱讀英文小說，有助於增進閱讀能力。

2　以 There 或 It 開頭（There / It ＋動詞）

句型 1　There ＋ be 動詞……

以 there 為首的句型，後接 be 動詞，真正的主詞是接在 be 動詞之後的名詞詞組，因此 be 動詞的單複數變化，必須配合接在動詞之後的主詞。

❶ There <u>is</u> <u>a book</u> on the table.　　桌上有本書。
　　　　↑主詞
　　　　用單數動詞 is

❷ There <u>are</u> <u>30 boys</u> in the class.　　班上有 30 個男孩。
　　　　↑主詞
　　　　用複數動詞 are

句型 2　It ＋動詞……

以 it 為首的句型一定接單數動詞，此句型帶有強調的語氣，比較以下句子。

❶ <u>It is</u> <u>my job</u> to take care of those children.　　我的工作就是照顧那些小孩。
　　強調「我的工作」，語氣上比例 2 和例 3 更強烈

❷ My job is to take care of those children.
❸ To take care of those children is my job.

❹ <u>It is</u> <u>not easy</u> to pass the exam.　　通過考試真的不容易。
　　強調「not easy」，語氣比例 5 更強烈

❺ To pass the exam is not easy.

❻ <u>It was</u> <u>midnight</u> when Annie finally fell asleep.　　直到午夜時分，安妮才終於睡著。
　　強調「直到午夜才……」

❼ Annie finally fell asleep at midnight.

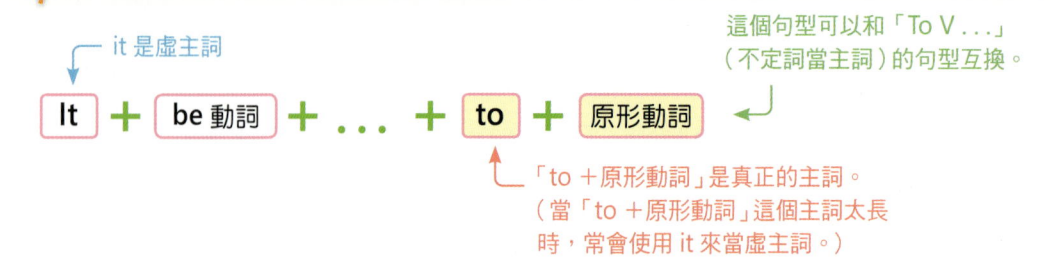

3 「It ＋ be 動詞＋ ... ＋ to ＋原形動詞」的句型

it 是虛主詞

| It | ＋ | be 動詞 | ＋ ... ＋ | to | ＋ | 原形動詞 |

這個句型可以和「To V ...」（不定詞當主詞）的句型互換。

「to ＋原形動詞」是真正的主詞。（當「to ＋原形動詞」這個主詞太長時，常會使用 it 來當虛主詞。）

❶ It is a good habit to get up early every day.
 ＝ To get up early every day is a good habit.
 每天早起是個好習慣。

❷ It is important to practice speaking English every day.
 ＝ To practice speaking English every day is important.
 每天練習說英語是很重要的。

4 「It is not until ... that ...」（直到……才……）的句型

| It is not until | ... | that | ...

＝ | 主詞 | ... | not | ... | until | ...

❶ It was not until three in the morning that he went to bed.
 ＝ He did not go to bed until three in the morning.
 一直到凌晨三點，他才就寢。

5 「I am afraid that ＋主詞＋動詞＋...」（我恐怕……）

「I am afraid that ＋主詞＋動詞＋...」（我恐怕……）的句型，用來**婉轉地提出異議**，或是**婉拒建議**，或是**表達不好的消息**。

I am afraid that ＋ 主詞 ＋ 動詞 ...（我恐怕……）

1. **I am afraid that** I won't attend the cocktail party.
   我恐怕不會參加雞尾酒會。
2. **I am afraid that** I have to leave now.
   我恐怕現在得離開了。

6 「否定字＋ without」的句型

「否定字＋ without」（沒有……，就無法……）的句型有**雙重否定**的意思，表示「**肯定**」語氣。without 是介系詞，後面要接名詞或動名詞。

no ＋名詞
not ＋動詞 ... without ＋ 名詞 / 動名詞 ...（沒有……，就無法……）
never ＋動詞

1. The project **couldn't** have been accomplished **without** you.
2. I could **never** realize my dream **without** my mother's help.
3. Grandmother **can't** read the newspaper **without wearing** glasses.
   （without+動名詞）
   = Grandmother **can't** read the newspaper **without glasses**.
   （without+名詞）

1. 這個計畫沒有你就無法完成。
2. 沒有我媽媽的幫忙，我永遠無法實現夢想。
3. 祖母看報紙時，一定要戴起眼鏡。

57

7 「All (that) ...」的句型

「**All (that) ...**」的句型，指「某人所（要／能／想）做的事，是……」的意思。

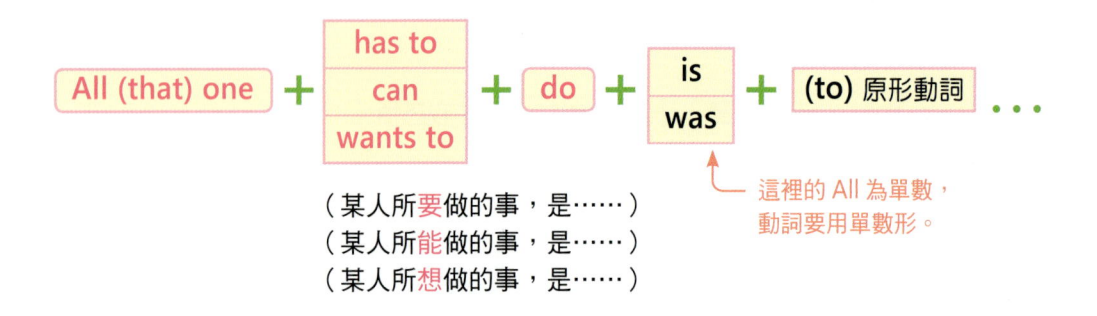

All (that) one + [has to / can / wants to] + do + [is / was] + (to) 原形動詞 ...

（某人所要做的事，是……）
（某人所能做的事，是……）
（某人所想做的事，是……）

這裡的 All 為單數，動詞要用單數形。

❶ **All (that) we can do is (to) practice every day.** 我們能做的就是每天練習。

4 多種句型混合套用

上述幾種句型也可以彼此套用在同一個句子中，形成較為複雜的句型。

1. I asked her to buy us the concert tickets. 我請她為我們買演唱會的門票。

→ 句型 5　主詞 ＋ 動詞 ＋ 直接受詞 ＋ 受詞補語

　　I ＋ asked ＋ her ＋ to buy us the concert tickets
　　主詞　動詞　直接受詞　　　　　受詞補語

→ 句型 3　主詞 ＋ 動詞 ＋ 間接受詞 ＋ 直接受詞

　　to buy ＋ us ＋ the concert tickets
　　動詞　間接受詞　　直接受詞

2. It is my sister who needs to find a job to support herself. 就是我妹妹要找工作維生。

→ 常用句型 2　It... 為首的句型。
　　　　　　　↑ 強調 my sister

→ 句型 2　主詞 ＋ 動詞 ＋ 受詞

　　who ＋ needs ＋ to find a job to support herself
　　主詞　 動詞　　　　　　受詞

　→ 用來修飾 my sister

→ 句型 5　主詞 ＋ 動詞 ＋ 直接受詞 ＋ 受詞補語

　　to find ＋ a job ＋ to support herself
　　動詞　　直接受詞　　受詞補語

→ 句型 2　主詞 ＋ 動詞 ＋ 受詞

　　to support ＋ herself
　　　動詞　　　受詞

Quiz 1

句子重組

將作答線下方所有的提示字詞組合成一個有意義的句子，且不能隨意增加字詞。

提示 先找出此句子的主詞和動詞，然後再放入受詞、受詞補語、主詞補語等。

1 last month / Japan / took a trip / to

My friends and I _____

2 rained / at that time / heavily / It / in Japan

_____

3 senior high school / Jimmy / is / a / student

_____

4 feel / We / in / excited / English class / our

_____

5 took / the medicine / She / a day / four times

_____

6 bread / very much / loves / Andrew

_____

7 Lynn / bought / a ring

Kenny _____

8 sent / a postcard / Barbie / also

Cliff _____

9 Levy / powerful / considered / leader / a

We _____

10 sad / made / us / The news

_____

Quiz 2

請根據下列中文短文，將題目的英文句重組，並且指出這個句子所用的句型。
（一個句子可能使用不止一個句型。）

【一個小氣的妹妹】
我最要好的朋友 Karen 是我的同班同學，Karen 很喜歡運動，同時她也是班上最漂亮的女孩。有一天，她到我家來，我老哥看到她，對她非常感興趣，便問我她是誰。我不想跟他說她的名字，老哥就直接問她，然後立刻邀請她參加學校舞會。我非常生氣。

1 is / my classmate / My best friend

   My best friend is my classmate.

2 Karen / Her name / is

3 likes / Karen / to exercise

4 the prettiest girl / in my class / She / is also

5 she / One day / to my house / came

6 her / My brother / saw

7 in her / was / He / very interested

8 who my friend was / asked / me / My brother

_____

9 him / her name / want / I / didn't / to tell

_____

10 asked / My brother / her name / directly / my friend

_____

11 her / he / invited / Immediately, / to attend / the school party

_____

12 very angry / I / was

_____

Note

Quiz 2

Unit 3 常見片語與連接詞

Warm-up 暖身

你可以從短文中分辨出各個連接詞組的意義嗎？

Both Charles and Tess live in this area. Charles is not only a businessman but also a person with great ideals. Tess is not only a teacher but also a person popular with her students. Either Charles or Tess will go to America next year. Neither Charles nor Tess is married.

暖身題解答

查爾斯和黛絲同住在一個地區。查爾斯不僅是一位生意人，還是一個擁有偉大理想的心；黛絲不僅是一位老師，而且還是一位受到學生歡迎的老師。不是查爾斯就是黛絲明年要去美國。查爾斯和黛絲都沒有結婚。

學習慣用語句型，是造句的開始，例如：

neither A nor B（既不……，也不……）
not only A but also B（不僅……，而且……）
either A or B（不是……，就是……）

好好熟讀本章，這裡介紹的都是英語考試中常會出現的句型和片語喔！

1 動詞片語

1 常見的短語動詞

短語動詞通常由 動詞 ＋ 介系詞 或 動詞 ＋ 副詞 組成。

- call on（拜訪）
- clean up（打掃）
- turn on（打開）
- get on（上車）
- get off（下車）
- turn off（關掉）
- put on（穿上）
- figure out（想出）
- take off（脫下；起飛）

1. Bruce cannot figure out the solution. 　布魯斯無法想出解答。
2. He always remembers to turn off the lights before he leaves the classroom. 　他總是記得離開教室前要把燈關掉。
3. He put on his best suit for the interview. 　他穿上最好的西裝去面試。

2 表示情緒的「動詞片語（動詞＋介系詞）＋名詞」句型

表示**情緒**的動詞片語，大多包含固定的**介系詞**，後面要接名詞或動名詞。

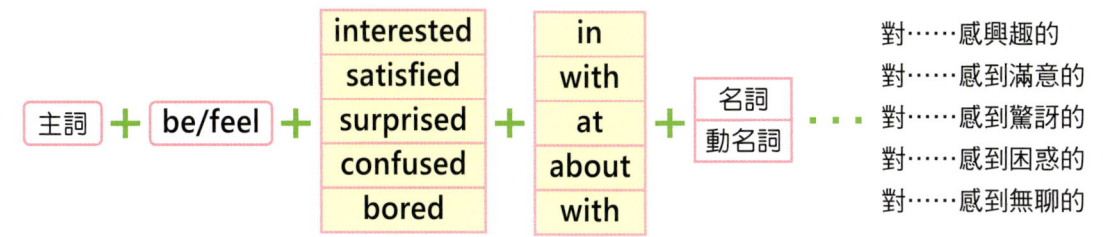

| 主詞 ＋ be/feel ＋ | interested / satisfied / surprised / confused / bored | ＋ | in / with / at / about / with | ＋ | 名詞 / 動名詞 | ⋯ | 對……感興趣的 / 對……感到滿意的 / 對……感到驚訝的 / 對……感到困惑的 / 對……感到無聊的 |

1. Pearl is interested in that book. 　珀兒對那本書感興趣。
2. She feels satisfied with his answer. 　她對於他的回應感到很滿意。
3. Jessie is surprised at the news. 　潔西對這個消息感到很驚訝。
4. Nicole is confused about this question. 　妮可對這個問題感到困惑。
5. Jonathan is bored with the routine work. 　強納森對於日常工作感到厭煩。

3 其他常見的「動詞片語＋動名詞／名詞」句型

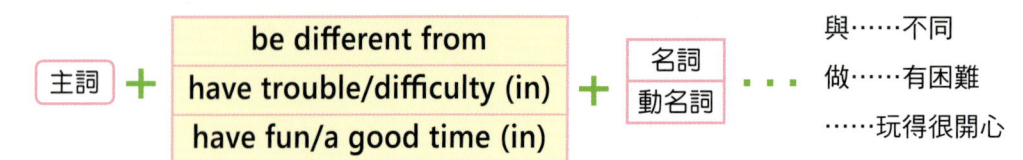

主詞 ＋ { be different from / have trouble/difficulty (in) / have fun/a good time (in) } ＋ 名詞／動名詞 … 與……不同／做……有困難／……玩得很開心

❶ Their uniforms **are different from** ours.（名詞；= our uniforms）
他們的制服和我們的不一樣。

❷ Zeus **has trouble (in)** doing his English homework.（動名詞）
宙斯做英文功課遇到困難。

❸ John **had a good time (in)** playing hide-and-seek.（動名詞）
約翰玩捉迷藏玩得很開心。

4 「be ＋ to ＋原形動詞」的句型

be 動詞 ＋ to ＋ 原形動詞 … → 用來表示預定、打算、意向等

否定用法：be 動詞 ＋ not ＋ to ＋ 原形動詞 …

❶ The airplane **is to** take off at eight a.m.（表示預定）
飛機預定將在上午八點起飛。

= The airplane **is going to** take off at eight a.m.

❷ The airplane **was to** land thirty minutes ago.（表示意向）
飛機本來要在三十分鐘前降落。

❸ The airplane **is not to** take off because of the bad weather.（表示打算）
因為天氣不好，所以飛機將不起飛。

5 表示「習慣」的用法

A 主詞 ＋ used to ＋ 原形動詞 … （以前常……）

→ 表「**過去的習慣**」或「**過去曾經持續的狀態**」，但現在已不存在。

① Elaine **used to** go to school by bicycle. 伊蓮以前常騎腳踏車上學。
（表示過去的習慣；原形動詞）

B 主詞 ＋ be used to / get used to ＋ 名詞／動名詞 … （習慣於……）

→ 表示「**現在的習慣**」，或是現在一直持續著的狀態。

① Elaine **is used to** taking a shower after she gets up. 伊蓮習慣在起床後沖澡。
（表示這個習慣現在仍保持；動名詞）

② They **get used to** the humid weather in Taipei. 他們習慣台北潮濕的天氣。
（表示現在一直持續著的狀態；名詞）

NOTE by 用來表示「手段、方法」，後面接交通工具時，表示「搭乘……」。

※ Molly goes to school **by bicycle**. 茉莉騎腳踏車上學。
※ Her father goes to work **by car**. 她爸爸開車上班。

- by bus 搭乘公車
- by bicycle 騎腳踏車
- by car 開車
- by MRT 搭乘捷運
- by motorcycle 騎機車
- by train 搭乘火車

6 spend、take、cost（花費……）

花時間

① 人 + spend + 時間 + V-ing ...
② 人 + spend + 時間 + on + 名詞 ...
③ It takes + 人 + 時間 + to + 原形動詞 ...

― spend 的主詞要用人
― spend 的後面要接「V-ing」或「on + 名詞」

❶ I **spend** an hour **finishing** my math homework every night.

= It **takes** me an hour **to finish** my math homework every night.

― take 的主詞要用 it
― 後面要接「to + 原形動詞」

我每晚花一小時寫完數學作業。

花錢

① 人 + spend + 金錢 + V-ing ...
② 人 + spend + 金錢 + on + 名詞 ...
③ It takes/took + 人 + 金錢 + to + 原形動詞 ...
④ 物 + cost(s) + 人 + 金錢

❷ He **spent** two hundred dollars **buying** the book.
　　　　　　　　　　　　　　　　動詞V-ing

= He **spent** two hundred dollars **on** the book.
　　　　　　　　　　　　　　　　on +名詞

= It **took** him two hundred dollars **to buy** the book.
　　　　　　　　　　　　　　　　　to +原形動詞

= The **book cost** him two hundred dollars.
　　物+cost

他花了 200 元買那本書。

> **NOTE**
> 要表達花費時間或金錢，可用 spend 或 take。
> cost 只用在「東西花費多少錢」，主詞要用物。
> 使用 take 時，主詞通常會用 it 帶出的句型。
>
> | | 主詞 | 花費 |
> |---|---|---|
> | spend | 人 | 金錢、時間 |
> | cost | 物 | 金錢 |
> | take | it | 金錢、時間 |

7 常見動詞片語

只有動詞單字有時無法完整表達某些概念，動詞片語能協助表達更多的意義。

1	**appeal to** 向……呼籲	The President **appealed to** the public to unite together.　　　總統呼籲民眾要團結起來。
2	**associate with** 把……聯想在一起	Business people would easily **associate** potential markets **with** profits. 商人很容易把潛在市場和利益聯想在一起。
3	**attach to** 附上	The salesperson **attached** the price tags **to** each product. 那位售貨員把價格標籤貼在每樣商品上。
4	**benefit from** 受惠於	Only a small number of people will **benefit from** the newly amended tax regulation. 只有小部分的人將受惠於新修訂的稅制條款。
5	**tend to / combine with** 有……的傾向／結合	Young children **tend to combine** reality **with** imagination when they listen to a story. 幼童聽故事時容易將現實跟想像結合在一起。
6	**concentrate on** 全神貫注於……	The newly elected lawmaker **concentrated on** her new task. 這位新當選的立法委員全神貫注於她的新工作。
7	**consult with** 商議	The premier **consulted with** ministers before making the decision. 在做決定之前，總理與各部長進行商議。
8	**contribute to** 捐助；幫助	Mr. Kao **contributed** lots of money **to** the relief work and reconstruction after the earthquake. 高先生熱心捐款，幫助地震後的救災和重建。

69

9	**cope with** 處理	The construction contractor should figure out ways to cope with the flood. 建築包商應該想出方法來處理淹水問題。
10	**devote to** 將……奉獻給	The mayor devoted herself to the rescue work. 市長專心一致地處理救援行動。
11	**differ from** 與……不同	Everyone is entitled to express his or her opinions that may differ from others. 每個人都有權表達與別人不同的意見。
12	**disagree with** 與……意見不同	Mr. Lee gets angry easily when others disagree with him. 當別人和李先生意見不合時,他很容易生氣。
13	**disapprove of** 反對;不贊成	Many people disapprove of domestic violence.　許多人反對家庭暴力。
14	**distinguish from** 區別;辨別	People tend to distinguish right from wrong based on their own experience. 人們通常基於經驗辨別對與錯。
15	**equip with** 配備	The World Trade Center was equipped with all kinds of hi-tech devices. 世貿中心配有各種高科技設備。
16	**interfere with** 妨礙;干涉	His drinking problem interferes with his ability to think straight. 他的酗酒問題妨礙了他的理性思考能力。
17	**participate in** 參加	All of our managers have to participate in the annual board meeting tomorrow. 全體經理都必須參加明天的年度董事會。
18	**prohibit from** 禁止;阻止	More and more restaurants prohibit customers from smoking. 愈來愈多的餐廳禁止顧客在室內抽菸。
19	**rely on** 仰賴	Single-parent families sometimes need to rely on support from relatives. 單親家庭有時需要仰賴親戚的資助。

2 常見的關係連接詞組

關係連接詞要成對使用，連接兩個平行結構，例如兩個名詞、兩個動詞、兩個子句等，而動詞要和最靠近動詞的主詞一致。常見的關係連接詞如下：

1 both A and B（A 和 B 兩者都）

1. Both **brother** and **sister** are safe and sound.　哥哥和妹妹兩人都相安無事。
   （名詞　名詞）

2. Both **Lora** and **May** like to walk their dogs in the evening.　蘿拉和玫都喜歡在傍晚時遛狗。
   （名詞　名詞）

3. Walking a dog is both **relaxing** and **delightful**.　遛狗既輕鬆又令人愉快。
   （形容詞　形容詞）

2 either A or B（不是 A，就是 B）

↑ A、B 為主詞時，動詞要和最靠近動詞的主詞一致。

1. Either **you** or **I** have to go.　不是你要去，就是我要去。
   （名詞　名詞）

   動詞 is 和主詞 Scott 一致。

2. Either **they** or **Scott** is often late for class.　不是他們就是史考特上課常遲到。
   　　　　　　　（名詞）

3. They are either **late** for class or **noisy** in class.　他們不是上課遲到，就是在課堂上吵鬧。
   （名詞）　（形容詞）　　　　　（形容詞）

71

3 neither A nor B（A、B 皆非）

A、B 為主詞時，動詞要和最靠近動詞的主詞一致。

1. My sister eats neither fish nor chicken.
   　　　　　　　　　 名詞　　　名詞
   我姊姊不吃魚，也不吃雞。

2. The movie is neither interesting nor instructive.
   　　　　　　　　　　 形容詞　　　　　形容詞
   這電影既無趣，也缺乏教育性。

3. Neither Megan nor Jill enjoys the movie.
   　　　　 名詞　　　名詞
   梅根和吉兒都不喜歡這部電影。

4 not only A but (also) B（不僅 A，而且 B）

also 可省略。

連接兩個主詞時，動詞的人稱和單複數，要和 B 一致。

1. Mrs. Colin is not only a great teacher but also a super mom.
   　　　　　　　　　　　 名詞　　　　　　　　　 名詞

2. Mark is not only a doctor but also a person with great ideals.
   　　　　　　　　 名詞　　　　　　 名詞

3. Not only he but also his friends want to contribute to our society.
   　　　　 名詞　　　　 名詞
   動詞 want 的單複數形，要和靠近的主詞 his friends 一致。

1. 柯林太太不僅是一位好老師，還是一位超級媽媽。
2. 馬克不但是個醫生，也是一位擁有偉大理想的人。
3. 不僅他，他的朋友們也都想對我們的社會有所貢獻。

5 whether A or B（不管是 A，或是 B）

whether ＋ 主詞 ＋ (be) 動詞 ＋ 受詞／地方副詞
＋ or ＋ whether ＋ 主詞 ＋ (be) 動詞 ＋ 受詞／地方副詞
↑ 藍字部分通常省略

1 I don't know whether he is at home or (whether he is) in the office.
↑ 通常省略
我不曉得他人在家，還是在辦公室。

2 I must do it whether I like or (whether I) dislike it.
↑ 通常省略
無論我是否喜歡，我都得去做。

其他常見的連接詞組合

❶ too . . . to . . .（太……，而不能……）

1. 這裡連接的不是對等詞性，too 後面接**形容詞**，to 後面則接**原形動詞**。
2. 也可以使用「so . . . that . . . cannot」來表達相同的意思。

※ The pineapple is **too** sour **to** eat. 這鳳梨太酸了，不能吃。
   　　　　　　　　　形容詞　原形動詞
   = The pineapple is **so** sour **that** we **cannot** eat (it).

※ The tea is **too** hot **to** drink. 這茶太燙了，不能喝。
   　　　　　　形容詞　原形動詞
   = The tea is **so** hot **that** I **cannot** drink (it).

❷ so . . . that; such . . . that（很……，所以……）

1. so 為副詞，後面要接**形容詞**或**副詞**；such 為形容詞，後面要接**名詞**。
2. 「so ＋形容詞＋ that」＝「such ＋ a/an ＋（形容詞）＋名詞＋ that」

※ The teacher is **so** kind **that** every student likes her.
   　　　　　　　　形容詞
   = The teacher is **such** a kind person **that** every student likes her.
   　　　　　　　　　　　　名詞
   這位老師好親切，每個學生都喜歡她。

Quiz 3

句子合併

請依照題目指示，將兩句合併成一句。

1 Ashley likes to collect stamps.
May likes to collect stamps, too.（用 both . . . and . . .）
_____.

2 Trent enjoyed the movie.
His friends also enjoyed the movie.（用 not only . . . but also . . .）
_____.

3 Grandmother can't read the newspaper.
She has to wear glasses.（用 without）
_____.

4 His umbrella is green. My umbrella is black.（用 different from）
_____.

5 The coffee is so hot. I can't drink (it).（用 too . . . to . . .）
_____.

6 Joy goes to school. She rides her bicycle to school.（用 by）
_____.

7 Joseph is so nice. He has many friends.（用 such . . . that . . .）
_____.

8 Jenny went to school by bicycle when she was a junior high school student.（用 used to）

_____.

9 Alexander is doing his English homework.
He doesn't know how to do it.（用 have trouble）

_____.

10 The book is not interesting.
The book is not instructive either.（用 neither ... nor ...）

_____.

Unit 4 時態變化

Warm-up 暖身

對英語學習者來說,「時態」是英文文法中與中文邏輯思考很不一樣之處。中文的時態多用時間副詞來修飾動詞,英文則是直接運用動詞進行時態變化。

中文多用副詞帶出時態	英文使用動詞變化表時態
你剛剛去哪兒?	Where have you been?
你昨天去哪兒?	Where did you go yesterday?
你等會兒要去哪兒?	Where are you going?

1 現在式的時態變化

1 變化 1：現在簡單式

簡單現在式 = 主詞 + 現在式動詞 →
① 表示目前的動作、狀態、事實。
② 用來表示習慣動作或事情，常和頻率副詞連用，例如 every day, often, always。
③ 也用來表示不變的真理或格言。

1. **Tim is a fashion designer.** → 表目前的狀態　提姆是一位時裝設計師。
2. **I get up at six every day.** → 表習慣　我每天早上六點起床。
3. **The sun rises in the east.** → 表事實　太陽在東方升起。

2 變化 2：現在進行式

現在進行式 = 主詞 + be 動詞 + V-ing →
① 表示目前正在進行的時態。
② 用來描述說話時正在進行的事情，強調進行中的動作。
③ 也用來表示動作的反覆或習慣，此用法常和 always, usually 等頻率副詞連用。

1. **"What is Jim doing?" "He is surfing the Net."**　「吉姆正在做什麼？」「他正在上網。」
   → 強調進行中的動作
2. **He is looking for a job at the moment.**　他目前正在找工作。
   → 調進行中的動作
3. **Jim is always spending a lot of time on the Internet.**　吉姆總是花很多時間在上網。
   → 表示動作的反覆或習慣

> **NOTE**：現在進行式用於目前或暫時的情況，簡單現在式則用於經常、不變的情況。

3　變化 3：現在完成式

主詞 ＋ have / has ＋ 過去分詞

① 表示動作在過去開始，持續到現在，或對現在有影響。

② 表示過去發生的動作，但不強調當時動作開始的確切時間。

🍀 I have studied French for two years.　　我學法文已經兩年了。
　→ 已經學了兩年的法文，所以現在法文程度很好，或指現在還有在學法文。

4　變化 4：現在完成進行式

主詞 ＋ have been / has been ＋ 現在分詞

① 表示動作在過去開始，現在仍持續進行中，未曾間斷。

② 表示動作已經結束，但對現在產生影響。

🍀 I have been cleaning my room for two hours. 我已打掃房間兩小時了。
　→ 已經打掃房間兩小時，很可能現在還持續打掃中。

過去　　　　打掃2小時　　　　現在

2 過去式的時態變化

1 變化 1：過去簡單式

簡單過去式 = 主詞 + 過去式動詞 →
1. 用來表示過去的動作、狀態。
2. 常和表過去的時間副詞連用，例如 yesterday, last year 等。
3. 也用來表示過去的習慣動作。

1. <u>Richard studied</u> in New York two years ago.
   理查兩年前在紐約念書。

2. <u>He often went</u> to the theater when he was there.
   他在那裡時，常去劇院看表演。

2 變化 2：過去進行式

過去進行式 = 主詞 + was/were + V-ing →
和過去正在進行的事有關，表示某個動作在過去的某時正在進行或繼續中。

1. At eight last night, <u>we were talking</u> about our weekend plans over the telephone.
   昨晚八點時，我們正在電話中討論週末的計畫。

3 變化 3：過去完成式

主詞 + had + 過去分詞

■ 過去的某個時間之前，某動作已經完成。
■ 比較兩個過去的動作，先完成的動作需使用過去完成式。

I had studied Chapter 10 before Mom came home.

媽媽回到家前，我已經讀了第十章。

過去 — 讀完第十章 — 媽媽回家 — 現在

4 變化 4：過去完成進行式

主詞 + had been + 現在分詞

說明動作在過去開始，持續進行到過去某個時間點。

I had been studying Chapter 10 until Mom got home.

媽媽回到家前，我一直在讀第十章。

過去 — 一直在讀第十章 — 媽媽回家 — 現在

3 未來式的時態變化

1 變化1：未來簡單式

主詞 + will / be going to + 原形動詞

表示未來會發生或預期的動作，多搭配未來時間副詞，有時可以用現在簡單式取代。

① **I will see** a movie tomorrow. 　　我明天會看電影。
② **I am going to see** a movie tomorrow. 　　我明天會看電影。

2 變化2：未來進行式

主詞 + will be + V-ing

表示未來的某個時刻正在進行的動作，未來進行時態也可以指已經確定或已經決定的未來事件（沒有正在進行的含意）。

① **I will be studying** English tomorrow evening in the library. 　　我明天晚上會在圖書館念英文。
　→ 已經決定了的未來事件，不代表正在進行

3 變化3：未來完成式

主詞 + will have + 過去分詞

表示某一動作現在還未完成，但在未來的某時間點前將會完成。

① **I will have finished** the English assignments by 6 p.m. 　　我晚上六點前會寫完英文作業。

4 變化 4：未來完成進行式

主詞 ＋ will have been ＋ 現在分詞

強調未來某段時間前，動作的持續進行。

🍀 **I will have been studying English for three hours by 6 p.m.**
到傍晚六點時，我將已經念了三小時的英文。

比較：

完成式　　　　**完成進行式**

說明動作已完成　　特別強調動作當時的進行

---

have/has been 與 have/has gone 的用法區別

1. **have/has been**：用來表**經驗**，表示「曾經到過……」、「曾經來過……」。
2. **have/has gone**：用來表**動作的完成**，表示「已經到……去了」。

✽ Justin **has been** to Taipei many times. 賈斯汀到過台北很多次了。
　→ 表示他現在不在台北。
✽ Justin **has gone** to Japan. 賈斯汀已經去日本了。
　→ 表示他現在人在日本。

現在完成式與簡單過去式的區別

1. **現在完成式**把過去與現在連在一起，**簡單過去式**則是只說過去的事情。
2. 提及**確定的過去時間**時（如 last night, two days ago），只能使用**簡單過去式**。如果談及**不確定的過去時間**至現在（如 ever, never, recently），就使用**現在完成式**。

✽ Pat **has worked** in London for ten years. 沛特已經在倫敦工作十年了。
　→ 用現在完成式，表示現在他仍在倫敦工作。
✽ Pat **worked** in London for ten years. 沛特以前在倫敦工作長達十年。
　→ 用簡單過去式，表示他現在已不在倫敦工作。
✽ **Has** Pat ever **been** to France? 沛特曾經去過法國嗎？
✽ **Did** Pat go to France last week? 沛特上星期去了法國嗎？

4 被動與時態搭配

不是所有動詞都可以轉換成被動形式，只有**及物動詞**，也就是可接受詞的動詞能轉為被動形式。以下介紹三種被動的時態。

1 變化 1：簡單式

1. The budget report is reviewed by the manager.
2. That report was prepared by the marketing department.
3. The annual report will be compiled by the vice president.

> 1 預算報告是經理審閱的。 2 報告是由行銷部準備的。 3 年度報告將由副總匯編。

2 變化 2：進行式

1. The budget report is being reviewed by the manager at the moment.
2. That report was being prepared by the marketing department at 9 yesterday morning.
3. The annual report will be being compiled by the vice president in December.

> 1 預算報告現正由經理檢閱。 2 報告昨天上午9點由行銷部準備中。 3 年度報告將在12月由副總匯編。

3 變化 3：完成式

1. The budget report has been reviewed by the manager.
2. That report had been prepared by the marketing department before it was sent to the headquarters.
3. The annual report will have been compiled by the vice resident by the end of next year.

> 1 經理已經看過了預算報告。 2 報告在送到總部之前，就已經由行銷部準備好了。 3 年度報告在明年底，將由副總匯編完成。

挑錯並訂正

將下列句子中動詞不正確的地方劃線並訂正。

1 The sun always set in the west.
_____.

2 Jimmy walk to school every day.
_____.

3 Katherine is play the violin now.
_____.

4 Walter goes to the USA last year.
_____.

5 Larry go to the baseball game tomorrow.
_____.

6 Maria lived in Taiwan since she was ten.
_____.

7 I has been to Japan many times.
_____.

8 They swim in the river last Friday.
_____.

9 We eat some seafood last night.
_____.

10 We visit our friends in Taipei next Sunday.
_____.

Quiz 5

挑錯並訂正
將下列句子中動詞不正確的地方劃線並訂正。

填寫正確的時態、主動、被動形式。(注意:有些句子可以有一種以上的時態選擇。)

【Susie Wang 的志向】

My name ① _____ (be) Susie Wang. I ② _____ (be) a senior student in college. Apart from being a student, I ③ _____ (work) part time since the first year in college. My previous job ④ _____ (be) in a convenience store. I ⑤ _____ (work) every day from 9 p.m. to midnight. Before I ⑥ _____ (quit) that job, I ⑦ _____ (witness) two robberies. That ⑧ _____ (be) really frightening. Now, I ⑨ _____ (work) at a big restaurant as a waitress. I ⑩ _____ (wait) at table in that restaurant for six months. After graduation, I ⑪ _____ (have) a chance to get a raise and promotion if I choose to become a full-time employee. I ⑫ _____ (not know) what I am going to do at the moment, but I am sure that I ⑬ _____ (become) somebody in the future. I ⑭ _____ (make) a lot of money by the age of 50. From 50 to 60, I ⑮ _____ (travel) around the world to realize my childhood dream. After that, I ⑯ _____ (live) in a small village peacefully for the rest of my life.

PART 2

英文句子的種類與結構

Unit 5　直述句與疑問句

Unit 6　直接問句與間接問句

Unit 7　主動與被動

Unit 8　祈使句

Unit 9　比較句型

Unit 10　對等連接詞

Unit 11　從屬連接詞與副詞子句

Unit 12　名詞子句

Unit 13　形容詞子句

Unit 14　分詞片語／分詞構句

Unit 5 直述句與疑問句

Warm-up 暖身

猜猜看：在湯姆和艾瑞克兩人的對話中，哪些分別是直述句、疑問句和附加問句？

Tom	What's playing at the theater?
Eric	It's *The Lord of the Rings*. This movie is a big hit. Do you want to see it?
Tom	Sure.
Eric	Keep an eye on my belongings while I am buying the tickets, won't you?

暖身題解答

直述句 It's *The Lord of the Rings*. This movie is a big hit.

疑問句 What's playing at the theater? Do you want to see it?

附加問句 Keep an eye on my belongings while I am buying the tickets, won't you?

1 直述句的肯定與否定用法

1 直述句

直述句 = 主詞 S + 述部 Predicate

又稱平述句，用來陳述事實或可能性，句尾以句號結尾。

述部是描述主詞的動作、狀態或性質等，通常包含述語動詞（V）、受詞（O）、補語（C）、修飾語等。

1. <u>Ken</u> <u>came to Taipei last week.</u>
   主詞　　述部
   肯上週來到台北。

2. <u>Taipei</u> <u>is a crowded and busy city.</u>
   主詞　　述部
   台北是一個擁擠忙碌的城市。

3. <u>Shopping at the night market</u> <u>interests him.</u>
   主詞　　　　　　　　述部
   他對在夜市購物逛街很感興趣。

4. <u>It</u> <u>shocks him to watch the violent TV news.</u>
   主詞　　述部
   看到電視上的暴力新聞讓他很震驚。

5. <u>He</u> <u>eats an apple every day.</u>
   主詞　　述部
   他每天吃一顆蘋果。

→ 表示肯定意思的句子，稱為肯定句，以上的例子都是直述句中的肯定用法。

2 直述句的否定用法

直述句的否定：
- 主詞 + be 動詞 + not ...
- 主詞 + 助動詞 + not + 原形動詞 ...

否定的寫法依句中為 be 動詞、助動詞或一般動詞而有所不同。

一個句子用來表示否定意思者，便稱之為否定句。

否定的部分可用縮寫的方式表示。

❶ **Matthew is not a senior high school student.** 馬修不是高中生。
   = isn't

❷ **The weather did not remain hot all week.** 炎熱的氣候並沒有持續一整個星期。
   = didn't＋原形動詞

❸ **It didn't rain very hard last night.** 昨晚雨下得不大。
   = did not

❹ **Matthew cannot speak French fluently.** 馬修無法說流利的法文。

❺ **Matthew shouldn't stay up.** 馬修不該熬夜。
   = should not

NOTE

上述的否定句中都有 not，如果想要寫作方式更有變化，可以使用其他表示否定的字，如副詞 never, seldom, hardly 等。

* Albert **never** keeps his words. 艾伯特從不守信用。
* He **seldom** tells the truth. 他很少說實話。
* I can **hardly** believe his words. 我幾乎無法相信他的話。

NOTE

否定副詞（no, little, few, neither 等）在句中的擺放位置：
「be 動詞或情態動詞後面、一般動詞前面」。

* There **is no** water in this river. 這條河沒有水。
* We **have little** snow in Taiwan. 台灣很少下雪。
* There **are few** trees in the forest. 這座森林樹木稀少。
* **Neither** of us **likes** the weather in Keelung.
  我們兩人都不喜歡基隆的天氣。

NOTE

表否定的代名詞：nobody, none

* **Nobody likes** to talk to her. 沒有人喜歡和她講話。
* **None** of us **know/knows** who she is. 我們沒有人知道她是誰。
  → 美式英語常用複數動詞，英式英語則常用單數動詞。

Quiz 6

A 句子重組

將下列題目中所有提示字詞整合成一個有意義的句子。
答案中須使用所有提示字詞,且不能隨意增加字詞。

1 Angus _____.
   breaks/his/never/promise

2 Luke _____.
   last/to/week/come/Taipei/didn't

3 Max _____.
   in/stay/won't/for/weeks/Taipei/two

4 Josephine _____.
   speak/Chinese/cannot

5 They _____.
   little/have/winter/snow/in

B 句子改寫:將以下的句子改為否定句。

1 Frank is a junior high school student.

_____.

2 He walks to school every day.

_____.

3 He was chased by a dog on his way to school this morning.

_____.

4 He has studied English for three years.

_____.

5 He will be on vacation in Australia with his family next summer.

_____.

2 疑問句的肯定與否定用法

1 疑問句的種類

> 疑問句用來提出問題，以 be 動詞、助動詞或疑問詞開頭，並以問號結尾。

1 be 動詞 + 主詞 ...?

be動詞 主詞
1. **Are** <u>you</u> a student?　你是學生嗎？
2. **Was** <u>the teacher</u> surprised at the news?　老師對這個消息感到驚訝嗎？
3. **Was** <u>Larry</u> absent yesterday?　賴瑞昨天缺席嗎？

2 助動詞 + 主詞 + 原形動詞 ...?

助動詞 主詞 原形動詞
1. **Does** <u>Cindy</u> <u>read</u> the newspaper every day?　辛蒂每天看報紙嗎？
2. **Will** <u>you</u> <u>go</u> on a picnic in the park this Sunday?　這星期天你會到公園野餐嗎？
3. **May** <u>I</u> <u>ask</u> you a question?　可以問你一個問題嗎？

3 疑問詞 + be 動詞 + 主詞 ...?

疑問詞 be動詞 主詞
1. **What** <u>is</u> <u>your favorite song</u>?　你最喜歡的歌是哪一首？
2. **Where** <u>is</u> <u>the nearest post office</u>?　最近的郵局在哪裡？
3. **How** <u>are</u> <u>you</u>?　你好嗎？

2 常見的疑問詞（5W1H）

常見的疑問詞 what, who, where, when, why, how，被稱為 **5W1H**：

1. **What** 用來詢問**事物**或**人的身分、職業**
2. **Who** 用來詢問**人**
3. **Where** 用來詢問**地方**
4. **When** 用來詢問**時間**
5. **Why** 用來詢問**原因**或**理由**
6. **How** 用來詢問**方法**和**狀態**

1. 疑問詞 ＋ 助動詞 ＋ 主詞 ＋ 原形動詞 ...？

疑問詞　助動詞　主詞　原形動詞

① **When will** they **get** to the airport?　他們什麼時候會抵達機場？
② **Why did** you **cry**?　你為什麼哭了？

2. 疑問詞 ＋ 動詞 ＋ 主詞 ＋ ...？

疑問詞　動詞

① **Who told** you the news?　誰告訴你這個消息？
② **What makes** you so happy?　什麼事使你這麼高興？

3 疑問句的否定

1 在肯定疑問句的助動詞或 be 動詞後面加上 not，縮寫成一字，句尾加問號，即形成否定語態。

2 如果助動詞或 be 動詞沒有和 not 縮寫成一字，not 就要緊跟在主詞後面。

肯定的疑問句	Are you a student? 你是學生嗎？
否定的疑問句	Aren't you a student? = Are you not a student? 你不是學生嗎？

在助動詞或 be 動詞後面加上 not，縮寫成一字，句尾加問號，即形成否定語態。

如果助動詞或 be 動詞沒有和 not 縮寫成一字，not 就要緊跟在主詞後面。

肯定疑問	Can you speak English?	你會說英語嗎？
否定疑問	Can't you speak English? =Can you not speak English?	你不會說英語嗎？

肯定疑問	Where will you go this summer?	今年夏天你會去哪裡？
否定疑問	Where won't you go this summer? =Where will you not go this summer?	今年夏天你不會去哪裡？

> **NOTE**
> ❶ 否定疑問句中將助動詞或 be 動詞和 not 縮寫的使用，較為常見。
> ❷ 通常可以用標點符號來判斷是**直述句**（以句號結尾）或**疑問句**（以問號結尾）。

4 附加問句

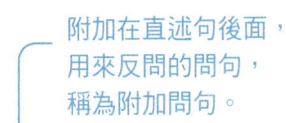

附加在直述句後面，用來反問的問句，稱為附加問句。

① 附加問句和直述句的搭配：直述句和附加問句「正負相反」，例如直述句為肯定，附加問句就要否定，反之亦然。
② 附加問句中的主詞，要用**人稱代名詞**。

附加問句 = 直述句 , 附加問句 ?

附加問句和直述句之間要用逗號分開。

1 <u>Becky **went** to the Taipei Zoo with her friends by MRT</u>, **didn't she**?
　　　肯定句　　　　　　　　　　　　　　　　　　　　　　否定　代名詞

　　附加問句要的主詞，要使用人稱代名詞 she。
　　前面的直述句為肯定句，後面的附加問句就要用否定。

貝琦和朋友搭捷運到台北木柵動物園，不是嗎？

2 They **didn't see** the baby koala, **did they**?
　　　否定句　　　　　　　　　　　　　　肯定　代名詞

　　前面的直述句為否定句，後面的附加問句就要用肯定。

他們沒有看到無尾熊寶寶，是嗎？

Quiz 1

Ⓐ 句子重組

將下列題目中所有提示字詞整合成一個有意義的句子。答案中須使用所有提示字詞,且不能隨意增加字詞。

❶ Can _____ ?
Sharon/piano/play/the/well

❷ Will _____ ?
be/pianist/a/she/in the future

❸ Did _____ ?
eat/restaurant/the/they/last/night/at

❹ Does _____ ?
every day/walk/she/to/school

❺ Is _____ ?
yours/umbrella/different/my/from

Ⓑ 句子改寫:依題目之提示,將原句改寫成指定型式。

❶ Anna keeps an English diary every day.（加入附加問句）

_____ .

❷ They didn't play basketball yesterday.（加入附加問句）

_____ .

❸ Do you like to play basketball?（改成否定句）

_____ .

❹ Did they have a good time?（改成否定句）

_____ .

❺ What will you do this summer?（改成否定句）

_____ .

3 直述句改為疑問句

1 直述句的動詞為 be 動詞或助動詞時

要將直述句（動詞為 be 動詞或助動詞時）改為疑問句，步驟如下：

步驟一 將 be 動詞或助動詞移到主詞前面，並大寫。
步驟二 將原本的主詞，改為小寫（專有名詞例外）。
步驟三 其餘內容照抄，最後將句尾的句號改成問號。

直述句　主詞 + be動詞/助動詞 ...

① 將 be 動詞或助動詞移到主詞前面，並大寫。

疑問句　be動詞/助動詞 + 主詞 ...? ③ 其餘內容照抄，最後將句尾的句號改成問號。

② 將原本的主詞，改為小寫（專有名詞例外）。

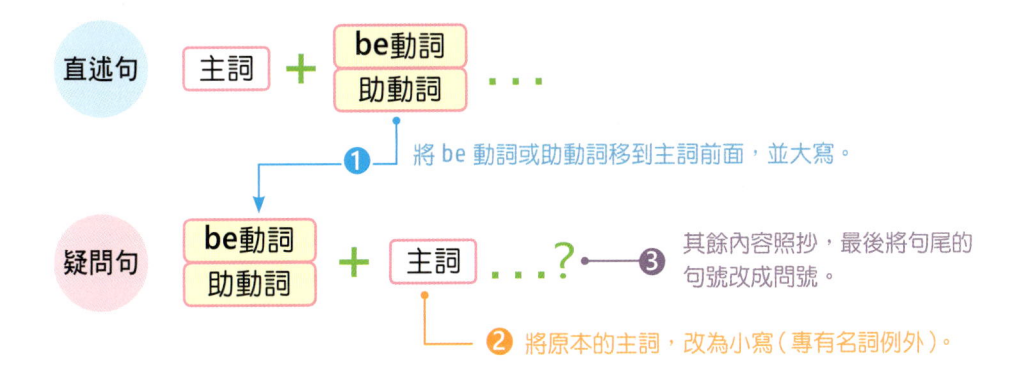

1 That little girl is an elementary school student.

① 將 be 動詞 is 移到主詞前面，並大寫成 Is。
③ 其餘內容照抄，最後將句尾的句號改成問號。

→ Is that little girl an elementary school student?

將原本的主詞 That little girl，改為小寫開頭 that little girl。

那個小女孩是小學生。
這女孩是小學生嗎？

2 This little girl can play the violin very well.

→ Can this little girl play the violin very well?

這個小女孩小提琴拉得很好。
這個小女孩的小提琴拉得很好嗎？

2 直述句的動詞為一般動詞時

要將直述句（動詞為一般動詞時）改為疑問句，步驟如下：

步驟一 主詞前面加大寫的助動詞 Do、Does（用於現在式）或 Did（用於過去式）。
步驟二 將原直述句中的動詞改為原形動詞。
步驟三 將原本的主詞，改為小寫（專有名詞例外）。
步驟四 其餘內容照抄，最後將句尾的句號改成問號。

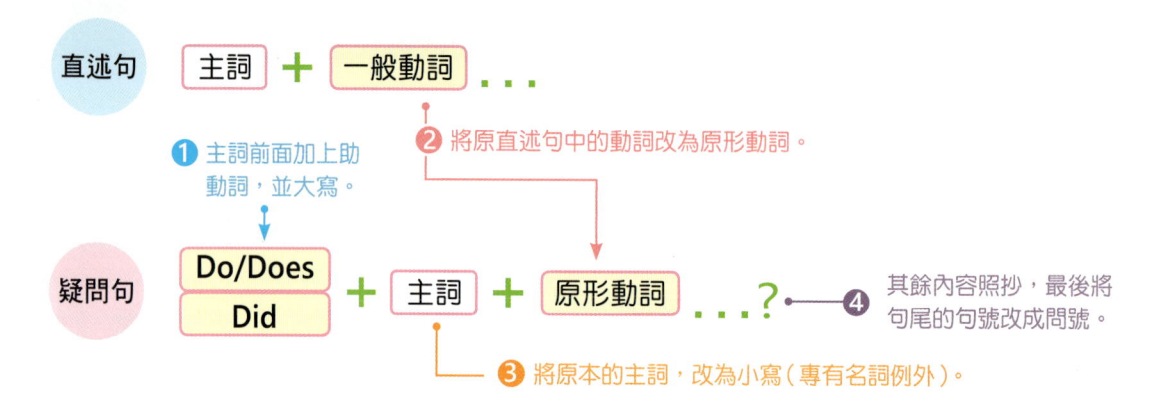

直述句： 主詞 + 一般動詞 ...

❶ 主詞前面加上助動詞，並大寫。
❷ 將原直述句中的動詞改為原形動詞。

疑問句： Do/Does / Did + 主詞 + 原形動詞 ... ?

❸ 將原本的主詞，改為小寫（專有名詞例外）。
❹ 其餘內容照抄，最後將句尾的句號改成問號。

❶ Maggie gets up early every day.　　　　　瑪姬每天早起。
→ Does Maggie get up early every day?
　　↑加入 Does，並大寫。　↑一般動詞 get 使用原形。

❷ Maggie and her family eat bread for breakfast.
→ Do Maggie and her family eat bread for breakfast?
瑪姬和家人早餐吃麵包。

❸ They ate pasta at an Italian restaurant last night.
→ Did they eat pasta at an Italian restaurant last night?
昨晚他們在義式餐廳吃義大利麵。

❸ 將完成式的直述句變成疑問句的句型

直述句　主詞 ＋ have/has ＋ 過去分詞 ...

完成式（have/has ＋過去分詞）的 have/has 被當作助動詞，所以將 have/has 移至主詞前，就可以形成疑問句。

疑問句　Have/Has ＋ 主詞 ＋ 過去分詞 ...？

❶ Vicky **has** played the guitar for many years.　維姬彈了好幾年的吉他了。

→ **Has** Vicky played the guitar for many years?　維姬已經彈了好幾年的吉他嗎？

❷ She **has** studied English for three years.　她學英語已經有三年了。

→ **Has** she studied English for three years?　她學英語已經有三年了嗎？

4 直述句改為以疑問詞開頭的疑問句

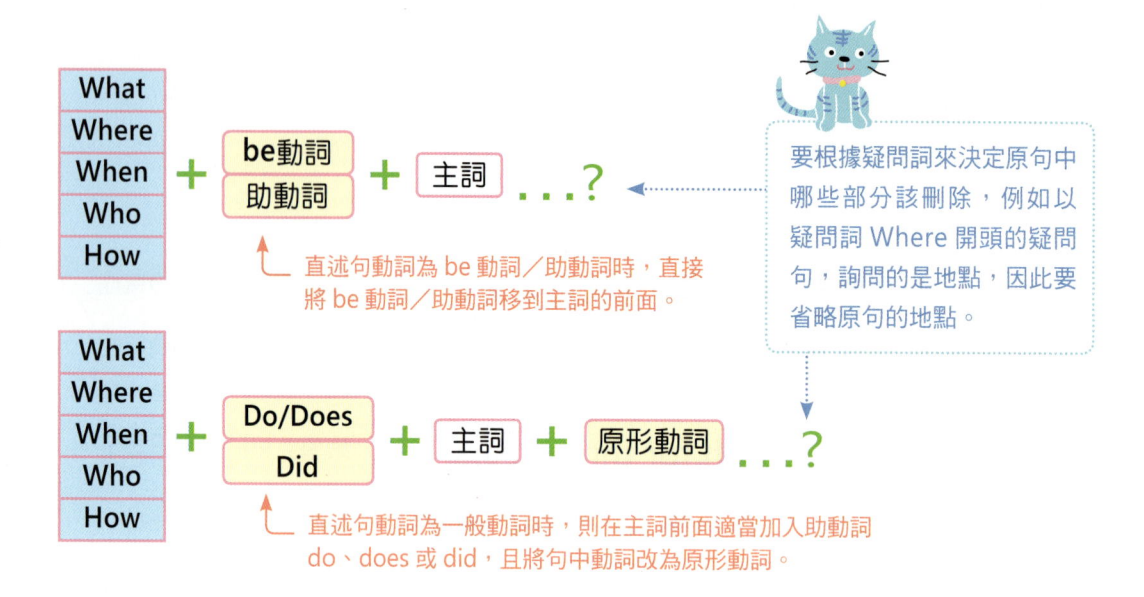

| What |
| Where |
| When |
| Who |
| How |

+ be動詞 / 助動詞 + 主詞 …？

↳ 直述句動詞為 be 動詞／助動詞時，直接將 be 動詞／助動詞移到主詞的前面。

| What |
| Where |
| When |
| Who |
| How |

+ Do/Does / Did + 主詞 + 原形動詞 …？

↳ 直述句動詞為一般動詞時，則在主詞前面適當加入助動詞 do、does 或 did，且將句中動詞改為原形動詞。

要根據疑問詞來決定原句中哪些部分該刪除，例如以疑問詞 Where 開頭的疑問句，詢問的是地點，因此要省略原句的地點。

1 琳達將待在美國一個月 → 琳達會在美國待多久？

Linda will stay in the USA ~~for a month~~.

→ How long will Linda stay in the USA?
　　↳ 以疑問詞 How 開頭的問句

How long 詢問「多久時間」，因此要刪去句中的 for a month。

2 琳達去年去過美國 → 琳達去年去了哪裡？

Linda went ~~to the USA~~ last year.

→ Where did Linda go last year?
　　↳ 以疑問詞 Where 開頭的問句

Where 詢問「地點」，因此要刪去句中的 to the USA。

Quiz 8

句子改寫

依題目之提示，將原句改寫成指定型式。

1 Roger came to Greece last week.

When _____?

2 He will stay in Greece for two weeks.

How long _____?

3 Sean and his friends went to the Taipei Zoo by MRT last Saturday.

How _____?

4 He usually goes to bed at 11:00 p.m.

What time _____?

5 I went to the Sun Moon Lake last Sunday.

Where _____?

6 That tall boy is my brother.

Who _____?

7 They went swimming in the river yesterday.（改成疑問句）

_____?

8 Tomorrow will be a fine day.（改成疑問句）

_____?

9 William walks to school every day.（改成疑問句）

_____?

10 That little boy can sing the song.（改成疑問句）

_____?

Unit 6

直接問句與間接問句

Warm-up 暖身

以下是警方和崔西的對話中，哪些是直接問句，哪些是間接問句？

A burglar broke into Tracy's house last night and robbed her of lots of valuable jewelry. The police are investigating this robbery, and they ask Tracy to give them some clues in order to catch the burglar.

The police	Do you remember what the burglar looks like?
Tracy	Yes, he's got dark skin and short hair.
The police	Good. How tall is he?
Tracy	He is medium height. I think he's around 1.7 meters tall.
The police	Can you guess how old he is?
Tracy	I guess he's middle-aged.

暖身題解答

直接問句　How tall is he?
間接問句　Do you remember what the burglar looks like?
間接問句　Can you guess how old he is?

1 何謂間接問句?

前面介紹的疑問句都屬於直接問句,我們可以把這些疑問句接在主要子句後面,構成由**疑問詞**引導的從屬子句,形成**間接問句**。間接問句可當作**名詞子句**,作主詞、受詞或補語。間接問句的結構和**直述句**相同:

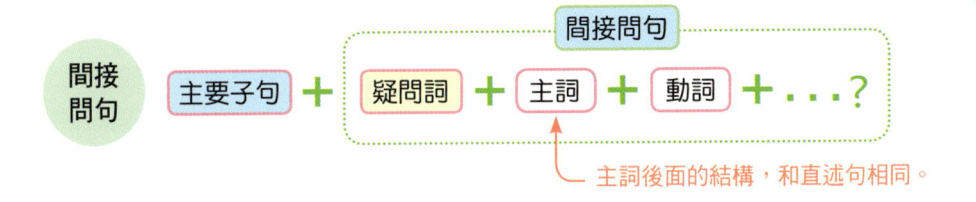

間接問句 = 主要子句 + [疑問詞 + 主詞 + 動詞 + ... ?]（間接問句）

主詞後面的結構,和直述句相同。

直接問句 What does the burglar look like?
小偷的長相為何?

間接問句 Do you remember what the burglar looks like?
　　　　　　（主要子句）　　　（疑問詞）（主詞）（動詞）（間接問句）
你記得小偷的長相嗎?

1. **Where he lives** is still unknown.
   （間接問句作主詞）（動詞）（副詞）（主詞補語）
   他住在哪裡仍是未知。

2. The police want to know **how tall the burglar is**.
   （主詞）（動詞）（間接問句作受詞）
   警方想知道小偷有多高。

3. The question is **how the police are going to catch him**.
   （主詞）（動詞）（間接問句作主詞補語）
   問題是警方要如何逮捕他。

103

2 直接問句與間接問句的結構差異

直接問句和間接問句的結構差異，可以從以下方面來分析：
① 主詞、動詞的位置（兩者的位置剛好相反）
② 標點符號（句尾有句號和問號的差別）
③ 依助動詞的種類做不同的變化

1 主詞、動詞的位置和標點符號

1 主詞、動詞的位置相反：直接問句的主詞要放在 be 動詞或助動詞後面；間接問句的主詞要放在 be 動詞或助動詞前面。

2 判斷主要子句是肯定句或疑問句：直接問句一律以**問號**結尾；而當間接問句的主要子句為疑問句時，要用**問號**結尾，肯定句時則用**句號**。

直接問句 Where is the nearest supermarket?
　　　　　疑問詞　be動詞　　　　主詞

最近的超級市場在哪裡？
請問最近的超級市場在哪裡？

間接問句 Could you tell me where the nearest supermarket is?
　　　　　　　　　　　　　 疑問詞　　主詞　　　　　　be動詞

└ 主要子句為疑問句，所以間接問句以問號結尾。

直接問句 What can't we do in class?
　　　　　疑問詞　否定助動詞　主詞

間接問句 Tell us what we can't do in class.
　　　　　　　　　疑問詞　主詞　否定助動詞

└ 主要子句為肯定句，所以間接問句以句號結尾。

我們在課堂上不可以做什麼事情？
告訴我們在課堂上不可以做什麼事情。

2 依助動詞的種類做不同的變化

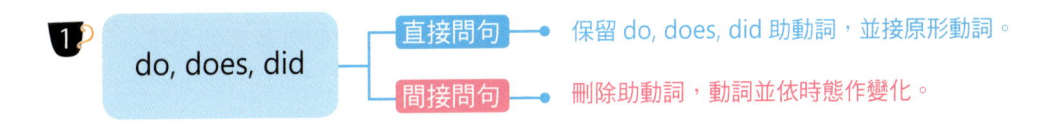

❶ do, does, did
- 直接問句 → 保留 do, does, did 助動詞，並接原形動詞。
- 間接問句 → 刪除助動詞，動詞並依時態作變化。

直接問句 Where **did** you **go** last weekend?
　　　　　助動詞過去式　原形動詞
上週末你到哪裡去了？

間接問句 Tell me where you **went** last weekend.
　　　　　主要子句　　　　　動詞過去式
告訴我上週末你到哪裡去了。

↑ 刪去 did 後，因時態是過去式，動詞用過去式 went。

❷ 否定式的助動詞 don't, doesn't, didn't
- 直接問句
- 間接問句
→ 不論是直接問句還是間接問句，這些助動詞都要保留。

直接問句 Why **didn't** you **show up** last weekend?
　　　　　否定助動詞過去式　原形動詞
為什麼你上週末沒到場？

間接問句 Tell me why you **didn't** **show up** last weekend.
　　　　　主要子句　　　否定助動詞過去式　原形動詞
告訴我為什麼你上週末沒到場。

↑ 否定式助動詞 didn't 要保留。

❸ can, can't, will, won't 等其他助動詞
- 直接問句
- 間接問句
→ 不論是直接問句還是間接問句，這些助動詞都要保留。

直接問句 How long **will** Nelly **stay** in Hong Kong?
　　　　　　　助動詞　　　原形動詞

間接問句 Do you know how long Nelly **will** **stay** in Hong Kong?
　　　　　主要子句　　　　　　　　　助動詞　原形動詞

↑ 助動詞 will 要保留。

妮莉要在香港待多久？
你知道妮莉要在香港待多久嗎？

105

Quiz 9

句子重組
請將題目中所有提示字詞，整合成一個有意義的句子。

1 Where _____?
John/is

2 Do you know _____?
is/John/where

3 The problem is _____.
arrest/are/we/how/to/him/going

4 Tell me _____.
where/last night/went/you

5 Tell me _____.
didn't/you/why/do/homework/your

6 Do you know _____?
Lydia/in/how long/stay/will /Singapore

7 Tell me _____.
what/do/I/should

8 I don't know _____.
can/how/I/help/you

9 Do you know _____?
what/to/likes/Stella/do/after school

10 Tell me _____.
you/school/usually/how/go/to

3 如何將直接問句改為間接問句

1 be 動詞或助動詞為首的直接問句

間接問句： 主要子句 + whether / if + 主詞 + be 動詞 / 助動詞 ...

以 be 動詞或助動詞為首的直接問句，要改成間接問句時，通常用連接詞 whether 或 if（是否）來引導。

通常 whether（是否）引導的子句後面，可以加 or not；但 if 引導的子句，則不適用。

直接問句 Is everyone surprised at this big news?

間接問句 I don't know whether everyone is surprised at this big news (or not).
　　　　　　主要子句　　　　以 whether 引導，形成間接問句。

每個人都對這天大的消息感到驚訝嗎？
我不知道是否每個人都對這天大的消息感到驚訝。

直接問句 Will she attend Kay's wedding?

間接問句 Tell me if she will attend Kay's wedding.
　　　　　　主要子句　　以 if 引導，形成間接問句。

她會參加凱的婚禮嗎？
告訴我她是否會參加凱的婚禮。

2 疑問詞為首、動詞為 be 動詞的直接問句

間接問句： 主要子句 + 疑問詞 + 主詞 + be 動詞 ...

以疑問詞為首、動詞為 be 動詞的直接問句，改成間接問句時，僅需要將主詞、動詞位置調換。

直接問句 Who is the singer?

間接問句 Tell me who the singer is.
　　　　　　主要子句　疑問詞

那歌手是誰呀？
你知道那個歌手是誰嗎？

3 疑問詞為首、動詞為助動詞 do 的直接問句

助動詞為肯定: 主要子句 ＋ 疑問詞 ＋ 主詞 ＋ 動詞 ...
(動詞依原句時態變化)

直接問句: When did Iris get to the airport?
　　　　　　　助動詞（過去式）　原形動詞

間接問句: He wants to know when Iris got to the airport.
　　　　　　　主要子句
(直接問句為過去式，間接問句的動詞要用過去式。)

艾莉絲何時抵達機場？
他想知道艾莉絲何時抵達機場。

助動詞為否定: 主要子句 ＋ 疑問詞 ＋ 主詞 ＋ don't / doesn't / didn't ＋ 原形動詞 ...

直接問句: Why don't you listen carefully in class?
　　　　　　　　助動詞（否定）　原形動詞

間接問句: Tell me why you don't listen carefully in class.
　　　　　　　主要子句　　　　助動詞don't＋原形動詞
(間接問句的否定助動詞 don't 要保留。)

你為什麼上課不仔細聽？
告訴我你為什麼上課不仔細聽。

4 疑問詞為首，動詞為其他助動詞的直接問句

間接問句: 主要子句 ＋ 疑問詞 ＋ 主詞 ＋ 助動詞 ＋ 原形動詞 ...

直接問句: How long will that movie star stay in Taiwan?
　　　　　　　　　　　　　　　　　　　　原形動詞

間接問句: He asks how long that movie star will stay in Taiwan.
　　　　　　　主要子句　　　　　　　　　　　　助動詞 原形動詞

直接問句: Why can't the movie star come to Taiwan again?
　　　　　　　　助動詞（否定）　　　　　原形動詞

間接問句: Tell me why the movie star can't come to Taiwan again.
　　　　　　　主要子句　　　　　　　　　助動詞can't＋原形動詞

那位電影明星會在台灣待多久？
他問那位電影明星會在台灣待多久。

為什麼那位電影明星不能再來台灣？
告訴我為何那位電影明星不能再來台灣。

Quiz 10

句子改寫
將下列句子改寫成間接問句。

---

1 Where is the nearest bank?

　Tell me _____ .

2 Why were you late yesterday?

　Tell me _____ .

3 Where did you go last Monday?

　Tell me _____ .

4 What do you usually do in your free time?

　Could you tell me _____ ?

5 Why didn't Carrie show up last Sunday?

　Tell me _____ .

6 Why doesn't Audrey like Dennis?

　Do you know _____ ?

7 How long will Jeffery stay in South Korea?

　Do you know _____ ?

8 What can I do to make it better?

　I don't know _____ .

9 Will she attend Kim's recital the day after tomorrow?

　Do you know _____ ?

10 Are your parents satisfied with what you have done?

　Tell me _____ .

Unit 7 主動與被動

Warm-up 暖身

猜猜看：以下哪些是主動語態，哪些是被動語態？

Sue is holding a birthday party next Friday. Rita and I have been invited to the party. We wonder what we should buy as her birthday present. It is said that clocks, handkerchiefs, shoes, and umbrellas may bring bad luck. After a discussion, we decide to buy her a jigsaw.

暖身題解答

直接問句 How tall is he?
間接問句 Do you remember what the burglar looks like?
間接問句 Can you guess how old he is?

1 將主動句改為被動句

1 何謂主動句、被動句？

1 **主動句**表示由**主詞**所產生的動作或行為。
2 主詞是動作的接受者，稱為**被動句**。

1 **Sue has invited** Rita and me to the party.
　主詞　動詞（主動語態）　　has invited（邀請）是由 Sue 行動的，故用主動語態。

2 **We tasted** the red wine.
　主詞　動詞（主動語態）　　tasted（品嚐）是由 we 行動的，故用主動語態。

3 **Rita and I have been invited** to the party by Sue.
　　主詞　　　動詞（被動語態）　　主詞 Rita and I 是 have been invited
　　　　　　　　　　　　　　　　　（被邀請）的接受者，故用被動語態。

4 **The red wine was tasted** by us.
　　主詞　　　動詞（被動語態）　　主詞 The red wine 是 was tasted
　　　　　　　　　　　　　　　　　（被品嚐）的接受者。

1. 蘇邀請我和麗塔參加派對。

2. 我們品嚐了這紅酒。

3. 麗塔和我被蘇邀請去參加派對。

4. 這紅酒被我們品嚐了。

2 主動改為被動的步驟

步驟一 把主動語態的受詞，改成被動語態的主詞。
步驟二 被動語態的動詞形式為「be 動詞＋過去分詞」。
步驟三 把主動語態的主詞，以「by ＋行為者」改成被動語態
（by 後面要接受格）。

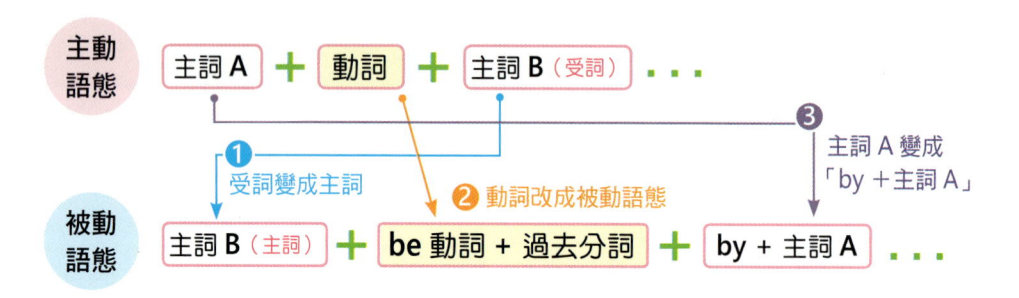

主動語態　主詞 A ＋ 動詞 ＋ 主詞 B（受詞）…

① 受詞變成主詞
② 動詞改成被動語態
③ 主詞 A 變成「by ＋主詞 A」

被動語態　主詞 B（主詞）＋ be 動詞＋過去分詞 ＋ by ＋主詞 A …

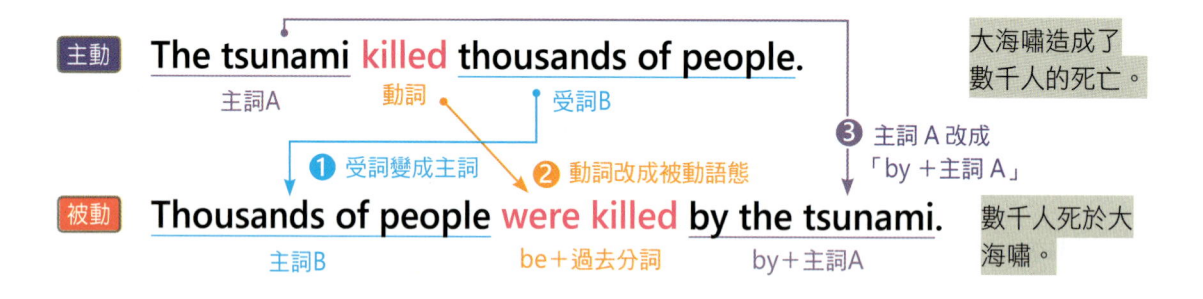

主動 The tsunami killed thousands of people.
　　　　主詞A　　　動詞　　　受詞B

大海嘯造成了數千人的死亡。

① 受詞變成主詞
② 動詞改成被動語態
③ 主詞 A 改成「by ＋主詞 A」

被動 Thousands of people were killed by the tsunami.
　　　　主詞B　　　be＋過去分詞　　by＋主詞A

數千人死於大海嘯。

> **NOTE** 主詞或受詞為一般名詞（Sue, the red wine, the tsunami）時，在主動改被動的情況下，只要移動位置，不需要變化。但如果主動句中是以「**人稱代名詞**」作主詞或受詞，改成被動句時，就要依位置改變成主格或受格。

3 主動句中的動詞為**一般動詞**時

1. 被動句中，要在**一般動詞**前加入 **be 動詞**，並根據原句判斷**時態**和**單複數**。
2. 原本的一般動詞不論時態如何，都要改為用**過去分詞**。

🍀 蘇珊娜用她迷人的嗓音唱這首歌。 → 這首歌用蘇珊娜迷人的嗓音來被唱出。

主動 Suzanne sang the song with her fascinating voice.
　　　　主詞A　　過去式動詞　　受詞B

被動 The song was sung by Suzanne with her fascinating voice.
　　　　主詞B　was＋過去分詞　by＋主詞A

主詞是單數 the song，動詞是「be 動詞＋過去分詞」（was sung）。

主動語態的主詞變成被動語態的「by ＋行為者」（by Suzanne）。

4 主動句中的動詞為**情態助動詞**時

1. 主動句中的動詞為**情態助動詞**，要改為被動句時，在助動詞後加上 **be 動詞原形**。
2. 原句中的**一般動詞**，一律改為**過去分詞**。

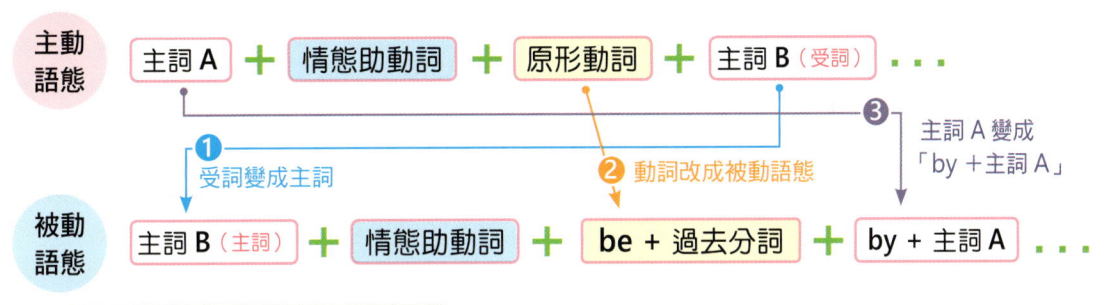

主動語態　主詞 A ＋ 情態助動詞 ＋ 原形動詞 ＋ 主詞 B（受詞）...

❶ 受詞變成主詞
❷ 動詞改成被動語態
❸ 主詞 A 變成「by ＋主詞 A」

被動語態　主詞 B（主詞）＋ 情態助動詞 ＋ be ＋ 過去分詞 ＋ by ＋ 主詞 A ...

🍀 我們可以烤個蛋糕慶祝她的生日。

主動 We can bake a cake for her birthday.
　　　　主詞A　情態助動詞　原形動詞　受詞B

被動 A cake can be baked for her birthday (by us).
　　　　主詞B　情態助動詞　be＋過去分詞　　　　　by＋主詞A

因被動句子沒有特別強調誰烤蛋糕，所以 by us 可以省略。

主動動詞是 can bake，改為被動句時，動詞要改成 can be baked。

🍀 每個人都該為她唱生日快樂歌。

主動 Everyone should sing the happy birthday song for her.

被動 The happy birthday song should be sung for her (by everyone).

5 主動句中的動詞為**進行式**時

1 主動句中的動詞為**進行式**，改為被動時，原句 be 動詞時態不變，但要依照被動句中主詞的**單**、**複數**而更改。

2 在原來的 be 動詞和現在分詞間加入 **being**。原本的現在分詞一律改為**過去分詞**。

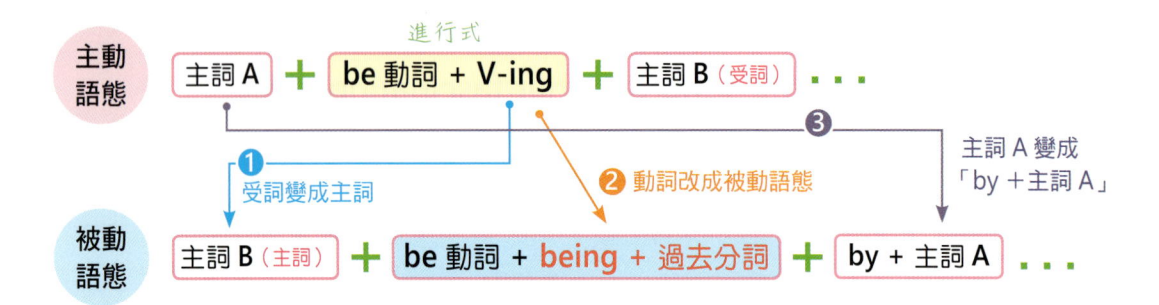

主動語態： 主詞 A ＋ [be 動詞 + V-ing] (進行式) ＋ 主詞 B（受詞）...

① 受詞變成主詞
② 動詞改成被動語態
③ 主詞 A 變成「by + 主詞 A」

被動語態： 主詞 B（主詞）＋ [be 動詞 + being + 過去分詞] ＋ by + 主詞 A ...

🍀 **1** 奧立佛說：「記者正在報導東南亞的最新消息。」

主動　"The correspondent **is reporting** the latest news from southeast Asia," said Oliver.
（主詞A）（is+V-ing）（受詞B）

被動　"The latest news from southeast Asia **is being reported** by the correspondent," said Oliver.
（主詞B）（is+being+過去分詞）（by+行為者（主詞A））

被動語態的動詞是「be + being + 過去分詞」（is being reported）。

🍀 **2** 華特說：「老闆正當著大家的面批評奧立佛。」

主動　"The boss **is criticizing** Oliver in public," said Walter.

被動　"Oliver **is being criticized** in public by the boss," said Walter.

6 主動句中的動詞為**完成式**時

1 主動句中的動詞為**完成式**，改為被動時，原來的**過去分詞**保持不變，並在前面加上 **been**。

2 原本的助動詞 have 時態不變，但要依被動句中的主詞作**單複數變化**。

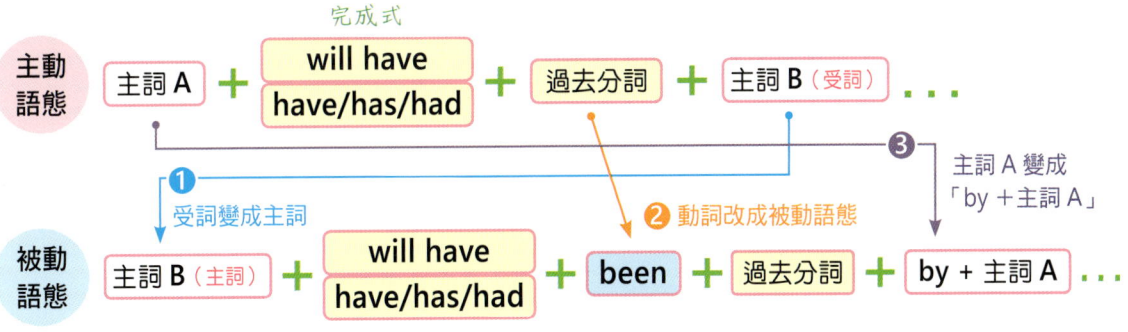

主動語態	主詞 A + [完成式 will have / have/has/had] + 過去分詞 + 主詞 B（受詞）...
被動語態	主詞 B（主詞）+ will have / have/has/had + been + 過去分詞 + by + 主詞 A ...

❶ 受詞變成主詞
❷ 動詞改成被動語態
❸ 主詞 A 變成「by + 主詞 A」

1 凱倫已邀請我們參加她的婚禮。

主動 Karen has invited us to her wedding.
　　　主詞A　has＋過去分詞　受詞B

被動 We have been invited by Karen to her wedding.
　　　主詞B　have＋been＋過去分詞　　by＋主詞A

↑ 主詞 we 是複數，所以用 have。

2 婚禮費用已由新娘家支付。

主動 The bride's family has paid for the wedding.

被動 The wedding has been paid for by the bride's family.

Quiz 11

挑錯並訂正
把下列句子錯誤的地方劃線並訂正。

1. Flora was invited to the seminar by I.

2. My money was steal.

3. The cake was made by he.

4. The card was written by we.

5. The house was painted by they.

6. The report was wrote by Mia.

7. My car was fix by that old man.

8. The roof repaired last night.

9. The house built ten years ago.

10. The book wrote by my teacher.

2 被動句要注意的事項

1 「主詞＋及物動詞＋間接受詞＋直接受詞」句型改為被動語態

「主詞＋及物動詞＋間接受詞＋直接受詞」句型改為被動語態，有以下兩種方式。

主動語態

主詞 ＋ 及物動詞 ＋ 間接受詞（通常是人）＋ 直接受詞（通常是物）...

🍀 Martin gave her a watch.　馬丁給了她一隻錶。
　　 主詞　及物動詞　間接受詞　直接受詞

被動語態A

間接受詞作主詞時，直接受詞要放在「be ＋過去分詞」後面。

間接受詞（通常是人）＋ be 動詞＋過去分詞 ＋ 直接受詞（通常是物）＋ by ＋主詞

🍀 She was given a watch by Martin.
　　　 was＋過去分詞　直接受詞
　　 間接受詞作主詞

> 以人（間接受詞）作主詞的被動語態 A，比以物（直接受詞）作主詞的被動語態 B，更為常見。

被動語態B

直接受詞作主詞時，間接受詞要放在「be ＋過去分詞＋介系詞」後面。

直接受詞（通常是物）＋ be 動詞＋過去分詞 ＋ 介系詞＋間接受詞（通常是人）＋ by ＋主詞 ...

🍀 A watch was given to her by Martin.
　　　　 was＋過去分詞　間接受詞
　　 直接受詞作主詞

2 「主詞＋及物動詞＋受詞＋受詞補語」句型改為被動語態

主動語態： 主詞 ＋ 及物動詞 ＋ 受詞 ＋ 受詞補語 …

被動語態： 受詞 ＋ be 動詞＋過去分詞 ＋ 受詞補語 ＋ by＋主詞

要用受詞作主詞，並將受詞補語放在過去分詞之後。（不可使用受詞補語作主詞）

❶ 我們推選亞歷山大為我們的主席。

主動 We elected Alexander our chairman.
主詞　及物動詞　　受詞　　　受詞補語

被動 Alexander was elected our chairman (by us).
用受詞 Alexander 作主詞

❷ 寶琳解釋道：「我們稱牠為海狸。」

主動 "We call it a beaver," Pauline explained.
　　　主詞 及物動詞 受詞 受詞補語

被動 "It is called a beaver," Pauline explained.
用受詞 it 作主詞

3 「It is thought...」和「It is said...」兩種被動語態句型

「It is thought . . .」（一般認為）和「It is said . . .」（據說；聽說）兩種被動語態句型，分別用來描述人們普遍所認為、所稱說的事。

被動語態A： It ＋ be 動詞＋過去分詞 ＋ that 子句 . . .

被動語態B： 主詞 ＋ be 動詞＋過去分詞 ＋ to ＋ 原形動詞 . . .

1. 他們認為瑪格莉特想要時鐘當聖誕禮物。

主動 They think that Margaret wants a clock as her Christmas gift.
　　　 主詞　　動詞　　受詞（由that引導子句，作think的受詞）

被動 It is thought that Margaret wants a clock as her Christmas gift.
　　　 It＋be動詞＋過去分詞　　　　that子句

　＝ Margaret is thought to want a clock as her Christmas gift.
　　　主詞　　be動詞＋過去分詞　to＋原形動詞

2. 據說時鐘和雨傘會帶來壞運。

主動 People say that clocks and umbrellas may bring bad luck.
　　　 主詞　　動詞　　受詞（由that引導的子句，作say的受詞）

被動 It is said that clocks and umbrellas may bring bad luck.
　　　 It＋be動詞＋過去分詞　　that 子句

　＝ Clocks and umbrellas are said to bring bad luck.
　　　　主詞　　　　　be動詞＋過去分詞　to＋原形動詞

4 「by +行為者」可省略的情況

被動語態中,在下列情況時,「by +行為者」可以省略:

1. 行為者為**泛稱的人們**。
2. 從句意或上下文,**可以推知行為者**。
3. **行為者不清楚**時。

1. **Cars and motorcycles can be seen everywhere in Taipei.**
   → 行為者泛指一般人們,因此省略。

2. **Mandarin is spoken in Taiwan.**
   → 從句意可以推知行為者是人。

3. **Stores in Taiwan are usually closed round 10:00 at night.**
   → 不清楚行為者是誰,通常為一般人。

1. 在台北,到處可見汽車和摩托車。

2. 在台灣,人們說國語。

3. 台灣的商店大約在晚上 10 點左右打烊。

NOTE 寫作時,在什麼樣的情況下,可以使用被動語態?

❶ 當我們**不清楚**某件事是什麼人或物所做時,例如:

❋ **Our car was stolen.** 我們的車子被偷了。
   → 不知道誰偷了車子。

❷ 當我們**不需要說明**某件事是由什麼人或物所做時,例如:

❋ **It is said that clocks, handkerchiefs, shoes, and umbrellas may bring bad luck.**
   據說時鐘、手帕、鞋子和雨傘會帶來壞運。
   → 誰是說話者,並不是重點。

❸ 當我們**不想說明**某件事是由什麼人或物所做時,例如:

❋ **The party will be finished by 11:00 p.m.**
   在晚上 11 點前會結束派對。

Quiz 12

句子改寫

將下列句子改寫成被動語態。

1. Eileen put the card in a drawer.

2. Lillian sang the song with her beautiful voice.

3. She sent Steve a Christmas card.

4. Lynn's teacher wrote the novel.

5. Juliet will ask Jim for a dance.

6. Nina has invited us to the ball.

7. That tsunami killed two thousand people.

8. I will have finished the work by Monday.

9. Many people in Canada speak both English and French.

10. They think that she wants a necklace as her valentine.

Unit 8 祈使句

在以下談論餐桌禮儀的段落中,包含五個祈使句(加底線的句子),用來指出用餐的基本禮儀,表達強烈的建議。觀察一下,這些祈使句在句型結構上的有什麼樣的特點?

Good table manners will make a favorable impression. Here are some tips for you:

1. Don't smoke while dining out.
2. Sit up straight at the table.
3. Don't talk with your mouth full.
4. If you need something that you cannot reach, politely ask someone to pass it to you. For example, "Pass me the salt and pepper, please."
5. Never make loud noises when you eat.

1 何謂祈使句？

1. 祈使句有多種用途，除了可用來表達**強烈建議**外，還可用來表示**命令**、**請求**、**警告**、**禁止**、**邀請**或**招待**等意思。
2. 祈使句的句型結構有以下特點：
   1. 通常**省略**主詞，但如果需要強調祈使的對象時，可加上**名詞**或**代名詞**。
   2. 都是將**原形動詞**放**句首**來表達。
   3. 如果要表示**否定**，則在**句首的原形動詞**前加 don't（或 never）。
3. 祈使句依對象人稱的不同，分為對第二人稱、第一、三人稱的祈使，以及表示條件的祈使句，以下分別介紹之。

1 祈使句主詞為第二人稱 you

You … → ① 原形動詞 …
② be 動詞 ＋ 形容詞 …

祈使句表請求、命令，以第二人稱（you）為主詞時，通常會將 you 省略，

　　　　　通常將 you 省略

1. (You) **Help** me with the baggage, please.　　請幫我拿行李。　→ 表達請求
   原形動詞
2. (You) **Be polite** to passengers.　　對旅客要有禮貌。　→ 表達命令
   Be＋形容詞

2 祈使句主詞為第一人稱、第三人稱

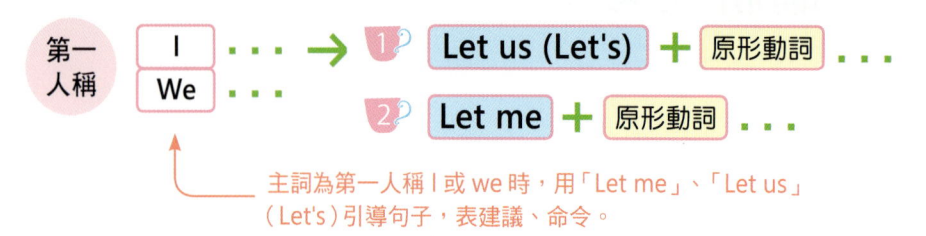

第一人稱 I / We ... → ① Let us (Let's) + 原形動詞 ...
② Let me + 原形動詞 ...

主詞為第一人稱 I 或 we 時，用「Let me」、「Let us」（Let's）引導句子，表建議、命令。

① **Let us go** swimming this afternoon, shall we?　　今天下午我們去游泳，好嗎？
　　第一人稱 us，使用「Let's ＋原形動詞」。

② **Let me stay** with you.　　讓我陪著你。
　　第一人稱 me，使用「Let me ＋原形動詞」。

第三人稱 him / her / it / them / 名詞 ... → Let + 受詞（him/her/it/them/名詞）+ 原形動詞 ...

主詞為第三人稱 he、she、it、they 或任何名詞時，也是使用 Let 的句型。

③ **Let Mickey go** with you.　　讓米奇跟你們一起去。
　　第三人稱 Mickey，使用「Let ＋ Mickey ＋原形動詞」。

3 祈使句否定句型

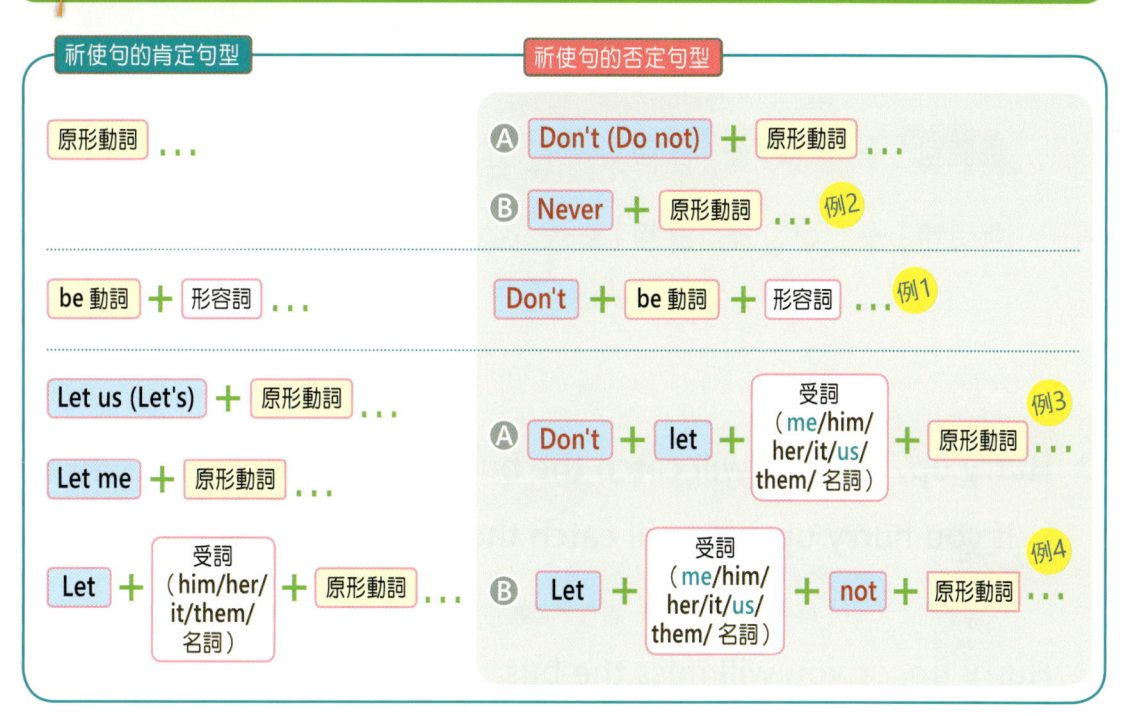

祈使句的肯定句型	祈使句的否定句型
原形動詞 ...	Ⓐ Don't (Do not) ＋ 原形動詞 ... Ⓑ Never ＋ 原形動詞 ... 例2
be 動詞 ＋ 形容詞 ...	Don't ＋ be 動詞 ＋ 形容詞 ... 例1
Let us (Let's) ＋ 原形動詞 ... Let me ＋ 原形動詞 ... Let ＋ 受詞（him/her/it/them/名詞）＋ 原形動詞 ...	Ⓐ Don't ＋ let ＋ 受詞（me/him/her/it/us/them/名詞）＋ 原形動詞 ... 例3 Ⓑ Let ＋ 受詞（me/him/her/it/us/them/名詞）＋ not ＋ 原形動詞 ... 例4

❶ **Don't be** so noisy, will you?　可以不要這麼吵嗎？　→ 表達請求、警告
　　└ Don't be ＋形容詞

❷ **Never smoke** in the cabin.　絕對不可以在機艙裡抽菸。　→ 表達禁止
　　└ Never ＋原形動詞

❸ **Don't let** him go swimming alone.　別讓他獨自去游泳。　→ 表達禁止、警告
　　└ Don't let ＋受詞＋原形動詞

❹ It is raining. **Let's not** go swimming, all right?　開始下雨了。我們不要去游泳了，好嗎？　→ 表達請求、建議
　　└ Let ＋受詞＋ not ＋原形動詞

4 表條件的祈使句

表條件的祈使句，有以下兩種句型：

1. 祈使句 + and + 子句 = If you ..., you ...
（如果做了某事，就會……）

2. 祈使句 + or + 子句 = If you +否定助動詞 ..., you ...
（如果不做某事，就會……）

「祈使句＋and ...」，表示「如果……，就……」。

❶ **Hurry up, and** you will catch the bus.
　= If you hurry up, you will catch the bus.

快點，你才能趕得上公車。

「祈使句＋or ...」，表示「如果不……，就……」。

❷ **Hurry up, or** you will miss the bus.
　= If you **don't** hurry up, you will miss the bus.

趕快，不然你會錯過這班公車。

「祈使句＋and ...」，表示「如果……，就……」。

❸ **Study hard, and** you will pass the exam.
　= If you study hard, you will pass the exam.

用功點，你就能通過考試。

「祈使句＋or ...」，表示「如果不……，就……」。

❹ **Study hard, or** you will fail the exam.
　= If you **don't** study hard, you will fail the exam.

用功點，否則會不及格。

Quiz 13

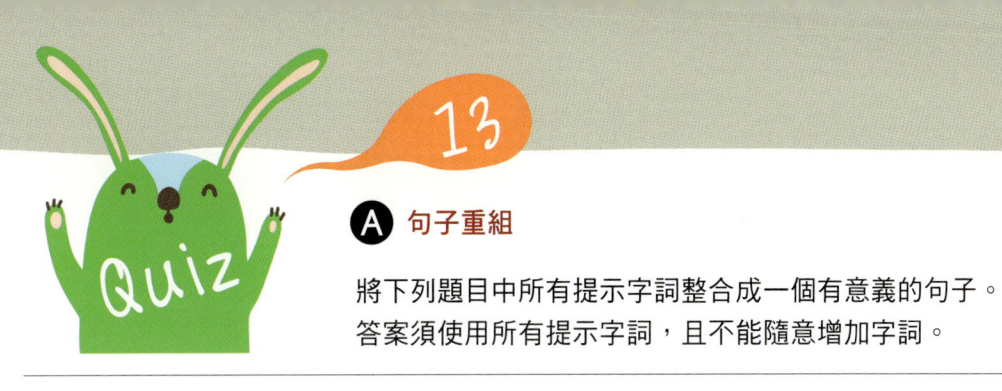

A 句子重組

將下列題目中所有提示字詞整合成一個有意義的句子。
答案須使用所有提示字詞，且不能隨意增加字詞。

1 Please _____.
the/handout/me/pass

2 Please _____.
noise/stop/making/that

3 Don't _____.
talk/mouth/with/full/your

4 _____.
Jacob/play volleyball/let/with/you

5 _____.
go/don't/let/fishing/alone/Glen

6 _____.
not/go/let's/hiking

B 句子合併：用 and 或 or 將下列句子合併成一句。

1 Get up. / You will see the shooting stars.
_____.

2 Get up. / You will miss the fascinating performance.
_____.

3 Get started. / You will finish the work ahead of time.
_____.

4 Get started. / You cannot finish your work on time.
_____.

2 祈使句的附加問句

1 第二人稱的祈使句

肯定句的附加問句
- Ⓐ 第二人稱祈使句 ， + will you?
- Ⓑ 第二人稱祈使句 ， + won't you? ← 語氣較客氣，或有勸誘的意思。

否定句的附加問句
- 第二人稱祈使句 ， + will you?

1. Go to bed, will you?　　去睡覺！　　→ 表命令
2. Go to bed, won't you?　　去睡覺好嗎？　　→ 表勸誘
3. Don't make noises, will you?　　不要製造噪音好嗎？　　→ 表命令

2 第一人稱和第三人稱的祈使句

肯定句的附加問句
- 第一、第三人稱祈使句 ， + shall we?

否定句的附加問句
- Ⓐ 第一、第三人稱祈使句 ， + OK?
- Ⓑ 第一、第三人稱祈使句 ， + all right?

1. Let's go swimming, shall we?　　我們去游泳吧！
2. Let's not shout in the classroom, OK?　　不要在教室裡吼叫好嗎？
3. Let's not dance, all right?　　我們不要跳舞好嗎？

Quiz 14

將下列句子加入附加問句。

1 Be quiet.

_____ .

2 Behave well.

_____ .

3 Let's talk in English.

_____ .

4 Let's not play badminton.

_____ .

5 Don't shout.

_____ .

3 如何將直述句改為祈使句

祈使句可分為對第二人稱和對第一、三人稱的祈使句，更改為祈使句時要注意：
1. 以直述句主詞的**人稱**，決定要改為何種人稱的祈使句。
2. 依據直述句的內容和意義，決定改為祈使句的**肯定**或**否定**用法。

1 改為對第二人稱的祈使句

步驟一 省略直述句的主詞 you。
步驟二 直述句的動詞改為**原形動詞**；如果有助動詞，要**去掉助動詞**。

| 肯定祈使句 | 原形動詞 ... | | 否定祈使句 | Don't / Never + 原形動詞 ... |

❶ 將主詞 you 省略
直述句：You are friendly to others. 你對人很友善。
❷ 將 be 動詞 are 改成原形動詞 be
祈使句：Be friendly to others. 待人要友善！

❶ 將主詞 you 省略
❷ 將助動詞 should 去掉
直述句：You should sit up straight at the table. 你應該端正地坐在餐桌前。
❸ 以原形動詞 sit 開頭
祈使句：Sit up straight at the table. 在餐桌前要端正坐好。

❶ 將主詞 you 省略
❷ 將助動詞 must 去掉

直述句 You ~~must~~ not smoke at this restaurant. 你不可以在這家餐廳抽菸。

❸ 表示否定，用「Don't + 原形動詞」開頭。

祈使句 Don't smoke at this restaurant. 不可以在這家餐廳抽菸。

> **NOTE** 肯定的祈使句，可用助動詞 **do** 來加強語氣。
> ✽ **Do** be friendly to others. 對人一定要友善。
> ✽ **Do** sit up straight at the table.
> 　一定要端正地坐在餐桌前。

2 改為對第一、三人稱的祈使句

步驟一 用 let 引導肯定祈使句，用 don't let 引導否定祈使句。
步驟二 直述句的主詞改為 let 的**受詞**。
步驟三 直述句的動詞改為**原形動詞**；如果有助動詞，要**去掉助動詞**。

肯定祈使句： **Let** ＋ 受詞（me/him/her/it/us/them/ 名詞）＋ 原形動詞 ...

否定祈使句：
Ⓐ **Don't** ＋ **let** ＋ 受詞（me/him/her/it/us/them/ 名詞）＋ 原形動詞 ...
Ⓑ **Let** ＋ 受詞（me/him/her/it/us/them/ 名詞）＋ **not** ＋ 原形動詞 ...

直述句 Fred remodels and decorates his house before Christmas.
　　　　　主詞　　動詞
費德會在聖誕節之前裝修他的房子。

❶ 改為由 let 引導
❷ Fred 變成 let 的受詞
❸ 動詞皆改為原形動詞

祈使句 Let Fred remodel and decorate his house before Christmas.
　　　Let＋受詞 Fred　　原形動詞
讓費德在聖誕節之前裝修他的房子。

直述句　He will shovel the snow in front of his house.
　　　　主詞　助動詞　動詞

❸ 刪去助動詞 will

❶ 改為由 let 引導
❷ he 變成 let 的受詞 him

祈使句　Let him shovel the snow in front of his house.
　　　　Let＋受詞him　原形動詞

他會把門前的雪鏟掉。

讓他把門前的雪鏟掉吧。

❸ 刪去助動詞 must

直述句　He must not go skiing alone.
　　　　主詞　助動詞　動詞

他不可以獨自去滑雪。

❶ 否定句由 don't let 引導
❷ he 變成 let 的受詞 him

祈使句　Don't let him go skiing alone, OK?
　　　　Don't let＋受詞him　原形動詞

　　　　＝ Let him not go skiing alone, all right?
　　　　　　Let＋受詞him　not＋原形動詞

不要讓他單獨去滑雪，好嗎？

Quiz 15

句子改寫

將下列直述句改為祈使句。

❶ You are kind to others.

　_____.

❷ You are so innocent as to believe his words.

　_____.

❸ You should be quiet at the temple.

　_____.

❹ You are not allowed to smoke in the hospital.

　_____.

❺ Janice washes her car once a week.

　_____.

❻ We take care of the orphans.

　_____..

❼ Steve will build a snowman in front of his house.

　_____.

❽ Arthur must not go scuba diving alone.

　_____.

❾ The baby is so noisy in the theater.

　_____.

❿ They won't go to the Taipei Zoo this weekend.

　_____.

Unit 9 比較句型

暖身 下列短文中，劃底線的部分就是我們這一章節要討論的「比較級」和「最高級」。觀察一下，這些部分字有什麼共通處？

Ivy's wedding is coming, but it's snowing harder and harder. However, the bad weather doesn't affect Ivy's mood at all. As the wedding gets closer, she becomes more and more excited, yet more and more nervous. We believe that Ivy will be the most beautiful and charming lady on her wedding day.

1 何謂比較句型？

形容詞和副詞不會因性別、數目、人稱或主受格的不同而改變拼法，但在比較性質、數量、狀態等程度時，例如「他比我高」則有「比較級」和「最高級」的變化。

1 比較級（更……；較……）

當我們比較兩個東西（所比較的對象須是**對等同類**），用來表示其中一個比另一個「更……」，就要用**比較級**。比較級的句型要使用 than（比……）：

形容詞和副詞的**比較級**構成通常為：❶ 字尾 ＋ -er
❷ more ＋ 原級

比較級句型：A ＋ 動詞 ＋ 形容詞或副詞的比較級 ＋ than ＋ B （A 比 B 更……）

than 所引導的子句，通常將助動詞或動詞省略，所以要注意代名詞的主受格。

形容詞 tall 加上 -er，形成比較級。

形容詞 tall　Lucy is tall**er than** Carl.　　露西比卡爾高。
　　　　　　　比較級＋than
　　　　　　　than 之後接比較的對象（比較的對象 Lucy 和 Carl，都是人）。

副詞 fast 加 -er，形成比較級。

副詞 fast　Carl runs fast**er than** Lucy.　　卡爾跑得比露西快。
　　　　　than 之後接比較的對象（比較的對象都是人）。

形容詞 young 加 -er，形成比較級。

形容詞 young　Carl is young**er than** I (am)/me.　　卡爾年紀比我小。
　　　　　　　　than 之後接比較的對象（比較的對象都是人）。

> 在較不嚴謹的英文中，可在 than 之後使用受格代名詞，如 me、him、her 等。但在寫作時，建議使用主格，這是較嚴謹的用法。
> * I like dogs better than she (does). 我比她還喜歡狗。
> * I like dogs better than her.
>   意一 我喜歡狗勝過喜歡她。
>   意二 我比她還喜歡狗。
>
> 這種寫法造成兩種意義，所以 than 後面最好用主格，而不用受格，以免意義含混。

2 最高級（最……的）

三者或三者以上作比較，要表示其中一個為「最……」時，要用**最高級**。最高級形容詞前要加定冠詞 the，但如果前面有名詞或代名詞的所有格時，就不加 the。

形容詞和副詞的最高級構成通常為：❶ 字尾 ＋ -est　❷ most ＋ 原級

最高級句型　A ＋ 動詞 ＋ the ＋ 形容詞或副詞的最高級 ...　（……是最……）

└ 副詞則無 the。

① **Sherry studies hardest of all the students.**　雪莉是學生中最用功的。
  - 副詞 hard 加上 -est，形成最高級。
  - 最高級副詞
  - 最高級副詞的前面，通常不加 the。

② **Rebecca is the most beautiful of the three girls.**　麗貝卡是這三個女生中最漂亮的。
  - 形容詞 beautiful 的前面加上 most，形成最高級。
  - 最高級形容詞
  - 最高級形容詞的前面，要加 the。

③ **Madeline is my closest friend.**　梅德琳是我最親密的朋友。
  - 形容詞 close 加上 -est，形成最高級。
  - 代名詞　最高級形容詞
  - 前面有代名詞的所有格 my，故不加定冠詞 the。

④ **Joshua learns most slowly of the three.**　約書亞是三人中學習速度最慢的。
  - 副詞 slowly 的前面加上 most，形成最高級。
  - 最高級副詞
  - 最高級副詞的前面，通常不加 the。

2 形容詞的比較級和最高級

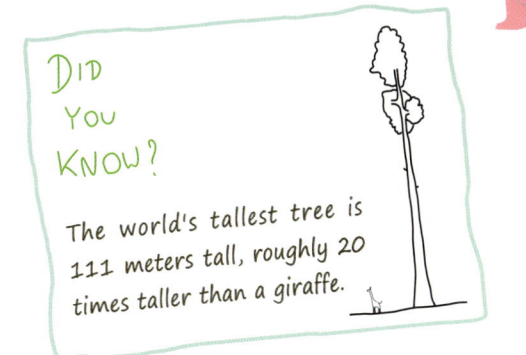

> DID YOU KNOW?
> The world's tallest tree is 111 meters tall, roughly 20 times taller than a giraffe.

　　為什麼有些比較級的構成是「原級＋-er」，但有些是「more＋原級」？而有些最高級的構成是「原級＋-est」，有些則是「most＋原級」？以下分別說明形容詞和副詞的比較級和最高級的構成。

1 形容詞的比較級與最高級的規則變化

1 單音節和以 -y 結尾的雙音節

	原級字尾	→ 比較級	→ 最高級
單音節	一般	字尾＋-er 例1	字尾＋-est
單音節	-e	字尾＋-r	字尾＋-st 例5
單音節	短母音＋單子音	重複字尾＋-er 例4	重複字尾＋-est 例6
雙音節	子音＋y	去 y ＋ -ier 例2	去 y ＋ -iest
雙音節	母音＋y	＋ -er 例3	＋ -est

2 不以 -y 結尾的雙音節，以及兩個音節以上的形容詞

比較級 → **more** ＋ 原級　　　最高級 → **most** ＋ 原級

1 Nina is young**er** than Jill. 　　　妮娜比吉兒年輕。

→ 形容詞 young（單音節）加上 -er，形成比較級。

2 Jill is bus**ier** than Nina. 　　　吉兒比妮娜忙碌。

→ 形容詞 busy（以 y 結尾的雙音節）去 y ＋ -ier，形成比較級。

❸ **Jill's hair is grayer than Nina's.**   吉兒的頭髮較妮娜的灰白。
→ 形容詞 gray（母音＋y）加 -er，形成比較級。

❹ **Nina is fatter than Milo.**   妮娜比米羅胖。
→ 形容詞 fat 重複字尾 t 加上 -er，形成比較級。

❺ **Nina is the wisest of the three.**   妮娜是三個人當中最有智慧的。
→ 形容詞 wise 加上 -st，形成最高級。

❻ **Jill is the thinnest of the three.**   吉兒是三個人當中最瘦的。
→ 形容詞 thin 重複字尾 n，加上 -est，形成最高級。

NOTE

① 以 -y 結尾的雙音節形容詞，加上 un- 之後的反義字（如 unhappy），雖然變成三音節，但其比較級和最高級仍要去 -y 加 -ier/-iest。
* **Derek was unhappier than Ernie at the meeting.**
  在會議上，德瑞克比恩尼還不開心。

② 以下這些字雖然是雙音節，卻是 ＋ -er 形成比較級，＋ -est 形成最高級。

quiet（安靜的）	quieter	quietest
clever（伶俐的）	cleverer	cleverest
simple（簡易的）	simpler	simplest

③ 上述提到雙音節的形容詞，也可以加上 more、most，來形成比較級和最高級（但 ＋ -er 和 ＋ -est 更正規）。

quiet（安靜的）	more quiet	most quiet
clever（伶俐的）	more clever	most clever
simple（簡易的）	more simple	most simple

---

② 形容詞的比較級與最高級的**不規則變化**

■ 形容詞比較級和最高級的不規則變化，沒有加 -er 或 -est 的規則可循。例如：

原級字尾 →	比較級 →	最高級
bad	worse	worst 例2
good/well	better 例1	best
many/much	more	most

① **This book is better than that one.** 這本書比那本好。
  → 形容詞 better 是 good 的比較級。

② **This is the worst book I have ever read.** 這是我讀過最糟的書。
  → 形容詞 worst 是 bad 的最高級。

2 有些形容詞的比較級和最高級會有兩種形式，例如：

原級字尾	→ 比較級	→ 最高級	
old	older 例1	oldest	（用來比較年齡或新舊）
old	elder 例2	eldest 例3	（用來指長幼順序，英式用法）
late	later	latest 例5	（指時間上的晚）
late	latter 例4	last 例6	（指順序上的晚）
far	farther	farthest 例7	（指空間距離上的遠）
far	further 例8	furthest	（指抽象距離或程度上的遠）

① **I am older than Jenny.** 我年紀比珍妮大。

② **Brian is my elder brother.** 布萊恩是我的哥哥。
  → 美式用 older brother。

③ **Anna is her eldest daughter.** 安娜是她的大女兒。
  → 美式用 oldest daughter。
  → 英式的 elder 和 eldest 只能用在名詞前面，不能和 than 連用；older 和 oldest 則可以和 than 連用。

④ **We will discuss the issue in a latter chapter.** 我們將在後面的章節討論這個議題。

⑤ **This is the latest news from CNN.** 這是 CNN 的最新新聞。

⑥ **We will take the last train to Hualien.** 我們會搭最後一班火車到花蓮。

⑦ **We got to the farthest village in a day.** 我們在一天之內就到達了最遠的村莊。
  → 英式也可以用 furthest。

⑧ **Cathy plans to go abroad for further study.** 凱西打算出國深造。

3 副詞的比較級和最高級

1 副詞比較級和最高級的規則變化

1 副詞比較級和最高級的規則變化和形容詞相同：雙音節、三音節以上的副詞，加上 more 形成比較級，加上 most 形成最高級。

比較級 → more ＋ 原級　　　最高級 → most ＋ 原級

2 單音節副詞的字尾加上 -er 形成比較級，加上 -est 形成最高級。

原級字尾	→ 比較級	→ 最高級
soon	sooner	soonest
near	nearer	nearest

3 以 y 結尾的雙音節副詞：去 y 加 -ier 及 -iest。

原級字尾	→ 比較級	→ 最高級
early	earlier	earliest

2 副詞比較級和最高級的不規則變化

原級字尾	→ 比較級	→ 最高級
well（很好地）	better	best
badly（不好地）	worse	worst

3 形容詞和副詞同形

形容詞和副詞同形的字，例如 early、fast、hard、late、little、much。這些字形容詞和副詞同形，也常出現在考試中，要熟記喔！

1 Norman's father drives more carefully than Eliza's (father).
→ 副詞 carefully 加 more，形成比較級。

2 Eliza's father works harder than Norman's (father).
→ 副詞 hard 加 -er，形成比較級。

3 Norman's father usually gets up earlier than Eliza's (father).

1. 諾曼的爸爸開車比伊萊莎的爸爸小心。
2. 伊萊莎的爸爸工作比諾曼的爸爸努力。
3. 諾曼的爸爸通常比伊萊莎的爸爸早起。

副詞 far 的比較級與最高級

| far | → farther | → farthest | （指**空間距離**上的遠） |
| far | → further | → furthest | （指**抽象距離**或**程度**上的遠） |

* I ran farther than I had planned. 我跑得比我計畫中的還遠。
  → 英式也可以用 further
* I will assist you further. 我會進一步地協助你。

副詞 late 的比較級與最高級

| late | → later | → latest | （指**時間**上的晚） |
| late | → latter | → last | （指**順序**上的晚） |

* The superstar arrived later than had scheduled.
  這位超級巨星比預定時間晚到。
* His fans left the airport last. 他的影迷最後離開機場。

Quiz 16

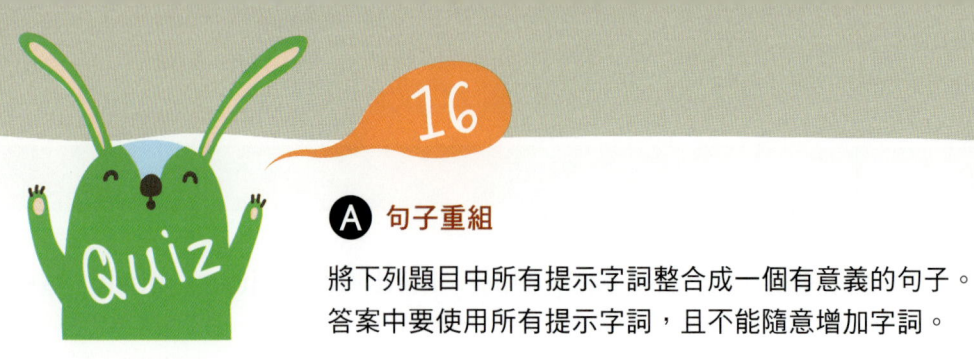

A 句子重組

將下列題目中所有提示字詞整合成一個有意義的句子。
答案中要使用所有提示字詞，且不能隨意增加字詞。

1 _____ .
fat/Morris/is

2 Sandra _____ .
more/is/Winnie/beautiful/than

3 Wayne _____ .
learns/than/Oswald/faster

4 Tess _____ .
studies/hardest/students/all/of/the/in her class

5 He _____ .
most/of/the/learns/slowly/three

6 The red album _____ .
older/the black/is/one/than

7 _____ .
latest/from/this/the/news/BBC/is

B 寫出下列各字的比較級和最高級。

原級	比較級	最高級
1 happy	a.	b.
2 thin	c.	d.
3 good	e.	f.

4 比較句中的常見詞組與句型

1 「as . . . as . . .」（像……一樣……）

這是比較**程度相等**的兩者時所用的句型，其中的形容詞和副詞用**原級**表示。

肯定句： A ＋ 動詞 ＋ as ＋ 原級形容詞或副詞 ＋ as ＋ B （A和B一樣……）

否定句： A ＋ 動詞 ＋ not so / not as ＋ 原級形容詞或副詞 ＋ as ＋ B （A不像B那樣……）

❶ Jay is active in class. ＋ Faith is active in class, too.
 ＝ Jay is as active as Faith (is active) in class.

 傑在課堂上很活潑。＋ 斐絲在課堂上也很活潑。
 ＝ 傑像斐絲一樣在課堂上很活潑。

❷ Our art teacher was dressed as beautifully as our history teacher (was dressed).

 我們美術課的老師穿得和歷史老師一樣漂亮。

❸ The English class is boring. ＋ The math class is interesting.
 ＝ The English class is not so (/as) interesting as the math class (is).
 ⇒ The math class is not so boring as the English class (is).

 英文課很無趣。＋ 數學課很有趣。
 ＝ 英文課不像數學課一樣有趣。
 ⇒ 數學課不像英文課一樣無聊。

143

❹ June finished the quiz **not so (/as) fast as** Ralph.
⇒ Ralph finished the quiz **not so slowly as** June.

茱恩做測驗的速度不像拉夫那樣快。
⇒ 拉夫做測驗的速度不像茱恩那樣慢。

2 其他包含「as . . . as . . .」的慣用語

A as ＋ 原級 ＋ as can be （至為；非常）

❶ Colin is **as happy as can be**. 　　　　　　　　　柯林非常高興。

B as ＋ 原級 ＋ as ＋ 主詞 ＋ can （儘可能；儘量）
＝ as ＋ 原級 ＋ as possible

❶ I will send the gift **as soon as I can**. 　　　　　我會儘快把禮物寄出去。
＝ I will send the gift **as soon as possible**.

❷ Please sing the happy birthday song **as loudly as you can**. 　　請儘量大聲唱生日快樂歌。
＝ Please sing the happy birthday song **as loudly as possible**.

C A ＋ 動詞 ＋ as good as ＋ B （A和B幾乎一樣……）

❶ This used book is **as good as** new. 　　這本二手書幾乎和新的一樣。

「as ＋原級＋ as ＋名詞」的常用比喻

* **as cool as a cucumber** 　像黃瓜一樣冷靜的（冷靜沉著的）
* **as poor as a church mouse** 　像教堂老鼠一樣窮（一貧如洗）
* **as easy as ABC** 　像 ABC 一樣簡單（非常簡單的）
* **as busy as a bee** 　像蜜蜂一樣忙（非常忙碌的）
* **as proud as a peacock** 　像孔雀一樣愛炫耀的（非常驕傲的）

as proud as a peacock

3 含最高級的慣用語

* the last 最不想……的
* the least 最小的……；最少的……
* make the best (/most) of . . . 充分利用……；把最好的發揮出來

1. Dave is **the last** person that I want to see. 　戴夫是我最不想見到的人。
2. It's **the least** I can do. 　這是最起碼我能做的事。
3. You should **make the best of** the opportunity. 　你應該要充分把握這個機會。

4 比較級的加強用法

要加強比較級，可在比較級前加上以下的詞語來修飾：

修飾比較級	
very much（非常）	
much（很）	
a lot（很）	＋ 比較級
rather（相當）	
far（很；極）	
a little（一點點）	
a little bit（一點點兒）	

1. This wedding dress is **much** more expensive than that one.
   用 much 來加強比較級 more expensive。
   這件結婚禮服比那件貴多了。

2. The blue shirt is **a bit** cheaper than the white one.
   用 a bit 來加強比較級 cheaper。
   藍色的襯衫比白色的便宜一點。

5 「越……越……」的句型

英文中用來表示「越……越……」的句型為：

少音節的形容詞或副詞： 比較級 + and + 比較級 （越……越……）
例 hotter and hotter 越來越熱

多音節的形容詞或副詞： more + and + more + 原級形容詞或副詞 （越……越……）
例 more and more interesting 越來越有趣的

1. The day is getting **closer and closer**. 　日子越來越接近。
   形容詞比較級 + and + 形容詞比較級

2. Joanna becomes **more and more** excited. 　瓊安娜越來越興奮。
   more and more + 原級形容詞

3. It snowed **harder and harder**. 　雪下得越來越大。
   副詞比較級 + and + 副詞比較級

6 最高級的加強用法

要加強最高級時，通常使用 by far。

修飾最高級： by far（非常） + 比較級

1. Emily is **by far** the tallest in her family.
   by far 用來加強最高級 the tallest

2. The movie is **by far** the best.

3. Soccer is **by far** the most popular sport in Britain.

1. 艾蜜莉在她家是最高的。

2. 這部電影顯然是最好看的。

3. 足球確實是英國最受歡迎的運動。

Quiz 17

句子重組
依照題目指示，將兩句合併成一句或改寫句子。

1. Andrew is noisy in English class.
   Donald is noisy in English class, too.（用 as . . . as . . .）
   _____.

2. Kenneth plays the violin beautifully.
   Christina plays the violin beautifully.（用 as . . . as . . .）
   _____.

3. My father drives carefully.
   Her father drives carelessly.（用 not so . . . as . . .）
   _____.

4. They sang the happy birthday song.
   They sang the song loudly.（用 as . . . as possible）
   _____.

5. The new book is exciting. / The old book is boring.
   （用 not so . . . as . . .）
   _____.

6. Leah is 1.50 meters tall. Alfred is 1.48 meters tall.（用比較級合併）
   _____.

7. The red shirt costs NT$ 300.
   The black shirt costs NT$ 3,000.（用比較級合併）
   _____.

8. Duncan is 65 kilos. Alex is 60 kilos. Greg is 50 kilos.（用最高級合併）
   _____.

9. Math is more difficult than Chinese.
   English is more difficult than math.（用最高級合併）
   _____.

10. Amanda becomes attractive.（用 more and more 改寫）
    _____.

Unit 10 對等連接詞

Warm-up 下文中，加底線的部分是這一章要討論的對等連接詞。觀察一下，這些字有什麼共通處？

Emma <u>and</u> Denise are very good friends. Emma is short <u>and</u> thin, <u>but</u> Denise is tall <u>and</u> fat. They often study together in the school library <u>or</u> in the coffee shop. They study at the same school, <u>yet</u> they are not in the same class.

1 常見的對等連接詞

and（和；及；而且）
but, yet（但是；然而）
or（或；抑；否則）
nor（也不）
so（因而；所以）
for（因為）

1 and（和；及；而且）

1. 用 and 連接兩個**詞組**時，通常不用逗點；但如果連接三者以上時，要用逗點分開這些詞組，並且將 and 放在最後一個詞組的前面。
2. and 來連接兩個獨立的**子句**時，通常要加逗點。
3. and 可表示「**結果**」的含意。
4. and 也可以用來表示**時間順序的先後**。

① They will take a trip to Spain and France. 他們要到西班牙和法國旅行。
　　　　　　　　　　　　　　名詞　　　名詞
（連接兩個對等的名詞，不用逗點。）

② Don't forget to take your passport, visa, tickets, baggage(,) and a camera with you.
（三個以上詞組要用逗號分開，and 放在最後一個詞組前，其前的逗號在英式用法可省略，但美式用法不能省略。）

③ The scenery is fantastic, and the people there are friendly.
　　　子句　　　　　　　　　　　　　　　　子句
（連接兩個子句，and 前要加逗號。）

④ It is an unforgettable experience, and we will ever forget this trip.
　　　子句　　　　　　　　　　　　　　　　　　　子句
（and 在這裡表示「結果」的含意。）

⑤ We bought some postcards and (we) sent them to our friends.
　　　動詞片語　　　　　　　　　　　動詞片語
（這裡的 and 表示先後順序（買了明信片之後寄給朋友），這兩個子句的主詞相同，可以省略 and 後面的 we，這樣就不是並列句，而變成了簡單句。）

2. 別忘了攜帶你的護照、簽證、機票、行李和你的相機。

3. 景色很迷人，而且那裡的人們很友善。

4. 這是一次難忘的經驗，我們永遠不會忘記這趟旅程。

5. 我們買了些明信片，然後寄給了我們的朋友。

2 but、yet（但是；然而）

❶ but 和 yet 用來表示「相反」或「對照」的意思。含義上 yet 比 but 強些。
❷ 句型「not . . . but . . .」表示「不是……，而是……」。

❶ The seafood is delicious but (/yet) too expensive.
   　　　　　　　形容詞　　　　　　　　　　形容詞
   海鮮很美味，但是太貴了。

❷ I am starving to death, but (/yet) I don't want to eat seafood at all.
   　　　子句　　　　　　　　　　　子句
   連接兩個子句，通常 but 前會有逗號。
   雖然我快餓死了，但我一點也不想吃海鮮。

❸ I tried hard to find an Italian restaurant, yet I failed.
   　　　　　　　子句　　　　　　　　　　　　　　子句
   我努力想找一間義式餐廳，卻還是沒找到。

❹ This is not scampi but lobster.
   　　　　　　名詞　　　名詞
   這不是明蝦肉，這是龍蝦肉。

3 or（或；抑；否則）

❶ 用 or 連接兩個主詞時，動詞要和最**靠近動詞的主詞**一致。
❷ 「either A or B」（不是 A 便是 B）的句型中，A 和 B 要是對等的字、片語或子句。
❸ 「or . . .」（否則……）祈使句的用法。

❶ Maria will be out of town for two or three days.
   　　　　　　　　　　　　　　　形容詞　　形容詞
   瑪麗亞會出城兩三天。

❷ Which country will she go to, Japan or Thailand?
   　　　　　　　　　　　　　　　名詞　　　名詞
   她會去哪個國家，日本還是泰國？

❸ Curt or Jason is her secretary.
   主詞　　主詞
   動詞要和最靠近動詞的主詞（Jason）一致，故用 is。
   柯特或傑森是她的祕書。

❹ She is either in Tokyo or in Bangkok now.
   　　　　　　介系詞片語　　介系詞片語
   她現在不是在東京就是在曼谷。

❺ You must work hard, or you will be fired.
　　子句　　　　　　　　　　　子句
（此句中的 or 帶有否定的含意）
你應該努力工作，否則你會被炒魷魚。

❻ Hurry up, or you will miss the flight.
　　祈使句
快點，否則你會錯過這班飛機。

= If you don't hurry up, you will miss the flight.

4　nor（也不）

1. nor 常用在 not, no, never 之後。
2. nor 放句首時，句子要倒裝（nor ＋助動詞或 be 動詞＋主詞），具否定意思。
3. 「neither A nor B」（既不是 A，也不是 B）具否定意思，A 與 B 要是對等的字、片語或子句。

❶ I have never written nor spoken to Jack since then.
　　　　　　　過去分詞　　　過去分詞
我從那時起就沒寫過信給傑克，也沒和他說過話。

❷ I don't like him, nor does Mia.
　　　　　　　　　　　　第三人稱單數助動詞
（nor 放在句首要倒裝，因 Mia 是第三人稱單數，故用 does。）
我不喜歡他，蜜兒也不喜歡他。

= I do not like him, and Mia does not like him, either.

❸ He isn't a journalist, nor is his father.
　　　　　　　　　　　　be 動詞　主詞
（nor 放在句首要倒裝，因 his father 是第三人稱單數，故用 is。）
他不是記者，他爸爸也不是。

= He is not a journalist, and his father is not a journalist, either.

❹ He is neither decent nor honest.
　　　　　　　形容詞　　　形容詞
他既不正直，也不誠實。

> **NOTE** 在英文裡，表達「也」有兩種最簡單的方法：
>
> ❶ **肯定句**：句尾加上「, too」，或句中加 also。
>
> ✽ Today is my birthday, and it is Jocelyn's birthday, too.
>   = Today is my birthday, and it is also Jocelyn's birthday.
>   今天是我的生日，也是賈思琳的生日。
>
> ❷ **否定句**：句尾加上「, either」，或句中加上 nor。
>
> ✽ He can't sing, and he can't dance, either.
>   = He can't sing nor dance. 他不會唱歌，也不會跳舞。

5 so（因而；所以）

so 用來表示「**推論**」或「**結果**」的意思。

🍀 The scenery was marvelous, so we took a lot of pictures.
景色很棒，所以我們拍了很多照片。

6 for（因為）

❶ for 用來為前述的事情提出**證據**或**說明**。
❷ 通常不放在句首，且 for 前面通常要加**逗號**。

🍀 It must have rained heavily last night, for the ground is still wet.

🍀 He must be sick, for he looks weak.

1. 昨晚一定下過大雨，因為地還是溼的。

2. 他一定是生病了，因為他看起來很虛弱。

> **NOTE** 使用 and, but, yet, or, nor, so, for 等來連接兩個獨立子句時，通常要在這些連接詞前加逗號。但如果兩個獨立子句簡短且對稱，逗號可省略。然而如果你舉棋不定，最保險的作法就是加逗點，在這種情況中加逗號永遠是正確的。

2 對等連接詞的重要性

在段落寫作時，要適時的運用連接詞結合，使句子有長有短。如果句子都一樣簡單且長度相等，這樣的文章一定死氣沉沉，呆板無趣。例如：

> I took a trip to Kenting National Park last Sunday. I set off early in the morning. I arrived in the evening. I saw many seafood restaurants. I was starving. I didn't want to eat seafood at all. I tried hard to find a fast food restaurant. I couldn't find it.

這個段落中使用太多短句，讓人覺得這篇文章沒有連貫性，累贅又乏味。為了讓段落更富變化，可以使用連接詞來變化句子的長度，使文章生動些。可改寫如下：

> I took a trip to Kenting National Park last Sunday. I set off early in the morning and arrived in the evening. I saw many seafood restaurants. I was starving, yet I didn't want to eat seafood at all. I tried hard to find a fast food restaurant (,) but (I) couldn't find it.

寫完一篇文章後檢查短句是否太多，並適時運用連接詞，但不要太過或不及。

連接詞在連接兩個子句時，會透露兩個子句之間的邏輯關係。如：

✲ It was getting late, so I decided to spend the night at Kenting.
天色漸漸晚了，所以我決定在墾丁過夜。
→ 因為晚上了，所以直接過夜。

✲ In the middle of the night, I woke up coughing, for I could not breathe. 我半夜時醒來咳嗽，因為我無法呼吸。
→ 半夜醒來的原因，是因為無法呼吸。

Quiz 18

A 句子合併
依照題目指示，將兩句合併成一句。

1. Judy plans to go to the US next month.
   Judy plans to go to Canada next month, too.（用 and 合併）

2. It is nice and warm today. / The birds are chirping.（用 and 合併）

3. This is not chicken. / This is turkey.（用 not . . . but . . . 合併）

4. The chicken soup is very delicious.
   The chicken soup is too greasy.（用 but 合併）

5. I am freezing. / I don't want to put on a thick coat.（用 yet 合併）

6. You must work harder. / You will be fired.（用 or 合併）

7. Lionel doesn't like cats. / Eva doesn't like cats, either.（用 nor 合併）

8. I have no time for the show.
   I have no money for the show.（用 neither . . . nor 合併）

9. She didn't go to school. / She caught a cold.（用 so 合併）

10. We must set off early.
    It will take three hours to get to the peak.（用 for 合併）

B 運用此章節提到的對等連接詞改寫下面的短文。

Leonard and Lucy went to Spain, France last summer. They brought their passports, visas, baggage, some traveler's checks, a camera with them. The scenery was fantastic. They took a lot of pictures. They also bought some postcards. They sent them to their friends, relatives. It was an unforgettable experience. They will never forget the trip.

Leonard and Lucy went to

Unit 11

從屬連接詞與副詞子句

Warm-up 暖身

下面短文中，劃底線的部分是本章節要討論的「從屬連接詞」，當中也包含了上一章所討論過的「對等連接詞」。觀察看看，對等連接詞和從屬連接詞有什麼差異？

I have enjoyed camping <u>since</u> I was a little child.
<u>Because</u> my parents love camping, we often go camping to get close to nature and away from our routine lives.
It refreshes our minds <u>when</u> we are close to nature.

1 從屬連接詞

1. **從屬連接詞**引導從屬子句，將主要子句和從屬子句連接起來，形成**複合句**。
   ⓐ **主要子句**：含有主詞和述部（動詞或動詞片語），本身具完整意義，亦稱為獨立子句。
   ⓑ **從屬子句**：以從屬連接詞開頭，也含有主詞和述部，但無法獨立存在。其功能在於修飾主要子句。

2. 常見的從屬連接詞，例如：
   - as 如同；因為
   - because 因為
   - if 如果
   - when 當……時
   - so that 以便
   - unless 除非
   - though/although 雖然
   - that（引導名詞子句）

3. 從屬連接詞引導的從屬子句，可以放在**句首**，也可以放在**主句**之後。

1 從屬子句放在句首（子句之間要加逗號）

從屬連接詞 + 主詞 + 動詞 ... , 主詞 + 動詞 ...
（從屬子句）　　　　　　　（逗號）（主要子句）

❶ **Because** I was so tired, I went to bed early.
　從屬連接詞　　從屬子句　　　　　主要子句
　　　　　　　　　　　　　　　　　因為我累壞了，所以提早上床睡覺。

❷ **Because** my parents love camping, we often go camping
　從屬連接詞　　　從屬子句　　　　逗號　　主要子句
　　　　　　　　　　　　　　　　從屬子句放在句首時，要用逗號隔開主要子句。
to get close to nature and (get) away from our routine work.
我爸媽很喜歡露營，所以我們常去露營，接觸大自然，遠離平淡的工作。

157

❸ **Although** Amy was sick, she went to school.　雖然艾咪生病了，她還是去上學了。
　　從屬連接詞　　　從屬子句　　　　　主要子句

中文的「雖然……，但是……」，在英文裡，although 和 but 不能同時出現，只能擇一使用。

2 從屬子句放在句中

| 主詞 | + | 動詞 | ... | (,) | 從屬連接詞 | + | 主詞 | + | 動詞 | ... |

主要子句　　　　　逗號可省略　　　從屬子句

兩個子句之間通常不加逗號，但從屬子句如果為非限定性，就要加逗號。

❶ **It refreshes our minds** when **we are close to nature.**
　　　主要子句　　　　　從屬連接詞　　從屬子句

❷ **I have enjoyed camping** since **I was a little child.**
　　　主要子句　　　　　從屬連接詞　　從屬子句

❸ **Lily promised to write from New York,** if **I remember correctly.**
　　　主要子句　　　　　　　　　　　從屬連接詞　從屬子句

if 引導的從屬子句放在主句後面，但因為這個從屬子句是非限定性的，所以 if 前面要加逗號。

1. 親近大自然，可以讓人精神為之一振。
2. 我從很小的時候就喜歡露營。
3. 如果我沒有記錯，莉莉答應在紐約會寫信回來。

NOTE　「對等連接詞」和「從屬連接詞」有什麼差異呢？

簡單來說，「從屬連接詞」只能用來連結兩個子句；「對等連接詞」則可以用來連接對等的字、片語或子句。

2 副詞子句的功能

副詞子句用來修飾：
1. 動詞
2. 形容詞
3. 副詞

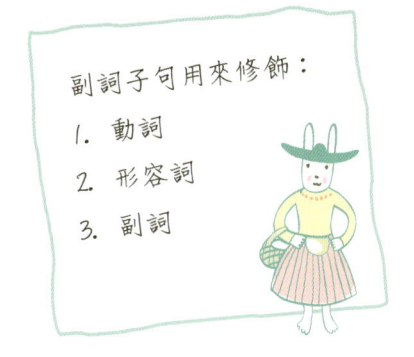

從屬子句依功能可分為**副詞子句**、**名詞子句**、**形容詞子句**。在本章節裡，我們要先介紹副詞子句。當從屬連接詞所引導的子句可以**修飾整個句子**時，便是副詞子句。副詞子句的功能如同副詞，可以用來修飾**動詞**、**形容詞**或**副詞**。

1 副詞子句用來修飾動詞

由從屬連接詞 until 帶出的副詞子句，用來修飾動詞 waited。

① We waited │until it cleared up.│
　　動詞　　　　　副詞子句

我們一直等到天氣放晴。

由從屬連接詞 while 帶出修飾動詞 were singing 的子句。

② We were singing │while we were waiting.│
　　動詞　　　　　　　　副詞子句

我們邊等邊唱歌。

2 副詞子句用來修飾形容詞

由從屬連接詞 because 帶出的副詞子句，用來修飾形容詞 disappointed 的子句。

① We felt disappointed │because we didn't go hiking as planned.│
　　　　形容詞　　　　　　　　　　　副詞子句

因為沒有如期去健行，我們覺得很失望。

❷ When the sun came out, we were all very happy. 當太陽露臉時，我們大家都好興奮。
　　　副詞子句　　　　　　　　　　　修飾 ↑ 形容詞

由從屬連接詞 when 帶出的副詞子句，用來修飾形容詞 happy。

3 副詞子句用來修飾**副詞**

❶ It was still raining heavily, so we didn't go hiking. 雨還是下得很大，所以我們沒有去健行。
　　　　　　　　　　副詞　　　　　副詞子句
　　　　　　　　　　　↑修飾

由從屬連接詞 so 帶出的副詞子句，用來修飾副詞 heavily。

由從屬連接詞 as 帶出的副詞子句，用來修飾副詞 worse。
　　　　　　　　　　　修飾 ↓
❷ The weather was getting worse as it was getting late. 天黑時，天氣也變壞了。
　　　　　　　　　　　　副詞　　　副詞子句

3 副詞子句的用法

> 從屬連接詞建立的副詞子句用來引導：
> 1. 時間
> 2. 地方
> 3. 原因
> 4. 條件
> 5. 情狀（as）
> 6. 比較（than）

從屬連接詞能建立起包含主要子句和從屬子句的副詞子句，用來修飾動詞、形容詞或其他副詞，常用來引導**時間**、**地方**、**原因**、**條件**、**情狀**（方式）、**比較**等。

1 用來引導時間

1	after	在……之後	→ 可用來描述某件事緊接另一件事發生。
2	before	在……之前	→ 可用來描述某件事緊接另一件事發生。
3	when, while, as	當……時	→ 可用來描述兩件事情同時發生。
4	as soon as	一……就……	
5	till, until	直至……	
6	since	自……以來	→ 表示從過去的某時間一直持續到現在。

❶ **Fred is used to taking a shower after he gets up.**
　　主要子句（事件 B）　　　　　　副詞子句（事件 A）
　　某件事（事件 B）緊接另一件事（事件 A），使用表時間的從屬連接詞 after。

費德習慣在起床後沖澡。

❷ **Fred likes to drink some milk before he goes to bed.**
　　主要子句　　　　　　　　　　　副詞子句

費德喜歡在睡覺前喝些牛奶。

❸ **He was listening to music when the doorbell rang.**
　　主要子句　　　　　　　　　副詞子句

當門鈴響時，他在聽音樂。

❹ **He often listens to the radio while he is having breakfast.**
　　主要子句　　　　　　　　　　　副詞子句

他常在吃早餐時聽廣播。

5 **As** he was answering the door, the telephone rang.
　　　副詞子句　　　　　　　　　　主要子句

當他在應門時，電話響了。

6 He will give you a call **as soon as** he figures out
　　主要子句（未來式）　　　　　　副詞子句（現在式）
a solution to the problem.

↳ 副詞子句中的時態要用現在式代替未來式

他一想出問題的解決方法，就會打電話給你。

7 We didn't know the news **till** he told us.
　　　主要子句　　　　　　　副詞子句

直到他告訴我們，我們才得知消息。

8 Fred has played the piano **since** he was a little child.
　　主要子句（完成式）　　　　　副詞子句（過去式）

↳ 描述從過去某段時間開始的行為，主要子句用**完成式**。

費德從很小的時候就開始練鋼琴。

> **NOTE**
> ❶ 從屬連接詞 when, before, after, as soon as 等引導的副詞子句，通常要用**現在式**代替**未來式**。
> ❷ 以 since 引導的副詞子句通常要用**過去式**，而主要子句則用**完成式**。

2　用來引導地方

1　where　　在……地方
2　wherever　無論何處

　　　　　　　　　　　　　描述見面的地點，故用表示地方的
　　　　　　　　　　　　　從屬連接詞 where。

1 Greg and Ann will meet **where** they first met.
　　　主要子句　　　　　　　　副詞子句

葛格和安將會在他們初次見面的地方會面。

2 **Wherever** she goes, he will always follow her.
　　　副詞子句　　　　　　主要子句

不管她到那裡，他總是會跟隨她。

3 用來引導原因

1	because	因為
2	as	因為
3	so	因此；所以
4	since	因為；既然
5	so . . . that	如此……，以致於……
6	such . . . that	如此……，以致於……

1 because 和 for

在描述兩件事的**因果關係**時，要用表示**原因**的從屬連接詞：

1 because：通常用來表示發生結果的**必然原因**，引導**從屬子句**。
2 for：通常用來表示推測的原因，引導**獨立子句**，且一般不放在句首。

We don't have to go to school **because** the typhoon is coming.
　　　　　主要子句　　　　　　　　　　　　　副詞子句

= **Because** the typhoon is coming, we don't have to go to school.

因為颱風要來了，所以我們不用上學。

2 so 和 such

1 so：用於**形容詞**或**副詞**之前。
2 such：用於**名詞**之前（也可以是前面加上形容詞的名詞）。

so + 形容詞或副詞 + **that** . . .

such + (a/an) + 形容詞 + 名詞 + **that** . . .

The food was **so** bad **that** I would never go to the restaurant again.
　　　　　　　　so ＋形容詞

那個食物那麼難吃，我再也不會去光顧那家餐廳了。

❷ It was **such a** horrible experience **that** I would never forget.
　　such ＋名詞（a ＋形容詞＋名詞）

　　那是一個如此可怕的經驗，我永遠不會忘記。

3 其他用語

❶ 表示因果關係時，雖然中文裡會說「**因為……，所以……**」，但在英文裡只能用一個連接詞來連接，亦即 **as**、**because**、**so** 不可以並用。

❶ Trees are important to us, **so** we must protect them.
　　＝ **As** trees are important to us, we must protect them.
　　＝ **Because** trees are important to us, we must protect them.

樹木對我們很重要，所以要加以保護。

❷ **since** 可用來引導原因，也可引導時間，這要從句子上下文來推知。表示時間時，since 引導的副詞子句要用**過去式**，主要子句要用**完成式**。

❶ **Since** the typhoon is coming, people have to be alert to the landslide.

因為颱風將近，大家要小心土石流。

4 用來引導條件

❶	if	如果	→ if 引導的從屬子句，通常要用現在式代替未來式。
❷	even if	即使；雖然	
❸	even though	即使；雖然	→ even though 的語氣較 although 強。
❹	though	雖然；儘管	→ though 在較不拘謹的語法時，可用來代替 although。
❺	although	雖然；儘管	
❻	as long as	只要	→ 表示從過去的某時間持續到現在。

❶ **If** it rains tomorrow, we won't go camping.
副詞子句（要用現在式代替未來式）　　　主要子句

由「It will rain tomorrow.」和「We won't go camping.」兩個未來式句子組合而成。

如果明天下雨，我們就不會去露營。

if 後的副詞子句，要用現在式代替未來式。

❷ **If** we don't go camping tomorrow, we will go to the movies.

由「We won't go camping tomorrow.」和「We will go to the movies.」兩個未來式的句子組合而成。

假如我們明天沒有去露營，我們會去看電影。

❸ **Although** (= **Though**) my father is usually very tired after work, he still expresses great concern about my school life.

= My father is usually very tired after work, **but** he still expresses great concern about my school life.

雖然我父親在下班後常常很疲憊，但他還是非常關心我在學校的生活。

> **NOTE** although 的用法要特別注意，中文裡會說「雖然……但是……」，但是在英文裡，一句個子裡不能同時使用 although 和 but。

❹ **Even though** (= **Even if** = **Although**) he is in his 50's, he still looks very young.

❺ He will go to the orphanage to take care of the children on weekends **as long as** he has free time.

4. 他雖然五十多歲了，但是看起來還很年輕。

5. 他只要有空，週末就會去孤兒院照顧那些孩子。

165

5　用來引導情狀：as（依照、像……一樣）

這裡的 as（像……一樣）和引導時間的 as（當……時）不同，可由上下文推知是表時間或情狀。

🍀 **You should take the medicine as the doctor told you.**
　　　　主要子句　　　　　　　　　　　副詞子句
你應該要按醫囑服藥。

🍀 **The medicine is not so bitter as you imagine.**
　　　主要子句　　　　　　　　　　副詞子句
這藥不像你想像的苦。

6　用來引導比較：than

1. 用 than（比……）來表示「跟……做比較」。
2. than 所引導的子句中，**助動詞**或**動詞**的部分通常會省略。
3. 因為是比較兩樣東西，所以要使用**比較級**，表達其中一個比另一個「更……」。

🍀 **I like chicken more than (I like) beef.**
　　主要子句　　　　　　　　副詞子句
我喜歡雞肉勝過於牛肉。

than 之後的 I like 因和主要子句的主詞、動詞相同，所以可省略。

🍀 **I am fatter than Belinda (is).**
我比碧琳達胖。

🍀 **I run faster than Carol (does).**
我跑得比卡蘿快。

Quiz 19

句子合併

依照題目指示，將兩句合併成一句。

1. Evelyn is having breakfast. / Her husband is still sleeping.
（用 while 合併）

2. Vernon will give you the answer. /
He will figure it out.（用 as long as 合併）

3. Viola has lived in Italy. / She was a little girl.（用 since 合併）

4. The traffic was heavy. /
Cliff didn't make it to the meeting on time.（用 because 合併）

5. I didn't walk my dog. / It was raining hard.（用 so 合併）

6. Barry studied hard. / He passed the exam.（用 so . . . that . . . 合併）

7. It was a horrible experience. / I would never forget.
（用 such . . . that . . . 合併）

8. It will rain tomorrow. /
We won't go on a picnic at the beach.（用 if 合併）

9. Harold looks like a middle-aged man. / He is 25 years old.
（用 although 合併）

10. Gilbert always checks the answers carefully. /
He hands in the answer sheet.（用 before 合併）

Unit 12 名詞子句

Warm-up 暖身

短文中，畫底線的部分是本章要討論的「名詞子句」。你能不能從這些句子中，歸納出共通點？

It makes me excited that the Edinburgh International Festival has opened. I believe that the Festival is full of fun. It is clear that not only children but also adults will enjoy the Festival very much.

1 名詞子句的特性與功能

上一單元已經介紹過「**從屬連接詞**引導**從屬子句**，在連接**主要子句**後，形成一個**複合句**」的概念，本章我們要介紹名詞子句。

名詞子句有以下特色：

① 名詞子句是主要子句本身不可或缺的一部分，少了名詞子句，主要子句就不完整。

② 名詞子句的功能如同**名詞**，可當作：

　①　主詞　　　　　②　真正主詞（it 當虛主詞）　　③　動詞的受詞
　④　介系詞的受詞　⑤　主詞補語　　　　　　　　　⑥　同位語

1 名詞子句作主詞

以 that 引導的名詞子句作主詞，雖然文法上無誤，但主詞太長，造成頭重腳輕，像這樣的句子，多以虛主詞 it 來引導。

從屬連接詞 that 帶出的名詞子句（作主要子句的主詞）

❶ **That** the Arts Festival **has opened** makes me excited.
　　　（從屬子句的主詞）　　（從屬子句的動詞）　　　　主要子句

藝術節開始了，我感到很興奮。

從屬連接詞 that 帶出的名詞子句（作真正主詞）

= **It** makes me excited **that** the Arts Festival has opened.
　虛主詞　　主要子句

2 名詞子句作真正主詞

從屬連接詞 that 帶出的名詞子句（作真正主詞）

❶ **It is** clear **that** not only children but also adults
　虛主詞 主要子句　　　　（從屬子句的主詞）
　will enjoy the Festival very much.
　（從屬子句的動詞）

很明顯地，不僅是小孩，連大人都會很喜歡這個藝術節。

169

3 名詞子句作動詞的受詞

> 從屬連接詞 that 帶出的名詞子句（作動詞的受詞）

① I believe **that the Festival is full of joy.**
  主要子句

我相信這個藝術節會充滿歡樂。

4 名詞子句作介系詞的受詞

> 從屬連接詞 that 帶出的名詞子句（作介系詞的受詞）

① We are talking about **whether we should go to the Festival or not.**
  主要子句

我們正在討論是否要去藝術節。

5 名詞子句作主詞補語

> 從屬連接詞 that 帶出的名詞子句（作主詞補語）

① The question is **where we should stay in Edinburgh.**
  主要子句

問題是在愛丁堡我們要住在哪兒。

6 名詞子句作同位語

> 從屬連接詞 that 帶出的名詞子句（作同位語）

① The idea **that we will stay overnight at the train station** sounds crazy.
  主要子句

由 that 引導的名詞子句是 idea 的同位語，來補充說明 idea。

我們要待在火車站過夜的主意，聽起來很瘋狂。

> **NOTE**
> ❶ 同位語通常放在名詞旁邊，用來補充說明或解釋該名詞。
> ❷ 「副詞子句」和「名詞子句」有什麼差異？簡單來說，把從屬子句去掉後，如果不影響主要子句的完整性，此從屬子句就是「**副詞子句**」；如果把從屬子句去掉後，主要子句變得不完整，此從屬子句就是「**名詞子句**」。

Quiz 20

句子重組

將下列題目中所有提示字詞整合成一個有意義的句子。
答案中要使用所有提示字詞，且不能隨意增加字詞。

1 That _____.
makes/has opened/me/the exhibition/happy

2 It _____.
surprises/they have been to/that/me/the exhibition

3 It _____.
people/clear/enjoy the exhibition/is/that/from all over the world

4 I believe _____.
the fair/that/is/entertaining

5 We are _____.
what/talking about/should buy/at the exhibition/we

6 The problem _____.
where/is/park/to/our car

7 The thought that _____.
we/sounds crazy/on foot/go

8 Whether _____.
or not/depends on/we will/the weather/go shopping

9 I _____.
the book/that/think/is/helpful

10 The latest news _____.
that/the criminal/is/still/is/at large

2 名詞子句的種類

寫作時常會運用來形成名詞子句的從屬連接詞有 that、whether（= if）和 what，以下我們就分別介紹用法。

1 that 引導的名詞子句

that 引導的名詞子句，在句中可作主詞、補語、受詞、同位語等。

1 作主詞

that 子句作主詞時，常可改寫成以 it 作虛主詞的句子，然後以 that 子句作主詞補語。一般來說，此類句子多以虛主詞 it 引導，較符合語言習慣。

❶ **That** the night market is a shopping paradise is certain.　夜市的確是購物的天堂。
　　　That 帶出的名詞子句作主詞

= **It** is certain **that** the night market is a shopping paradise.
　it 為虛主詞帶出的句子　　　　　　　主詞補語

❷ **That** you can buy many cheap things there is true.　你真的可以在那裡買到很多便宜的東西。
　　　That 帶出的名詞子句作主詞

= **It** is true **that** you can buy many cheap things there.
　it 為虛主詞帶出的句子　　　　　主詞補語

2 作主詞補語

❶ The trouble is **that** I don't have money.　苦惱的是我沒有錢。
　主詞　　　動詞　that 帶出的名詞子句作主詞 the trouble 的補語

❷ Another problem **is** **that** the food in the night market may not
　　　主詞　　　　　　動詞　　　that 帶出的名詞子句作主詞 another problem 的補語
be clean.
　　　　　　　　　　　　　　　　　　　　另一個問題是，夜市的食物可能不是很衛生。

3 作動詞的受詞

　　that 引導的名詞子句，在「主詞＋動詞＋受詞」句型中作受詞時，連接詞 that 通常會被省略，這在口語英語中尤其常見。

　　　　　　　　that 帶出的名詞子句作動詞 think 的受詞
❶ I think (that) our night market is a special spot for foreign visitors.
主詞　動詞
　　　　　　　　　　　　　　　　　　　　　　我想我們的夜市對外國觀光客
　　　　　　　　　　　　　　　　　　　　　　而言，是個很特別的景點。
　　　　　　　　that 帶出的名詞子句作動詞 believe 的受詞
❷ I believe (that) they will have a lot of fun in the night market.
主詞　　動詞
　　　　　　　　　　　　　　　　　　　　　　我相信他們在夜市會玩得很開心。

4 作介系詞的受詞

　　that 子句作介系詞的受詞，只用在「except that」（除了……之外）。

　　　　　　　　　　　　　　that 帶出的名詞子句作介系詞 except 的受詞
❶ The night market is fun **except** **that** it is too crowded.
　　　　　　　　　　　　　　介系詞
　　　　　　　　　　　　　　　　　　　　　　除了太擁擠外，夜市很好玩。

5 作同位語

　　that 子句常接在名詞 idea, fact, belief, report, news 等後面，作該詞的同位語。

　　　　　　　that 帶出的名詞子句作名詞 belief 的同位語
❶ The **belief** **that** "I already gave my best, and thus I have no
　　　主詞
regrets at all" **makes** William Hung famous overnight.
　　　　　　　　主要動詞
　　　　　　　　　　　　　　「我毫無遺憾，因為我盡了最大的努力」的信念，
　　　　　　　　　　　　　　使得孔慶翔一夕之間聲名大噪。

　　　　　　　that 帶出的名詞子句作名詞 belief 的同位語
❷ The **fact** **that** he couldn't carry a tune **made** the judges shake
　　　主詞　　　　　　　　　　　　　　　　　主要動詞
their heads.
　　　　　　　　　　　　　　　　　　　　　　他的走音讓評審員搖頭。

2 「whether . . . (or not)」＝ if（是否……）引導的名詞子句

1. whether 後面可以接 or not；但 if 後面不可接 or not。
2. whether 引導的名詞子句，可作句中的主詞、主詞補語或受詞。

1 作主詞

由 whether 引導的名詞子句作主詞時，通常不可用 if 代替，但可改寫成以 it 為虛主詞的句子。

① **Whether we will go camping tomorrow (or not) depends on the weather.**
　　whether 帶出的名詞子句作主詞　　　　　　　主要動詞

　＝ **It depends on the weather whether we will go camping tomorrow (or not).**
　　以 it 為虛主詞帶出的句子　　　whether 帶出的名詞子句作補語

　我們明天是否會去露營視天氣而定。

② **Whether the typhoon will go away (or not) is doubtful.**
　　　whether 帶出的名詞子句作主詞

　＝ **It is doubtful whether the typhoon will go away (or not).**
　　以 it 為虛主詞帶出的句子　whether 帶出的名詞子句作補語

　颱風是否會遠離，令人懷疑。

2 作主詞補語

由 whether 引導的名詞子句作主詞補語時，可以用「if」句型代換。

① **The problem is whether Tom will propose to Helen (or not).**
　　主詞　　動詞　　whether 帶出的名詞子句作主詞補語

　＝ **The problem is if Tom will propose to Helen.**
　　　　　　　由 whether 引導的名詞子句作主詞補語時，可以用 if 句型代換。

　問題是湯姆會不會跟海倫求婚。

② **Our question is whether Helen will accept his proposal (or not).**
　　主詞　　　動詞　　whether 帶出的名詞子句作主詞補語

　＝ **Our question is if Helen will accept his proposal.**

　我們的問題是海倫會不會接受他的求婚。

3 作動詞的受詞

由 whether 引導的名詞子句作受詞時，可以用「if」句型代換。

❶ I wonder **whether** they will go to Italy for their honeymoon (or not).
　主詞　動詞
　↑ whether 帶出的名詞子句作動詞的受詞

　= I wonder **if** they will go to Italy for their honeymoon.

❷ I don't know **whether** it will snow at that time (or not).
　主詞　　動詞
　↑ whether 帶出的名詞子句作動詞的受詞

　= I don't know **if** it will snow at that time.

1. 我想知道他們是否會到義大利度蜜月。
2. 我不知道那時候是否會下雪。

3　what（所……的事物或人）引導的名詞子句

what 引導的名詞子句，可作句中的主詞、主詞補語及受詞。

1 作主詞

❶ **What** makes me excited **is** the whale-watching activity on the Pacific Ocean.
　what 帶出的名詞子句作主詞　動詞　主詞補語

使我興奮的是在太平洋上的賞鯨活動。

❷ **What** worries me **is** the unpredictable weather.
　what 帶出的名詞子句作主詞　動詞　主詞補語

令我擔心的是無法預料的天氣。

2 作主詞補語

❶ The Turtle Mountain Island is not what it was before.
　　　主詞　　　　　　　　　動詞　　what 帶出的名詞子句作主詞補語

= The Turtle Mountain Island is not what it used to be.
　　　主詞　　　　　　　　　動詞　　what 帶出的名詞子句作主詞補語

❷ My question is what made the residents in the island move out.
　　主詞　　　動詞　　what 帶出的名詞子句作主詞補語

1. 龜山島已今非昔比。
2. 我的疑問是島上的居民為什麼會遷出。

3 作動詞的受詞

❶ Please tell me what happened yesterday.
　　　　動詞　　what 帶出的名詞子句作動詞的受詞

❷ Do you know what they are talking about?
　　　　動詞　　what 帶出的名詞子句作動詞的受詞

1. 請告訴我昨天發生了什麼事。
2. 你知道他們正在說什麼嗎？

Quiz 21

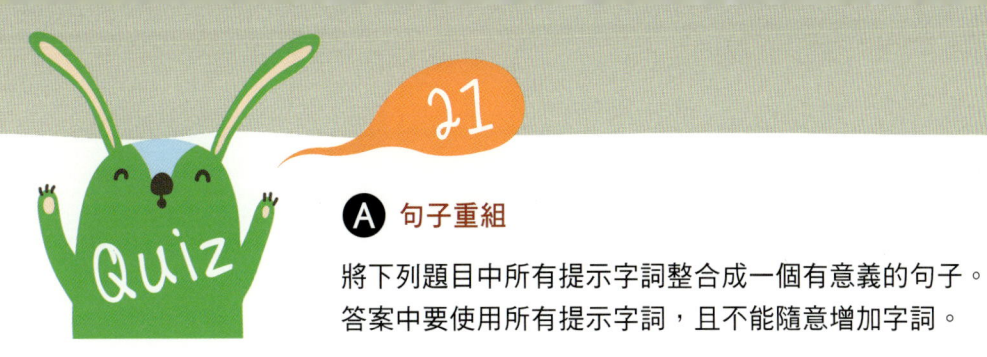

A 句子重組

將下列題目中所有提示字詞整合成一個有意義的句子。
答案中要使用所有提示字詞，且不能隨意增加字詞。

1 I _____.
   talk to/am afraid/you/I can't/that/now

2 I told you that _____.
   couldn't/make it/Stanley/to work today

3 What _____.
   want/is/we/your money

4 Sonia asked Jason _____.
   he/if/do her a favor/could

5 I thought that _____.
   I/myself/understood/had made

B 請依指示改寫句子。

1 Whether we will go hiking tomorrow or not depends on the weather.

   It _____.

2 That Romeo loves Juliet is certain.

   It _____.

3 The students will benefit a lot from this activity.
   I believe it.（用 I believe . . . 合併）

   _____.

4 Ask Laura whether she can come or not.（用 if . . . 改寫）

   _____.

5 That Pamela didn't catch the train this morning was true.

   It _____.

Unit 13 形容詞子句

Warm-up 暖身

下列短文中,畫底線的部分是本章節要討論的重點「形容詞子句」。觀察看看,它們有什麼特性或共通點?

The woman <u>who is wearing a pair of sunglasses</u> is a column writer. She is the leading actress of the TV series <u>which we watch every night</u>. <u>What she wears</u> is in fashion these days.

1 如何形成形容詞子句（關係子句）

前面討論了副詞子句和名詞子句，接著要來學習形容詞子句。兩個句子（主要子句和關係子句）中以相同的名詞為基礎，用關係代名詞把兩個句子連接起來，這樣的從屬子句就稱為「**形容詞子句**」或「**關係子句**」。在寫作時應用此句型，不僅能做多樣變化，亦可以展現自己的英文程度。

1 何謂形容詞子句（關係子句）？

1 何謂形容詞子句？簡單來說，形容詞子句就是由**關係代名詞**開頭的子句。關係代名詞的**人稱**、**單複數**、**性別**要和**先行詞**一致（先行詞乃是「關係代名詞所代表的名詞或代名詞」）。關係代名詞可分成兩大類：

ⓐ **簡單**關係代名詞：who, whom, whose, which, that
ⓑ **複合**關係代名詞：what

2 關係代名詞的「格」，依關係代名詞在其引導形容詞子句中的作用而定。

先行詞	主格	所有格	受格
人	who	whose	whom
事物、動物	which	whose	which
人、事物、動物	that	—	that

先行詞
1. The woman <u>who</u> is wearing a pair of sunglasses is a column writer.
   ↑ 關係代名詞 who 帶出形容詞子句，修飾先行詞 the woman。

   那個戴著太陽眼鏡的女人是一位專欄作家。

2. She is the leading actress of the TV series 先行詞
   <u>which</u> we watch every night.
   ↑ 關係代名詞 which 帶出形容詞子句，修飾先行詞 the TV series。

   她是那位我們每晚收看的電視影集的女主角。

② 如何將兩句直述句合併為形容詞子句？

步驟一 找出兩句中指同一人事物的詞（名詞或代名詞），通常以第一句的名詞或代名詞來當作「**先行詞**」。

步驟二 接著把第二句中相同的名詞或代名詞，用適當的「**關係代名詞**」代替，並將關係代名詞放至**句首**，形成「**形容詞子句**」。

步驟三 最後把形容詞子句放到第一句的**先行詞**後面，就形成一個複合句。

1 關係代名詞的主格

❶ 找出兩個句子中相同的名詞「the girl」來作先行詞。

1. The girl is my classmate. ＋ The girl is wearing a red skirt.

❷ 先行詞 the girl 是人，又是主格，故要用關係代名詞 who 或 that 代替，形成形容詞子句「who/that is wearing a red skirt」。

= The girl **who/that** is wearing a red skirt is my classmate.
　先行詞　　　　　　　　　形容詞子句

❸ 把形容詞子句放在先行詞 the girl 的後面。

> 那位穿紅裙的女孩是我的同班同學。

❶ 找出兩個句子中相同的名詞「an apartment」來作先行詞。

2. She lives in an apartment. ＋ The apartment is close to our school.

❷ 先行詞是事物，所以關係代名詞用 which 或 that，形成形容詞子句。

= She lives in an apartment **which/that** is close to our school.
　　　　先行詞　　　　　　　　形容詞子句

❸ 把形容詞子句放在先行詞 an apartment 的後面。

> 她住在我們學校附近的公寓。

2 關係代名詞的所有格

❶ 找出兩個句子中，指同一人事物的詞「the girl, her」，先行詞是第一句中的「the girl」。

1. The girl is my classmate. ＋ Her mother is our English teacher.

❷ 因代名詞 her 是人，而這個代名詞在原句中是所有格，故要用關係代名詞 whose 代替，形成形容詞子句「whose mother is our English teacher」。

= The girl **whose** mother is our English teacher is my classmate.
　先行詞　　　　　　形容詞子句

❸ 把形容詞子句放在先行詞 the girl 的後面。

> 那個女孩是我的同班同學，她的媽媽是我們的英文老師。

② She has a dog. ➕ The dog's name is Coco.　　她有一隻小狗叫蔻蔻。

找出兩個句子中，指同一人事物的詞「a dog, the dog」，先行詞是第一句中的「a dog」。

＝ She has a dog whose name is Coco.

因代名詞在原句中是所有格 the dog's，故要用關係代名詞 whose 代替。

先行詞　形容詞子句

把形容詞子句放在先行詞 a dog 的後面。

3 關係代名詞的受格

① This is the dog. ➕ We saw it on the poster at the train station yesterday.

先找出兩個句子中所指同一人事物的詞 the dog, it，先行詞是 the dog。

＝ This is the dog which/that we saw on the poster at the train station yesterday.

因第二句中的 it 是動詞 saw 的受詞，故要用受格 which 或 that 代替，並將關係代名詞放至句首，形成形容詞子句。

先行詞　形容詞子句

把形容詞子句放在先行詞 the dog 的後面。

② This is the girl. ➕ Tim asked the girl out for dinner last Friday.

先找出兩個句子中所指同一人事物的詞 the girl，用來當作先行詞。

＝ This is the girl whom/that Tim asked out for dinner last Friday.

因第二句中的 the girl 是動詞 asked 的受詞，故要用受格 whom 或 that 代替，並將關係代名詞放至句首，形成形容詞子句。

先行詞　形容詞子句

把形容詞子句放在先行詞 the girl 的後面。

1. 這是昨天我們看到張貼在火車站海報上的小狗。

2. 這是提姆上星期五邀請出去吃飯的女孩。

Quiz 22

A 填空

在下列的空格中填入 who、which、whom、whose 或 that。（每一題的正確解答也許不只一種）

1. The man _____ is wearing a black shirt is my teacher.
2. We live in a house _____ is near the park.
3. He is my English teacher _____ name is Clark Chang.
4. He has a beautiful wife _____ he loves very much.
5. This is the ring _____ Mr. Lin bought for their anniversary.

B 句子合併：將下列句子用形容詞子句合併成一個複合句。

1. The man will join the cocktail party.
   + He is singing the happy birthday song.
   _____.

2. This is the book. + I borrowed it from the school library.
   _____.

3. He is a writer. + His daughter is a friend of mine.
   _____.

4. They have a cat. + The cat's name is Kitty.
   _____.

5. This is the girl.
   + We met the girl in the bookstore last week.
   _____.

2 形容詞子句的功用和種類

1 形容詞子句的功用

1. 形容詞子句在整個複合句中的功能就像**形容詞**，可以用來修飾名詞、代名詞或其他形式的名詞。
2. **關係代名詞**具有連接詞和代名詞的功用，一方面可當代名詞以代表**先行詞**，另一方面當**從屬連接詞**，以引導從屬子句，將從屬子句和主要子句連接成一個句子。

1 The movie star **whom/that** we just talked about won the Best Actress of the Academy Awards.
　　先行詞　　　關係代名詞　　　（從屬子句）　　　　（主要子句）

> 原句 The movie star won the Best Actress of the Academy Awards.
> ＋ We talked about the movie star.

2 The woman **whose** hair is blond is my idol.
　　先行詞　　關係代名詞（從屬子句）　　（主要子句）

> 原句 The woman is my idol. ＋ The woman's hair is blond.

1. 我們剛剛談論的那個電影明星，獲得奧斯卡的最佳女主角獎。

2. 那個金髮女郎是我的偶像。

2 形容詞子句的「限定」與「非限定」用法

1 「限定」與「非限定」的定義：
  a「限定」的形容詞子句：用來限定或修飾先行詞，以幫助辨識先行詞的身分。
  b「非限定」的形容詞子句：不幫助辨識先行詞的身分，因先行詞的身分已確認，形容詞子句只是在提供更多先行詞的訊息。
2 **逗號的用法**：通常在**非限定**的形容詞子句前，要加逗號；如果非限定的形容詞子句插在主句中間，那麼形容詞子句前後都要用逗號。
3 **分辨「限定」與「非限定」的形容詞子句**：假如形容詞子句刪除後，主句的意思仍然完整，便可判定為「非限定性」子句；反之，則為「限定」子句。
4 在「**非限定**」的形容詞子句中，不能使用關係代名詞 that。
5 如果先行詞是**專有名詞**，則一定要用**非限定**的用法。

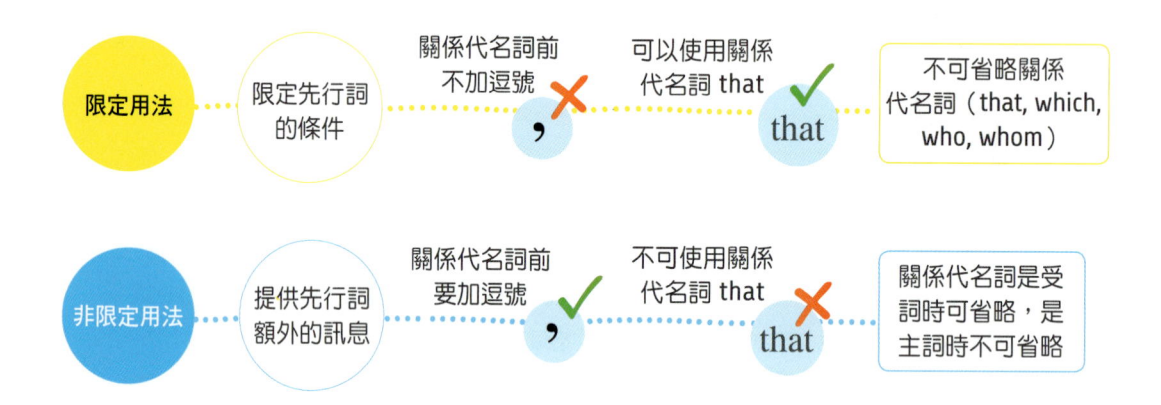

限定用法	限定先行詞的條件	關係代名詞前不加逗號 ✗	可以使用關係代名詞 that ✓	不可省略關係代名詞（that, which, who, whom）
非限定用法	提供先行詞額外的訊息	關係代名詞前要加逗號 ✓	不可使用關係代名詞 that ✗	關係代名詞是受詞時可省略，是主詞時不可省略

1 限定用法

這個形容詞子句是限定用法，用來指定「朱里安買的花」。

❶ The flowers **which**/**that** Julian bought are very beautiful.
　先行詞　　　　形容詞子句

朱里安買的花很漂亮。

原句 The flowers are very beautiful. ＋ Julian bought the flowers.

❷ He is talking to **the person** <u>who</u>/<u>that</u> will deliver the flowers.
　　　　　　　　　先行詞　　　形容詞子句

這個形容詞子句是限定用法，用來指定「送花的人」。

他和要去送花的人在講話。

原句 He is talking to the person. ＋ The person will deliver the flowers.

2 非限定用法（關係代名詞不可用 that 替代）

這個形容詞子句在此沒有辨識的作用，因為我們已知道所說的是 Hilary，此形容詞子句只是提供了更多關於先行詞的訊息。

❶ **Hilary**, <u>who</u> is Julian's girlfriend, has just received the flowers.
　先行詞　　　形容詞子句

原句 Hilary has just received the flowers. ＋ Hilary is Julian's girlfriend.

Suburb　　**Downtown**

❷ **Hilary's office**, <u>which</u> is in the suburbs, is far away from Julian's.
　　先行詞　　　　　形容詞子句

這個形容詞子句提供 Hilary 辦公室的額外地理訊息。

原句 Hilary's office is far away from Julian's. ＋ Hilary's office is in the suburbs.

1. 希拉蕊是朱里安的女朋友，她剛剛收到花。
2. 希拉蕊的辦公室在郊區，離朱里安的辦公室很遠。

加不加逗號的差別

❋ Jim has **three brothers** <u>who</u> have become doctors.
　吉姆有三位當醫生的哥哥。
　→ 限定形容詞子句：吉姆可能不只有三個哥哥，現在提的是當醫生的哥哥。

❋ Jim has **three brothers**, <u>who</u> have become doctors.
　吉姆的三位哥哥都是醫生。
　→ 非限定形容詞子句：吉姆只有三個哥哥，而且都在當醫生。

3　關係代名詞 who, that, which, whom 的省略問題

1 在**限定**的形容詞子句中，關係代名詞如果是形容詞子句的動詞**受詞**，則關係代名詞可以省略；如果關係代名詞是形容詞子句的**主詞**，則關係代名詞就不能省略。

2 **非限定**的形容詞子句，則不可省略 who 或 which。

① The movie (which/that) we saw yesterday was entertaining.
　　　　　　　　限定形容詞子句

（受詞：關係代名詞 which/that 是動詞 saw 的受詞，故可以把關係代名詞省略，後面直接接代名詞 we。）

② That was the movie (that/which) we had been waiting for.
　　　　　　　　　　限定形容詞子句

（受詞：關係代名詞 that/which 是動詞 wait 的受詞，故可以把關係代名詞省略，後面直接接代名詞 we。）

③ The man who/that was coughing all the time in the theater sat next to me.
　　　　　　　　　　限定形容詞子句

（主詞：who/that 是子句中的主詞，如果省略，形容詞子句的開頭是 was，而不是名詞，故不能省略。）

④ Lady Gaga, whom/who we talked about yesterday, is our idol.
　　　　　　　非限定形容詞子句

（主詞：這是非限定形容詞子句，關係代名詞不可省略。）

1. 我們昨天看的電影很富娛樂性。
2. 那是我們等待已久的電影。
3. 在電影院裡一直咳嗽的人就坐在我旁邊。
4. 我們昨天聊到的女神卡卡，是我們的偶像。

4　一定要用關係代名詞 that 的情況

1 在限定子句中，如果先行詞有下列的字詞時，關係代名詞一定要用 that：

- all
- every
- any
- no
- the very
- the only
- the same
- the little
- the few
- the first
- the last

2 先行詞有**人**和**物**時，也一定要使用關係代名詞 that。

① **This is the only subject that interests me.** 這是唯一讓我感興趣的科目。

　　先行詞有 the only，關係代名詞只能用 that。
　　that 是形容詞子句的主詞，因此不能省略。
　　先行詞　　that 帶出形容詞子句

② **All (that) I have to do every day is (to) study.** 我每天得做的就是讀書。

　　先行詞是 all，關係代名詞要用 that。
　　that 是 do 的受詞，可省略。
　　先行詞　that 帶出形容詞子句

③ **The poem describes a little boy and his Teddy Bear that are sitting under a giant tree.**

　　先行詞是 a little boy（人）和 his Teddy Bear（物），所以要用關係代名詞 that。
　　先行詞
　　that 帶出形容詞子句

　　這首詩描述坐在大樹下的小男孩和他的泰迪熊。

5 介系詞與關係代名詞

1. 關係代名詞用作介系詞的**受詞**時，介系詞的位置可以在句尾或在關係代名詞之前。
2. 如果介系詞放在關係代名詞前，關係代名詞就要用**受格**（介系詞＋受格）。
3. 關係代名詞 that 不可直接放在介系詞後面。

① **This is the house.** ＋ **She lives in the house.**

＝ **This is the house which/that she lives in.** 這就是她住的房子。

＝ **This is the house she lives in.** ← 口語用法，省略關係代名詞。

＝ **This is the house in which she lives.** ← 不可以寫成「…in that she lives」，關係代名詞 that 不可接在介系詞 in 的後面。

② **She is the person.** ＋ **I talked to the person just now.** 我剛剛就是和她講話。

＝ **She is the person whom/that I talked to just now.**

＝ **She is the person I talked to just now.** ← 口語用法，省略關係代名詞。

187

= She is the person to whom I talked just now.

> 不可以寫成「... to that I talked」，
> 關係代名詞 that 不可接在介系詞 to 的後面。

6 關係詞 what 的用法

由 what 所引導的子句，在句中通常為名詞子句，作句中的主詞、受詞或補語。

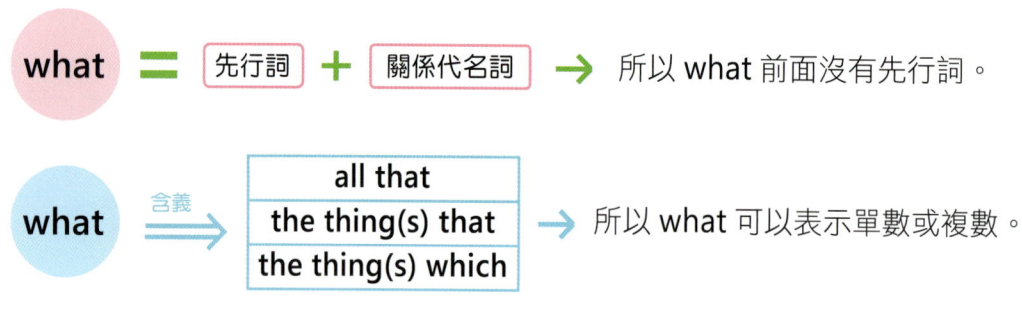

what = 先行詞 + 關係代名詞 → 所以 what 前面沒有先行詞。

what 含義 → all that / the thing(s) that / the thing(s) which → 所以 what 可以表示單數或複數。

❶ What she bought were/was very expensive. 她買的東西很昂貴。

= The thing(s) that/which she bought were/was very expensive.

❷ This is exactly what I want.

= This is exactly the thing that/which I want. 這正好是我想要的東西。

❸ I have no idea what she is talking about. 我不了解她在說什麼。

= I have no idea the thing that/which she is talking about.

> 看到這裡，有沒有覺得似曾相識？沒錯，在 Unit 12 裡我們從名詞子句的角度來討論 what 的用法，現在再翻回 Unit 12 複習 what 的用法，是不是有恍然大悟的感覺呢？

7 使用 where、when、why、how 的形容詞子句

以關係副詞 where、when、why、how 引導形容詞子句，其中 why 及 how 通常只用於限定用法。

地方先行詞 + where + 完整子句
時間先行詞 + when + 完整子句
原因先行詞 + why + 完整子句 ┐
方法先行詞 + how + 完整子句 ┘ why 和 how 通常只用於限定用法

❶ This is the apartment where he lives. 【限定用法】
　　　地方先行詞　　　　形容詞子句
　= This is the apartment in which he lives.

❷ Roy will take a trip to Athens, where he will stay for two weeks. 【非限定用法】
　= Roy will take a trip to Athens, in which he will stay for two weeks.

❸ Tell me the time when the train should arrive. 【限定用法】

❹ Roy got home on June 7th, when his niece was born. 【非限定用法】

❺ This is (the reason) why he can't come. 【限定用法】

❻ This is (the way) how he earns his travel expenses. 【限定用法】

1. 這就是他住的公寓。
2. 羅伊要到雅典旅行，他將在那裡待上兩星期。
3. 告訴我火車應該抵達的時間。
4. 羅伊在六月七日回到家，他的姪女也在當天出生。
5. 這就是他不能來的原因。
6. 這就是他賺得旅費的方法。

8 先行詞的省略

以 when、where、why、how 引導的形容詞子句，其先行詞如下時，通常會把先行詞省略：

當先行詞是 the place	+	where
當先行詞是 the time	+	when
當先行詞是 the reason	+	why
當先行詞是 the way	+	how

以上的先行詞通常會省略

❶ Tell me **when** you will be free. 　　告訴我你什麼時候有空。

= Tell me the time **when** you will be free.

when 和先行詞 the time 通常不會一起出現，但是在文法和意思上無誤。

❷ This is **where** we live. 　　這就是我們住的地方。

= This is the place **where** we live.

where 跟先行詞 the place 通常不會一起出現，但是在文法和意思上無誤。

= This is the place **in which** we live.

= This is the place **which/that** we live in.

= This is the place we live in.

❸ That is **why** it's my treat today. 　　那就是為什麼今天我請客。

= That is the reason **why** it's my treat today.

why 跟先行詞 the reason 通常不會一起出現，但是在文法和意思上無誤。

❹ That was **how** he won the lottery. 　　那就是他贏得樂透的方法。

= That was **the way** he won the lottery.

how 跟先行詞 the way 通常不會一起出現，兩個中選擇一個造句即可。

Quiz 23

A 挑錯並訂正

把下列句子錯誤的地方劃線並訂正。

1. Judy who is John's sister is my good friend.

2. The woman which wears a pair of glasses is a teacher.

3. The picture shows a little girl and her pet which are playing in the park.

4. The Olympic Games will take place in Athens which is the capital of Greece.

5. This is the only program which arouses my interest.

B 句子合併：將下列句子用形容詞子句合併成一個複合句。

1. The movie was very interesting. ✚ We saw the movie yesterday.

2. Anthony is my high school classmate.
   ✚ He will go to Australia next summer.

3. This is the house. ✚ He lives in the house.

4. The story seems very exciting. ✚ He told me the story last month.

5. This is the most delicious food. ✚ I have ever tasted the food.

Unit 14

分詞片語／分詞構句

Warm-up 暖身

下面短文中，有前面章節討論過的從屬連接詞（如 after, as），也包含了本章節的重點「分詞片語」。劃底線的部分是分詞片語。觀察看看，它們有什麼共通處？

While/When <u>checking in</u> at the hotel, we asked the receptionist whether we could exchange some money. <u>After having settled</u>, we made a call to the front desk to ask how to get an outside line. <u>As being</u> very tired that night, we went to bed early.

1 認識分詞構句

1 何謂分詞片語？

由**分詞**引導而兼含**連接詞**和**動詞**功用的片語，稱為分詞片語或分詞構句。分詞片語的重點在於將副詞子句改為**分詞片語**。分詞片語可區分為**現在分詞**（V-ing）和**過去分詞**兩種。一般來說，現在分詞表**主動**，過去分詞表**被動**，和時態無關。

原句為主動，故用現在分詞 Swimming。

❶ <u>Swimming</u> in the swimming pool, Daisy saw a plane flying across the sky.
　　　分詞片語（分詞構句）

使用 while 引導的分詞片語，這種用法更常見。

= <u>While swimming</u> in the swimming pool, Daisy saw a plane flying across the sky.

意思為「被遺忘」，用過去分詞 forgotten，表被動。

❷ Daisy lives alone in the countryside, <u>forgotten</u> by everyone.
　　　　　　　　　　　　　　　　　　　　分詞片語（分詞構句）

1. 在泳池游泳時，黛西看見一架飛機在空中飛過。
2. 黛西獨自住在鄉間，被每個人遺忘了。

2 將副詞子句改為分詞片語／分詞構句的步驟

步驟一 將引導副詞子句的連接詞刪除。

步驟二
❶ 主詞1＝主詞2時 → 去掉主詞1
❷ 主詞1≠主詞2時 → 保留主詞1

步驟三
❶ 動詞為主動時 → 改成現在分詞（V-ing）
❷ 動詞為被動時 → 改成過去分詞（V-ed）

副詞子句句型

步驟一 將引導副詞子句的連接詞刪除

步驟三
- 動詞為主動時 → 改成現在分詞（V-ing）
- 動詞為被動時 → 改成過去分詞（V-ed）

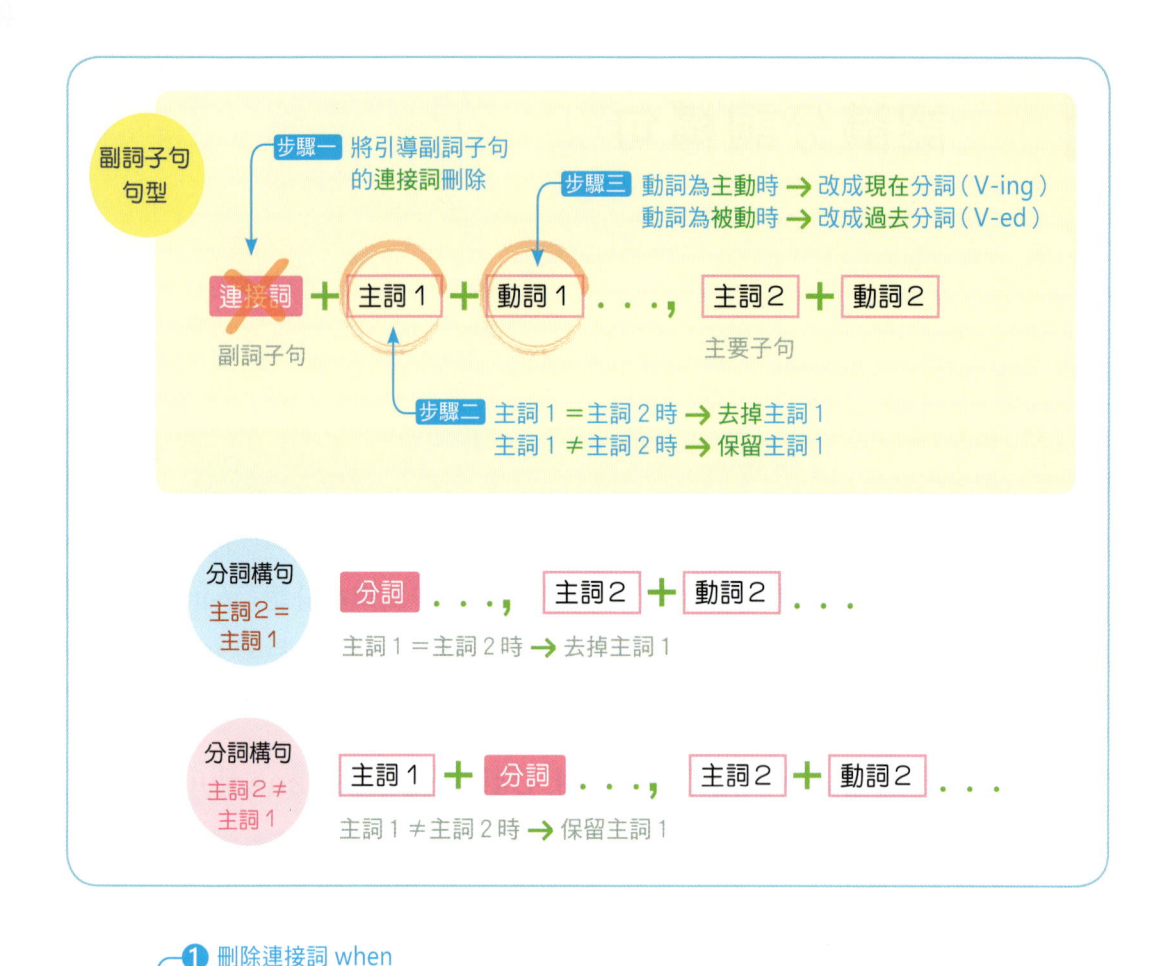

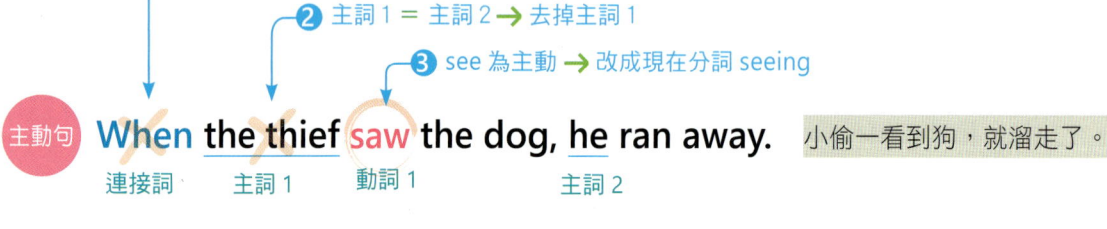

~~連接詞~~ ＋ 主詞1 ＋ 動詞1 ..., 主詞2 ＋ 動詞2

副詞子句　　　　　　　　　　　主要子句

步驟二
- 主詞1＝主詞2時 → 去掉主詞1
- 主詞1≠主詞2時 → 保留主詞1

分詞構句 主詞2＝主詞1

分詞 ..., 主詞2 ＋ 動詞2 ...

主詞1＝主詞2時 → 去掉主詞1

分詞構句 主詞2≠主詞1

主詞1 ＋ 分詞 ..., 主詞2 ＋ 動詞2 ...

主詞1≠主詞2時 → 保留主詞1

主動句

❶ 刪除連接詞 when
❷ 主詞1＝主詞2 → 去掉主詞1
❸ see 為主動 → 改成現在分詞 seeing

~~When~~ ~~the thief~~ ~~saw~~ the dog, he ran away.　　小偷一看到狗，就溜走了。
連接詞　主詞1　動詞1　　　　　主詞2

→ **Seeing** the dog, the thief ran away.
　　分詞片語（分詞構句）

被動句

❶ 刪除連接詞 if
❷ 主詞1＝主詞2 → 去掉主詞1
❸ was seen 為被動 → 改成 being seen，省略 being 之後，只留 seen。

~~If~~ ~~it~~ ~~was seen~~ from a distance, it looked like a cat.　　從遠處看，就像隻貓。
主詞1　被動語態　　　　　　　　主詞2

→ **Seen** from a distance, it looked like a cat.

NOTE

❶ **分詞的否定**：副詞子句中有否定詞時，將否定詞放在分詞前，形成否定分詞片語。

❊ Since Samuel **didn't know** what to do, he kept silent.
　　　主詞1　　否定詞　動詞（主動）　　　　　主詞2

→ **Not knowing** what to do, Samuel kept silent.
　否定詞　現在分詞

　因為山繆不知道該怎麼辦，所以他保持沉默。

❷ **完成式的分詞**：否定詞 not 放在 having 之前或之後皆可。

❊ Because Sam **hadn't heard** from May for a long time, he wrote her an email.
　　　主詞1　　　動詞（主動）　　　　　　　　　　　　主詞2

→ **Not having heard** from May for a long time, Sam wrote her an email.
　否定詞　現在分詞

→ **Having not heard** from May for a long time, Sam wrote her an email.

　山姆很久沒有梅的消息，所以寫電子郵件給她。

---

❸ 副詞子句的動詞為**主動**時，如何改成分詞片語／分詞構句？

1️⃣ 一般動詞時 → 把動詞改成現在分詞。
2️⃣ 進行式時 → 把 be 動詞去掉。
3️⃣ 完成式時 → 把動詞改成「having ＋過去分詞」。

　　　　　　　　　　　　　一般動詞時 → 把動詞 heard 改成現在分詞 hearing
　主詞1

🍀 After Nick **heard** a scream, he ran out to see what had happened.
　　　　　　一般動詞　　　主詞2

= **Hearing** a scream, Nick ran out to see what had happened.
　現在分詞

　尼克聽到尖叫聲後，他跑出去查看發生什麼事了。

195

❷ When Nick ~~was studying~~ in the park, he saw a flock of swallows flying across the sky.
　　　(進行式時 → 把 be 動詞 was 去掉)
　　主詞 2　　　　　　　　　　　　　　主詞 2

= **Studying** in the park, Nick saw a flock of swallows flying across the sky.
　現在分詞

尼克在公園讀書時，看到一群燕子從空中飛過。

= **While studying** in the park, Nick saw a flock of swallows flying across the sky.

在這種例句中，由 while 引導的分詞片語更常見。

❸ As Nick ~~has failed~~ in the exam many times, he doesn't want to study any more.
　　　(完成式時 → 把動詞改成「having ＋過去分詞」)
　主詞 1　　　　　　　　　　　　　　　主詞 2

= **Having failed** in the exam many times, Nick doesn't want to study any more.
　having ＋過去分詞

因為尼克考試好幾次都沒有考過，所以他不想再讀書了。

4　副詞子句的動詞為**被動**時，如何改成分詞片語？

❶ 為 be 動詞時 → 把動詞改為「being ＋過去分詞」。
❷ 完成式時 → 把動詞改為「having ＋ been ＋過去分詞」。
❸ 被動的分詞片語在句首時 → 有時可省略 being 或 having been，只保留過去分詞。

❶ Although ~~he was told~~ many times, Ray still made the same mistake again and again.
　　　(為 be 動詞時 → 把動詞改為「being ＋過去分詞」)
　　　主詞 1　　　　　　　　主詞 2

雖然瑞被警告很多次，他依然再三犯下相同的錯誤。

= **Being told** many times, Ray still made the same mistake again and again.
　being ＋過去分詞

= **Though being told** many times, Ray still made the same mistake again and again.

由 though 引導的分詞片語更常見。

完成式時 → 把動詞改為「having + been +過去分詞」

❷ As he has been deceived too many times, Ray has become
　　主詞 1　　被動語態　　　　　　　　　　　主詞 2
very sensitive.

= (Having been) deceived too many times, Ray has become
　　having + been +過去分詞
very sensitive.

因為瑞經常受騙，所以他變得非常敏感。

❸ After the lyrics were written, Ray sang the song for his lover.
　　　　主詞 1　　　被動語態　　主詞 2

= The lyrics being written, Ray sang the song for his lover.
　　　　　　being +過去分詞

瑞寫完歌詞後，他唱這首歌獻給他的愛人。

NOTE 分詞片語的位置

❶ 分詞片語的位置可以放在句首、句中（主詞後）、句尾，而且都要用**逗點**將分詞片語隔開。

❷ 分詞片語最適當的位置，要依上下文意思來決定。

❸ 一般來說，放在**句中**和**句尾**的分詞構句，在**小說**中尤其常見。在**英文考試**裡，以使用在**句首**的分詞構句為多（本章節的範例與練習，以放置句首的分詞構句為主）。

　句首　Being very happy, Hazel was moved to tears.

　句中　= Hazel, being very happy, was moved to tears.

　句尾　= Hazel was moved to tears, being very happy. → 較不自然

　　　　= As she was very happy, Hazel was moved to tears.

　　　　因為海柔很高興，所以感動得眼淚都掉下來了。

Quiz 24

句子改寫

將下列句子改寫成分詞片語。

1. When we were rowing in the river, we saw a flock of ducks swimming.
   _____.

2. After the sun had set, the swallows flew south.
   _____.

3. Because we were invited to a barbecue, we had to bring some eating utensils.
   _____.

4. As Nigel has been told many times, he begins to behave well.
   _____.

5. While Jim was sunbathing on the beach, he saw a big wave coming.
   _____.

6. When Beryl was watching TV, she heard a dog barking.
   _____.

7. When Florence was taking a walk, she came across her old friend.
   _____.

8. Because Frank lives far away from the downtown, he seldom goes there.
   _____.

9. Since I didn't know how to answer the question, I kept silent.
   _____.

10. Because she knew that you wanted to see the movie, she bought a ticket for you.
    _____.

2 分詞片語的用法

在 Unit 11 討論了引導時間、原因、條件、讓步、附帶狀況的**從屬連接詞**，我們也可以用**分詞片語**來表示這些意思。而分詞片語的原意，要視其還原後的連接詞來決定。熟悉分詞片語的用法，寫作時交互運用從屬連接詞和分詞片語，寫作會更生動！

1 表時間

1 常用以下的詞語所引導的副詞子句，來表示**時間**：

- when
- as soon as
- as
- after
- while

2 分詞片語可以用來表達多種不同的連接詞意思，可從句子的前後關係來判斷。

3 為了讓句意明確，有時會將連接詞放在分詞前面，成為「連接詞＋分詞構句」。

❶ <u>After having settled</u>（分詞片語（分詞構句）），we made a call to the front desk to ask how to get an outside line.

= <u>After</u> we had settled（表時間的副詞子句）, we made a call to the front desk to ask how to get an outside line.

我們安頓好之後，打電話問櫃台要如何撥打外線電話。

❷ <u>After entering the house</u>（分詞片語（分詞構句）），she got a big surprise.

= <u>After</u> she entered the house（表時間的副詞子句）, she got a big surprise.

進家門後，她發現一個大驚喜。

❸ Checking in at the hotel, we met our friends Doris and Arthur.
　　　分詞片語（分詞構句）

　　　表時間的副詞子句
= While we were checking in at the hotel, we met our friends Doris and Arthur.

在旅館報到時，我們遇到朋友多莉絲和亞瑟。

2 表原因、理由

常用以下的詞語所引導的副詞子句，來表示**原因、理由**：
- because
- as
- since

❶ Being very tired that night, we went to bed early.
　　分詞片語（分詞構句）

= As we were very tired that night, we went to bed early.
　　表原因的副詞子句

我們那晚很累，所以很早就上床睡覺了。

❷ The hotel being a long way from the downtown, we spent a boring but quiet night.
　　　　　　分詞片語（分詞構句）
　主詞1　　　　　　　　　　　　　　　　　　　主詞2

主詞1（the hotel）和主詞2（we）不同，所以要保留。現在較少使用像這句的分詞片語，不太自然。

= Since the hotel was a long way from the downtown, we spent a boring but quiet night.
　　表原因的副詞子句

飯店距市中心很遠，所以我們過了一個無聊但寧靜的夜晚。

❸ Having checked the map, we knew how to get to the train station.
　　分詞片語（分詞構句）

= Because we had checked the map, we knew how to get to the train station.
　　表原因的副詞子句

因為我們查了地圖，所以我們知道怎麼到火車站。

3 表條件

常用 if 所引導的副詞子句，來表示**條件**。

① **Waiting** a moment, I'll go and tell the manager that you are here.　　〔分詞片語（分詞構句）〕

= **If** you wait a moment, I'll go and tell the manager that you are here.　　〔表條件的副詞子句〕

等一下，我去告訴經理你到了。

② **Turning** to the right, you will find the theater you are looking for.　　〔分詞片語（分詞構句）〕

= **If** you turn to the right, you will find the theater you are looking for.　　〔表條件的副詞子句〕

往右轉，你就會找到你要找的戲院。

4 表讓步

常用以下的詞語所引導的副詞子句，來表示**讓步**：

- although
- though
- even if
- even though

① **Being** drenched to the skin, we still enjoyed the show very much.　　〔分詞片語（分詞構句）〕

= **Even though** we were drenched to the skin, we still enjoyed the show very much.　　〔表讓步的副詞子句〕

雖然我們淋得像落湯雞，但我們還是沉醉在這個表演中。

② **The tickets being** expensive, **we** still thought the show worth seeing.

主詞1　　　　　　　　主詞2

主詞 the ticket 和 we 不同，所以要保留。
分詞片語（分詞構句）現在較少用。

= **Although** the tickets were expensive, we still thought the show worth seeing.　　〔表讓步的副詞子句〕

雖然票價很貴，但我們覺得這個表演值回票價。

5 表附帶狀況

附帶狀況的分詞片語，通常可以改為由對等連接詞 and 所引導的**對等子句**。

🍀 We stood up to applaud, <u>saying</u> bravo to the actors.
　　　　　　　　　　　　　　　↑ 分詞片語（分詞構句）

= We stood up to applaud, <u>and</u> we said bravo to the actors.
　　　　　　　　　　　　　　　　↑ 由對等連接詞 and 所引導的對等子句

我們起身鼓掌，並向演員們喊讚。

🍀 The actors came to the front of the stage, <u>the audience</u>
　　主詞 1　　　　　　　　　　　　　　　　　　主詞 2
<u>continuing</u> to applaud.
　↑ 主詞 the actors 和 the audience 不同，所以兩個主詞都要保留。
　　分詞片語（分詞構句）現在較少用。

= The actors came to the front of the stage, <u>and</u> the audience
continued to applaud.
　　　　　　　　　　　　　　　　　　　　　　　↑ 由對等連接詞 and 所引導的對等子句

演員來到舞台前，觀眾繼續鼓掌。

Quiz 25

A 句子改寫
將下列句子改寫成分詞構句。

1. As Lois had read the book, she knew how to answer the questions.
   _____.

2. If you don't get up at six, you will miss the flight.
   _____.

3. Even though the shirt was very expensive, I thought it worth buying.
   _____.

4. When the sun rises, the sea sparkles in the sunlight.
   _____.

5. We said goodbye to Judith, and we went home.
   _____.

B 句子重組：將下列題目中所有提示字詞整合成一個有意義的句子。
答案中要使用所有提示字詞，且不能隨意增加字詞。

1. _____.
   Susie/being/enjoyed/soaked to the skin/very much/still/the performance

2. _____.
   said/after kissing/the baby/Samantha/good night/on the forehead

3. _____.
   Rosalie/entering/she/the house/turn off the light/found that/had forgotten to

4. _____.
   Having failed/he/study harder/the entrance exam/decided to

5. _____.
   Virginia/lay on/being/the bed/very exhausted

PART 3

英語段落寫作

本章以英檢寫作的題目（看圖寫作）來設計練習，主要是看三張連環圖，依據圖中所提供的訊息，寫一篇約50字的段落。段落寫作要注意的地方，是回答所有的重點或問題，並且以完整的段落方式作答，不能用單句或片語方式簡答。要在段落寫作拿高分，除了靈活運用前面所提及的觀念來形成完整的句子，更重要的還包含段落中結構的安排、短文的開頭、承接、結尾等。

Unit 15 段落結構的安排

Unit 16 短文的開頭（起）：主題句

Unit 17 短文的中間（承、轉）：支持句

Unit 18 短文的結尾（合）：結論

Unit 15 段落結構的安排

1 文體：敘述文和描寫文

該如何運用約 50 個字，寫出一個完整且精確的段落呢？首要注意的就是**結構的安排**。結構安排得好，文章脈絡清晰有條理，寫作便已成功了一半；反之，如果安排得不好，會使文章顯得雜亂無章，甚至毫無組織可言。

1 敘述文

1	時態	**敘述文**像說故事般，描述一件發生的事情，常以**過去式**來描寫。
2	人稱	常以**第一人稱**（I, we）或**第三人稱**（he, she, they）來寫作。以第一人稱來寫作時，會較為主觀、逼真；以第三人稱來寫作時，則較客觀、超然。
3	內容要素	基本要素包括 5W1H（when, where, who, what, why, how）。
4	直述法	通常按時間的順序來推展段落。

1 以第一人稱敘述：表現逼真

段落範例

Once I stayed up late to prepare for an exam. Because I felt very tired, it seemed to me that the room was spinning. All of a sudden, the books on my bookshelf fell down and hit me on the head. Then I realized it was an earthquake.

- who（當事人）主角是「我」
- what（做了什麼事）熬夜
- when（時間）曾有一次
- why（為什麼要熬夜）準備考試
- how（當事人感覺如何）感到非常疲憊
- where（地點）房間

> 有一次我熬夜準備考試。因為太累，整個房間感覺上好像在旋轉。突然，書架上的書掉下來，砸到我的頭，我才意識到原來是地震。

2 以第三人稱敘述：客觀陳述

段落範例

One night when Natalie was reading a newspaper, a burglar broke into her house. The evil burglar shouted loudly, "This is a holdup. Don't move, or I will hurt you! Show me the money!" Then Natalie put her money on the table. She was so afraid that she began to shake.

- when（時間）某天晚上
- who（當事人）娜塔莉
- who（當事人）夜賊
- where（發生地點）娜塔莉的家
- what（發生什麼事）夜賊闖空門
- why（為何娜塔莉開始發抖）她非常害怕

某天晚上，娜塔莉在看報紙時，夜賊破門闖入她家。兇惡的夜賊大喊道：「搶劫！不要動，不然你就慘了！把錢拿出來！」娜塔莉於是把錢放在桌上。她非常害怕，開始發抖。

NOTE

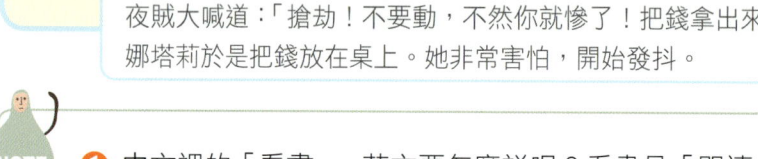

❶ 中文裡的「看書」，英文要怎麼說呢？看書是「閱讀」，所以要用 read，看報紙、漫畫、雜誌等，也要用 read：

- read the book
- read a book
- read books
- read the newspaper
- read the comic book
- read the magazine

❷ 說到「看」，有幾個英文裡固定的用法，要熟背它們，別用錯了！

- watch TV 看電視
- see the movie 看電影
- go to the movies 看電影

→ 如果是 watch the movie，通常是表示收看在電視上播放的電影。

2 描寫文

❶ 時態 用文字客觀地再現事件的內容，而事件通常是靜態的人、物或地。一般而言，常用現在式（例如人物描寫、景物描寫）；如果事情發生在過去，則用過去式（例如個人的經驗等）。

❷ 內容要素 基本要素包括 5W1H（when, where, who, what, why, how）。

❸ 敘述順序 在寫作時要留意順序的發展：

ⓐ 描寫旅遊：通常以時間發展順序來陳述。

ⓑ 描寫地方或景物：依空間順序來陳述，例如由前而後、由上而下。

1 用現在式描寫人物

> 段落範例
>
> My father is tall but fat. He usually wears a pair of glasses. Although he is far from being handsome from a little girl's point of view, he is very friendly. Even though he is in his 50's, he still looks young.
>
> 我的父親高高的，但胖胖的，他常戴著一副眼鏡。從一個小女生的角度來看他，他一點也稱不上帥，但是他很友善。儘管他已經五十幾歲，但是看起來還是很年輕。

2 用過去式描寫個人經驗

> 段落範例
>
> When I got <u>home</u> <u>last night</u>, <u>I</u> had <u>a big surprise</u>.
>   where when who what
> As I entered the house, all the lights in my house were
>   how
> <u>suddenly turned on</u> and my friends were singing the happy birthday song for me. They also bought me a birthday cake. I was so happy that I was moved to tears.
>
> 昨晚我回到家時，我收到一個好大的驚喜。我一踏進家門，屋內的燈突然全部亮了起來，這時朋友們對我唱生日快樂歌。而且他們還替我買了個生日蛋糕。我很高興，感動得眼淚都掉出來了。

> **NOTE**
>
> **敘述文 vs. 描寫文**
>
> **敘述文**主要敘述事物的**動作變化**，屬於**動態**敘述；**描寫文**主要以記敘事物的**狀態**、**性質**為主，屬於**靜態**敘述。在實際寫作時，不會特別區分這兩種文體，寫作內容也並不一定純粹屬於某種文體，因為兩者通常會同時穿插使用。

2 短文的架構

> 1. 起：主題句（topic sentence）
> 2. 承、轉：支持句（supporting sentences）
> 3. 合：結論（conclusion）

1 短文的基本架構

短文的基本架構可分為三部分：主題句（**起**）、支持句（**承**、**轉**）、結論（**合**）。

1. **主題句** 短文通常由主題句引導出來，主要功用在介紹短文的中心思想，通常提供一個廣泛、清楚的大綱。
2. **支持句** 根據主題句加以擴展，用來支持主題句的概念。
3. **結論** 用來總結前述的重要部分或感想，再次加深主題句的觀念，有時也是主題句類似想法的呈現。

段落範例

My family and I took a trip to Canada last winter. 〔主題句（起）〕
We spent a lot of time skiing at Mt. Whistler. We also took a lot of pictures and bought many souvenirs for our friends. 〔支持句（承、轉）〕 **It was a wonderful trip, and I will never forget that experience.** 〔結論（合）〕

> 我和我的家人去年冬天到加拿大旅行。我們在惠斯勒山滑雪滑了好久。我們也照了很多相片，為朋友買了很多紀念品。那次旅行真的很棒，我會永遠記得那個經驗。

NOTE

❶ 「照相」英文要用 take pictures。「吃藥」英文要用 take the medicine（不可說成 eat the medicine）。

❷ 清楚的主題句可以讓人立即了解短文的中心思想，漂亮的結尾會讓人印象深刻而獲得高分，評分老師是在看了結論後才給分數的喔！

2 短文結構安排的步驟

步驟一 快速瀏覽三張連環圖，把浮現在腦海中的片段場景、主要句子甚至是整個故事，約略地寫下來，用意在掌握心中浮現的點子。（即使只是想到一個簡單的字，也可以寫下來。）

步驟二 按前面所說過的「起承轉合」基本架構，來布局短文。

步驟三 利用 5W1H 來幫助構思，使段落完整，可利用以下的步驟：

1. **What** 發生什麼事？
2. **Why** 為什麼發生？
3. **Where** 發生的地點？
4. **How** 如何發生？
5. **Who** 主角是誰？
6. **When** 發生的時間？

寫作範例

上個星期日，John 和同學到公園野餐。請根據下列三張圖，想像你是 John，以第一人稱的方式寫出他在公園裡的所見所聞。

步驟一 下筆前快速瀏覽連環圖，觀察畫中的人和物，以及所顯示的時間和地點。利用 5W1H 幫助構思事件中的元素。

1. **What** 到公園野餐；有很多人、很多花草樹木
2. **How** 開心、愉快
3. **Why** 畫中呈現的結果和原因是什麼？（沒有明確答案）
4. **Who** John 和同學
5. **Where** 公園
6. **When** 上週日

211

步驟二 依照事件的邏輯和圖片順序來安排故事。因為短文的字數有限制，按「題目、圖一、圖二、圖三」，盡量將故事安排在四句到五句。

題目	John 和同學上週日去公園野餐
圖一	公園裡很多人，也有很多花草、樹木
圖二	有人和狗玩，也有人躺在草地上
圖三	John 和同學坐在大樹下聊天

步驟三 構想出每張圖的重點句後，發現圖片上沒有透露出明確的結尾。這時，為了使整個事件連貫、完整，以不改變整個事件過程的基本框架為原則，想出四大劇情點，列出所設想到的短文結尾：

A	我們就這樣度過了愉快的一天
B	那次的野餐真是一個很開心的經歷
C	我們一整天都像這樣在公園裡快樂地度過
D	我們一直聊天，開心得差點忘了回家的時間

步驟四 最後，依照邏輯性和趣味性篩選構成短文的句子，完整的短文便成形！

我和同學上週日去公園野餐。公園裡很多人，也有很多花草、樹木。
　　　主題句（起）　　　　　　　支持句（承、轉）
有人和狗玩耍，也有人躺在草地上，我們則坐在大樹下聊天。
我們一整天都像這樣在公園裡快樂地度過。
　　結論（合）

只要不改變圖片中事件過程的基本要求，短文的變化有很多。你可以在既定的限制下，開展不一樣的短文內容。以上面的連環圖為例，你也可以這樣安排：

　　　　主題句（起）　　　　　支持句（承、轉）
我和同學上週日到公園野餐。我們一整天都坐在大樹下聊天，還看到有人躺在草地上和狗玩耍。因為是星期天，所以有很多人來公園。
那真是一次愉快的野餐經驗。
　　結論（合）

3 短文結構安排的技巧

1 為了在有限字數下寫出涵蓋所有圖片的內容，要準確掌握短文的起承轉合：

- **起** 文章開頭直接切入短文主題。
- **承** 延伸主題句的內容，留意空間或時間順序的發展。
- **轉** 運用轉折語或連接詞連貫文句。
- **合** 除了圖片中已告知的故事結局外，可加上自己的結論或看法，使整篇文章更有可讀性。

2 安排短文架構時，可同時將可應用的單字寫出來，當作選擇內容時的考量。

寫作範例

上週六你到台北（Taipei）去拜訪 Rachel，參考連環圖寫出你當天的行程活動。

進階技巧一

假設你根據短文安排的步驟與技巧，已大致決定短文的內容和架構有以下兩種。檢查看看以下的句子是否反映出概念中提到的技巧。

A 上週六我到台北拜訪 Rachel。我們中午 12 點約在餐廳吃飯，然後 2 點半去台北 101，5 點再去看電影。真是愉快的一天。

B 上週六我過得非常愉快。我到台北去拜訪 Rachel。中午在餐廳吃過飯後，我們去逛台北 101，還在下午看了一場電影。我們約好下次還要再見面。

NOTE

❶ 如果圖中的時間可以有很大的變化彈性，你可以寫出確實時間（如上 A），或用適當的轉折詞表示時間的先後順序（如上 B），亦可以兩種混合。

❷ 由於圖片只表示出時間順序和事件內容，事件的前因後果並不明顯，這時可以簡單的根據圖片順序安排，最後再自訂一個結論「真是愉快的一天」（如上 A），或是更靈活地在一開始便點出短文敘述的重點，再跟自訂的結論呼應「我們約好下次還要再見面」（如上 B），整個短文的故事性便增加了。

進階技巧二 故事大綱決定好之後，需要運用英文單字撰寫內容。如果遇到不確定的拼字或用法時，用其他較簡單的單字替換，或是將句子換句話說。這時趁機再次確定短文架構。例如：

	英文寫法	換句話說
✓ 拜訪 Rachel	visit Rachel	go to see Rachel / have a date with Rachel
✓ 中午	at noon	at 12 p.m.
✓ 在餐廳吃午飯	eat at a restaurant	have lunch in the mall
✓ 去台北 101 逛街	go shopping at Taipei 101 Mall	go to Taipei 101 Mall
✓ 看電影	see a movie	go to a movie
✓ 過得非常愉快	have a good time	have a very happy day

Quiz 26

將下列的幾個句子，按編號重組成一篇結構完整的短文。

1 Then we went to Taipei 101 Mall to do some shopping, and we also saw a movie.

2 I went to Taipei last Saturday to visit my friend Rachel.

3 Although we were very tired, we really had a good time.

4 It was her birthday, so we celebrated at a restaurant at noon.

_____ → _____ → _____ → _____

Unit 16 短文的開頭（起）：主題句

暖身 Warm-up 閱讀以下短文，看了開頭第一句之後，你是否覺得一頭霧水？你猜得到下面這個段落接下來要傳達什麼樣的內容嗎？

All of us enjoyed his performance very much. My company held the year-end party last Friday. A famous singer was invited to perform. What excited me most was that I won the biggest prize. We expressed our wishes to each other and had a wonderful night.

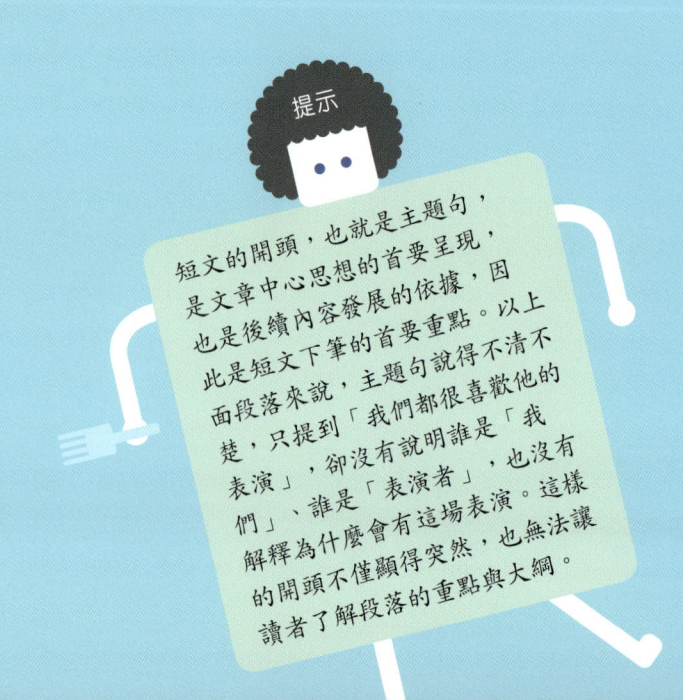

提示

短文的開頭，也就是主題句，是文章中心思想的首要呈現，也是後續內容發展的依據，因此是短文下筆的首要重點。以上面段落來說，主題句說得不清不楚，只提到「我們都很喜歡他的表演」，卻沒有說明誰是「我們」、誰是「表演者」，也沒有解釋為什麼會有這場表演。這樣的開頭不僅顯得突然，也無法讓讀者了解段落的重點與大綱。

1 撰寫主題句的技巧與注意事項

1 範例分析

前面講到，短文架構可分為主題句（起）、支持句（承、轉）和結論（合）。本單元首先針對**主題句**進行實際寫作練習。主題句的撰寫技巧和注意事項如下：

1. **列點** 清楚的點出人、事物、時間、地點，釐清文章大綱及中心思想。
2. **選擇** 利用學習過的句型來表達和搭配，考量全文的脈絡走向，從中選擇最適切的來當作主題句。
3. **簡潔** 主題句較長時，應盡量利用子句來達到簡單明瞭的目的，這樣的寫法也可以展現出英文能力的靈活應用。

寫作範例一

下圖是昨晚你和媽媽所發生的事情。

進階技巧一	列出要點（記得清楚點出地點、動作、人和事件）
圖一	地點在超級市場。
圖二	買了許多食材（雞肉、西瓜、甘藍菜、雞蛋、牛奶），共花了 380 元。
圖三	主角跟媽媽付錢時，才發現忘記帶錢包。

進階技巧二 短文安排

我和媽媽昨晚去超級市場時發生了一件很尷尬的事。我們花了 380 元
　　　主題句（起）　　　　　　　　　　　　　　　　　　　（承）
買了好多東西：有西瓜、甘藍菜、一打雞蛋、雞肉和兩公升的牛奶。

沒想到，付帳時我們發現竟然忘了帶錢包，真是糗大了。
　　　　（轉）　　　　　　　　　　　　　（合）

進階技巧三 利用所學過的句型變化出多種主題句，把它們寫在草稿紙上。

我和媽媽昨晚去超級市場。

A　My mother and I went to the supermarket last night. 簡單直述句

B　I went to the supermarket with my mother last night. 簡單直述句

（昨晚）發生了一件很尷尬的事。

C　An embarrassing thing happened (last night). 簡單直述句

D　Something (that was) embarrassing happened (last night). 形容詞子句

進階技巧四 以適當的連接詞合併主題句，作出不同的句子搭配，並從其中選擇你認為最適當的。可以是以下幾種組合：

A + C　My mother and I went to the supermarket last night, and an embarrassing thing happened.

A + D　My mother and I went to the supermarket last night, and something embarrassing happened.

B + C　I went to the supermarket with my mother last night, and an embarrassing thing happened.

B + D　I went to the supermarket with my mother last night, and something embarrassing happened.

　　　如果要強調有「一件尷尬的事」發生「在某人身上」，可以將 B + D 的句子改為：
　　　Something embarrassing happened to us last night while my mother and I were in the supermarket.

寫作範例二

圖中的男生是 Jonathan 及 Felix，根據圖的內容描述他們所發生的事情。

進階技巧一 列出要點（清楚點出人物、共同的興趣和事件。圖中沒有明確指出地點在哪邊，但根據第三張圖，可以推測是在街道上打球，所以才會有車子經過。）

圖一　Jonathan 和 Felix 兩人喜歡打棒球。
圖二　兩人會一起練習打棒球。
圖三　某天兩個人打棒球的時候，差點被一輛車子撞到。

進階技巧二 短文安排

Jonathan 和 Felix 兩人很喜歡打棒球。他們常常在一起打棒球。
　　　主題句（起）　　　　　　　　　　（承）
有一天，他們在街道上打棒球，結果差點被車子撞到。從此以後，
　　（轉）　　　　　　　　　　　　　　　　　　（合）
他們倆再也不敢在街道上打球了。

進階技巧三 利用所學過的句型變化出多種主題句，把它們寫在草稿紙上。

Jonathan 和 Felix 兩人很喜歡打棒球。

A　Jonathan and Felix like to play (= enjoy playing) baseball very much. 　簡單直述句

B　*Not only* Jonathan *but also* Felix likes to play (= enjoys playing) baseball very much. 　not only A but also B

C　*Playing baseball* is Jonathan and Felix's favorite sport. 　以動名詞作主詞

進階技巧四 A、B、C 都可以當作此文的主題句，可視整段文章的字數或整段文章的句型變化，來決定要用哪一句。舉例說明，如果短文裡簡單直述句比較多時，為求變化，可考慮使用 B 或 C。

NOTE

play 的用法

❶ 表示做什麼運動時，用「**play ＋運動名稱**」來表示。

- 打棒球　→　play baseball
- 打籃球　→　play basketball
- 打網球　→　play tennis

❷ 彈鋼琴、拉小提琴等樂器演奏，用「**play ＋ the ＋樂器名**」來表示。

- 彈鋼琴　→　play the piano
- 拉小提琴　→　play the violin
- 彈吉他　→　play the guitar

寫作範例三

下圖是對 Daphne 的一些介紹。

進階技巧一　列出要點（清楚點出人物的身分、興趣、志願。像這類單純描述個人的題目，可以加進更多細節，讓文章變得生動。例如 Daphne 喜歡烹飪，所以時常做菜給別人吃，或是她以後的志願是當廚師等。）

　　圖一　　Daphne 是一位國中生
　　圖二　　Daphne 喜歡烹飪
　　圖三　　Daphne 想要當廚師

進階技巧二　短文安排

Daphne 是個國中生，而且她對烹飪很有興趣，她常在放學回家後為家
　主題句（起）　　　　　（承）

人做菜。此外，有空閒時間時，她喜歡烹飪。她希望長大後可以做個廚師。
　　　（轉）　　　　　　　　　　　　　　　（合）

進階技巧三　利用所學過的句型變化出多種主題句，把它們寫在草稿紙上。

Daphne 是個國中生。

A　Daphne is a junior high school student.　　簡單直述句

她對烹飪很有興趣。

B　She is interested in cooking.　　以人為主詞
C　Cooking interests her.　　以物為主詞（此種用法較不常用）

進階技巧四 以適當的連接詞合併主題句，作出不同句子搭配，並從其中選擇你認為最適當的。可以是以下幾種組合：

A + B　Daphne is a junior high school student, and she is interested in cooking.

A + C　Daphne is a junior high school student, and cooking interests her.

A + B　Daphne is a junior high school student who is interested in cooking.

為了顯示對英文寫作的熟練度和增加句型變化，在此例中，主題句用 A + B 的形容詞子句最佳。

2 容易混淆的形容詞：V-ing 和 V-ed

有些形容詞使用「V-ing」形式，通常主詞是**物**，指「某物令人感到……」；使用「-ed」形式時，主詞通常是人，指「某人感到……」，此外所搭配的介系詞也不同。

物 + be 動詞 + 動詞 -ing　→　某物令人感到……

人 + be 動詞 + 動詞 -ed + 介系詞 + 物　→　某人對某物感到……

物 + be + V-ing 形容詞		人 + be + V-ed 形容詞 + 介系詞	
interesting	令人感到有趣的	be interested in	感到有興趣的
satisfying	令人滿意的	be satisfied with	感到滿意的
confusing	令人困惑的	be confused about	感到困惑的
surprising	令人驚訝的	be surprised at	感到驚訝的
boring	令人乏味的	be bored with	感到無聊的

1. The book is interesting.　　那本書很有趣。
   　物
2. Lee is interested in the book.　　李對那本書感興趣。
   　人
3. It is not a satisfying answer.　　這不是一個令人滿意的回答。
   　　　　　　　　物
4. Jean feels satisfied with his answer.　　琴很滿意他的回答。
   　人

Quiz 27

選出最適合的主題句（可複選）。

1 這是 Justin 的功課表（timetable）

9:30–10:15	10:30–11:15	13:00–13:45	14:00–14:45	15:00–15:45
英文	國文	數學	音樂	體育

下列哪幾句適合作主題句？ _____

A. The table shows Justin's timetable.
B. The second class is Chinese.
C. English class starts at nine-thirty.
D. This is Justin's timetable.

2 你是王小明，以下是你的簡短自我介紹。

姓名	王小明（Wang, Xiao-ming）
出生年月日	2001 年 5 月 10 日
學歷	永吉（Yong-Ji）國中 2014–2016
出生地	台北（Taipei）
興趣	聽音樂、上網、打籃球

下列哪幾句適合作主題句？ _____

A. My name is Wang Xiao-ming.
B. I was born in Taipei.
C. I would like to introduce myself.
D. I studied at Yong-Ji High School from 2014 to 2016.
E. I like to listen to music, surf the Net, and play basketball.

Unit 17

短文的中間（承、轉）：支持句

Warm-up 暖身

把下列短文中劃底線字的部分刪去，再來閱讀下面的段落，是不是覺得句子之間少了些什麼？這些重要的元素關係著以下要討論的重點：短文的承接。

When he woke up this morning, Clement found that it was eight-thirty. He got up immediately, brushed his teeth, and washed his face. <u>After that</u>, he rode his bicycle to school as fast as he could. <u>However</u>, when he got to school, the school was empty. He <u>then</u> realized that today was Mid-Autumn Festival.

1 撰寫支持句的技巧與注意事項

在撰寫支持句時，有以下的技巧與注意事項：

1. 承接主題句時，語意要順暢。
2. 在動詞的地方多做變化，運用貼切的片語來表達。
3. 要依情況來選擇適當的轉折語。

1 短文架構（一）

我和媽媽昨晚去超級市場時發生了一件很尷尬的事。我們花了 380 元
　　　　主題句（起）　　　　　　　　　　　　　　支持句（承）
買了好多東西：有西瓜、甘藍菜、一打雞蛋、雞肉和兩公升的牛奶。

沒想到，付帳時我們發現竟然忘了帶錢包，真是糗大了。
　　支持句（轉）　　　　　　　　　　　（合）

進階技巧一　將零散的詞組用學過的句型變化出多種句型。這裡的組合共有
A＋D、A＋E、B＋D、B＋E、C＋D、C＋E 等六種。

我們花了 380 元買了好多東西：有西瓜、甘藍菜、一打雞蛋、雞肉和兩公升的牛奶。

A	We spent three hundred and eighty NT dollars buying/on a watermelon, a cabbage, a dozen eggs, chicken, and two liters of milk.	簡單直述句
B	We bought many/a lot of things, such as a watermelon, a cabbage, a dozen eggs, chicken, and two liters of milk. The total amount was NT 380 dollars.	兩個簡單直述句
C	We bought a watermelon, a cabbage, a dozen eggs, chicken, and two liters of milk that came to three hundred and eighty NT dollars in total.	主句和形容詞子句

沒想到，付帳時我們竟然發現忘了帶錢包。

D　However, when we were about to pay the bill, we then realized that we forgot to bring our purse. 　副詞子句＋簡單直述句

E　To our surprise, we couldn't find our purse when we were about to pay the bill. Then we realized that we forgot the purse. 　簡單直述句＋副詞子句／主句＋名詞子句

進階技巧二　選擇讀起來最順暢、最貼切題意的內文組合，加在主題句後面，形成：

> Something embarrassing happened last night while I 主題句（起）
> was in the supermarket with my mother. We bought a
> 　　　　　　　　　　　　　　　　　　　　支持句（承）
> watermelon, a cabbage, a dozen eggs, chicken, and two liters of milk. The total amount was three hundred and eighty NT dollars. However, when we were about to pay
> 　　　　　　　　　　　　　支持句（轉）
> the bill, we then realized that we forgot to bring our purse.
>
> 段落共 58 字

進階技巧三　決定好上面的句子後，會發現短文還未寫完就超過 50 個字。這時需要減少字數，例如將購買物品的明細刪去，改用較短的句子來代替，因此形成：

> Something embarrassing happened last night while I was in the supermarket with my mother. We bought a lot of things that came to NT 380 dollars in total. However, when we were about to pay the bill, we then realized that we forgot to bring our purse.
>
> 段落共 47 字

❶ 用 a lot of things 取代了「a watermelon, a cabbage, a dozen eggs, chicken, and two liters of milk」。
❷ 用 NT 380 dollars 取代原本的「three hundred and eighty NT dollars」。

進階技巧四 你也可以直接選擇 A 句，並將價錢用數字表示以減少字數：

> Something embarrassing happened last night while I was in the supermarket with my mother. We spent NT 380 dollars buying a watermelon, a cabbage, a dozen eggs, chicken, and two liters of milk. However, when we were about to pay the bill, we then realized that we forgot to bring our purse.
>
> 段落共 52 字

❶ 用 NT 380 dollars 取代原本的「three hundred and eighty NT dollars」。
❷ 保留「a watermelon, a cabbage, a dozen eggs, chicken, and two liters of milk」。

NOTE

❶ 用「such as ＋細目」可提供較完整的資訊，但仍要以字數為整體考量，來評估是否刪減或保留內容。

❷ 如果字數太多或遇到不確定的購買品項名稱，可以用「we spent ＋錢＋ buying many things」，來代替所買的細目。

❸ 中文裡沒有名詞數量，但寫英文時要考量到**名詞的單、複數**，例如：
　● a cabbage　　● eggs

❹ 適當運用 however, to our surprise, then 等轉折詞，不但加強了故事的張力，也能讓短文語氣更流暢。

2 短文架構（二）

Jonathan 和 Felix 兩人很喜歡打棒球。他們常常在一起打棒球。
　主題句（起）　　　　　　　　　　　　　（承）

有一天，他們在街道上打棒球，結果差點被車子撞到。從此以後，
　　　（轉）　　　　　　　　　　　　　　　　　（合）

他們倆再也不敢在街道上打棒球了。

進階技巧一 將零散的詞組用學過的句型變化出多種句型。A + B 或 A + C 的組合都可以；其中以 A + C 的組合為佳，因為使用了分詞片語，不僅使句型富變化，也展現了寫作者的英語應用能力。

他們常常在一起打棒球。

A They often play baseball together. 　簡單直述句

有一天，他們在街道上打棒球，結果差點被車子撞到。

B One day they played baseball on the street and (they) were almost hit by a car. 　簡單直述句

C One day while playing baseball on the street, they were almost hit by a car. 　分詞片語

進階技巧二 接著加入主題句，檢查語意是否順暢，字數是否適當。因此形成：

Playing baseball is Jonathan and Felix's favorite sport.
主題句（起）
They often play baseball together. One day while playing
支持句（承）　　　　　　　　　　　　　支持句（轉）
baseball on the street, they were almost hit by a car.

段落共 28 字

NOTE

❶ 時間的轉折語
* 有一天　　→　one day
* 後來　　　→　then, later, after
* 同時　　　→　meanwhile
* 有時候　　→　sometimes
* 最後；終於 →　at last, finally, in the end, in the long run

❷ 次序的轉折語
* 第一、第二、第三 →　the first, the second, the third
* 其次　　　→　next, then

3 短文架構（三）

Daphne 是個國中生，而且她對烹飪很有興趣，她常在放學回家後為家
　　　　　　主題句（起）　　　　　　　　　　　　　　　（承）

人做菜。此外，有空閒時，她喜歡烹飪，她希望長大後可以當個廚師。
　　　　　　（轉）　　　　　　　　　　　（合）

進階技巧一 將零散的詞組用學過的句型變化出多種句型。

她常在放學回家後為家人做菜。

A　She often cooks for her family after school.　簡單直述句

此外，有空閒時，她喜歡烹飪。

B　Besides, she likes to cook in her leisure time/ whenever she is free.　簡單直述句＋副詞子句

C　In addition, she enjoys spending her free time cooking.　簡單直述句

進階技巧二 A＋B 或 A＋C 的組合都可以，棄普遍為人熟知的 besides 改用 in addition，可表現英語能力。將 A＋C 句加上主題句，觀察語意是否正確順暢。

Daphne is a junior high school student who is interested
　　主題句（起）

in cooking. She often cooks for her family after school.
　　　　　　　　　　支持句（承）

In addition, she enjoys spending her free time cooking.
　　支持句（轉）

段落共 29 字

NOTE

❶ 採用較具難度的片語或表達方式，並不是寫作最重要的元素，文意的順暢才是短文撰寫最重要的訴求。除非你已經確定了片語及措辭的用法，並兼顧了文意的流暢性，否則不要隨便選用沒有把握的詞彙。

❷ 表附加性的轉折語：besides（此外）、in addition（而且）。

Unit 18 短文的結尾（合）：結論

Warm-up 暖身

下列這篇短文看到最後，你是否會質疑——「然後呢？」

My name is Eugene, and I am a junior high school student. I was born on October 11th in Hsinchu. Playing basketball and playing the guitar are my hobbies. In addition, I like to sing and dance.

提示

文章結束時要有結論，來總結前述的重要部分或感想。不論短文的主題句和支持句寫得有多完美，如果沒有適當的結尾，整篇文章便不完整。接下來，我們要討論的重點就是短文的結尾。

1 撰寫結論的技巧與注意事項

　　結論有重複加深**主題句**的作用，有時也是主題句的**同義改寫**。在段落寫作時，除了圖片提供的結局，也可以加上自己的結論或看法，使整篇文章更有可讀性。撰寫時的技巧和注意事項包括：

1. 結論要和主題句相呼應，文句也要流暢通順，才能賦予短文生命力。
2. 選擇句子時，避免使用重複的句型與詞彙，力求豐富、變化。
3. 再次調整字數，反覆檢查文法細節，例如時態是否統一、拼字是否正確等。

1 範例分析

1 短文架構（一）

我和媽媽昨晚去超級市場時發生了一件很尷尬的事。我們花了 380 元
　　　　主題句（起）　　　　　　　　　　　　　　　　（承）
買了好多東西：有西瓜、甘藍菜、一打雞蛋、雞肉和兩公升的牛奶。

沒想到，付帳時我們發現竟然忘了帶錢包，真是糗大了。
　（轉）　　　　　　　　　　　　　　　　總結（合）

進階技巧一　用前面學過的句型，來變化出多種句型。

真是糗大了。

A	That was an embarrassing situation.	簡單直述句
B	That was really embarrassing.	簡單直述句
C	We felt so embarrassed.	簡單直述句
D	What an embarrassing experience!	感嘆句

進階技巧二 選擇適合的結論句，並整合前面已決定的主題句與支持句，形成短文內容：

> Something embarrassing happened last night while I was in the supermarket with my mother. We spent NT 380 dollars buying a watermelon, a cabbage, a dozen eggs, chicken, and two liters of milk. However, when we were about to pay the bill, we then realized that we forgot to bring our purse. What an embarrassing experience!
>
> 段落共 56 字

❶ 選擇用D句來結尾，主要的考量是增加短文中句型的多樣性。
❷ 用感嘆句結尾，使得經驗的描述更顯生動。

2 短文架構（二）

Jonathan 和 Felix 兩人很喜歡打棒球。他們常常在一起打棒球。
　　　主題句（起）　　　　　　　　　　　　（承）
有一天，他們在街道上打棒球，結果差點被車子撞到。從此以後，
　　　　　　　（轉）　　　　　　　　　　　　　　　（合）
他們倆再也不敢在街道上打棒球了。

進階技巧一 用前面學過的句型，來變化出多種句型。

從此以後，他們倆再也不敢在街道上打球了。

A	After that, they would never play baseball on the street anymore.	簡單直述句
B	From then on, they learned a lesson from that experience and (they) would never play baseball on the street anymore.	簡單直述句

進階技巧二 選擇適合的結論句，整合前面已決定的主題句與支持句，形成短文內容：

> Playing baseball is Jonathan and Felix's favorite sport. They often play baseball together. One day while playing baseball on the street, they were almost hit by a car. From then on, they learned a lesson from that experience and would never play on the street anymore.
>
> 段落共 46 字

使用B句結尾的原因，一方面是字數上的考量；另一方面，B句除了敘述「再也不敢在街道上玩球」，還指出「從中學到一些經驗」，使文章更添可讀性。

3 短文架構（三）

Daphne 是個國中生，而且她對烹飪很有興趣，她常在放學回家後為家
主題句（起）　　　　　　　　　　　　　　　　　　　（承）
人做菜。此外，有空閒時間時，她喜歡烹飪，她希望長大後可以當個廚師。
　　　　（轉）　　　　　　　　　　　　　　　　　（合）

進階技巧一 將零散的詞組用學過的句型變化出多種句型。

她希望長大後可以當個廚師。

A　She wants to be a cook when she grows up. 　簡單直述句＋副詞子句

B　To become a chef in the future is her dream. 　不定詞作主詞的句型

C　It is her dream to become a chef in the future. 　虛主詞作主詞的句型

D　She likes/loves cooking so much that she wants to be a chef in the future. 　〔句型〕so . . . that . . .

233

進階技巧二 選擇適合的結論句，整合前面已決定的主題句與支持句，形成短文內容：

> Daphne is a junior high school student who is interested in cooking. She often cooks for her family after school. In addition, she enjoys spending her free time cooking. She loves cooking so much that she wants to be a chef in the future.
>
> 段落共 44 字

❶ 在這個例子中，字數上留給結尾很大的彈性，所以可以選擇較長的D句作結尾。
❷ D句利用了「so . . . that . . .」的句型，承接前面「Daphne loves cooking . . .」的說法，給予文章一個完整的結尾，因此是最適合的句子。

❷ 文章完成之後：最後的檢查清單

1	語意連貫	☐ 連貫性：至少從頭到尾唸過整篇短文一次，以確定語氣和文意的連貫和一致性。 ☐ 避免重複：盡量不重複使用相同的單字、片語、句型。
2	標點符號	☐ 句子的結尾：肯定句用句點，疑問句用問號。
3	大小寫	☐ 句子的開頭：要大寫。 ☐ 專有名詞（人名、地名、星期、月分等）：要大寫。
4	拼字	☐ 拼寫檢查：務必確定字拼寫正確。 ☐ 用確定的用語：如果不是很確定某單字或片語時，可以想想別的變通寫法，或是用別的字來替換。
5	時態	☐ 檢查整篇文章時態是否一致。
6	主詞與動詞一致	☐ 第三人稱單數現在式時，動詞要加 s 或 es。
7	名詞的單複數	☐ 可數名詞：要特別注意名詞的單複數。 ☐ 不可數名詞：不可加定冠詞 a 或 an。

寫完短文後，記得反覆閱讀，並做最後的檢查，才能避免失分喔！

Quiz 28

今天是 Fanny 的音樂會（concert），
請依照下圖內容寫出約 50 個字的短文。

PART 4

中譯英的步驟與技巧

Unit 19 中譯英類型破解

Unit 20 中譯英的翻譯步驟

Unit 21 中譯英的翻譯技巧

Unit 22 中譯英的特殊用法與常犯錯誤

Unit 19 中譯英類型破解

在外商公司工作常發生一個情況，同事拿來一篇中文譯成英文的信件，表示信中內容寫得很清楚，但是外國老闆看不懂。等到仔細閱讀英譯的信件後，才發現原來信中的英文完全是對應中文結構的翻譯。

同樣地，當老師也會面對同樣的情況。試舉學生的作文句子為例：「Every day have many people crime.」。一開始還讀不懂這個句子的意義，只能確定這是一句不符合文法的句子，後來才發現原來這也是一句中文逐字翻成英文的句子：Every day（每天）、have（有）、many people（很多人）、crime（犯罪）。因此這句的中文句意為「每天有很多人犯罪。」這類型問題的出現，都是因為不了解英文字詞與基本句型的關係所致。希望讀者開始閱讀後，可以清楚地看出這樣的錯誤。

✗ **Every day have many people crime.**
　　每天　　有　　很多人　　犯罪
✓ **There are many people who commit crimes every day.**

> 這是一句中文逐字翻成英文的句子，中文句意為「每天有很多人犯罪。」但卻是一句不符合文法的句子，讓人有讀沒有懂。

翻譯考試沒有制式的標準答案，因為同一句中文可以有千變萬化的英文翻譯。良好的文法基礎，配合不同的規則變化，就可以讓同一句中文演變出許多不同的英文句型。

參加國際研討會時，代表上台以英文進行簡報。介紹各項休閒設施時，不斷地說著「we have this . . . , we have that . . .」，重複了七八次，很明顯可以發現這是中文翻成英文的結果：「我們有這個……，我們有那個……」。其實這句話要加點變化一點都不難，只要會用國中課本所教的「there is . . .」、「there are . . .」，或「there will be . . .」，就可以讓翻譯的句子不單調。

1 譯法的技巧轉換

　　中譯英最常出現的情況是擺脫不了主詞的魔咒，常常都會出現 I 或 we 開頭的句子。若能利用不同譯法的技巧轉換，就可以讓句子呈現變化，如：

1 我要照顧弟妹。

① I have to take care of my brother and sister.
② **It is** my job to take care of my brother and sister.
　　└─ 使用以 It is 開頭的句型

2 這次考試可能很難。

① The exam might be difficult.
② **It** might be difficult **to** pass the exam.
　　└─ 使用以 It . . . to . . . 開頭的句型

3 我要舉個例子說明我的論點。

① I want to give you an example to explain my argument.
② **An example** will explain my argument.
　　　　└─ 將 An example 提前成為「主詞 + 動詞 + 受詞」的句型

　　以上三題翻譯不見得第二句一定優於第一句，必須視整篇文章的前後文而定。讀者可以在閱讀本單元的過程中，試著利用中英翻譯的轉換練習，慢慢體會翻譯的變化與技巧。

Unit 20 中譯英的翻譯步驟

→ 先斷句，將中文內容切割成符合英文句型的結構
→ 參考中文句型結構，標示每個句子中可能的主詞與動詞
→ 決定時態，逐步完成翻譯
→ 最後再加以潤飾

1 步驟❶：句子的分割與組成

　　中文與英文很大的不同點在於標點符號，中文也許三、四行或更多行形成一段，段落間可以全用逗號分隔句子，只需要在最後段落結束時使用句號；但是英文則不同，一個英文句的句意完整結束時，就必須使用句點。也就是说，即使句子再短（最短的英文句也許只有主詞加動詞兩個字），句尾仍需以句點作結束。因此中譯英時，首先須斷句，將中文內容切割成符合英文句型的結構。

中譯英斷句 | 範例 Ⓐ

中文原文

上個星期天我和母親到百貨公司逛街。中午在一家餐廳用餐時，我們突然聽到有人大喊：「小心！」原來是有個小男孩不小心從椅子上摔下來。之後，餐廳經理送小男孩到醫院檢查。雖然小男孩受了一點傷，但應該沒有大礙。

英文斷句（以 ¶ 區分）

上個星期天我和母親到百貨公司逛街。¶ 中午在一家餐廳用餐時，我們突然聽到有人大喊：「小心！」¶ 原來是有個小男孩不小心從椅子上摔下來。¶ 之後，餐廳經理送小男孩到醫院檢查。¶ 雖然小男孩受了一點傷，但應該沒有大礙。¶

中譯英斷句 | 範例 Ⓑ

中文原文

許多人不知如何增強英文聽力。其實多看英語影片對增強你的（英文）聽力非常有幫助。此外，你可以嘗試學英文歌，甚至結交外國朋友。總之，只有靠不斷地練習，你的英文聽力才會進步。

英文斷句（以 ¶ 區分）

許多人不知如何增強英文聽力。¶ 其實多看英語影片對增強你的（英文）聽力非常有幫助。¶ 此外，你可以嘗試學英文歌，甚至結交外國朋友。¶ 總之，只有靠不斷地練習，你的英文聽力才會進步。¶

2　步驟❷：決定主詞與動詞

　　將文章斷句之後，讀者可以參考中文句型的結構，將每個句子中可能的主詞與動詞標示出來。主詞與動詞是英文句的靈魂，找出主詞與動詞後，這個句子可說是完成了一半。

　　當然，有時候句子屬於句型套句型的結構，句子中可能會出現不只一組主詞與動詞，這時可考慮用對等連接詞或片語（and、but、or、not only . . . but also、either . . . or、neither . . . nor）連接。

　　標示主動詞時，也可順便將句子中的其他詞類標示出來，增加翻譯的速度。以下是同一篇中譯英〈範例A〉，方框中的圈選文字為句子的主詞和動詞。

範例A

上個星期天 我和母親 到百貨公司 逛街 。

中午在一家餐廳用餐時， 我們 突然 聽到 有人大喊：「小心！」

原來是有個 小男孩 不小心從椅子上 摔下來 。

之後， 餐廳經理 送 小男孩 到 醫院檢查。

雖然 小男孩 受 了一點傷，但應該 沒有大礙 。

1 主詞與動詞的一致性

單數主詞 + **單數動詞**　　**複數主詞** + **複數動詞**

有些名詞以 -s 結尾，看起來像複數，但其實是不可數名詞，需搭配單數動詞，而有些名詞雖為複數形式，搭配複數動詞，但有單數意義，須特別留意。

2 形式為複數，意義為單數的不可數名詞

1 學科類

多以 -s 結尾，看起來像複數，但為不可數名詞，其後應接單數動詞。但是如果這些名詞的意義不當學科，而是兼具一般事物的性質，此種狀態下就有接複數動詞的情況出現。如：

- economics 經濟學／經濟
- physics 物理學
- civics 倫理學／倫理觀念
- news 新聞學／新聞報導
- statistics 統計學／統計（資料）
- optics 光學
- mathematics 數學／數學運算
- politics 政治學／政治
- gymnastics 體育／體操

❶ **Politics** has been more popular than economics among college students in recent years.
　　└─ 政治學，作單數

近幾年來，對大學學生來說，政治學比經濟學更受歡迎。

❷ **Politics** is the game of politicians.
　　└─ 為政治，作單數

政治是政客的遊戲。

❸ **Statistics** is a very difficult subject.
　　└─ 統計學，作單數

統計學是一門很難的學科。

❹ The latest **statistics** have been released on the Internet.
　　　　　　└─ 統計資料，作複數

最新的統計資料已經在網路上發表了。

2 抽象名詞

多為不可數名詞，雖然字尾以 -s 結尾，但其後應接單數動詞。

- access 進入
- darkness 黑暗
- status 地位
- happiness 快樂
- loneliness 孤寂
- progress 前進；進步
- sadness 難過

1. The <u>status</u> of women in Taiwan has changed a lot over the years.
   近年來，台灣女性的地位改變了很多。

2. Free <u>access</u> to computers is available for every high school student around the island.
   島上的每位中學生都可以免費使用電腦。

3 衣物或工具

具有單數意義的複數名詞，以 -s 結尾，其後多接複數動詞。

- glasses 眼鏡
- scissors 剪刀
- trousers 長褲
- jeans 牛仔褲
- pants 褲子

1. Willie's <u>glasses</u> are broken.
   威利的眼鏡破掉了。

2. These <u>pants</u> don't look good on me.
   我穿這幾條褲子都不好看。

3 人稱名詞的限定與未限定

　　中文的文字雖有直接對應英文不定冠詞 a、an 的字彙，但常常被省略。如中文說：「桌上有（一）本書（There is a book on the table.）」，中文句的「一」常常是省略的，這符合中文習慣用法，聽者也可以理解意義。但若是英譯也省略不定冠詞「a」，就會形成一句不符合英文文法的句子。

　　另一方面，中文較少使用直接對應英文定冠詞 the 的字彙，因此，很多應該使用定冠詞的字彙無法在中文句子中看出來。中譯英時，必須依照文章結構及名詞特性來作出判斷。

以〈範例A〉為例，文章的主角皆為人，分析後發現人稱名詞有些作主詞，有些則是受詞。英譯主詞或受詞時，必須根據人物出現的先後順序，及意念傳達是否清楚作為翻譯的原則，也就是第一次出現的人稱名詞。若不確定為何人時，單數時使用不定冠詞（a、an、one），多數時可用數詞（two、three、four . . .）或數量形容詞（some、many . . .）；而同樣的名詞第二次出現時，就可以使用代名詞（he、she、it、they . . .）、定冠詞（the）、或指示詞（this、that、these、those）。

以下〈範例A〉便對於人稱名詞作出分析，請看圈選中文：

> **範例 A**
>
> 上個星期天 我和母親 到百貨公司 逛街 。¶中午在一家餐廳用餐時， 我們 突然 聽到 有人大喊：「小心！」¶原來是有個 小男孩 不小心從椅子上 摔下來 。¶之後， 餐廳經理送 小男孩 到 醫院檢查。¶雖然 小男孩受 了一點傷，但應該 沒有大礙 。¶

1 我和母親／我們

雖然中文是「我和母親」，但英文習慣用法是將第一人稱放在最後，所以英譯為「my mother and I」。這已經是非常清楚的陳述，如果出現第二次，便可直接使用代名詞 we。

2 有人

「有人」並沒有點明為何人，在還不清楚事情狀況時，必須使用不定代名詞 someone。

3 小男孩

段落中共出現三次「小男孩」。第一次出現時，未特別指明是哪一個小男孩，所以需使用不定冠詞 a little boy 或數詞 one little boy；第二次出現時，因為已經知道是前面說明過的小男孩，所以可以使用定冠詞 the boy 或指示詞 that boy。第三次出現時，可以更簡化直接使用代名詞 he，以求譯文的精簡。

4 餐廳經理

只出現一次。雖然沒有說明是哪家餐廳，不過可以知道一定是主角和母親當時用餐的那家餐廳，可以直接使用定冠詞 the restaurant manager。

4　人稱名詞與所有格的搭配

所有格的使用，必須比定冠詞更加謹慎，尤其要注意人稱名詞與所有格的搭配。

> **範例 B**
>
> 許多人不知如何增強英文聽力。¶其實多看英語影片對增強你的（英文）聽力非常有幫助。¶此外，你可以嘗試學英文歌，甚至結交外國朋友。¶總之，只有靠不斷地練習，你的英文聽力才會進步。¶

🖊 第一句：許多人不知如何增強英文聽力。

「許多人」未指明哪些人，只知數量超過兩個以上，可用 **many people**。

「英文聽力」→ 許多人的英文聽力，主詞要搭配所有格 **their**

- ✔ their English listening ability
- ✘ your English listening ability

🖊 第二句：其實多看英語影片對增強你的（英文）聽力非常有幫助。

句中提到「你的（英文）聽力」，可以當成是針對閱讀文章的人來說話，因此可以譯成 your；也可以當作對一般人所提出增強英文聽力的建議，可指任何一個人。同時，「英文聽力」因為是第二次出現，所以可省略 English listening，簡化為 your ability。

🖊 第三句：此外，你可以嘗試學英文歌，甚至結交外國朋友。

此處的「你」跟第二句的「你的」相同。上一句譯為 your，此處譯為 you。

🖊 第四句：總之，只有靠不斷地練習，你的英文聽力才會進步。

1. 「你的英文聽力」在這裡是第三次出現。此處可以選擇省略不翻譯，把重點放在「不斷練習就會有進步（Constant practice is the only way to make progress.）」，「your English listening ability」不翻也不會改變整句意義。

2. 此處與第二句提過的「你的（英文）聽力」中間隔了一句話，同時又是整篇文章的最後一句，為了強調文章結束的力量，也可以將「英文聽力」逐字譯出：
Constant practice is the only way to improve your English listening ability.

步驟❸：決定時態

1 分析情境以決定時間

　　時態是整篇文章的基調，也是動詞變化的主要依據。以中級英檢的中譯英為例，它屬於短篇文章，約有五句左右的翻譯，較不會出現複雜的時態變化，因此整篇文章的時態基本上必須一致，也就是時態的基調必須先定好，決定是現在、過去，或未來。撰寫內容所使用的簡單式、完成式、進行式等，都必須在同樣的時態基調內作變化。決定時態須先分析文章情境，以〈範例A〉和〈範例B〉為例：

範例 A

上個星期天我和母親到百貨公司逛街……

→ 「上個星期天」很明顯是已經發生過的事情，所以必須要用過去式。

範例 B

許多人不知如何增強英文聽力。其實多看英語影片對增強你的（英文）聽力非常有幫助……

→ 陳述增進英文聽力的方法屬一般現象，使用現在式。

2　注意關鍵時態詞彙

注意每個英文句子的中文意思，辨別句中是否有出現明確的時間點，或是相關的時間詞彙。

1 明確的時間點

1. I will graduate from college **in two years**.　我將於兩年後從大學畢業。
2. My father went on a business trip to Kaohsiung **last weekend**.　我父親上週到高雄出差。
3. My sister had a baby boy **last summer**.　去年夏天我姐姐生了一個兒子。

2 相關時間詞彙

中譯英時，有關時間的中文詞彙有時不需要逐字逐字的翻譯，直接將時間以動詞時態變化表現即可，有時也會加入副詞配合語氣變化。

1. I **will** be rich.　我以後會很有錢。
2. He **has** (already) left.　他已經離開了。
3. He **just** left.　他剛離開。
4. He **has been** gone for some time.　他已經離開一陣子了。
5. They **are going to** move to Singapore.　他們即將搬到新加坡。
6. I **am** still a student.　我目前還是學生。
7. I **used to** walk to school.　我以前都走路上學。
8. I **was** deeply in love with her.　我曾經深愛過她。

249

9 I **cannot** forget her. 我忘不了她。
　　↑ 現在式：陳述事實

10 I **have not been** able to forget her. 我一直忘不了她。
　　↑ 完成式：強調從當初到現在都忘不了

11 I **have not been** able to forget that relationship. 我至今無法忘懷那段感情。

12 I **have been** on a diet. 我最近在節食。

NOTE

表達能力的 be able to 片語

1. be able to = can 能夠
2. be unable to = cannot = be not able to 不能夠

句子可以直接使用 can 時，就不需要用 be able to；當 can 無法配合某些動詞的變化時，可藉助 be able to 來表達能力等語氣的變化。

未來式　I hope I will **be able to** buy a house of my own in 10 years. 我希望 10 年內可以買一棟自己的房子。

完成式　I was lucky to **have been able to** complete this project with your help. 由於你的幫助，我很幸運能夠完成這項計畫。

動名詞片語　She is excited about **being able to** deliver a speech to 200 people. 她很興奮能夠對兩百人發表演說。

4 步驟❹：選擇句型

要避免翻譯出現中式英文，就要盡量避免死板的字對字英譯。若能熟練運用所有的英文常用句型，就可以寫出簡單又正確的英文句。

中翻英時，先觀察中文句子，找出主詞與動詞，看看選擇哪種英文句型套用最適當。接下來根據時間和地點等元素，加入其他詞類完成句子翻譯。以下根據〈範例A〉的句型進行練習。

中譯英範例 A-1 ｜上個星期天我和母親到百貨公司逛街。

句型二　　主詞 ＋ 及物動詞 ＋ 受詞

❶ <u>my mother and I</u> <u>went shopping</u>　　我和母親去逛街
　　　主詞　　　　　　　動詞

❷ 加入時間副詞 last Sunday（上個星期天）

❸ 加入地方副詞 in a department store（到百貨公司）

→ Last Sunday my mother and I went shopping in a department store.

---

1 「逛街」的英譯可直接使用片語「go shopping」，與游泳、釣魚、爬山等相同（go swimming、go fishing、go hiking）。

2 此句還可以 I 作主詞，利用介系詞 with 表達「和……一起」的意義。

→ <u>I</u> went shopping <u>with</u> my mother in a department store last Sunday.

中譯英範例 A-2 ｜ 中午在一家餐廳用餐時，我們突然聽到有人大喊：「小心！」

句型五　　主詞 ＋ 動詞 ＋ 直接動詞 ＋ 受詞補語

❶ **We heard someone scream, "Look out!"**
　主詞　動詞1　　　　　　　動詞2
　　　　　　　　　　　　　　　　我們（突然）聽到有人大喊：「小心！」

❷ 加入時間副詞子句 while we were having lunch in a restaurant,（中午在一家餐廳用餐時）

❸ 加入副詞 suddenly（突然）

➔ While we were having lunch in a restaurant, we heard someone scream, "Look out."

---

[1] 感官動詞 hear、feel、see、watch、smell 後，可接原形動詞或現在分詞，二者差異很小，此處兩者皆可。

　🍀 **I heard them talk about the exam.**
　　　　　　　└─ 聽到他們討論考試，talk 用原形，強調動作已經完成
　　　　　　　　　　　　　　　我聽到他們討論考試。

　🍀 **I heard them talking about the exam.**
　　　　　　　└─ 用 talking，強調聽見他們談話時，他們正在談論考試
　　　　　　　　　　　　　　　我聽到他們正在討論考試。

[2] 片語「小心」：look out = watch out

NOTE

英文引號的使用

在美式英語的文法中,引號後面如果接了另一個標點符號,通常有幾種搭配方式:

1 逗號和句號一定置於引號內,引號內句子的第一個字母需大寫。

2 冒號和分號應該置於引號外。

3 問號和驚嘆號則根據句義,決定擺放的位置。

※ 問號和驚嘆號屬於引言的一部分 → 放引號內

※ 不屬於引言的一部分 → 放引號外,當作整個句子的結尾

1 He told her, "We have to go home."　他告訴她:「我們必須回家了。」

2 She asked, "Do we really have to go home now?"
　　　　　　　　　　　　　　　　她問:「我們一定要現在回家嗎?」

3 "The time is getting late," he explained, "and we have to get up
　　　　　　　接續前句未完的內容,所以不需大寫。↗
early tomorrow."
　　　　　　他解釋:「時間已經很晚了,而且我們明天還要早起。」

4 "Let's go!" she said.　　　　　　　　她說:「我們走吧!」

中譯英範例 A-3 ｜原來是有個小男孩不小心從椅子上摔下來。

句型二　　主詞 ＋ 及物動詞 ＋ 介系詞片語

❶ A little boy fell down from a chair.
　　主詞　　　動詞
　　　　　　　　　　　　　　　　有個小男孩從椅子上摔下來。

❷ 加入副詞 accidentally（不小心）
→ A little boy accidentally fell down from a chair.

---

1 看到「有」這個中文時，英文可以試著運用「there」來做變化。

🍀 **There was** a little boy who accidentally fell down from a chair.　　有個小男孩不小心從椅子上摔下來。

2 中文句出現「原來……」這個特殊的語氣，有幾種處理方式。

🍀 **It was** a little boy who accidentally fell down from a chair.
　　└─ 用「it」作主詞帶出句型
　　　　　　　　　　原來是一個小男孩不小心從椅子上摔了下來。

🍀 **It turned out** that a little boy accidentally fell down from a chair.
　　　　└─ 利用動詞片語 turn out 帶出名詞子句

254

> **NOTE**
>
> 「there was . . .」、「it was . . .」、「it turned out . . .」的比較
>
> 〈範例A-3〉提到了三種「有……」的句型。
>
> ❶ 「there was」：雖然文法正確，但未帶出「原來」的語氣，又顯得累贅不簡潔，不建議選用此句翻譯。
>
> ❷ 「it was」與「it turned out」句型有強調程度上的差異。「it was」句型強度適中，不像「turn out」的句型過於強調。不過如果文章內容較長，故事迂迴曲折，最後發現「原來……」，此時使用 turn out 較切合上下文的承接。

中譯英範例 A-4 ｜之後，餐廳經理送小男孩到醫院檢查。

句型五 　主詞 ＋ 動詞 ＋ 直接受詞 ＋ 受詞補語

❶ **The restaurant manager took the boy to the hospital for an examination.**
　　主詞　　　　　　　動詞
餐廳經理送小男孩到醫院檢查。

❷ 加入連接副詞 after that（之後）

→ After that, the restaurant manager took the boy to the hospital for an examination.

中譯英範例 A-5 ｜看來小男孩受了一點傷，但應該沒有大礙。

句型四　　主詞 ＋ 連綴動詞 ＋ 主詞補語

❶ <u>He</u> <u>was injured</u>. He should be fine.
　　主詞　　　動詞

小男孩受了傷。他應該沒有大礙。

❷ 加入副詞 slightly（輕微地）

→ He was slightly injured. He should be fine.

❸ 加入連接詞 but（但）

→ He was slightly injured, but he should be fine.

---

1. 中文句裡「看來……」是這句翻譯的重點字，因為不知道小男孩到醫院檢查的結果如何，所以這個「看來」是根據觀察之後的印象。利用動詞 seem 可以表達出「看來好像」的意思，配合不同主詞可以有兩種寫法：

　❶ He **seemed to** be slightly injured.　　看來他受了一點傷。
　　＝ It **seemed that** he was slightly injured.

2. 「受傷」常用的單字是「injure」和「hurt」。
　說某人受傷了，會用「sb. was injured」＝「sb. was hurt」

3. 「但……」，有「雖然……但是」或「然而」的語氣，翻譯時可選擇不同連接詞作運用。

　❶ **Although** he was slightly injured, he should be fine.
　❷ **While** he was slightly injured, he should be fine.
　❸ He was slightly injured, **but** he should be fine.

4. 雖然他受了一點輕傷，不過他應該會沒事。
　「沒有大礙」可以引申不同解釋：
　ⓐ 指「小男孩」沒有大礙：He should be fine / all right / OK.
　ⓑ 指「傷勢」沒有大礙：It was not serious.

5 步驟❺：文章修飾

根據前面四個步驟，重新將整段中文翻譯後再讀一遍，檢查**標點符號**、**拼字**、**時態變化**、**大小寫**、**單複數**和**語氣**。以下是〈範例A〉的完整英文翻譯：

中文段落
❶ 上個星期天我和母親到百貨公司逛街。
❷ 中午在一家餐廳用餐時，我們突然聽到有人大喊：「小心！」
❸ 原來是有個小男孩不小心從椅子上摔下來。
❹ 之後，餐廳經理送小男孩到醫院檢查。
❺ 看來小男孩受了一點傷，但應該沒有大礙。

英文翻譯
❶ Last Sunday my mother and I went shopping in a department store. ❷ While we were having lunch in a restaurant, we suddenly heard someone scream, "Look out!" ❸ It was a little boy who accidentally fell down from a chair. ❹ After that, the restaurant manager took the boy to the hospital for an examination. ❺ He seemed to be slightly injured, but he should be fine.

上述英譯的第三句話選擇以「it was」句型以配合文章的語氣，而最後一句也有不同的譯法，但是在語氣上沒有太大差異，可自由選擇。因為第三句話已經用了「it was」句型，所以最後一句選擇 He 作主詞的直譯。

一般來說，翻譯沒有標準答案，只有參考答案，而一般坊間翻譯考試的評分標準就是根據標點符號、拼字、時態變化、大小寫、單複數、語氣、字詞運用等文法規則，作為給分或扣分的依據。

一個句子可以有好幾種譯法，端視讀者在文章修飾時對句子所作的判斷。不管如何選擇，考試時記住拿分的基本前提「**不確定拼法的字不用，沒有把握的句子不寫**」。

Unit 21 中譯英的翻譯技巧

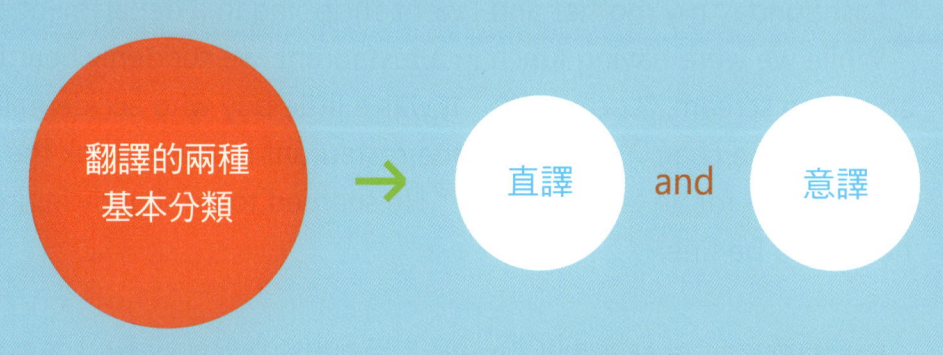

翻譯的兩種基本分類 → 直譯 and 意譯

1 直譯

「直譯」就是字對字的翻譯，通常出現在中文和英文句型結構相近的句子中，做法是直接將中文句的字詞對應轉換成英文。如：

1. I am still a student.　　我還是學生。
2. I like traveling, hiking in the mountains, and listening to music.　　我喜歡旅遊、爬山和聽音樂。

> **NOTE**
>
> **英文的「爬山」**
>
> 　　一般認知中，「爬山」的英文會想到 mountain climbing，其實 mountain climbing 意義較接近「登山」。若「爬山」意指在山中步道散步兼運動，其英譯較接近「健行」= hiking in the mountains。所以上面〈例2〉的翻譯寫「hiking in the mountains」或「mountain climbing」皆可。
>
> 　　但若中文為「星期天上午我和父親去爬山，一路上欣賞美景及呼吸清新的空氣。」在這個句子中，爬山的意義較接近健行，譯為 hiking in the mountains 較適合。

採用「直譯」技巧可以順利完成翻譯，但前提是讀者需熟悉中英對照的片語或詞彙，也就是看到中文可以馬上想到對應的英文。因此，在準備翻譯前，應多熟記中英對照的詞彙及片語。

當然，如果只有這麼簡單，有何翻譯技巧可言？問題在於許多讀者在學習英文過程中，通常只會學到對應英文的一種中文表達，如：看到「交朋友」馬上想到「make friends (with...)」，談到「（與……）相處」，腦中浮現的片語就是「get along (with...)」。

在外語學習的初期階段，這是大家都有的經驗，但若希望提升語言程度，就必須練習拋開中文字詞的束縛，理解真正的涵義，這就是翻譯的另一層次「意譯」。

2 意譯

「意譯」是指理解中文意義後,以同等或類似意義的英文譯出。

1 因為我還在就學,所以沒有工作。

　　這句話沒有難字,意義很清楚,但若想以「直譯」的方式翻譯這句話,而又不能查字典時,「就學」該怎麼說?是 in school 還是 at school?英文可以這樣表達嗎?這是中式英文嗎?考試時該怎麼辦?此時若能真正理解中文的意義,便可以發揮「意譯」的技巧。

　　理解中文後可得出「我還在就學」=「我還在唸書」=「我還是學生」,所以上述文字就可以輕鬆譯成「I am still a student, so I don't have a job.」。
請看下列翻譯的變化:

	直譯	意譯	意譯
我還在就學	= I am still a student.	≒ I am still studying at school.	≒ I am still at school.
我還在唸書	= I am still studying at school.	≒ I am still a student.	≒ I am still at school.
我還是學生	= I am still at school.	≒ I am still studying at school.	≒ I am still a student.

→「at school」片語有三種意義:在上課、在學校裡、在求學。

中譯英考試時不能查字典,以「我的嗜好(興趣)是旅遊、爬山、聽音樂。」這句為例,萬一「嗜好」拼法不確定、「興趣」也不知道該怎麼說,只要記得拿分的前提「不確定拼法的字不用,沒有把握的句子不寫」,加上利用「意譯」的技巧,避開不會寫的字,直接使用最簡單的文法「I like traveling . . .」。

有時利用「意譯」技巧寫出來的英譯,會與中文原意有些差異,但總勝過寫成錯字或空白不寫。在理解中文真正意義後,當然要選擇最有把握的正確句子完成翻譯。

2 我的嗜好(興趣)是旅遊、爬山、聽音樂。

直譯 My hobbies are traveling, hiking in the mountains, and listening to music.

意譯 I like traveling, hiking in the mountains, and listening to music.

3 直譯與意譯的交互運用

對以中文為母語的人們來說，掌握中文的文字變化是輕鬆自然的，但進入中譯英階段，中文意義的理解雖不是問題，卻苦於英文無法發揮。其實這只是陷入中文的文字障礙，只要擺脫掉一個個的中文字就可發現，其實簡單的英文也可以在中譯英時應付自如。只要真正理解中文句的意義，就可交互運用「直譯」與「意譯」，為中譯英帶來多樣面貌。

試譯下列二句，利用「意譯」的技巧，發揮創意，這二句話的關鍵片語曾在本章前面提及。

1 當我搬到一個新城市時，我就必須認識新朋友。

這句的中文基本上沒有難字，可以發揮創意的關鍵字在「認識」，英文究竟應該是 know 還是 meet？若讀者有注意到本章一開始介紹的片語「make friends」，中文原意雖為「交朋友」，若能理解「認識新朋友」其實等同於「交朋友」，這句就可以順利的翻譯出來。

> **翻譯** When I move to a new city, I will have to make new friends.
> 當我搬到一個新城市時，我就必須認識新朋友。

2 我的父母很高興我和姐姐相親相愛。

這句的中文意義很清楚，但也許有讀者會被「相親相愛」這個詞給嚇到，若能試著理解它的意義後，可以瞭解「相親相愛」＝「相處融洽」＝「相處地很好」，「get along with」加上副詞 well，就能夠表達出類似或相近的意義。

> **翻譯** My parents are pleased that I get along well with my sister.
> 我的父母很高興我和姐姐相親相愛。

「意譯」在處理不同語言與文化有關的表達時也常能派上用場。因為東西文化的差異，許多中文俗語在譯成英文時，若以直譯方式翻譯，外國人士可能無法理解。此時需以「意譯」，也就是用解釋的方式翻譯，或以英文中有對等意義的片語或成語翻譯。如：

3 俗話說一個巴掌拍不響。

直譯 It is said that one hand cannot clap to make a sound.
→ 雖然譯出英文，但外國人士較難理解。

解釋 It is said that it takes two hands to clap (in order to make a sound).
→ 較易理解，但仍須根據上下文加以引申解釋。

意譯 It is said that it takes two to tango.
→ 對應英文慣用語，直接傳達中文意義。

對翻譯有興趣的讀者，也可以利用「意譯」的技巧做反向練習，也就是先練習「英譯中」。在閱讀英文文章時，若看到某些特殊的英文表達，可以盡量理解其意義，再想想看中文有那些對應的説法。透過日常閱讀的「英譯中」練習，就可以持續累積「中譯英」的能力。

如「It takes two to tango.」，中文除了譯為「一個巴掌拍不響」之外，還有什麼中文句子可以表達同一意義？另一個成語「孤掌難鳴」是不是也很切題？下次英譯看到「孤掌難鳴」時，就可以搭配上下文，以意譯的方式聯想英譯，千萬不要被中文字困住。

4 不同譯法的轉換練習

「直譯」與「意譯」可以展現一個人對兩種語言的掌握能力。不同的人翻譯同一句子，常會出現許多不同的譯法；同樣地，同一個人也可以利用同一個句子，練習說出不同的譯法。這種不同譯法的轉換練習，是主修翻譯的學生常用來提升外語程度的方法之一，稱為「paraphrasing（不同譯法的轉換練習）」。

許多人在語言學習出現停滯，或不知如何更進一步提升程度時，也可以利用「不同譯法的轉換練習」來突破瓶頸。利用同一句中文，練習說出兩種以上的英譯，可以協助學習者認識字詞片語的正確用法，不僅提升外語程度，中文程度也會相對獲益。

試利用下列例子，練習不同的譯法：

1 錢要花在刀口上。

直譯 Money should be spent on the cutting edge of a knife.
→ 雖然譯出英文，但完全無法令人理解。

意譯 先理解意義：錢其實不是真的花在刀口上，而是必須用在最需要的地方，有效的使用金錢。由此引申出的相關解釋，都可以作為中譯英的「意譯」基礎。

句型 1　以「錢」作主詞

1. Money should be used in effective ways. 　應該有效使用金錢。
2. Money should be used to maximal effect. 　金錢使用應該達到最高效用。
3. Money should be used to address the key issues. 　錢應該花在重要事物上。
4. Money should be used in a way based on priorities. 　花錢應該遵照優先順序。
5. Money should not be wasted. 　不應該亂花錢。

句型 2 以「花錢」作主詞

1. Spending should fully reflect one's true needs.　　錢應該花在個人真正需要的東西上。

句型 3 以「人花錢」作主詞

1. People should spend their money in practical ways.　　人花錢應該講求實際。
2. People should use money wisely.　　人應該聰明地花錢。
3. People should make smart spending choices.　　人花錢時應該做出精明選擇。

句型 4 以「祈使句」帶出強調語氣

1. Spend your money wisely!　　花錢要聰明點！
2. Be smart when it comes to money.　　對於錢要謹慎點。

句型 5 「否定」成句

1. Don't throw away your money.　　不要亂花錢。
2. Don't spend money like water.　　不要花錢如流水。
3. Spending money like water.
   → 可對應中文成語「揮金如土」。

　　上述種種不同的英譯表達，都在說同一個中文句，該如何選擇呢？必須根據上下文的情境作出判斷。也許有人會問，為什麼同樣的中文句要寫出這麼多的英譯句？只要會一句不就夠了！其實這是希望讀者在翻譯時不要太拘泥中文字眼，要放寬思考的角度，翻譯時就不容易受到字詞的限制，變化也會更具創意。

　　以下介紹的五種轉換方法，是「中譯英」時可以運用的技巧，也是以「不同譯法的轉換練習」為基礎發展而來。

1 詞性轉換

中譯英時，利用「詞性轉換」可以讓同一句中文展現多樣化的英譯，如中文句中的關鍵字可以譯為名詞，也有可能譯為動詞或形容詞。同樣地，選擇作為主詞的字也可以轉為受詞。利用詞性轉換的技巧，可以選擇自己最有把握的英譯句子，減少扣分的機會。

1 動詞變名詞；主詞變受詞

中文 我的英文聽力開始進步了。

直譯 My English listening comprehension (主詞) begins to improve.

變化 I start making improvements in my English listening comprehension (受詞).

→ 動詞 improve 變成名詞 improvements

2 名詞變形容詞；受詞變主詞

中文 一個老師應該要有能力吸引學生的注意力。

直譯 A teacher should have the ability to attract students' attention (受詞).

變化 1 A teacher should be capable of attracting students' attention.

→ 名詞 ability 變成形容詞 capable

變化 2 The ability to attract students' attention (主詞) is very important for a teacher.

3 動詞變形容詞；受詞變主詞

中文 貧窮家庭通常買不起電腦。

直譯 Poor families often cannot afford to buy computers (受詞).

變化 Computers are not often affordable to poor families.
　　　　主詞
→ 動詞 afford 變成形容詞 affordable

4 副詞變形容詞；動詞變名詞

中文 我學得很快。

直譯 I learn quick/quickly.
　　　　　　　動詞

變化 I am a quick learner.
　　　　　　　名詞
→ 副詞 quick/quickly 變成形容詞 quick

5 利用虛主詞

中文1 There is an improvement in my English listening comprehension.　　　　　　　　　　　我的英語聽力有進步。

中文2 It is very important for a teacher to have the ability to attract students' attention.
→ 第二句的英譯與中文原始意義稍有不同，但傳遞了類似或接近的意念。

老師擁有吸引學生專心的能力十分重要。
（原句：一個老師應該要有能力吸引學生的注意力。）

2 同義詞代換

若翻譯時有單字拼不出來，又無法查詢，可以利用同義字代換的技巧，也就是利用「意譯」技巧，先理解中文後，再使用較簡單的英文表達類似的意義。

以先前出現過的兩句範例來作練習。

🍀 當我搬到一座新城市時，我就必須認識新朋友。
→ 可以運用片語「make friends with」，或是想想其他衍生意義。

➜ When I move to a new city, I will have to meet new people / get to know new people.

266

❷ 我的父母很高興我和姊姊相親相愛。
→ 若沒學過「get along with」片語，可以思考姐妹相親相愛時，彼此間的相處行為、感受等。

→ My parents are pleased that my sister and I love each other / support each other.

❸ 我的英文聽力開始有進步了。
→ 「進步」的基本定義＝越來越好。

→ My English listening comprehension is getting better.

❹ 一個好老師應該要有能力吸引學生的注意力。
→ 有能力＝能夠＝ can ＝ be able to。

→ A good teacher should be able to attract students' attention.

❺ 多數人對考試成績很不滿意。

ⓐ Most people are dissatisfied with their test results.
→ 「不滿意」＝ unsatisfied ＝ not satisfied

ⓑ Most people feel disappointed about their test results.

ⓒ Most people are not pleased with their test results.
→ not pleased ＝ unhappy

ⓓ The test results are unacceptable for most people.

❻ 學生應該要專心課業。
→ 專心課業常用的片語為「concentrate on」和「focus on」。

ⓐ Students should concentrate on their studies.

ⓑ Students should focus on their studies.
→ 另外還可以聯想到「專心」＝全部注意力＝一心想著。

• Students should give all the attention to the studies.

• Students should think of the studies only.
→ 另外談到「課業」，也會聯想到課業＝學業＝學習。

• Students should do their best to learn.

3 相反詞的運用

意義相反的詞彙及否定詞 not 的交互運用，可表達類似意義。

1 意義相反的字或片語

① Robert still **remembers** his ex-girlfriend. 羅柏還在懷念前任女友。
 = Robert **cannot forget** his ex-girlfriend.
 = Robert still **thinks about** his ex-girlfriend.

② We must find out ways **not to increase** costs.
 = We must find out ways to **reduce** costs.
 = We must find out ways to **cut down** costs.
 我們必須找到減少開銷的方法。

2 以 un- 或 dis- 開頭的相反詞

① They **don't agree** with me. 他們不贊同我的意見。
 = They **dis**agree with me.

② The food in the refrigerator **is in**adequate. 冰箱裡的食物不夠。
 = The food in the refrigerator **is not adequate**.

③ The truth should always be **un**covered. 真相不應被隱瞞。
    cover 隱藏

④ The truth will be **un**covered one day. 真相有一天會被揭發的。
    cover 掩蓋

⑤ Readers may **dis**cover new ways of thinking from this book.
    cover 掩飾、覆蓋　　讀者能從這本書發現新的思考方向。

⑥ His sickness **dis**abled him, and he was unable to work.
    able 有能力的　　他的疾病使他殘廢了，他也無法工作。

⑦ He was **un**able to work because of his sickness.
    able 有能力的　　因為他的疾病，他無法工作。

⑧ An **un**qualified coordinator cannot handle this job.
    qualified 符合資格的　　一位不合格的協調人無法做好這份工作。

9 People who don't meet the qualifications will be disqualified during the interview.

— qualified 符合資格的

不符合資格的人在面試時會被淘汰。

4 人稱名詞的使用

1 中文的人稱名詞有非常多樣的表達，如「人」、「人們」、「許多人」、「大家」等。此外，也有些表達是省略了人稱，像是「俗話說」、「常言道」等。真正理解其意義後，可以發現其實這類表達的意義都是「人們說」。

2 人稱名詞沒有固定的譯法，可以選擇直譯方式處理，如：

- 有些人 → some people
- 大家 → people
- 許多人 → many people

以下為中譯英時可以參考的技巧：

1 人稱的單複數

中文 在台灣，大家都很注重英文的學習。

直譯1 In Taiwan, people think that learning English is very important.

直譯2 In Taiwan, everyone pays a lot of attention to learning English.

→「大家」一般翻作 people，但「大家」通常也指每一個人，所以也可以用 everyone 取代多數人稱。

2 人稱的對象

第一人稱	we	指包含自己在內，或自己所屬的團體，如學校、社區、家人、或國家。
第二人稱	you	針對閱讀文章的人而言。
第三人稱	they	指不包含自己的其他對象，泛指人們。

中文 在台灣，大家都很注重英文的學習。

直譯3 In Taiwan, we all stress the importance of learning English.

→ 使用 we 代表作者假設讀者皆為台灣人，為包含自己在內的團體。

3 虛主詞

中文常說「常言道」、「俗話說」，其實就是指「人們認為」、「人們相信」。在英譯時，可以避開人稱名詞，使用虛主詞取代。

中文 常言道：「早起的鳥兒有蟲吃。」
（早起的鳥兒有蟲吃＝先下手為強＝捷足先登……）

- **人稱英譯法** People believe that the early bird gets the worm.
- **虛主詞譯法 1** It is said that the early bird gets the worm.
- **虛主詞譯法 2** It is thought that the early bird gets the worm.

4 連接副詞

中文 俗話說：「學習外語愈早愈好」。

- **虛主詞譯法** It is believed that it's never too early to learn a foreign language.
- **連接副詞譯法** Generally speaking, children are never too young to learn foreign languages.

5 轉折語氣的轉換

1 轉折語氣是中譯英時需要特別留意的部分，若是語氣沒有翻譯出來，有時就像忘了放鹽的菜，沒有味道。

2 與轉折語氣有關的基本詞彙，在前面幾章的對等連接詞、副詞子句連接詞，及連接副詞單元中做過介紹。當然，利用「意譯」技巧變化出來的相關詞彙，也可以帶出轉折語氣，像「……之後」不一定對應 after；「此外」也不一定就是 furthermore；有些副詞沒學到又該怎麼說？這時可以回到「意譯」的基本定義：**理解中文意義**。

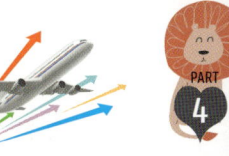

中文 1 湯米下定決心要用功念書,此外,他還要出國留學。

- **直譯** Tommy has decided to study hard. Furthermore, he wants to study abroad.
- **變化 1** Tommy has made up his mind to study hard. Not only that, he wants to study abroad.
- **變化 2** Tommy has committed himself to studying hard. What's more, he wants to study abroad.

中文 2 毫無疑問地,學校不准學生進入校園停車。

- **直譯** Without a doubt, the college doesn't allow students to park their cars on campus.
- **變化 1** Clearly, the college doesn't allow students to park on campus.
- **變化 2** It is obvious that students are not allowed to park on campus.

中文 3 經歷一連串的恐怖攻擊事件之後,人們心中始終堅信明天會更好。

- **直譯** After a series of horrible terrorist incidents, people still firmly believe that we will have a better tomorrow.
- **變化 1** Having gone through a series of horrible terrorist incidents, people still firmly believe that a better tomorrow lies ahead.
- **變化 2** Although there have been a series of horrible terrorist incidents, people never give up believing that there will be a brighter future.

　　「翻譯」是將一種語言轉換成為另一種語言,可協助不同語言人士相互溝通。除此之外,有些語言學者同意「翻譯」可以作為外語學習四個方法(聽說讀寫)之外的第五個方法,這是因為在學習過程中,如果搭配了母語的理解,透過翻譯的練習,可以加深學習者在外語與母語之間的相互對應,提升學習成效。

Unit 22 中譯英的特殊用法與常犯錯誤

中譯英最忌翻成中式英文,只要掌握本章重點,熟悉英文特殊語彙的正確用法,就能譯出合乎邏輯與英文文法的譯文。

1 與 to 有關的特殊用法

to 常與動詞或名詞搭配形成片語，表達特定的意義，有時當介系詞用，有時當不定詞用，需格外留意。

Ⓐ to 當不定詞用　　to ＋ 原形動詞

Ⓑ to 當介系詞用　　to ＋ 動名詞／名詞

1 used to

1 「**used to ＋ 原形動詞**」過去常做（現在不再做）
2 「**be used to ＋ 動名詞**」＝「**be accustomed to ＋ 動名詞**」習慣於
   → to 是介系詞，後面需要接動名詞或名詞。

❶ I used to ride a bike to school.　　我過去常常騎車上學（現在沒有了）。
   → used to ＋ 原形動詞

❷ I am used to walking to school.　　我習慣走路上學。
   → be used to ＋ 動名詞

❸ I used to stay up late.　　我過去習慣熬夜。

❹ I am accustomed to getting up early.　　我習慣早起。

2 prefer to

① 「(would) prefer to ＋ 原形動詞」寧願；……較喜歡……
② 「prefer ＋ 動名詞 ＋ to ＋ 動名詞」寧願……而不願……

🍀 I (would) prefer to lie on the sofa and watch TV the whole day.
我比較喜歡躺在沙發上整天看電視。

🍀 I prefer staying at home to going out.
　　　　動名詞　　　　　　　　　動名詞
我寧願待在家，也不願出門。

3 would rather; would like to

① 「would rather ＋ 原形動詞 ＋ than ＋ 原形動詞」較願意……而不是……
② 「would like to ＋ 原形動詞」想要

🍀 I would rather stay here than go with you.
我寧願待在這裡，也不要和你去。

🍀 I would like you to go with me.
我想要你和我一起去。

4 had better (not) + 原形動詞

① 「had better ＋ 原形動詞」最好
② 「had better not ＋ 原形動詞」最好不

🍀 You had better hurry, or you will miss the bus.
你最好快一點，否則會錯過公車。

🍀 You had better not oversleep, or you might miss the exam.
你最好不要睡過頭，否則你會錯過考試。

2 「形容詞」與「副詞」的運用

中譯英時，中文句的「地」與「的」可以作為讀者用來判斷該譯為「副詞」或是「形容詞」的方法，如：

1. 她開心地收下這份生日禮物。
   She happily accepted this birthday gift.

2. 今天是她一生中最開心的日子。
   Today is the happiest day in her life.

3. 他犯了一個明顯的錯誤。
   He made an obvious mistake.

4. 他明顯地犯了一個錯誤。
   Obviously, he made a mistake.

3 以 -ly 結尾的形容詞（副詞）

形容詞如何形成副詞，可歸納出一些基本規則，一般副詞是在形容詞後面加上 -ly，如：

- recent → recently（最近的／最近地）
- public → publicly（公眾的／公開地）
- evident → evidently（明顯的／明顯地）
- beautiful → beautifully（美麗的／美麗地）

但是也有許多以 -ly 結尾的字看起來像副詞，但其實是形容詞，中譯英時須特別留意這種易混淆的情況。

1 以 -ly 結尾的形容詞

- costly（代價）昂貴的
- friendly 友善的
- likely 很可能的
- lively 活潑的
- lonely 孤獨的
- silly 可笑的
- ugly 醜陋的
- lovely 可愛的；令人愉快的
- manly 有男子氣概的

1. This **costly** mistake made him lose his job.　這個代價慘重的錯誤讓他丟了工作。
2. This **lovely** weather is perfect for a picnic.　晴朗的天氣很適合去野餐。
3. The old man next door leads a **lonely** life.　隔壁的老人過著孤獨的生活。
4. He put on a **manly** pose to attract women.　他擺出男子氣概的樣子來吸引女性。

2 同時兼具副詞與形容詞功能的 -ly 結尾詞

- early 早的；早
- daily 每日的；每日
- weekly 每週的；每週
- quarterly 季度的；一季一次
- hourly 每小時；每小時地
- nightly 每夜的；每夜
- monthly 每月的；每月
- yearly 每年的；一年一度

❶ We have to get up **early** tomorrow morning.
　　　　　　　　　　副詞
　　　　　　　　　修飾動詞 get up
我們明天早上必須早起。

❷ If you want to lose weight, having an **early** dinner is one of the most effective ways.
　　　　　　　　　　　　　　　　　形容詞
　　　　　　　　　　　　　　　　形容名詞 dinner
假如你要減重，其中一個有效的方法是早一點吃晚餐。

❸ This conference will be held **yearly**.
　　　　　　　　　　　　　　　副詞
　　　　　　　　　　　　　修飾動詞 held
這個會議將每年舉行一次。

❹ This conference is an important **yearly** event.
　　　　　　　　　　　　　　　　形容詞
　　　　　　　　　　　　　　　　形容名詞 event
這個會議是一年一次的重要活動。

❺ We have to turn in the report **monthly**.
　　　　　　　　　　　　　　　　副詞
　　　　　　　　　　　　修飾動詞片語 turn in
我們必須每個月提交報告。

❻ The **monthly** report is due on Monday.
　　　形容詞
　　　形容名詞 report
星期一要交月報。

4 動詞變化

1 動詞三態同形

有些動詞的三個時態變化（現在式、過去式、過去分詞）皆為同一字，不做任何改變，寫作時需須特別留意，此類字包括：

- burst 爆發
- cost 價值
- cut 切
- hit 打；撞
- hurt 受傷
- let 讓
- put 放置
- quit 放棄；停止
- read 閱讀
- rid 使免除
- set 放；安裝
- shed 流出
- shut 關上
- spread 伸展；張開
- upset 弄翻；心煩意亂

1. The Keelung River burst its banks and made many people homeless.
   基隆河潰堤讓許多人無家可歸。

2. The flood spread from the riverside to the downtown area.
   洪水從河畔淹到市區。

3. Many people read about this accident in the next day's newspaper.
   許多人在隔天的報紙看到了這件意外。
   → read 雖然三態同型，讀音卻不同：[rid] → [rɛd] → [rɛd]

2 動詞變化的陷阱

某一動詞的現在式可能是另一動詞的過去式，須小心不要混淆。

- find → found → found 發現
- found → founded → founded 成立
- lie → lay → lain 躺
- lie → lied → lied 說謊
- lay → laid → laid 放置
- wound → wounded → wounded 受傷
- wind → wound → wound 上發條；彎曲通過

1 Sarah **found** a purse on the floor.
→ 動詞「發現」三態 find → found → found

莎拉在地上發現了一個錢包。

2 This prestigious college was **founded** in 1945.
→ 動詞「建立」三態：found → founded → founded

這所頗負盛名的大學成立於 1945 年。

3 Charles **lay** down to take a nap.
→ 動詞「躺」三態：lie → lay → lain

查爾斯躺下來小睡一下。

4 Beautiful women tend to **lie** about their age.
→ 動詞「說謊」三態：lie → lied → lied

美麗的女人通常會謊報年齡。

5 The teacher asked the students to **lay** their textbooks aside and take out a piece of blank paper for the exam.
→ 動詞「放置」三態：lay → laid → laid

老師叫學生把書本放到旁邊，拿出一張空白的紙考試。

6 The speakers **wound** their way through the crowds to get to the stage.
→ 動詞「彎曲通行」三態：wind → wound → wound

主講人迂迴繞過群眾，才到達台上。

7 One passenger was **wounded** in this pileup accident.
→ 動詞「受傷」三態：wound → wounded → wounded

一位乘客在這次連環車禍中受傷了。

3　不適用進行式的動詞

動詞通常為描述動作，所以可使用進行式，如：Alice was reading a book when her boyfriend called.（愛麗絲的男友打來時，她正在看書。）。另外有些動詞如感官動詞、連綴動詞，或描述心理狀態的動詞，不適合使用進行式，此類字包括：

• appear 顯露	• believe 相信	• belong 屬於	• hate 恨
• contain 包含	• doubt 懷疑	• feel 感覺	• know 知道
• hear 聽見	• imagine 想像	• include 包括	• need 需要
• like 喜歡	• look 看	• love 愛	• realize 了解
• own 擁有	• prefer 寧可	• possess 擁有	• smell 聞
• remember 記得	• seem 似乎	• see 看見	• wish 希望
• want 想要	• sound 聽起來	• taste 嚐	
• consist of 由……組成		• understand 認識到	

❶ This house **belongs** to my brother.　這棟房子是我哥哥(弟弟)的。
　　　　　　↑ 不可寫為 is belonging。

❷ He **prefers** a house to an apartment.　他喜歡平房勝過公寓。

❸ I **wish** I could **own** a house like that.　我希望我能擁有一棟像那樣的房子。

4　同字不同義的動詞

有些動詞兼具兩種特性，意思也不同。

have a bath　英式英語
take a bath　美式英語

❶ I **have** two dogs.　我有兩隻狗。
　　↑ = own 擁有

❷ They are **having** a bath now.　他們現在正在洗澡。
　　　　　　↑ 指動作，可用進行式

❸ You seem to have worked all night, and you **look** terribly tired today.　你似乎整晚都在工作，今天看起來疲倦極了。
　　　↑ 連綴動詞

❹ I have been **looking for** a solution to this problem.　我一直在找這個問題的答案。
　　　　　　↑ 指動作，可用進行式

5 時態混用

1 錯誤的時態混用

一般而言,一個句子中如果同時出現現在式與過去式,這個句子很可能不正確。

1. ✗ I **take** a long bath when I **felt** tired.
   現在式 　　　　　　　　　過去式
   我累的時候會好好洗個澡。
   → 這句話的時態邏輯前後不合,需將子句與主句的時態調整一致

2. ✓ I **take** a long bath when I **feel** tired.
   我累的時候會好好洗個澡。
   → 動詞皆為現在式,指現在習慣

3. ✓ I **took** a long bath when I **felt** tired yesterday.
   → 動詞與時間皆是指過去,全句時態相同
   昨天我覺得很累的時候,好好的洗了個澡。

2 名詞子句的時態混用

在名詞子句的句子中,現在式與過去式有可能同時出現。

1. I **agree** with what you **have** just **said**.
   現在式　　　　　　　　完成式
   我同意你剛剛說的話。

2. I **am** sure that you **knew** the truth last week.
   現在式　　　　　　過去式
   我確定你上週就知道真相。

> **NOTE**
>
> **時態混用的原則**
> 1. 避免寫出時態不一致的句子。
> 2. 寫出時態混用的句子時,需確定句子的意義符合邏輯。

6 語氣連接詞

中文常說「雖然……但是」、「因為……所以」，不過在英文的寫作上必須擇一連接詞運用，不可二者同時使用，使用時需注意句子的邏輯關係。

❶ 雖然老闆是我父親，但是他不會給我特別的待遇。
- Although the boss is my father, he won't treat me any differently.
- The boss is my father, but he won't give me any special treatment.

❷ 因為我在這家公司上班，所以我必須遵守公司規定。
- Because I work for this company, I have to follow the company's rules.
- I work for this company, so I have to abide by the company's rules.

7　中英對應的易犯錯誤

某些中文詞與英文對應時，直譯不一定符合字義，需真正理解中文原意，以及特別留意英文既有的習慣用法，才能選擇正確的翻譯字詞。

1 因為土地有限，所以台灣的房子通常蓋得很高。
The **buildings** in Taiwan are often very tall because of the limited land.
→ 這句話的「房子」指的是建築物，避免譯為 houses，讀者可參考英英字典對 house 的解釋

2 根據最新資料顯示，明天氣溫會降五度。
According to **the latest information**, the temperature will drop 5 degrees tomorrow.
→ 「最新資料」避免譯為 the newest information

3 最近幾年，他的健康每況愈下。
In recent years, his health **has been getting worse**.
→ 因為是最近幾年一直持續發生的情況，所以要用完成進行式 has been getting worse

4 最近五年來，醫療費用不斷增加。
Over the last five years, the medical expenses have increased.
→ 「over the last five years」這樣的用法，搭配了數字，所以需要使用 last

Quiz 29

單句翻譯

1. 準備考試的訣竅。

2. 有些人很怕考試。

3. 其實考試沒有想像中那麼可怕。

4. 有些步驟可以幫助你準備考試。

5. 首先,你必須擬訂一個讀書計畫,能讓你在考試前把所有資料複習一遍。

6. 接下來,在考試前一天好好的休息。

7. 熬夜念書只會增加你的壓力和焦慮。

8. 考試當天記得吃早餐,穿著舒適的衣服。

9. 盡量提早出門,以避免塞車。

10. 最後,盡自己最大努力應試。

11. 如果成績不理想,就只好下次多努力。

Quiz 30

整段翻譯

1 我 12 歲時父母送我一台收音機。從此它就成為我最好的朋友,並為我帶來許多快樂。有時我會打電話到電台回答許多有趣的問題。更重要的是,它讓我的生活更充實且多采多姿。

2 上個月我第一次參加了一場演講比賽。我既緊張又興奮。比賽當天,其他參賽者的表現讓我印象深刻。如預期般我沒有贏得任何獎項,但是我學到了重要的一課:成功是要努力才能獲得。

3 一星期前,我和妹妹在街上發現一隻流浪狗。牠看起來是這麼可愛又無辜,讓我們決定帶牠回家。回到家後,媽媽告訴我們養狗不是一件輕鬆的事。幸好爸爸表示可以幫忙照顧。現在牠已經成為家裡的一分子。

4 今年開始,我自願在一家當地醫院擔任義工。我每星期花一個下午的時間在醫院幫助人們。雖然我比以前更忙,但是我學會充分利用時間。我也學會對生命感恩,不再視一切為理所當然。

PART 5

英文作文題型破解

Unit 23 英文作文的寫作步驟

Unit 24 英文作文的寫作技巧

Unit 25 英文寫作的常犯錯誤與對策

Unit 23 英文作文的寫作步驟

英文學習者常常碰到的狀況是：看到作文題目，卻不知道要寫些什麼？現代社會的資訊爆炸，新資訊的出現還來不及消化吸收，下一波資訊又排山倒海而來，許多人因而養成被動接受資訊的習慣。

因資訊過度密集，讓人沒有時間消化吸收，間接讓許多人出現一種麻木狀況，也就是對許多事物或社會現象沒感覺。這種情形在寫作時可能會很痛苦，因為不是英文不會寫，而是不知道該寫些什麼。

作文與翻譯最大的差異在於：**翻譯是寫別人的句子**，進入別人的思考；而作文則是**根據一個既定的題目**，寫出自己的話，可能是自我生活經驗、對事物的看法、回憶過往事物，甚至利用想像力創造新的情境。若是對題目沒有感覺，腦筋一片空白，真的是英文單字背再多，英文片語背再熟也幫不上忙。

不同檢定有不同的規定，舉全民英檢中級為例，英文作文的寫作長度約在120字左右，約為八到12個英文句子，段落數根據寫作內容自由決定，可為完整的一段或兩段不等。由於字數有限，寫作內容需更為精簡，直接切入主題。

有鑑於此，以下單元的重點希望提供讀者一些步驟及技巧，幫助讀者在看完考試題目後，有思考的方向，不致於腦中茫然一片，不知道要寫什麼，或是寫了一堆，內容卻沒有切中題意。在進入正題之前，先簡單介紹中級英檢寫作考試的三類題型。

1. **圖片申論**：根據題目中的圖片及提示文字，寫出對圖片現象的感想與看法。
2. **短文銜接**：將一篇只有開頭段落的英文作文完成，可自由決定內容的發展方向。
3. **書信寫作**：根據提示文字，完成一篇符合題意且完整的信件。

1 圖片申論

圖片申論的寫作提示有兩種：

1. 一張「圖片」，呈現一種社會現象，或一種生活情境。
2. 一段「提示文字」，闡述圖片中的現象。

因為圖片所能傳遞的意念非常多，每個人都可以有不同的眼光來看圖片現象，也可以有不同的角度來發揮。為了更清楚地傳遞主題意念，主試單位會在圖片外附上一段提示文字，這段文字內容主要是協助應試者集中寫作主題，避免發生太過天馬行空的情況。因此，這段提示文字可以作為寫作大綱的重要參考。圖片申論的寫作文體多為論說文，陳述圖片中現象的優缺點，再加以分析比較。

步驟 1　引言：描述圖片內容（1到2句）

1. 描述圖片內容時，可參考提示文字，以求正確解讀圖片所傳遞的意念。寫作重點可以摒除個人的好惡，以客觀的立場來描述圖片現象，也可以附上個人對圖片的主觀感受。
2. 第一段在整篇作文中所占的分量較輕，若字數較少可不需獨立為一段，選擇與下一段合併。

以下是兩張圖例，作為描述圖片的寫作練習：

A

可描述這是中國傳統的團圓飯景象，個人感覺到這是溫馨的時刻。

B

可描述這也許是上下班尖峰時間，許多人利用捷運代步，因此造成人潮。

步驟 2　申論：闡述論點（6到8句）

1 闡述主題句（1到2句）

主題句的重點在回答「提示文字」的問題，所以一定要參考提示文字內容，直接點出圖片現象產生的原因，來作為主題句。

圖A　除夕夜全家團圓吃飯

除夕夜全家團圓吃飯，是因為根據傳統習俗，在農曆新年前的除夕夜，家中成員共進團圓飯，象徵圓滿。

圖B　捷運人潮

許多人都利用捷運上下班及假日出遊，是因為捷運非常方便。

2 發展**支持**論點（3到4句）

此段為申論段落的重心，應占有較多篇幅，重點在說明上述主題句的論點，也就是進一步解釋主題句所分析的原因。

圖 A　除夕夜全家團圓吃飯	圖 B　捷運人潮
解釋農曆年的傳統習俗，如農曆新年是最重要的節日、平日散居各地的家人藉此時節團聚、大家圍爐品嚐母親的拿手菜、除夕夜守歲、初一共迎新年、互賀恭喜等。	支持捷運非常方便的論點：捷運準時、路線多、便捷、價格實惠、不會塞車、不用找車位、安全、不會製造空氣汙染、減輕市區的交通負荷等。

3 提出**反向**論點（1到2句）

在陳述支持論點之後，可以在此提出反向思考的論點與支持論點做比較，需注意反向論點的陳述只是做對比，其分量不應超過支持論點。

圖 A　除夕夜全家團圓吃飯	圖 B　捷運人潮
前面解釋過農曆年的傳統習俗，反向論點可以從「傳統與現代」對比的角度進行思考：社會進步、工作性質轉變、許多人無法放假回家過年、餐廳過年不打烊、大家到餐廳吃年夜飯等。	前面解釋捷運的優勢，反向論點可以從「優點與缺點」對比的角度進行思考：捷運人潮集中時必須依序上下車、不是每班車都擠得進去、有時無位子可坐、高架捷運會產生噪音、只有某些都市的居民才有機會搭乘，鄉村居民沒有便利的捷運可坐。

　　介紹支持論點與反向論點的對比觀念，是希望幫助讀者擴大思考角度，避免不知從何著手寫作的窘境。論點分析之後，可選擇較好發揮的部分，根據邏輯進行組織。因為這屬於短篇寫作，所以可從中挑選適合的部分發揮，不一定要全部都寫出來。

　　在擬定論點順序時，必須特別注意各論點間的邏輯關係，如果中間有不相干的觀點，即使想到非常好的英文表達，有時也必須將其捨去。同時因字數有限，所以必須將寫作集中於有限的重點發揮。集中式的重點表達才可以讓作文的邏輯前後貫通，不會形成東寫寫、西寫寫的零散組織。

步驟 3　結論：對未來的前景提出個人想法（1到2句）

結論時，可以綜合上述的支持及反向論點，提出自己的看法，可以朝「未來的前景」來構思結論句。

圖A　除夕夜全家團圓吃飯
→ 因應社會變化，大家對團圓飯的心態也隨之調整。未來的過年方式也許是我們所無法想像的等等。

圖B　捷運人潮
→ 希望未來捷運的服務可以推廣到更多城市，讓更多人都享受到捷運的便利。

實例應用　圖B

提示

每天搭乘捷運（metro）的人數這麼多，許多人都利用捷運代步、上下班、假日出遊，你認為捷運受到歡迎的原因為何？請說明你的看法。

寫作步驟

引言：描述圖片現象，這可能是上下班尖峰時間，許多人利用捷運代步、趕上下班。當然，這也可能是假日出遊的人潮。

申論

主題句：許多人都利用捷運上下班或假日出遊，是因為捷運非常方便。

支持論點：捷運方便的原因包括捷運準時、路線多、不會塞車、不用找車位、不開車可以減輕市區的交通負荷。

反向論點：可惜只有某些都市的居民才有機會搭乘捷運。

結論 希望未來捷運的服務可以推廣到更多地區，讓更多人享受到捷運的便利。

作文範例

引言 During rush hour, many people are busy getting on and off the metro, hoping to get to work on time or get home earlier. This is not an unusual scene on a weekday morning or evening.

主題句 The metro is popular because it is convenient to commute to work or to go to tourist attractions on holidays.

支持論點 Besides, it is always on time and provides many route lines. Metro passengers don't worry about being stuck in traffic or finding a parking space. With fewer people driving their cars, this rapid transit system helps cities relieve the traffic burden.

反向論點 However, currently in Taiwan, it is a pity that only certain cities provide this efficient and convenient service.

結論 I hope that it can be developed in more cities in the future.

2 短文銜接

短文銜接的寫作類似**敘述文**，主試單位會提供一個主題，及一段簡短的英文敘述作為一個故事的開頭。短文的題目會要求應試者根據所提供的故事情節寫出**後續內容**，並寫出**結局**。短文的種類多屬**生活情境**，如生日、吃喜酒、看電影、上圖書館、休閒娛樂等等，日常生活中所上演的各種場景都屬於命題的範圍。

步驟 1　確認主詞

短文銜接的主題設定了故事發展的方向，如題目是 An Embarrassing Situation，故事就一定要出現尷尬的場景，可能是主角忘了帶錢或褲子破掉等。若題目是 My Summer Vacation，故事的內容就需要圍繞著暑假來發展，如暑假的某次旅行、暑假的打工經驗等。

步驟 2　瀏覽短文第一段

從題目所提供的第一段文字內容，可以歸納出人、事、時、地等相關的故事情節。這段文字內容奠定了故事發展的基調。

閱讀時需留意：

時間　故事發生的時間。時間點決定整篇短文的時態。

人物　故事的主角。主角決定短文的敘述口氣是第一人稱（I）的自述，或第三人稱（Peter、Susan 或某人的故事）的敘述。

地點　故事的地點。可能在餐廳裡、火車上、家裡，或 KTV 等。

原因　瞭解故事發生的原因。可能是為了慶祝生日到餐廳聚餐、為了考試到圖書館念書，或是為了回家過節趕火車等。

事件　故事的內容。第一段文字通常會提供一個大架構，讓應試者在這個架構裡寫出後續的故事。

步驟 3　安排故事的起承轉合

短文銜接可以利用中文寫作常用的「起、承、轉、合」作為故事發展的順序。題目所提供的第一段文字內容，可作為整篇文章的「起」段，從中歸納出相關的人、事、時、地等故事情節後，就可開始構思故事內容。

短文銜接的表現手法類似「故事接龍」，故事的發展與寫作者的性格有密切關係，性格平實的人，可從個人生活經驗發展出四平八穩的故事；個性調皮的人，也可以利用豐富的想像力，寫出異想天開的情節。有時若能夠加入類似「腦筋急轉彎」的結局，也可達到出奇制勝的效果。

1 承（2到4句）

開頭第一段便是「起」，而「承」段的文句需呼應第一段的故事內容：相同的主角，在同樣的場景下，接續上一段的故事發展。

2 轉（3到4句）

此段為故事的高潮，通常為主角遇到事先無法預料的情況，而這樣的情況為主角帶來了某一種的情緒感受，可能是驚喜、怒氣、哀傷、快樂、窘境、氣憤等。

範例題目

An Embarrassing Moment

起 主角小明好不容易趕上回台中老家的巴士，要掏錢跟司機買票時，卻發現錢包不見了……。

承 小明摸遍口袋，翻遍手提袋，只找到一個十塊銅板。

轉 小明尷尬地向司機笑了一笑，因為沒錢，只好先下車，找提款機領錢後，再坐下一班車。此時忽然有人叫住他，原來是一位國中同學正好也搭同班車要回台中，小明趕緊跟同學借錢買車票。

3 合（2到4句）

為故事的結尾作準備，可以是完美大結局，也可以是主角內心的自我調適，或是記取教訓的經驗學習，或任何出人意料的結局。

範例題目

An Embarrassing Moment

起 主角小明好不容易趕上回台中老家的巴士，要掏錢跟司機買票時，卻發現錢包不見了……。

承 小明摸遍口袋，翻遍手提袋，只找到一個十塊銅板。

轉 小明尷尬地向司機笑了一笑，因為沒錢，只好先下車，找提款機領錢後，再坐下一班車。此時忽然有人叫住他，原來是一位國中同學正好也搭同班車要回台中，小明趕緊跟同學借錢買車票。

合 結尾一：兩人一路上聊天敘舊，愉快地抵達台中。
結尾二：小明心想下次絕對要更小心，千萬別再發生這種令人尷尬的情形。

作文範例

說明 請完成以下故事。寫作能力測驗的主題是「My Summer Trip」。

　　Last summer, my father decided that our family should spend some time together before the end of the summer vacation. Therefore, he planned a trip to the southern part of Taiwan. He didn't tell us the destination, because he wanted it to be a surprise. Therefore, one hot summer day, we began our journey. We were sitting in the car and stuck in the highway traffic. . . .

寫作步驟

1 確認主題 題目是 My Summer Trip（我的夏天之旅），故事發展應與某個夏天的旅程有關，可能是旅途中所發生的事情，或為了安排這趟旅行，寫作者做了哪些準備事項，也可以是這趟旅行的感想等等。

2 瀏覽短文 上述說明文字提供了故事的背景。

第一段
1. 時間：發生在去年暑假接近尾聲時，全篇應使用過去式。
2. 人物：「我及家人」，為第一人稱（I）的自述。
3. 地點：台灣南部某旅遊景點，因不確定地點，所以是可以自行發揮的部分。
4. 原因：父親希望全家人在暑假結束前能相聚共遊。
5. 事件：全家出遊。

3 安排故事的起承轉合

承「起」段故事內容包括家人正前往南台灣、天氣很熱、高速公路塞車。接著必須承接前段的故事內容：

在車上爸爸終於宣布目的地是「蝴蝶谷」，因為聽說那兒有成千上萬的蝴蝶飛舞，形成壯觀的景象。大家滿懷期待，到了目的地，迫不及待下車，但奇怪的是，卻沒看到半隻蝴蝶……

轉 提供一個出乎意料之外的情節。
1. 四平八穩版本：大家只看到滿谷野花，突然，上百隻蝴蝶出現在空中，原來滿谷野花都是蝴蝶。
2. 異想天開版本：蝴蝶王突然出現，並且會說話，主角嚇了一跳。

合
1. 四平八穩版本：大家覺得蝴蝶谷果然不虛此名。
2. 異想天開版本：原來蝴蝶王只是夏日之旅的一場夏日夢。

寫作實例

承 At that time, Father announced the destination. He wanted to take us to a place called "Butterfly Valley." He was told that it was a beautiful place. When we finally arrived at "Butterfly Valley," everyone couldn't wait to get out of the car. Strangely enough, there were no butterflies flying, and the valley wasn't very attractive.

四平八穩版本	異想天開版本
轉 There were only flowers all over the valley. Suddenly, hundreds of butterflies coming out of nowhere flew upward into the sky. Then, we realized that those flowers we had seen were actually butterflies resting on the grass.	Suddenly, one giant butterfly flew by the crowd and stopped in front of my face. Unbelievably, this giant butterfly opened its mouth and said, "Welcome to my valley!" Right after that, hundreds of butterflies coming out of nowhere flew upward into the sky.
合 That view was really magnificent. Even though we drove a long way to Butterfly Valley, we thought it was worthwhile to take this summer trip.	"What an impressive view!" I thought. Unexpectedly, I heard Mother's voice: "Wake up, son! We're here!" At that time, I realized that it was only a summer dream of my summer trip.

3 書信寫作

前述兩種作文題型的文體沒有太大的限制，但是第三類書信寫作的格式屬於應用文體裁，必須符合正確的格式，這是與前述兩種作文題型最大的差異。書信寫作步驟如下：

1 書信寫作的格式

書信寫作的格式涵蓋範圍相當廣泛，從信封的書寫方式，到寄信人的姓名抬頭等，都有一定的規範，此處僅將與中級英檢試題內容相關的部分列出。

1 日期

第一行左邊頂格（齊頭式）或**置中**或**靠右**寫上書信日期，如「December 10, 2016」。在現代信函中，日期左邊頂格是最常見的，寫作時也最不容易出錯。

2 稱謂

與日期間空出一行，從第三行最左邊寫起，字尾加上逗號（親朋好友之間）或冒號（商務信函）。如果是一般朋友，可直接在名字前加上「Dear」，如「Dear Mary,」或「Dear Mary and Tom,」；如果是稱呼長輩或商業往來，可稱呼「Dear Mr./Ms./Mrs. Wang:」。如果是親人，可寫為「My dear father/mother,」。

> **NOTE**
> 如果是商務信件或正式公文，在稱呼後面要用冒號，而且也要用尊稱，如「Mr./Ms.」等等，例如「Dear Mr. Wang:」。如果是親朋好友之間的信函，在稱呼後面可以用逗號，例如「Dear John,」。

3 正文

與稱謂中間空出一行，有兩種書寫方法：

1. **齊頭式** 信函每一行的第一個字，由最左邊第一格開始寫起。商業書信多採齊頭式的寫作方式。

2. **半平頭式（標準格式）** 日期行、結束語和寫信人的身分（姓名、職位），一律居中或靠右；其他所有內容都左起頂格。

內文段落**可以是齊頭式，也可以縮排**，即每段落的第一行空出五個字母的空格後，再開始書寫，寫到第二行要換行時，須由最左邊第一格開始寫起。全民英檢並未規定書信寫作的格式，但讀者需要注意格式的一致性。

4 結束語

與正文結束中間再多空一行。有兩種寫法：如果是齊頭式，在最左邊第一格寫上結束語，如果是半平頭式，日期寫在中間靠右處。總之，**結束語要與日期對齊**。結束語第一字母需大寫，字尾加逗號。如果是朋友間往來信件，常使用 With my best wishes! 或 Take care! 等；正式的商務信件會用 Sincerely、Yours truly、Sincerely yours，或 Respectfully 等，這些詞後面要用逗號。如果收信人為長輩，亦可用 Yours respectfully 或 Sincerely 等表示。

5 簽名

寫信人的姓名，直接寫在結束語的下方。

> **NOTE**
> 結束語下要有寫信人的親手簽名，然後才是在電腦上打出來的名字。從結束語到打出來的名字之間要空三行，即按 Enter 鍵四次。如果是電子信函，則不需要簽名，直接在結束語的下方打出名字就行了。

Basic business letter formats
商業信件基本格式

Quality Cosmetics, Inc.
302 Beauty Lane, Suite 5
San Bruno, CA 94066
(415) 748-9852

❶ 信頭：公司商標名稱和地址
Letterhead: Sending company's name and address

Catherine Davies
15 Qingtong Rd.-1011
Pudong New District,
Shanghai, PRC 201203

November 2, 2015

Permissions Department
Harbinger Publishing
309 Ditmas Ave.
Brooklyn, NY 11218-4901

July 9, 2015

Dear Permissions Editor:

I would like to use one of your illustrations in my in-house report titled "Third-Quarter Growth in the Cosmetics Industry." The illustration is called "Girl Applying Lipstick."

Thank you in advance for your attention to my request. Please contact me as soon as possible at (415) 748-9852.

Regards,
Irina Safarova
Analyst, Quality Cosmetics

❷ 收信人名稱與地址
Recipient's name and address

Ms. Nina Lin
Double Design
Room 205, Building 3
Lane 2498, Pudong Avenue
Shanghai, PRC

Dear Ms. Lin:

I am writing to request an interview regarding Double Design's opening for a graphic designer.

I am a recent graduate of the Academy of Art with a degree in graphic design. For the past six months, I have interned with Studio Design in Shanghai, learning to apply the skills I gained in school. I would appreciate an opportunity to learn more about the graphic designer position and to discuss how I can contribute to your company.

I have enclosed my résumé for your reference. Please feel free to contact me for any reason at (021) 5184-3155 or by email at cath.davies@yahoo.com. Thank you for your attention. I look forward to hearing from you.

❸ 信件內容
Body text

Best regards,
Catherine Davies
Catherine Davies

Enc (1)

cc: Flora Lopez

❹ 結尾和簽名
Closing and signature

Three business letter styles
三種商業書信格式

❶ 齊頭式（block style）：廣受歡迎

❷ 改良齊頭式（modified block style）：亦常見

❸ 縮排式（indented style）：逐漸式微

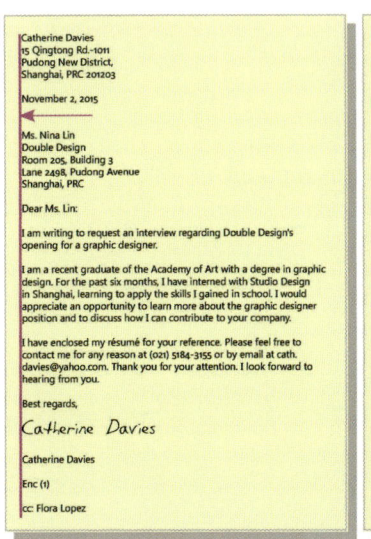

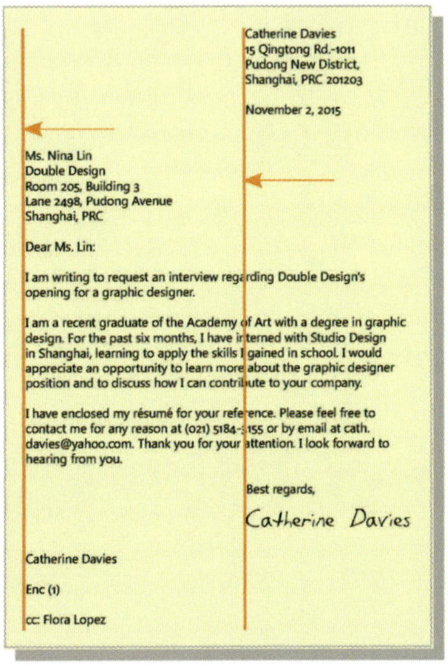

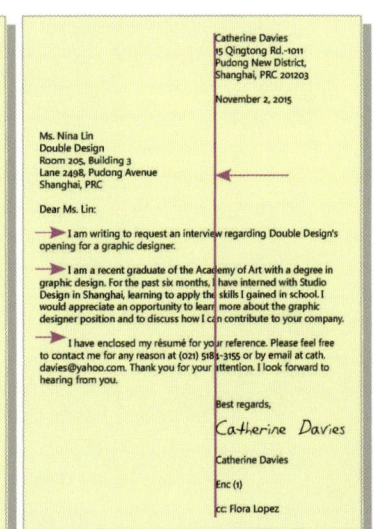

[Three sample letters shown side by side, each containing the same content addressed to Ms. Nina Lin from Catherine Davies, demonstrating block style, modified block style, and indented style formatting respectively.]

2 分析提示文字

根據提示文字,可以分析出**書信種類**、信件**書寫原因**、信中**應記載事項**等共三類。

1. **書信種類** 邀請函、感謝函、家書等等。因收信對象不同,信中的用字與語氣也有所區別。平輩的書信可以是輕鬆、不拘泥形式的寒暄;寫給長輩的信件就必須用字謹慎,語氣恭敬。
2. **信件書寫原因** 告知近況、詢問事項、恭喜對方等等。
3. **信中應記載事項** 提示文字會清楚說明信件內容應包含的細節,可將細節編號避免遺漏。細節內容的書寫順序也可以參考提示文字的順序。

作文範例

說明 上個星期,志明的弟弟志中前往美國攻讀兩年碩士,志明陪著母親到機場送機,當時母親非常擔心弟弟一個人出國。現在請你以哥哥志明的身分擬一封信給弟弟志中,詢問志中在美國生活適應的如何,並告訴他,母親非常掛念他。另外,順便要弟弟常打電話回家,好讓母親放心。

提示分析
1. **書信種類**:兄弟間的家書。
2. **信件書寫原因**:對弟弟志中的關心及叮嚀。
3. **信中應記載事項**:
   a 詢問美國的生活近況。
   b 告知母親的掛念。
   c 要弟弟常打電話回家,好讓母親放心。

3　擬列書信大綱

確定書信種類及書寫原因後，必須安排信件內容，擬列大綱。大綱內容除了參考提示文字中的應記載事項外，還必須自行構思符合內容的相關細節。

步驟 1　草擬大綱

1　信件開頭

收信人：從提示文字確認收信人的姓名及身分（志明的弟弟志中）。

寒暄問候：一般書信的開頭須先表達關心，問候對方近況，也可順便提起自己的近況。

2　切入主題：將提示中應記載事項逐一列出

① 詢問美國的生活近況。
② 告知母親的掛念。
③ 要弟弟常打電話回家，好讓母親放心。

3　信件結尾

期待回音、祝福對方。

書信大綱中除了制式的開頭寒暄問候語及結尾期待回音之外，主題內容是應試者必須自行構思的部分，以舉例說明的例子示範，則是指主題 ①②③ 的部分。

步驟 2　構思主題內容

進行主題內容構思時，同樣可參考提示文字前半段的背景說明，分析後可歸納出：

1 志中上星期剛前往美國。
2 志中一個人隻身前往美國。
3 志中的目的是攻讀碩士。
4 母親非常掛心。

從上述四點來構思的內容可能包括：詢問志中是否一切已安頓妥當（宿舍、學校等）；有無朋友照應；希望志中專心學業、早日學成歸國；不要忘記每個星期都要固定打通電話給母親等等。以上構思的內容可依順序插入主題大綱。

> **範例**
>
> ❶ 詢問美國的生活近況
> → 宿舍、學校是否安頓妥當,有無認識新朋友。
>
> ❷ 告知母親的掛念
> → 母親很擔心,所以希望他專心學業、早日學成歸國。
>
> ❸ 要弟弟常打電話回家,好讓母親放心
> → 每個星期都要固定撥通電話給母親。

4 常用句型

書寫時主要會遇到幾大類句型,如信件開頭的問候語、內容表達感謝之意並期待對方回音,以及信末的祝福語。只要把這幾類書信常用的句型熟記,寫作時將能更順利流暢。

1 問候寒暄

❶ I haven't heard from you for a long time. How have you been?
好久沒有你的消息,近來好嗎?

❷ How are you? I am thinking about you all the time. I hope you are doing fine.
你好嗎?我一直都很關心你,希望你一切都好。

❸ How are you? I haven't heard from you in a while. I hope that you are OK.
你好嗎?有一段時間沒有你的消息了,希望你過得不錯。

❹ It was really nice to hear from you.
聽到你的消息(收到你的信)真好。

❺ As usual, I was really happy to hear from you.
我非常開心能聽到你的消息(收到你的信總是令人開心)。

❻ I was so happy to hear from you!
我很高興聽到你的消息!

❼ How nice to hear from you again!
再聽到你的消息真好!

2 謝謝對方

1. Thanks so much for writing. — 謝謝你寫信給我。
2. Many thanks for your kind and warm letter. — 很感謝你體貼、令人感到溫暖的信件。
3. Thank you so much for your generous hospitality. — 很感謝你慷慨的款待。
4. Thank you for doing so much to make my trip(/visit) interesting. — 謝謝你做了這麼多，讓我的旅行（參觀）很有趣。
5. Thank you very much for your kind help on many occasions in the past. — 很謝謝你在過去許多時刻的協助。
6. Thank you for providing the information about . . . — 感謝你提供關於……的資訊。

3 期待回音

1. I love hearing from you. — 希望有你的消息。
2. I am looking forward to hearing from you soon. — 期盼早日有你的回音。
3. I am looking forward to your early reply. — 期待你早日回覆。
4. We hope that you will be able to join us and look forward to seeing you then. — 希望你可以加入我們，期待到時見面。

4 祝福對方

1. I hope that you have a happy day! — 希望你有快樂的一天！
2. Good luck in your new school year. — 祝你在新學年好運！
3. I hope you have a great year! — 希望你有很棒的一年（祝你來年順利）！
4. I'd like to take this opportunity to express my best wishes for you and your family. — 我想藉這個機會表達我對你和你家人的祝福。
5. I wish you great success in the future. — 祝你未來成功。

4 書信寫作範例

作文範例

說明 上個月，志明的大學同學Tom邀請他到家裡一起共進晚餐，用餐時大家享用了Tom的太太Mary所烹煮的美味晚餐，度過了一段愉快的時光。現在請你以志明的身分擬一封信給Tom，謝謝他的晚餐邀約，並告訴他當天晚上有哪些令你印象深刻的事。另外，順便邀請Tom和Mary在耶誕夜時到你家一起共進晚餐。

寫作步驟

1 書信寫作的格式：採齊頭式。

2 提示文字分析：
　① 書信種類：朋友間的書信。
　② 信件書寫原因：感謝及邀請。
　③ 信中應記載事項：
　　a. 謝謝Tom和Mary的晚餐邀請。
　　b. 當天晚上令你印象深刻的事。
　　c. 邀請Tom和Mary在耶誕夜時到你家共進晚餐。

3 擬列書信大綱：
　① 收信人：Tom。
　② 寒暄問候：近來好嗎？
　③ 謝謝上週的晚餐邀請。
　④ 令人印象深刻的事：稱讚Mary煮了好吃的晚餐及甜點、回憶大學的瘋狂事蹟等。
　⑤ 希望再辦個同學會，並邀請Tom和Mary在耶誕夜時共進晚餐。
　⑥ 期待回音，祝福對方及他們家人一切順利。

September 10, 2016

Dear Tom,

How have you been? Thank you for your invitation last week. Mary was a wonderful cook. I really enjoyed the dinner and the dessert.

I had a very pleasant time talking about the crazy things we did together in college. That night made me feel young again. That's why I have been thinking about having a class reunion party on Christmas Eve at my house. Would you and Mary like to join me? I will contact our other friends to come over. I am sure we will have a good time.

I look forward to hearing from you soon and hope everything is going well with you and your family.

Sincerely,

Chi-Ming

Chi-Ming

Unit 24 英文作文的寫作技巧

　　英文作文的寫作技巧與中譯英技巧有些類似。一般來說，很難要求英文非母語的讀者直接以英文思考，但若以中文來思考作文大綱時，**寫作上仍多半會運用到中譯英的技巧。**

　　下列所介紹的技巧中，包含了寫作時需注意的邏輯銜接，以及中譯英的相關技巧，技巧應用也包括了之前單元所介紹的「意譯」。

1 前後句的邏輯銜接

　　寫作是溝通的方法之一，寫作與說話最大的不同在於：說話時有手勢與面部表情可以輔助溝通，而寫作只能靠文字來溝通。因此，要將腦中的思想以文字方式呈現，文字的組成就必須謹慎而精確。

　　寫作最怕的就是跳躍性的思考，也就是作文的主旨沒有集中於一個題目上。常出現的情況是一篇作文中，前後句的主旨相差太遠或相互矛盾，而之後的文章內容又沒有解釋中間的變化，等於應試者寫了一大篇文章，但卻毫無重點可言。

1 利用圖例訓練邏輯寫作

　　以本圖為例，這張圖片可以發揮的角度很多，如果寫作時的大綱安排，沒有按照符合邏輯的方式處理，就很容易讓作文前後句相互矛盾。

以搭乘捷運的優缺點舉例來說：

優點
捷運方便、路線多、不會塞車、不用找車位。

缺點
捷運的停靠站數有限，有時還要轉乘公車。

優點　方便及路線多　←互相矛盾→　**缺點**　停靠站有限

　　雖然可以根據上述現象多加解釋，但是「方便及路線多」與「停靠站有限」的邏輯關係，可能需花費較多篇幅才能解釋其中的連接原因。中級英檢的作文句數需要在8到12句完成，所以某些論點必須捨棄，最好以單一貫通的主旨來連接前後文。

優點
捷運方便，大家不開車、街道不會塞車、可以減輕市區的交通負荷。

缺點
可惜只有都市居民才有機會搭乘捷運。

結論
希望未來捷運的服務可以普及化，讓更多人享受到捷運的便利。

　　用以上三點發展文章看來似乎流暢，但若深一層思考，可以發現「可惜只有都市居民才有機會搭乘捷運」的論點，與上一句「減輕市區交通負荷」產生矛盾。

優點　減輕市區交通負荷　←互相矛盾→　**缺點**　可惜只有都市居民才有機會搭乘捷運

矛盾處在於：

1 捷運的興建在幫助解決都市人口集中現象、紓解交通流量，所以捷運本來就是只有都市居民才會享受到的便捷服務。「可惜只有都市居民……」這句話出現了邏輯語病。

2 結論提到了「希望捷運普及化」，但論點的意義不夠明確，而捷運需要普及至郊區或鄉間的必要性待商榷。

因此上述邏輯可修正如下：

> **優點**
> 捷運方便，大家不開車、街道不會塞車、可以減輕市區的交通負荷。

> **缺點**
> 可惜只有某些都市的居民才有機會搭乘捷運。

> **結論**
> 希望未來捷運的服務可以推廣到更多城市，讓更多人享受到捷運的便利。

2 加強句子的邏輯概念

範例

My friend is an artist. He likes to eat pizza.
→ artist 和 pizza 似乎沒有什麼關聯

我的朋友是位藝術家。他喜歡吃披薩。

如果是要表達有個朋友喜歡吃披薩，可直接寫「I have a friend. He likes to eat pizza.」，不需特別寫出朋友的職業。若前一句寫出了朋友的職業，邏輯上後一句應該要接著陳述與朋友職業相關的內容。

下面針對以上例句作出修改，可以比較看看哪一句的邏輯性比較強。

1 My friend is an artist. He enjoys traveling around the world.
→ 「藝術家」和「喜歡旅遊」兩者有點相關，但邏輯關係還不夠明確。一般人也可以喜歡旅遊，不一定要是藝術家。

我的朋友是藝術家，他喜歡環遊世界。

2 My friend is an editor for a travel magazine. He enjoys traveling around the world.

我的朋友是旅遊雜誌的編輯，他喜歡環遊世界。

→ 因為是「旅遊雜誌的編輯」所以「喜歡旅遊」，兩者的關聯度與邏輯性比〈例1〉更強，也較具有說服力。

3 My friend is an artist. He enjoys traveling around the world in order to gain inspiration for his paintings.

我的朋友是藝術家。他喜歡環遊世界，因為可以汲取繪畫的創作靈感。

→ 「藝術家」和「喜歡旅遊是為了汲取創作靈感」，兩者呈現清楚而明確的因果邏輯。句子作出這樣的修正，可以幫助寫作主旨集中，不會偏離主題太遠。

3 短文分析「Is honesty always the best policy?」

英文短文

¹My friend is an artist. ²He often asks me how I feel about his paintings. ³I want to tell him how I honestly feel, but I am afraid that the truth might hurt his feelings. ⁴People always say that honesty is always the best policy. ⁵However, if being honest could hurt a friend's feelings, what should I do?

中文翻譯

我的朋友是藝術家。他常問我覺得他的繪畫如何。我想告訴他我真正的感覺，但我怕實話會傷人。人們總是說誠實為上策。然而，假如實話會傷了朋友的感覺，那我該怎麼做呢？

藉由觀察短文的關鍵字，可分析英文前後句的文字相關性或比較性。

句1 第一句的artist（藝術家）帶出第二句的paintings（繪畫）。

句2 第二句的ask帶出第三句的回答tell；第二句的feel帶出第三句的how I honestly feel。

句3 第三句的the truth might hurt his feelings，對應到第四句的honesty is always the best policy。

句5 第五句中的疑問what should I do，回應第三句所提到的問題（I want to tell him how I honestly feel）與可能的衝突（the truth might hurt his feelings）。

2 轉換主旨的語氣轉折詞

一篇文章的主旨需前後一致，才能發展出明確的邏輯概念，但若是想**轉換主旨**或**帶出新訊息**時，需藉助**語氣轉折詞**來帶出轉變。

同樣地，運用語氣轉折詞還是必須要有清楚的邏輯關係，像因果關係用 so/because，有對照比較用 but/although/however 等。常用的語氣轉折詞在對等連接詞、副詞子句連接詞，及連接副詞單元中作過介紹。

以捷運圖片為例，在草擬作文大綱時，不一定會將轉折的語氣列入大綱中，但**在陳述支持論點後，提出反向論點前**，常需利用語氣轉折詞來帶出對照比較。

捷運圖的例子剛好是正反意見的對照，所以可使用 however 作為兩句的語氣轉折詞。

> 正
> . . . With fewer people driving their cars, this rapid transit system helps cities relieve the traffic burden.

> 反
> **However**, currently in Taiwan, it is a pity that only certain cities provide this efficient and convenient service.

→ however 的使用，將前一句捷運的優勢，帶到下一句中討論捷運仍然有什麼缺點有待改善。

下面有七個例句，分別是組成一篇短文的各句。試分析下列例子，並且使用適當的轉折連接詞。

句 1 Learning a foreign language involves many things.

句 2 Learning a foreign culture is one of those many things.

→ Learning a foreign language involves many things. In fact, learning a foreign culture is one of those many things.

> 第一句陳述「學習外語包括許多事情」，第二句點出「學習外國文化就是其中之一」。分析後發現第一句與第二句的主旨相同，只是第二句清楚地點出主旨，因此在連接詞部分可考慮 and；連接副詞的選擇更多，有 moreover、in addition、in fact 等。這裡選擇使用 in fact，是希望達到強調的目的。

句 3 Culture determines many of the words or body language people say or use.

句 4 When Chinese get together, they tend to shake hands or ask each other whether they have eaten a meal.

→ Culture determines many of the words or body language people say or use. For example, when Chinese get together, they tend to shake hands or ask each other whether they have eaten a meal.

> 第三句說明「文化決定人們說的話與肢體語言」，第四句舉例說明「中國人見面的握手習慣或常用問候語『吃飽了沒』」。分析後發現，第四句是在加以解釋第三句，因此轉折詞可使用 for example、for instance。

句 5 Western people like to say hello and give a hug or a quick kiss on the cheek to greet each other.

→ **On the other hand**, Western people like to say hello and give a hug or a quick kiss on the cheek to greet each other.

> 第五句順著第四句的邏輯，舉了另一個文化影響問候語及身體語言的例子，轉折語可有兩種選擇：一是呈現對比的「on the other hand」，或直接提出另一例子「another example is that . . .」。

句 6 Many people don't realize the essence of learning a foreign language lies in learning its culture.

→ **Generally speaking**, many people don't realize the essence of learning a foreign language lies in learning its culture.

> 第六句話是陳述一般現象，轉折詞可用 generally speaking、in general 等。

句 7 They would probably miss the most interesting part of learning a foreign language.

→ **Therefore**, they would probably miss the most interesting part of learning a foreign language.

> 分析第七句與第六句的關係：第六句陳述「許多人不知道學外語的精華是在學習文化」，第七句表達「他們可能失掉學習外語的真正樂趣。」這兩句呈現了因果關係「因為不知道……所以失掉……」，可用的連接詞包括 so、because，或連接副詞 therefore、as a result 等。
> 這裡用 therefore 來連接。

3 以關鍵字發展句型

　　如先前所述，英文作文檢定拿分的基本前提是「不確定拼法的字不用，沒有把握的句子不寫」。在寫作時，須瞭解**學習語言的最佳方法是模仿，而不是創造**。若憑空寫出自己想像的句子，很有可能不符合文法結構。

　　因此在擬列寫作大綱時，**可以把每個句子的關鍵字圈出**，中文或英文皆可，然後在腦海裡搜尋與關鍵字相關的片語或句型，把曾經學過的類似句型應用出來。若想不起來可運用的片語，就利用中文關鍵字搭配意譯技巧，換個簡單的方式表達。

1 練習找出句中關鍵字

練習 1

詹姆士立志成為作家。

- 關鍵字：立志
- 相關片語：to decide to、to be determined to、to aspire to
- 例句：James aspired to become a writer.

練習 2

他閱讀各式各樣的書籍。

- 關鍵字：各式各樣
- 相關片語：a variety of ＋ 名詞、many different kinds of ＋ 名詞、to be various
- 例句：He reads a variety of books.

練習 3

他盡可能地到各地旅遊以擴展經驗。

- 關鍵字：盡可能地擴展經驗
- 相關片語：as . . . as possible、to acquire/gain/enlarge/enrich experience
- 例句：He tried to visit as many places as possible in order to enrich his understanding of the world.

練習 4

如果有機會出書，他不僅希望能贏得父母的讚揚，還希望獲得世界的認可。

- 關鍵字：贏得讚揚；不僅……還……
- 相關片語：to earn/win praise、to gain/obtain recognition
  not only . . . but also、both . . . and . . .
- 例句：If he has the chance to publish his works, he wishes not only to win his parents' praise but also to gain international recognition.

2　短文示範「The person who has an influence on me」

句 1

媽媽是影響我最深的人。

翻譯 1　My mother is the person who has influenced me the most.

翻譯 2　My mother is the person who has the most influence on me.

句 2

鄰居都知道她很有耐心，從不亂發脾氣。

翻譯 1　Everyone in the neighborhood knows that she is very patient and never loses her temper.

翻譯 2　In the neighborhood, she is known for being patient and never losing her temper.

句 3

媽媽常常鼓勵我追尋夢想，勇敢接受挑戰，永不放棄嘗試（與其放棄，不如勇敢接受挑戰）。

翻譯 1 My mother always encourages me to pursue my dreams and be brave to meet any challenges. She teaches me that I should never give up.

翻譯 2 My mother always encourages me to follow my dreams and bravely meet any challenges rather than give up.

句 4

她也讓我瞭解成功建築在努力之上，但努力不一定都導致成功。

翻譯 1 She also makes me understand that success is built upon hard work, but hard work doesn't always lead to success.

翻譯 2 She also lets me understand that one should work hard to achieve success, but hard work doesn't always result in success.

句 5

因此，我很能面對人生中的失敗與挫折。

翻譯 1 Therefore, I am good at dealing with failures and frustrations in life.

翻譯 2 That is why I don't have trouble facing failures and frustrations in life.

4 英文字詞的慣用搭配

在英文寫作時，需特別留意英文字詞的搭配。某個英文字一定會加上另一個固定的字使用，如特定動詞會與慣用的名詞作搭配。另外在練習將中文句轉換成英文句時，也會發現某些中文說法，未必就是直接翻譯的英文字，所以下面將介紹常用的搭配組合。

組合 1

養成習慣　to foster/make a habit of . . .
戒掉習慣　to abandon a habit of . . . /
　　　　　to break the habit of . . .

組合 2

吃午餐　eat lunch / have lunch
吃藥　✔ take medicine
　　　✘ eat medicine

吃午餐和吃藥的動詞雖都為「吃」，但吃食物通常會用 eat，吃藥則有「服用藥物」的意思，所以用 take。

組合 3

收拾玩具　✔ put away one's toys
　　　　　✘ collect toys

「收拾玩具」必須使用動詞片語 put away one's toys。
注意不要陷入中英對照的制式翻譯。

組合 4

持續／不斷／經常 continuous/unceasing/regular

以英文字詞搭配的習慣來看，與名詞練習（practice）搭配的形容詞多用 constant，因此這舉例而言，「學習英文最好的方法就是持續／不斷／經常的練習」這句話可以寫成：「The best way to study English is constant practice.」。

組合 5

大量的練習
- ✔ considerable/extensive practice
- ✘ big practice

英文字 big 比較沒有「大量的」之意，這裡不適用中文直譯。

組合 6

蘋果般的粉嫩臉蛋
- ✔ rosy cheeks
- ✘ apple face / pink face

「蘋果般的」是一種形容，如果真的看到「蘋果」兩字就用 apple，這種表現方式除了十分奇怪，也無法正確傳達意思。

1 動詞與名詞的慣用搭配，用紅色標示的文字可代換右方文字

❶ 寫日記 I keep a journal in English to improve my writing ability. — write

我用英文寫日記，以增進我的寫作能力。

❷ 交作業 The teacher asked us to turn in the homework on Monday. — hand in

老師叫我們星期一交作業。

❸ 欣賞風景 We were sitting in the car and admiring the scenery along the highway. — enjoying

我們坐在車裡，欣賞公路的風景。

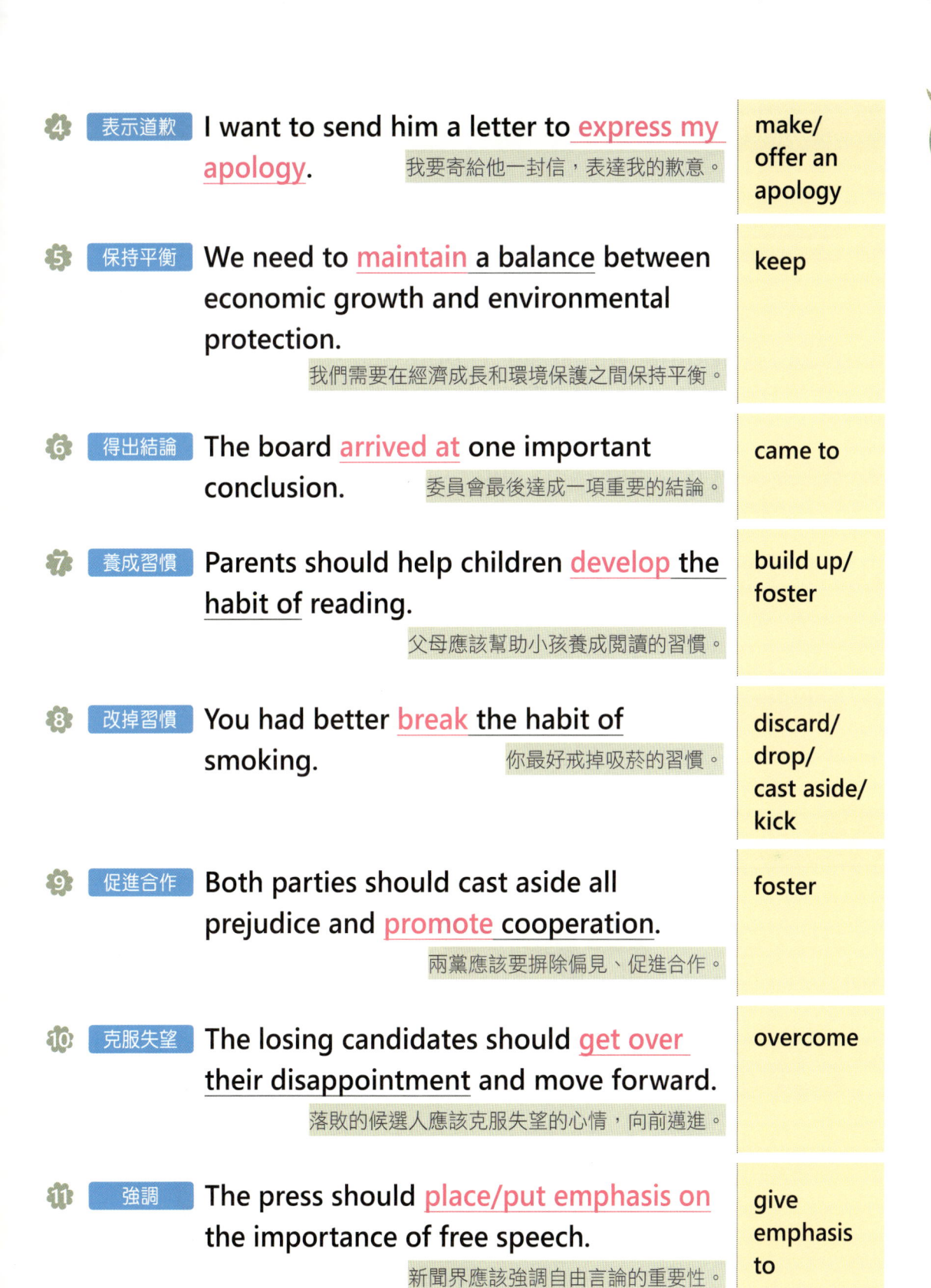

#	中文	例句	其他搭配
4	表示道歉	I want to send him a letter to <u>express my apology</u>. 我要寄給他一封信，表達我的歉意。	make/ offer an apology
5	保持平衡	We need to <u>maintain a balance</u> between economic growth and environmental protection. 我們需要在經濟成長和環境保護之間保持平衡。	keep
6	得出結論	The board <u>arrived at</u> one important conclusion. 委員會最後達成一項重要的結論。	came to
7	養成習慣	Parents should help children <u>develop the habit of</u> reading. 父母應該幫助小孩養成閱讀的習慣。	build up/ foster
8	改掉習慣	You had better <u>break the habit of</u> smoking. 你最好戒掉吸菸的習慣。	discard/ drop/ cast aside/ kick
9	促進合作	Both parties should cast aside all prejudice and <u>promote cooperation</u>. 兩黨應該要摒除偏見、促進合作。	foster
10	克服失望	The losing candidates should <u>get over their disappointment</u> and move forward. 落敗的候選人應該克服失望的心情，向前邁進。	overcome
11	強調	The press should <u>place/put emphasis on</u> the importance of free speech. 新聞界應該強調自由言論的重要性。	give emphasis to
12	樹立榜樣	His brother has <u>set an example</u> in his family. 他哥哥給家裡樹立了榜樣。	

321

2 動詞與副詞的慣用搭配，用紅色標示的文字可代換右方文字

一般而言，一個句子中如果同時出現現在式與過去式，這個句子很可能不正確。

1 熱烈地慶祝 We warmly celebrated grandmother's birthday.
我們熱烈地慶祝祖母的生日。

2 堅決反對 Mother was strongly opposed to his moving to Hualien.
媽媽強烈反對他搬去花蓮。

> actively/ firmly/ totally

3 傾盆大雨 It is raining cats and dogs.
→ cats and dogs 為副詞片語
現在正在下傾盆大雨。

4 受傷嚴重 Sam was hurt seriously.
→ 受重傷副詞可替換 severely/badly，輕傷應搭配 slightly
山姆傷得很重。

5 生動地描述 Max vividly described his trip to Disneyland.
馬克思生動描述他的迪士尼樂園之旅。

3 形容詞與名詞的慣用搭配，用紅色標示的文字可代換右方文字

1 負起完全的責任 The manager took full responsibility for this mistake.
經理為這個錯誤負起完全的責任。

2 非凡的成就 Brian's brilliant achievement made his parents proud.
布萊恩非凡的成就，讓他的父母很驕傲。

3 激烈的競爭　The newly-launched product has to face keen competition in the market.　　fierce/tough

新上市的商品必須面對市場的激烈競爭。

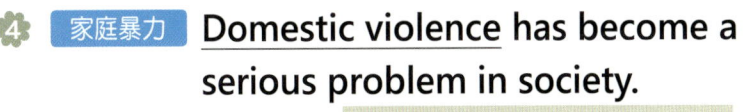

4 家庭暴力　Domestic violence has become a serious problem in society.

家庭暴力已成為嚴重的社會問題。

5 愉快的氣氛　Our neighbors really like the cheerful atmosphere in my family.　　pleasant

鄰居非常喜歡我們家的愉快氣氛。

6 工整的字跡　Her clear handwriting often helps her win extra points.　　good/neat

她工整的字跡常幫她獲得額外的分數。

7 呆板的個性　I don't like his boring personality.　我不喜歡他呆板的個性。

8 豐富的想像力　This writer was famous for his rich imagination.

這位作家以豐富的想像力著稱。

　　想要熟悉此類字詞搭配，可以透過一般的相關片語書籍來學習。另外，大量閱讀也可以增加字詞篩選的熟練度；或者也可以使用辭典來查閱相關資訊。

Unit 25 英文寫作的常犯錯誤與對策

句構、文法和詞彙是構成英文寫作的重要要素，若使用錯誤則不但會使作文閱讀困難，甚至會造成會錯意的情況，本單元整理一些常見的錯誤，並提供因應對策，增強寫作技能。

1 完整的英文句子結構

1 大寫字母與句點

中文寫作與英文相當不同，中文寫作的內容只要屬於同一主旨，是可以一整個段落皆以逗號分隔句子，只需在段落結束時，使用句號。

英文寫作則不同，只要一句話的語意已經完整，就需要用句點作結，因此要判斷英文句的結束，**大寫字母**與**句點**是句子完整與否的重要依據。

英文句的**第一個字母大寫**，**句尾以句點**（問號或驚嘆號）**結束**，是最基本的要求。常出現的錯誤形式包括：前一句以句點結束，後一句的第一個字母卻用小寫；或在逗號之後的句子以大寫字母開頭；又或用逗號連接過多的句子、未使用連接詞，或未適時斷句等。這些若在寫作時能稍加注意，寫作成績的失分便可減少。

2 主句與子句

一個完整的句子中至少要有一個**主詞**及一個**動詞**，若出現兩個以上的主詞或動詞時，就必須使用**連接詞**；而若想將兩個以上的句子連接成一個句子時，也不可隨意以逗號連接，需先分析句子間的邏輯關係，再選擇適當的連接詞。

對等連接詞連接兩個獨立對等句，而使用**附屬連接詞**時，必須區分**主句**與**子句**。因為英文文法結構嚴謹，建議讀者在連接句子時，以兩個句子為限，也就是主句和子句。主句和子句的關係清楚明確，較不易發生錯誤；超過三個句子的連接容易產生主句與子句混淆的情形，可盡量避免。

1 對等連接詞 and 連接兩組動詞

❀ Last summer, Joyce <u>quit her job</u> and <u>went to France to learn French for a month</u>.　去年夏天，喬伊絲辭去工作，去法國學了一個月的法文。

→ and 連接 quit her job 和 went to France 兩組動詞片語。

2 對等連接詞 but 連接兩個對等句

1 Joyce didn't expect a great improvement in her French, but she hoped to visit many famous places.

→ but 前後連接兩個意思對等的句子。

喬伊絲不期望法文能有多大的進步,但她希望去參觀許多著名的地方。

3 選擇兩句連接成為一句,避免三句以上的連接

1 She arrived in Paris.

她到達了巴黎。

2 She was so excited that she couldn't sleep the first night.

她非常興奮以至於在那裡的第一個晚上無法成眠。

3 She finally fell asleep at three in the morning.

她終於在早上三點的時候睡著了。

> **連接 1** 附屬連接詞 when 連接句一和句二
>
> When she arrived in Paris, she was so excited that she couldn't sleep the first night.
>
> 抵達巴黎的第一晚,她興奮地睡不著覺。

> **連接 2** 對等連接詞 but 連接句二和句三
>
> She was so excited that she couldn't sleep the first night there, but she finally fell asleep at three in the morning.
>
> 雖然在巴黎的第一晚,她興奮地睡不著覺,但她終於在早上三點時睡著了。

> **簡化連接 2**
>
> She was so excited the first night there that she didn't fall asleep until three in the morning.
>
> 在巴黎的第一晚,她興奮地睡不著覺,直到早上三點才睡著。

2 英文句的文法檢查

1 檢查名詞的單複數

名詞的單複數看起來很簡單，屬於初級文法，但若未培養敏感度，即使英文程度很好的人，也常會在這個地方犯錯。

1 主詞單複數決定動詞、名詞、補語、所有格等相關字詞的變化

❶ That **girl goes** to school every day.
　　主詞 girl 為單數，後接 goes
　那女孩每天上學去。

❷ Those **girls go** to school every day.
　　主詞 girls 為複數，後接 go
　那些女孩們每天上學去。

❸ **John and I are** good friends.
　約翰和我是好朋友。

❹ Not only my brother but also **my parents are** coming to visit me.
　不只我哥哥（弟弟），還有我的父母都來看我了。

❺ Either Charlie or **I am** going to join the school basketball team.
　不是查理就是我會加入籃球校隊。

2 區分虛主詞與真正主詞

❶ **There have been two men** standing at the entrance of that building all day.
　　　　　　　　真主詞
　有兩個男人站在那棟房子的入口，已經整整一天了。

❷ **There was some cheese** left in the refrigerator.
　　　　　　真主詞
　有一些起司放在冰箱裡。

327

3 區分主詞與介系詞受詞

❶ **One** of **my friends** failed the exam.
　主詞　　　介系詞受詞
　我的一個朋友沒有通過考試。

→ 真正決定動詞單複數的，是介系詞 of/to/in 等前面的主詞。

❷ **The key** to **the house** was left on the table.
　房門的鑰匙留在桌上了。

❸ **The answers** to **the question** are still open for discussion.
　這問題的解答仍待討論。

❹ **Listening** to **the radio** in the evenings is a good way to relax.
　在晚上聽廣播是放鬆的好方法。

4 all of / most of / some of / half of 作主詞

若主詞片語中出現 all of、most of、some of、half of 等，需注意主詞動詞的一致性。of 之後接複數可數名詞，需搭配複數動詞；of 之後接不可數名詞，需搭配單數動詞。

❶ **Some of** the **students** are from single-parent families.
　　　　　複數，接 are
　有一些學生來自單親家庭。

❷ **Some of** the **homework** involves using computers in the lab.
　　　　　單數，接單數動詞
　有些作業需要用到研究室的電腦。

❸ **All of** the assignments have to be returned.　全部的作業必須繳回。

❹ **All of** the information has been verified twice.
　所有的消息都查證過兩次。

2 檢查動詞的變化

需要注意動詞的時態、搭配助動詞的變化,以及肯定／否定／疑問句等,雖屬於初級文法,但仍須在寫作完成檢查錯誤時特別留意。

1 助動詞之後的動詞為原形動詞

❶ My parents may go to the United Sates to visit my sister this summer.
今年夏天,我的父母也許會去美國看我姐姐。

❷ If they go, they will stop by Hawaii.
假如他們去的話,他們會在夏威夷停留。

❸ I wish I could go with them.
我希望我可以和他們一起去。

❹ But I don't have time to join them.
但我沒有時間和他們一起去。

2 be 動詞之後的動詞,主動為現在分詞,被動為過去分詞

❶ Mother was preparing dinner when I called home.
→ 人主動準備晚餐
我打電話回家的時候,媽媽正在準備晚餐。

❷ The dinner was left in the refrigerator.
→ 晚餐被留了下來
晚餐被留在冰箱裡。

3 have/has/had 之後的動詞為過去分詞

❶ Alex has finished his homework.
艾力克斯已經寫完功課了。
→ 功課已經做完了,為「現在完成式」

❷ Tom had eaten dinner when his parents got home.
→ 兩件事情都發生在過去,吃晚餐比父母回家更早,所以用「過去完成式」
父母回到家時,湯姆已經吃過晚餐。

4 肯定句與否定句的比較

句型 1　簡單式否定

助動詞 + not + 原形動詞

肯定 Ron <u>walks</u> to school.　　　　　榮恩走路上學。
否定 Ron <u>doesn't like</u> to walk to school.　榮恩不喜歡走路上學。

句型 2　進行式否定

be 動詞 + not + 現在分詞

肯定 He <u>is walking</u> to school now.　　　他現在正走路去學校。
否定 He <u>is not enjoying</u> walking to school at all.
　　　　　　　　　　　　　　　　　　　他一點也不喜歡走路上學。

句型 3　完成式否定

have/has/had + not + 過去分詞

肯定 He <u>has arrived</u> at school.　　　　他已經到學校了。
否定 He <u>has not prepared</u> himself for his classes yet.
　　　　　　　　　　　　　　　　　　　他還沒準備好上課。

5 肯定句改為疑問句的方法

句型 1　簡單式句型

助動詞移至句首

肯定 He <u>prepares</u> dinner every day.　　他每天準備晚餐。
問句 <u>Does he</u> prepare dinner every day?　他每天準備晚餐嗎？

句型 2　進行式句型

be 動詞移至句首

肯定　He is preparing dinner now.　　他正在準備晚餐。
問句　Is he preparing dinner now?　　他正在準備晚餐嗎？

句型 3　完成式句型

have/has/had 移至句首

肯定　He has prepared dinner.　　他準備好晚餐了。
問句　Has he prepared dinner?　　他準備好晚餐了嗎？

6　祈使句

句型 1　將原形動詞放在句首

1. Open the door!　　開門！
2. Be a good student!　　要當個好學生！

句型 2　否定形式

助動詞 do ＋ not ＋ 原形動詞

1. Don't open the door!　　不要開門！
2. Don't be such a baby.　　不要這麼幼稚！

3 檢查時態的邏輯

一篇文章中需留意時態變化的邏輯，凡是出現與時間有關的詞彙時，就需注意**時態變化**。

`圖片申論` 須依據圖片內容及寫作方向來決定時態。

`短文銜接` 因屬生活經驗的敘述，所以多為過去式。

`書信寫作` 各種時態都有可能，需依文章內容作出判斷。

以下就一篇短文範例加以分析。

作文範例

My grandparents live in I-lan. I love to visit them because I-lan is a wonderful place.

Last weekend, my parents and I got up very early in the morning to go to I-lan. We took my uncle's car. Along the way we bought different kinds of fruit.

When we arrived at Grandma's house, she had cooked lunch. Everyone enjoyed Grandma's homemade meal. After lunch, we shared the fruit that we had bought on the way. It was really delicious.

In the afternoon, my uncle and I went for a walk to a nearby mountain. We climbed to the top. The view up there was really magnificent. Since coming home, I have thought about that view and hoped to climb that mountain many more times.

範例分析

短文共分四段，每一段根據事物發生的順序與時間邏輯，而使用不同的時態。

1. 第一段的第一、二句為事實的陳述，使用現在式 live 和 love。
2. 第二段開頭的關鍵字 last weekend，點出了文章的時態轉換，因此從這句開始就必須使用過去式配合 last weekend 的時間邏輯。
3. 第三段由 when 帶出過去式的子句，因此主要子句必須使用過去完成式 had cooked 配合時間順序；第三句中的 had bought 也是配合主句的動詞時態。
4. 第四段第四句的 since coming home，再次轉換時態，因此之後的句子皆需搭配現在完成式，用 have thought about。

中文翻譯

我的祖父母住在宜蘭，宜蘭是一個很棒的地方，所以我喜歡去拜訪他們。

上個週末，我的父母和我起了一大早要去宜蘭。我們搭叔叔的車，沿途還買了好幾種水果。

我們到達祖母家的時候，她已經煮好了午餐，每個人都享用了祖母自己煮的午餐。吃完午餐後，大家一起吃了路上買的水果，真的很好吃。

下午的時候，叔叔和我到了附近的一座山散步。我們爬上山，那裡的風景真的很壯觀。回到家之後，我一直想起那裡的風景，希望還能再多去爬幾次那座山。

3 易混淆的字詞

1 區分 make 和 do 的動詞片語

「make」和「do」在中文意義上很相近，都有「做……」之意。一開始學習相關片語時，若未加留意，很容易造成混淆。通常來說，「to make something」的中文意義是「**製造**某物」，而人要**完成一件事情**會使用動詞 do。

以下是「make」和「do」相關的動詞片語。

do 的動詞片語
- do the dishes 洗碗盤
- do the assignments/homework 做功課
- do the work 做工作
- do one's laundry 洗某人的衣服
- do somebody a favor 幫助某人
- do one's best 盡全力
- do the right thing 做對的事情

make 的動詞片語
- make one's clothes/curtains 製作某人的衣服／窗簾
- make coffee/a cake for a party 為派對作咖啡／蛋糕
- make a meal/lunch/dinner 煮一餐／午餐／晚餐
- make friends 交朋友
- make a mistake 犯錯
- make a response 作出回應

- make an effort 付出努力
- make an impression 留下印象
- make a difference 作出改變
- make (more) money 賺（更多）錢

2 區分現在分詞和過去分詞的形容詞

現在分詞（-ing 結尾）的形容詞帶有**主動**意味，**過去分詞**（規則變化類的動詞為 -ed 結尾）的形容詞帶有**被動**意味。在選擇之前，須確定形容詞與所修飾名詞間的關係為**主動**或**被動**。

❶ The movie we saw last night was really amusing.
→ amusing 修飾主詞 the movie；
電影帶來愉快的感覺，為**主動**含意

我們昨天晚上看的電影真有趣。

❷ We felt highly amused.
→ amused 修飾主詞 we；
我們因為看電影而覺得愉快，人受到電影的影響，為**被動**含意

我們覺得非常愉快。

❸ The man who was smoking was asked to go outside.
→ 人在抽菸，為**主動**；
但該男子被請到外面，為**被動**

那個抽菸的人男子被請到了室外。

❹ The smoked salmon was served on a toasted bagel.
→ 鮭魚「被煙燻過」增加食物風味，
貝果則是「被放入烤箱烤過」，兩者皆有**被動**含意

煙燻鮭魚被放在烤過的貝果上。

Quiz 31

段落改錯：直接在錯誤處劃線並訂正（括號中的數字為錯誤數目的提示）。

1 A tip on practicing English

I think it's good idea to practice English with foreigner. When we talk to them in English, we have to forgot our own language. By talking, we can improve our pronunciation. We can also learn many useful phrases and about Western culture. If you are afraid of talk to foreigners, you can try to practice English with your classmate and friend that have excellent English. You can share the happinesses of learning English. The most important thing are to read and listen to English extensively. Then open your mouth bravely. Remember practice makes perfect. (8)

2 Going to a movie

I readed an article about the movie *Brokeback Mountain* in the newspaper. I ask my father whether he can take some time off to watch it with me. Father was a very busy businessman, so I tryed to persuade him that it was a good movie and it had won many movie prizes. Father finally agreed to watch the movie on our TV. I was so happy, and I was sure we will have a good time together. (5)

3 Home alone

Saturday was my parents' wedding anniversary. My brother and me encouraged they to go out and have a romantic dinner. at first, mother was a little worried about leaving us alone at home, but I promised to take good care of my brother. Mother finally agreed with this idea. After them left, I made some fried rice for dinner. Then my brother and I watched a movie on HBO together. Before going to bed, I made sure my brother had taken a shower and brushed his teeth. I also left a light on in the living room for my parents. I hoped them had an unforgettable anniversary. (5)

Quiz 32

英文作文

1. 俗話說「一種米養百樣人」，在茫茫人海中，你如何尋找真正的朋友？是看成績好壞、外表、財富，還是身分地位？請描述你選擇真正朋友的方法。

2. 如果你有一天請假沒有上學（或上班），你覺得會是因為何種原因造成？請描述你的這一天。

3. 人們常在歲末年初時，為自己許下新年新希望（New Year's resolutions）。你是否也曾立下志願，要在新的一年中達成什麼目標？你會如何去實現新年新希望？

PART 6

十篇寫作練習與實例解析

本單元設計十回合的寫作測驗，透過實際的寫作練習，活用前面章節所學過的各種寫作技巧，同時複習並練習實際寫作，訓練作文的靈感發想，並熟悉寫作手感。

1 我的嗜好

說明	1. 依提示在「答案卷」上寫一篇英文作文。 2. 文長約 150 單詞（words）左右。
提示	以 My Favorite Hobby 為題，寫一篇英文作文，第一段說明你最喜愛的嗜好及原因；第二段說明這個嗜好和你的關係。

英文範文

My Favorite Hobby

  Listening to music is my favorite hobby. Music has led an essential role in my daily life. It reaches the depth of my soul. It not only cultivates my mind but also enriches my spiritual life. Most importantly, it provides an outlet to relieve the pressures in my daily life. I can imagine what the world would be like without music.

  Depending on the mood I am in, I choose different kinds of music. When I am sad or depressed, I listen to some soft music while indulging myself in crying. If I am in a good mood, I turn on some rock music and dance to it. Before I go to bed, I like to play some classical music or jazz. What more, New Age music is for studying. In a word, I think I would probably go crazy without music.

1 寫作指導

中心主旨	音樂是我最喜愛的嗜好。
第一段	在開頭點出主題句，之後舉出音樂的角色、對自己的重要性及影響，來說明音樂是最喜愛的嗜好的原因。 ✓ 主題句　　聽音樂是我最喜愛的嗜好。 ✓ 次要句　　（說明音樂是我最喜愛的嗜好的原因。） 　　　　　　1) 音樂在我的日常生活中扮演著不可或缺的角色。 　　　　　　2) 音樂能觸及我的心靈深處。 　　　　　　3) 音樂不僅陶冶了我的心靈，也豐富了我的精神生活。 　　　　　　4) 更重要的是，音樂提供了一個抒發我日常生活壓力的管道。 ✓ 結論　　　我無法想像要是沒有音樂的話，這個世界會變成什麼樣子。
第二段	利用例子來說明嗜好和我的關係。 ✓ 主題句　　依據不同的心情，我會聽不同類型的音樂。 ✓ 次要句　　（用舉例來支持說明主題句） 　　　　　　1) 當我難過或沮喪時，我會聽些輕音樂，然後放縱自己大哭一場。 　　　　　　2) 如果我心情好的話，我會放些搖滾樂且隨著音樂手舞足蹈。 　　　　　　3) 在我睡覺前，我會聽些古典樂或爵士樂。 　　　　　　4) 此外，當我在念書時，我會放些新世紀音樂。 ✓ 結論　　　總之，如果沒有音樂的話，我可能會瘋掉。

2 重要單字

1	**essential** [ɪˋsɛnʃəl]	(a.) 必要的;不可缺的 Air and water are essential to living things. 空氣和水是生命所不可或缺的要素。
2	**cultivate** [ˋkʌltə͵vet]	(v.) 陶冶;培養 Trista cultivates her mind by participating in artistic and cultural activities. 翠絲塔藉由參與藝術與文化活動來陶冶性情。
3	**enrich** [ɪnˋrɪtʃ]	(v.) 使豐富 Reading novels and listening to classical music enrich Jason spiritual life. 閱讀小說和聽古典音樂,豐富了傑森的精神生活。
4	**outlet** [ˋaʊtlɛt]	(n.)(感情或精力等的)發洩途徑 Keeping a diary is Lucy's only form of emotional outlet. 寫日記是露西發洩情緒的唯一方式。
		NOTE → outlet 後若要接名詞,要加介系詞 for,即「outlet for + 名詞」,表示為「……的發洩途徑」。 例 Playing the guitar provides an outlet for Rita's energy and talents. 彈吉他是莉塔展現活力與天分的方式。
5	**relieve** [rɪˋliv]	(v.) 紓解;使寬慰 Joanna felt relieved after she had received Tom's call. 接到湯姆的來電之後,喬安娜就感到安心多了。

3　重要句子及片語

1

Listening to music is my favorite hobby.
聽音樂是我最喜愛的嗜好。

以動名詞片語（listening to music）為主詞視為單數，所以要用單數動詞。以動作為句子主詞時，要將動詞改為動名詞（V-ing），這是常見且重要的用法。

2

Music has led an essential role in my daily life.
音樂在我的日常生活中扮演著不可或缺的角色。

lead/play ｛ an essential / an important / a vital / a critical / a indispensable ｝ role/part

「扮演一個不可或缺的角色」的用法後面常接「in + 名詞片語」，表示「在……當中（扮演不可或缺的角色）」，例如：

◆ play an essential role ｛ in my daily life（在我日常生活中）/ in my school life（在我的學校生活裡）｝

3

. . . what the world would be like without music.
要是沒有音樂的話，這個世界會變成什麼樣子。

這是一句假設語氣，與現在事實相反，所以要用過去式 would。

※ 好用句型：

I can't imagine what the world would be like without . . .
我無法想像要是沒有……的話，這個世界會變成什麼樣子。

4

It not only cultivates my mind but also enriches my spiritual life.
音樂不僅陶冶了我的心靈，也豐富了我的精神生活。

在「not only A but (also) B」（不僅 A 而且 B）的句型中，A 與 B 必須是對等的字、片語或子句。also 可省略。這個句子裡，是連接了兩個對等的動詞。
在以下例句中，它連接了兩個對等的子句：

‧ Not only is Bob an English teacher, but he is also the conductor of our church's choir. 鮑伯不但是一位英語老師，還是我們教會合唱團的指揮呢。

◆ not only 放在句首，句子要倒裝。

5	**Most importantly, it provides an outlet to relieve the pressures in my daily life.** 更重要的是，音樂提供了一個抒發我日常生活壓力的管道。 「most importantly」（最重要的是……）為副詞片語，通常放在句首，後面加逗號。可以替換成：「above all」或「most important of all」。
6	**Depending on the mood I am in, I choose different kinds of music.** 依據不同的心情，我會聽不同類型的音樂。 「depending on the mood I am in」是分詞片語。 「depend on」（依據；視……而定），後面接名詞、代名詞或動名詞。
7	**I listen to some soft music while indulging myself in crying.** 我會聽些輕音樂，然後放縱自己大哭一場。 「indulge (oneself) in . . .」（放縱自己於……當中）；in 為介系詞，故後面動詞要用動名詞（V-ing）的形式。 ◆ Jimmy indulges (himself) in playing computer games. 　　吉米沈迷於打電腦遊戲。
8	**If I am in a good mood, I turn on some rock music and dance to it.** 如果我心情好的話，我會放些搖滾樂且隨著音樂手舞足蹈。 「be in a good mood」（心情好）可以替換成「in high spirits」。 也可以簡單說成：「When I am happy . . .」。
9	**What's more, New Age music is for studying.** 此外，當我在念書時，我會放些新世紀音樂。 「what's more」（此外；甚者）通常放在句首，後面加逗號。 這是一個常用在作文中承先啟後的轉折語，且常用在列點說明。 可以替換成：・in addition　・besides　・moreover　・furthermore
10	**In a word, I think I would probably go crazy without music.** 總之，如果沒有音樂的話，我可能會瘋掉。 「in a word」（總之；一言以蔽之）通常放在句首，後面加逗號。在作文中常出現在文章結尾要下結論時，為文章作個總結。 可以替換成：・in short　・in brief　・to sum up　・all in all

4 Exercise

A 句子填空

1. 聽音樂是我最喜愛的嗜好。

   1) Listening to music _____ my favorite _____ .

   2) Of all my _____ , _____ to music is my favorite _____ .

   3) Of all my _____ , I like _____ to music the _____ .

2. 音樂在我的日常生活中扮演著不可或缺的角色。

   Music _____ an _____ _____ in my daily life.

3. 音樂不僅陶冶了我的心靈，也豐富了我的精神生活。

   Music not only _____ my mind but also _____ my spiritual life.

4. 我無法想像要是沒有音樂的話，這個世界會變成什麼樣子。

   1) I can't _____ _____ the world _____ be like _____ music.

   2) It _____ hard to imagine _____ the world _____ be like if _____ _____ no music.

5. 音樂提供了一個抒發我日常生活壓力的管道。

   1) Music provides an _____ to _____ the _____ in my daily life.

   2) Music gives me an _____ for the _____ in my daily life.

6. 依據不同的心情，我會聽不同類型的音樂。

   1) I choose different kinds of music, _____ on the _____ I am _____ .

   2) Based _____ my _____ , I listen to _____ kinds of music.

7. 如果沒有音樂的話，我可能會瘋掉。

   1) I think I _____ probably go crazy _____ music.

   2) If I _____ unable to listen to music, I would probably go nuts.

B 中譯英練習

1. 我們必須善加利用我們的空閒時間,並且妥善規劃。

2. 我是一個較內向的人,喜歡室內活動,像是集郵或看電影。

3. 上網是我最喜歡的休閒活動。

4. 看外國電影能擴展我的視野及對這世界的知識。

5. 我是個不折不扣的電影迷,所以在我有空的時候我喜歡看電影。

6. 我是個外向的人,所我我喜歡戶外活動,像是健行或打籃球。

7. 打籃球能強健我的體魄。

C 作文範例架構練習

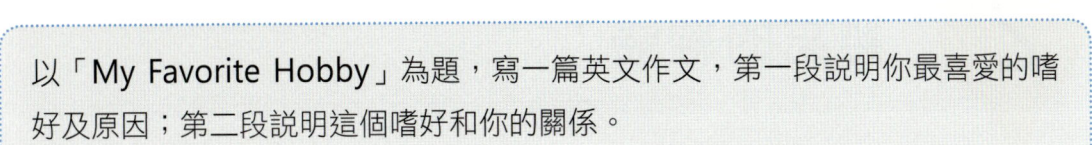

以「My Favorite Hobby」為題，寫一篇英文作文，第一段說明你最喜愛的嗜好及原因；第二段說明這個嗜好和你的關係。

★ Brainstorming（可根據以下的句子，來幫助你完成文章）

1. What do you usually do in your spare time?
2. Why are your hobbies important to you?
3. What are the characteristics of your hobbies?
4. What are the merits of your hobbies?
5. What negative effects do your hobbies have on you?
6. Give some specific examples to demonstrate your hobbies, and tell how they influence your daily life.

2 難忘的經驗

說明	1. 依提示在「答案卷」上寫一篇英文作文。 2. 文長約 150 單詞（words）左右。
提示	考試，可以說是你我成長過程中必經的一個步驟與經驗；有人甘之如飴、有人懂得苦中作樂，更多的人則是頭疼不已，真是如人飲水、冷暖自知。請寫一篇英文作文，文分兩段，第一段以「Exams have become an inevitable part in my learning process and also an important element of my school life.」為主題句；第二段則以「The most unforgettable exam I have ever taken is . . .」為起始句並加以發展。

英文範文

　　Exams have become an inevitable part in my learning process and also an important element of my school life. Preparing for an exam helps me review what I have learned. To be honest, taking an exam is the one of the least enjoyable things I do, but it seems as if I have no other choice but to take it because our educational system is exam-oriented. However, it cannot be denied that taking an exam is the easiest and fastest way for me to find out what I have learned.

　　The most unforgettable exam I have ever taken is my history final in senior high school. As I had previously failed my history class twice, I was determined not to get another "F." I studied very hard that semester. I also stayed up three nights in a row to cram for the exam. When it was time for the history final, I was so tired and drowsy that I started to doze off as soon as I got the exam paper. I did not wake up until it was time to hand in the answer sheet. Naturally, I flunked my history class and had to take the make-up exam.

1 寫作指導

第一段

主題句在題目部分已給予，接下來要以此主題句發展，可以利用 5W1H 來幫助構思這一小段。

1. **Why** are exams an inevitable part of my learning process?
2. **Why** are they so important?
3. **What** are the merits of exams? **What** do you think of exams?
4. **How** do exams work? **How** do exams help you?

利用中文寫作的「起、承、轉、合」作為段落發展的順序。

◆（起：點出主題句）
考試已成為我學習過程中不可避免的一部分，同時也成為我學校生活重要的一環。

◆（承：說明考試為何在我的學習過程中是不可避免，同時也是重要的一部分）
準備考試可以幫助我複習所學過的東西。

◆（轉：提出你對考試的看法）
老實說，考試是我覺得最無趣的事情之一，但似乎我沒有任何選擇的餘地只能接受，因為我們的教育制度是以考試為導向。

◆（合：結論）
然而，不可否認的是，考試是幫助我檢視所學最容易且最快速的方法。

第二段

主題句在題目部分已給予，接下來可以利用 5W1H 來幫助構思這一小段。

1. **What** happened?
2. **Where** did it take place?
3. **When** did it happen?
4. **Why** is it the most unforgettable exam?
5. **Who** gave you the exam?

利用中文寫作的「起、承、轉、合」作為段落發展的順序。

◆（起：點出主題句）
我所參加過的考試裡，最難忘的是高中的歷史期末考。

◆（承：承接主題句，描述這個難忘的經驗）
由於我的歷史已經被當了兩次，我下定決心不要再被當。那一學期，我非常努力用功。為了這個考試，我還一連熬了三天的夜來臨時抱佛腳。

◆（轉：提供一個出乎意料之外的情節）
到了考歷史那天，我好累、整個人昏昏欲睡，結果一拿到考試卷，眼皮重得打不開。一直到要交卷時我才醒過來！

◆（合）
當然我的歷史又被當了，且必須要參加補考。

2 重要單字

#	單字	說明
1	**review** [rɪˋvju]	(v.) 複習 Lillian always has to sit up late to **review** a pile of books whenever exams are approaching. 只要接近考試，莉莉恩就要熬夜 K 一大堆書。 ◆ review 可以替換成「go over」或「brush up（on）」
2	**fail** [fel]	(v.) 評定（學生）不及格；沒有通過考試 Our biology teacher **failed** one third of the class. 我們的生物老師當掉了全班三分之一的學生。
3	**cram** [kræm]	(v.) 死記硬背 Alice burned the midnight oil to **cram** for the English exam. 愛麗絲為了英語考試挑夜燈猛 K 書。
4	**drowsy** [ˋdraʊzɪ]	(a.) 昏昏欲睡的 After taking the medicine, George felt **drowsy**. 吃了那個藥之後，喬治覺得很想睡覺。
5	**flunk** [flʌŋk]	(v.) 不及格 Bill **flunked** his third year exams and was kicked out of the college. 比爾在三年級時考試被當掉，遭到退學。
6	**make-up exam** [ˋmek͵ʌp ɪgˋzæm]	補考 Vincent failed the math exam, so he had to take the **make-up exam**. 文森數學考試沒有過，所以需要補考。

3 重要句子及片語

1 **Preparing for an exam helps me review what I have learned.**
在準備考試時，可以幫助我複習所學過的東西。

1) 以動名詞（V-ing）當主詞，要視為單數，所以要用單數動詞。
2) help +（to）+ 原形動詞；help 後接動詞時可以省略不定詞 to，直接加原形動詞。

   若 help 後面接名詞時，通常要在 help 後加介系詞 with。
   ◆ Mia often helps her brother with his math homework.
      蜜兒常常幫她弟弟做數學作業。
3) 此處的 what（= the things that/which）為複合關係代名詞，相當於「先行詞 + 關係代名詞」，所以 what 前面沒有先行詞。

2 **To be honest, taking an exam is one of the least enjoyable things I do, but it seems as if I have no other choice but to take it because our educational system is exam-oriented.**
坦白說，我是最不喜歡考試了，不過我們的教育制度就是採取考試導向的，所以看來我也只好接受了。

1)「to be honest」（老實說），常放在句首，後面加逗點。可以替換成：

   ・honestly　　　・honestly speaking　　・to be frank
   ・frankly　　　 ・frankly speaking　　 ・to tell the truth
2)「one of the least enjoyable things」（最無趣的事情之一）：

   「one of the + 最高級形容詞 + 複數名詞」，但後面若接動詞要用單數動詞。
   ・One of the most beautiful countries I have visited is Britain.
      我去過最美麗的國家之一，就是英國。
3)「have no other choice but to + 原形動詞」（沒有選擇的餘地；不得不……）：
   這個用法裡的 other 可以省略，choice 可以替換成 option 或 alternative。

3. **As I had previously failed my history class twice, I was determined not to get another "F."**
   我的歷史課已經被當過兩次了,我決定不要再被當了。
   1) 談到「因為……」時,除了可以用 because 外,還可用連接詞 as。
   2) had failed 為過去完成式:在談到過去的事情時(回憶難忘的考試經驗),我們有時會提及更早發生的事情(歷史被當了兩次),這時就要用過去完成式。
   3) 大寫的 F 為「成績不及格」的意思,是由 fail 或 flunk 而來。通常在句子裡出現的形式是「to get an "F"」,複數形式是「to get 2 Fs/F's」。

4. **I also stayed up three nights in a row to cram for the exam.**
   我也是熬夜熬了三天來準備考試。
   1) stay up「熬夜」;可以替換成:
      ・sit up ・pull an all-nighter ・burn the midnight oil
   2) 「in a row」(一連;接連)。通常放在所強調的事物後面,如:
      three years in a row(一連三年)、two days in a row(一連二天)。

5. **When it was time for the history final, I was so tired and drowsy that I started to doze off as soon as I got the exam paper.**
   到了考歷史那天,我好累、整個人昏昏欲睡,結果一拿到考試卷,眼皮重得打不開。
   1) 「when it was/is time for sth.」(到了……的時候)
   2) 「so + 形容詞 + that + S1 + V1 ...」(如此……以致於……)
   3) 「doze off」(打瞌睡)

6. **I did not wake up until it was time to hand in the answer sheet.**
   我一直到要交考卷時才醒過來。
   1) 可改寫成:Not until it was time to hand in the answer sheet did I wake up.(Not until 放句首,主要子句要倒裝)
   2) 「hand in」(繳交);用法是「hand sth. in」或「hand in sth.」。意思同 submit。
      ・Diana forgot to hand in her assignment.
      = Diana forgot to hand her assignment in. 黛安娜忘了交作業了。

4 Exercise

A 句子填空

1. 準備考試可以幫助我複習所學過的東西。

   P_____ _____ an exam helps me to review _____ I have learned.

2. 坦白說，我是最不喜歡考試了，不過我們的教育制度就是採取考試導向的，所以看來我也只好接受了。

   To be _____, taking an exam is one of the _____ enjoyable _____ I do, but it seems as if I have no other _____ but to take it because our educational system is exam-o_____.

3. 然而，不可否認的是考試是幫助我檢視所學最容易且最快速的方法。

   1) However, it cannot be d_____ that taking an exam is the easiest and fastest way for me to find out _____ I have learned.

   2) Undoubtedly, the easiest and fastest way for me to find out _____ I have learned _____ to take an exam.

4. 由於我的歷史已經被當了二次，我下定決心不要再被當。

   1) As I _____ previously f_____ my history class twice, I was d_____ not to get another "F."

   2) Because I _____ previously f_____ my history class twice, I made up my _____ not to fail again.

5. 為了這個考試，我還一連熬了三天的夜來臨時抱佛腳。

   I also _____ up three nights in a _____ to c_____ for the exam.

6. 到了考歷史那天，我好累、整個人昏昏欲睡，結果一拿到考試卷，眼皮重得打不開。

   When it was _____ for the history final, I was _____ tired and d_____ that I started to d_____ off as soon _____ I got the exam paper.

7. 一直到要交卷時我才醒過來！

1) I _____ wake up until it was time to h_____ in the answer sheet.

2) Not until it was time to s_____ the answer sheet _____ I wake up.

8. 當然，我的歷史又被當了，而要參加補考。

Naturally, I _____ my history class again and had to take the _____ exam.

B 中譯英練習

1. 我們被無數的大大小小考試壓得喘不過氣來。

2. 由於升學的壓力,我們被迫放棄一些課外活動。

3. 放學後,我還得去補習班以求能趕得上班上的同學。

4. 對我而言,在高中最大的煩惱是滿臉的青春痘。

5. 我看過了無數的醫生,但都無法根治。

6. 我總是試著在念書和玩耍間取得平衡。

7. 當我玩耍放鬆時,我就把課業拋諸腦後。

8. 當我念書時,我就專注在課業上。

9. 好的成績使我有成就感。

10. 俗話說:「今日事今日畢。」我正努力養成每天複習功課的習慣。

C 作文範例架構練習

說明	1. 依提示在「答案卷」上寫一篇英文作文。 2. 文長約 150 單詞（words）左右。
提示	考試，可以說是你我成長過程中必經的一個步驟與經驗；有人甘之如飴、有人懂得苦中作樂，更多的人則是頭疼不已，真是如人飲水、冷暖自知。請寫一篇英文作文，文分兩段，第一段以「Exams have become an inevitable part in my learning process and also an important element of my school life.」為主題句；第二段則以「The most unforgettable exam I have ever taken is . . .」為起始句並加以發展。

★ Brainstorming（可根據以下的句子，來幫助你完成文章）

第一段
Do you like exams? Why or why not?
What is your opinion about exams?
What are the pros and cons of exams?
Why is it important to take exams?

第二段
What is your most unforgettable exam?
What happened during that exam?
When did it happen?
Where did it take place?
What did you learn from that experience?
How did you feel?

3 寫 Email

說明	1. 依提示在「答案卷」上寫一篇英文作文。 2. 文長約 150 單詞（words）左右。
提示	上個月妳（Linda）在美國的表姊（Miranda）寫了一封 email 給妳，信中邀請妳到美國玩，但因為妳忙著準備大學入學考試，所以遲遲未能回信。第一段請在簡單的問候之後，婉轉說明妳到現在才回信的原因；第二段說明妳考完試以後的計畫，同時也回應她的邀約。

英文範文

March 16, 2017

Dear Miranda,

　　It was really nice to hear from you. How have you been? I have been thinking about you all the time and hoping that you are doing well. I am so sorry that it has taken me so long to get back to you. Because the college entrance exam was approaching, I had to review a pile of books every day. I didn't have time and energy to write any emails. I hope you're not mad at me.

　　Thank you for your invitation, and I will definitely pay you a visit. Actually, my parents and I have planned to take a trip to the U.S. after my college entrance exam. First, we will go to Disneyland in California, which I have longed to visit for many years. Then, we will fly to the Big Apple, New York City, to enjoy its charm and to experience life as New Yorkers. Last but not least, we will also be sure to visit you.

　　I look forward to seeing you soon and hope everything is going well with you and your family.

Take care!

Linda

1 寫作指導

主旨	信中應記載事項：（參考提示文字的背景說明） ✓ 說明遲遲沒有回信的原因 ✓ 回覆 Miranda 的邀請 ✓ 考完後的計畫
信件開頭	收信人：Miranda 寒暄問候：聽到妳的消息真好。近來好嗎？我一直都在想妳，希望妳一切都安好。
切入主題	寫出要給對方知道的事情。 ✓ 說明遲遲沒有回信的原因：拖了這麼久才給你回信，真的感到很抱歉。因為大學入學考試就要到了，每天都要複習一堆功課。因此，我沒有時間也沒有精力寫 emails。希望妳不要生氣。 ✓ 回覆邀請：謝謝妳的邀請，我一定會去找妳玩。事實上，爸媽和我計畫在我考完大學入學考試後到美國遊玩。 ◆ 考完後的計畫： 　a.) 首先，我們會先去位在加州的迪士尼樂園，因為我已經夢想到那裡玩好幾年了。 　b.) 接著，我們要去有 Big Apple 之稱的紐約，享受它迷人的地方，且感受一下紐約人的生活。 　c.) 最後，我們當然會去看看你。
信件結尾	期待回音，祝福對方。 ◆ 期盼早日見到妳，也祝福妳和妳的家人一切安好。

② 重要單字

1	**long** [lɔŋ]	(v.) 渴望 Pete has **longed** to visit London for a long time. 彼特盼望能去倫敦玩已經盼望很久了。 第一個 long 為動詞「渴望」的意思；第二個 long 為形容詞「長久的」。
2	**fly** [flaɪ]	(v.) 搭飛機旅行 Jane will **fly** to Spain next week. 珍下星期會飛去西班牙。
3	**charm** [tʃɑrm]	(n.) 魅力 Britain is a country full of modern and old-world **charm**. 英國是一個兼具現代與古典魅力的國家。

3 重要句子及片語

1	**It was really nice to hear from you.** 聽到你的消息，真是太好了。 「hear from sb.」（收到某人的消息）：這個句型常用在信件開頭的問候寒暄。 也可說成： ・As usual, I was really happy to hear from you. 　聽到你的消息，總是那麼讓我高興。 ・I was so happy to hear from you! 聽到你的消息，真高興！ ・How nice to hear from you again! 能再聽到你的消息，真好！
2	**I am so sorry that it has taken me so long to get back to you.** 很抱歉這麼晚才回信給你。 1)「I am sorry（that）+ 子句」：例句裡子句的時態是現在完成式，表示在過去開始而持續至現在的動作。 2)「get back to sb.」表示「回信給某人」。
3	**Because the college entrance exam was approaching, I had to review a pile of books every day.** 因為大專院校的入學考試快到了，我每天都得複習一大堆書。 be approaching「接近」，可用在抽象（如例句）或具體事物（如 The train is approaching Taipei station. 火車快要進台北車站了。） 在這裡用過去進行式來表示「大學入學考試」在過去正在進行的持續動作。 可以替換成： ・be around the corner　・be at hand　・be coming near
4	**Thank you for your invitation, and I will definitely pay you a visit.** 感謝你的邀約，我一定會去拜訪你的。 「pay someone a visit」或「pay a visit to someone」（拜訪）。 這裡的 someone 若是人名或專有名詞時，則兩種用法皆可。 若 someone 為代名詞時，則只能用「pay someone a visit」。

5	**Actually, my parents and I have planned to take a trip to the U.S. after my college entrance exam.**
	事實上，我和我爸媽計畫在我的大專院校入學考試結束之後，去美國玩一趟。
	1) actually（事實上）為副詞，可用在句首或句中。
	可以替換成：・in fact　　・as a matter of fact
	2)「take a trip to ＋ 地方」：表示到某地旅行
6	**First, we will go to Disneyland in California, which I have longed to visit for many years.**
	我們會先去加州的迪士尼樂園玩，這我可期待好幾年了。
	1) first（首先），用於在文章列點時，常放在句首，後面接逗號。也可以用「first of all」。
	2) which 是指前半句中的 Disneyland in California。因先行詞（Disneyland in California）是專有名詞，所以要用非限定的形容詞子句，對先行詞只做補充說明。非限定形容詞子句前面要加逗號。
7	**Last but not least, we will also be sure to visit you.**
	最後，而且重要的是，我們一定也會去拜訪你的。
	「last but not least」（最後但不代表最不重要）是一個轉折語用在文章列點時，通常出現在文章的末尾。
8	**I look forward to seeing you soon.**
	期盼早日見到妳。
	「look forward to」為「期待」的意思，to 為介系詞，所以後面要接動名詞（V-ing）。書信中也常以「I look forward to hearing from you.」作結。書信中常見的結尾還有：
	・I would love to hear from you. 真高興聽到你的消息。
	・I am looking forward to your early reply. 期待你早日回信。

4 Exercise

A 句子填空

1. 聽到妳的消息真好。

   1) _____ was really nice to _____ from you.

   2) How n_____ to _____ from you!

2. 拖了這麼久才給你回信,真的感到很抱歉。

   1) I am so sorry that it has t_____ me so long to get _____ to you.

   2) I am so sorry for the d_____ in r_____ to your letter.

3. 因為大學入學考試就要到了,每天都要複習一堆功課。

   1) Because the college entrance exam was a_____, I had to review a p_____ of books every day.

   2) Owing _____ the advent of the college entrance exam, I had to go _____ a _____ of books every day.

4. 謝謝妳的邀請,我一定會去找妳玩。

   Thank you for your _____, and I will definitely _____ you a visit.

5. 事實上,爸媽和我計畫在我考完大學入學考試後到美國遊玩。

   Actually, my parents and I have p_____ to _____ a t_____ to the U.S. after my college entrance exam.

6. 首先,我們會先去位在加洲的迪士尼樂園,因為我已經夢想到那裡玩好幾年了。

   1) First, we will go to Disneyland in California, _____ I have l_____ to visit for many years.

   2) First of all, we will go to Disneyland, which is _____ in California, because I have been l_____ forward to visiting it for many years.

7 接著，我們要去有 Big Apple 之稱的紐約，享受它迷人的地方，且感受一下紐約人的生活。

1) Then, we will f_____ to the Big Apple, New York City, to enjoy its c_____ and to e_____ life as New Yorkers.

2) Then, we will h_____ towards New York City, which is also c_____ the Big Apple, to enjoy its c_____ and to e_____ life as New Yorkers.

8 最後，我們當然會去看看你。

Last but not _____, we will also be s_____ to visit you.

9 期盼早日見到妳。

I look _____ to _____ you soon.

B 中譯英練習

1. 大學入學考試將要結束，我終於可以自由了。

2. 我會一個星期什麼都不做，只想看些我一直想看的書。

3. 我會逛逛我家附近的書店，或到朋友家串串門子。

4. 我計畫和朋友到墾丁國家公園過些放鬆的日子。

5. 我會待在墾丁至少一個星期，享受燦爛的陽光和浩瀚的海洋。

6. 我想學衝浪和浮潛。（浮潛 dive (v.)）

7. 我會去打工來賺些零用錢。

8. 同時，我會不斷增進我的英文能力。

C 作文範例架構練習

說明	1. 依提示在「答案卷」上寫一篇英文作文。 2. 文長約 150 單詞（words）左右。
提示	上個月妳（Linda）在美國的表姊（Miranda）寫了一封 email 給妳，信中邀請妳到美國玩，但因為妳忙著準備大學入學考試，所以遲遲未能回信。第一段請在簡單的問候之後，婉轉說明妳到現在才回信的原因；第二段說明妳考完試以後的計畫，同時也回應她的邀約。

★ Brainstorming（信中應記載事項）

1. 因大學入學考試將近所以遲遲沒有回信
2. 回覆 Miranda 的邀請
3. 考完後的計畫

   a.) Do you have any plans after the entrance exam?
   b.) How are you going to spend your time after the entrance exam?
   c.) Do you have any dreams that haven't come true yet and that you would like to fulfill after the entrance exam?
   d.) Will you take a part-time job?
   e.) Are you going abroad for your summer vacation?
   f.) Do you want to learn anything this summer, for example, guitar, swimming, chess, or ballroom dancing?

4 昨天是情人節

說明	1. 依提示在「答案卷」上寫一篇英文作文。 2. 文長約 150 單詞（words）左右。
提示	請根據以下三張連環圖畫的內容，以「Yesterday was Valentine's Day.」為起始句，將圖中主角所經歷的事件作一合理的闡述。

英文範文

　　Yesterday was Valentine's Day. Almost everyone was having a special supper with his or her significant other, except for Jane. Instead of spending the special event with her loved one, she had to put in some overtime in the office. As a matter of fact, Jane did not have a boyfriend, and this was why she was willing to work late in the office.

　　Jane was so exhausted that she dozed off at her desk. Prince Charming showed up out of the blue and invited her out. They had a romantic candlelight dinner in a swanky restaurant to celebrate Valentine's Day. The handsome prince told Jane how much he loved her and he wanted to spend the rest of his life with her. Suddenly, the telephone rang and woke up Jane. It dawned on her that she had just experienced a lovely dream and a pile of work was still waiting for her. The telephone rang again, and she picked up the phone with a deep sigh.

1 寫作指導

主旨	瀏覽圖片，可以歸納出人、事、時、地等相關的故事情節。 Who: Jane; a man When: yesterday Where: in the office; in a restaurant What: What happened to Jane? Why: Why did Jane work in the office alone? Why did Jane have dinner with a man? How: How did Jane feel?
第一段	利用中文寫作的「起、承、轉、合」作為段落發展的順序。 （起） 昨天是情人節。 （承） 幾乎每個人都和他們的另一半共進特別的晚餐，只不過 Jane 例外。 （轉） 她必須在辦公室裡加班，而不是和她的愛人慶祝這個特別的日子。 （合） 事實上，Jane 沒有男朋友，這就是為什麼她願意在辦公室裡加班。
第二段	利用中文寫作的「起、承、轉、合」作為段落發展的順序。 （起） 由於太疲倦了，她就在辦公桌前打起瞌來。 （承） 她心目中的白馬王子意外出現，且邀她共進晚餐。他們在一家很華麗的餐廳共享浪漫的燭光晚餐，來慶祝情人節。英俊的白馬子告訴 Jane 他有多麼地愛她，及他希望下半輩子都能和她在一起。 （轉） 突然間，一通電話響起把 Jane 吵醒。 （合） 她才知道原來剛剛的只是一場美夢，而還有一堆等著她完成的工作。電話又再度響起，她邊嘆氣邊接起電話。

2 重要單字

1	**overtime** [ˈovɚˌtaɪm]	(n.)(adv.) 加班 (overtime 當副詞用) Jane is working **overtime**, trying to finish the pile of work on time. 珍正在加班，她想如期把一堆工作完成。 (overtime 當名詞用) Miranda was paid extra for **overtime**. 米蘭達有領加班費。
2	**exhausted** [ɪgˈzɔstɪd]	(a.) 精疲力竭的 After putting in a lot of overtime, Bob was **exhausted**. 鮑伯在加了很久的班之後，累壞了。
3	**swanky** [ˈswæŋkɪ]	(a.) 華麗的；時髦的 Owing to the limited budget, we will stay in that **swanky** hotel just for one night. 因為經費有限，我們只會在豪華的旅館住一晚。

3　重要句子及片語

1　**Almost everyone was having a special supper with his or her significant other except for Jane.**
幾乎所有的人都各自和情人共進了一頓特別的晚餐，除了珍。

1) 「significant other」（另一半），在這裡也指男朋友或女朋友。
2) 「except for sb./sth.」意思是「除了某人某物之外」，可以替換成「aside from」。

在諸如 all、every、no、everything、anything、anybody、everybody、nowhere、whole 等表概括性的詞之後，可以用 except 或 except for。若接子句，則只用 except。

2　**Instead of spending the special event with her loved one, she had to put in some overtime in the office.**
她沒有和情人共度，而是得在辦公室裡頭加班。

1) 「instead of . . .」（不……而……）：由於 of 為介系詞，所以後面的動詞要用動名詞（V-ing）的形式。
2) 「had to + 原形動詞」：是「必須」的意思。
3) 「put sth. in」或「put in sth.」：「花費很多時間或精力做某事」。
   - Jack has put in some extra hours today so he can have some time off tomorrow.
   傑克今晚加了幾個鐘頭的班，這樣他明天就可以請個幾個鐘頭的假。

3　**As a matter of fact, Jane did not have a boyfriend, and this was why she was willing to work late in the office.**
事實上，珍沒有男朋友，所以她願意在辦公室裡頭待得比較晚。

1) 「as a matter of fact」（事實上）通常用在文章轉折處，可替換成 in fact 或 actually。
2) 「This is why + 子句」（這就是為什麼……）是由「This is the reason why + 子句」簡化而來。
3) 「be willing to + 原形動詞」表示「願意」的意思。

4　Jane was so exhausted that she dozed off at her desk.
珍累得在桌子上打起瞌睡來了。

1)「so + 形容詞 + that + 子句」（如此……，以致於……）：
   so 為副詞，後面要接形容詞或副詞。
   另一個類似的用法是「such + a/an +（形容詞）+ 名詞 + that + 子句」
   such 為形容詞，後面要接名詞。
2)「doze off」的意思是「打瞌睡」。

5　Prince Charming showed up out of the blue and invited her out.
她的白馬王子突然出現，找她一起出去。

1)「Prince Charming」（白馬王子）兩個字都要大寫，因被視為專有名詞。
2)「show up」是「出現」的意思，可以替換成 appear。
3)「out of the blue」是「出乎意料」、「突然地」的意思。

6　It dawned on her that she had just experienced a lovely dream and a pile of work was still waiting for her.
她才知道原來剛剛的只是一場美夢，而還有一堆等著她完成的工作。

1)「事物 + dawn on + 人 + that + 子句」是「頓悟」、「明白」的意思，使用這個句型時，主詞為事物或虛主詞 it。

   也可說成：
   It occurred to her that . . .
   It struck her that . . .
   It came to her mind that . . .
   It came to her that . . .
   It flashed across her mind that . . .

2) had experienced 為過去完成式：
   在談到過去的事情時（「Jane 明白到」這件事），我們有時會提及更早發生的事情（「做美夢」這件事），這時就要用過去完成式。

4 Exercise

A 句子填空

1 幾乎每個人都和他們的另一半共進特別的晚餐，只不過Jane例外。

1) Almost everyone was having a special supper with his or her s_____ other, except _____ Jane.

2) Almost everyone was having a special supper with his or her s_____ other, but Jane was the _____.

2 她必須在辦公室裡加班，而不是和她的愛人慶祝這個特別的日子。

1) Instead of s_____ the special event with her loved one, she had to p_____ in some _____ in the office.

2) She didn't c_____ this special day with her lover; i_____ she needed to work o_____ in the office.

3 事實上，Jane沒有男朋友，這就是為什麼她願意在辦公室裡加班。

1) As a_____ of fact, Jane did not have a boyfriend and this was _____ she was w_____ to work late in the office.

2) The truth was that Jane didn't have a boyfriend, _____ was why she was w_____ to work in the office.

3) Jane was willing to w_____ late in the office because she didn't _____ have a boyfriend.

4) The _____ why Jane was w_____ to work in the office was that she didn't have a boyfriend.

4 由於太疲倦了，Jane就在辦公桌前打起盹來。

1) Jane was so e_____ that she _____ off at her desk.

2) Since Jane was w_____ out, she _____ off at her desk.

5. 她心目中的白馬王子意外出現，且邀她共進晚餐。

   Prince C_____ s_____ up out of the b_____ and i_____ her out.

6. 他們在一家很華麗的餐廳共享浪漫的燭光晚餐，來慶祝情人節。

   They were having a romantic _____ dinner in a s_____ restaurant to c_____ Valentine's Day.

7. 突然間，一通電話響起把 Jane 吵醒。

   1) Suddenly, the telephone rang and w_____ _____ Jane.

   2) Jane was suddenly a_____ by the s_____ of the telephone.

8. 她才知道原來剛剛的只是一場美夢，而還有一堆等著她完成的工作。

   1) It d_____ _____ her that she _____ just experienced a lovely dream and a p_____ of work was still waiting for her.

   2) She then r_____ that she _____ just experienced a lovely dream and a p_____ of work was still waiting for her.

B 中譯英練習

1. 藉著看漫畫書，我可以得到消遣。

2. 我常和家人到「吃到飽」型的自助餐廳吃飯。它也是我和三五好友聚會，並聊聊最新消息的好地方。

3. Kevin 中了樂透，所以他要請我們吃大餐。

4. 我很喜歡晚餐時間，因為我們可以一邊悠閒吃晚餐一邊聊聊身邊發生的事情。

5. Ian 不但人長得帥而且吉他彈得棒，是許多女孩的偶像。

6. 有一次 Ian 翹課和朋友去打撞球。爸爸得知後，他被狠狠教訓了一頓。

C 作文範例架構練習

說明	1. 依提示在「答案卷」上寫一篇英文作文。 2. 文長約 150 單詞（words）左右。
提示	請根據以下三張連環圖畫的內容，以「Yesterday was Valentine's Day.」為起始句，將圖中主角所經歷的事件作一合理的闡述。

★ Brainstorming（把圖中所看到及你想到東西先寫下來，以幫助自己寫出段落）

Picture 1　in the office / a lot of documents /
　　　　　　The office was almost empty. / Jane was the only one there.

Picture 2　Jane dozed off. / a dream / a man / in a restaurant /
　　　　　　having a candlelight dinner with the man

Picture 3　a telephone rang / Jane woke up. / in the office /
　　　　　　the pile of work not finished

5 母親節要到了

說明	1. 依提示在「答案卷」上寫一篇英文作文。 2. 文長約 150 單詞（**words**）左右。
提示	母親節就要到了。為了感謝媽媽的辛勞，你精心策畫了一個驚喜要送給她。請寫一篇英文作文，描述你打算送給媽媽的驚喜，並說明為何要給媽媽這個特別的驚喜。

英文範文

　　As Mother's Day is just around the corner, I have decided to give my mother some surprises in order to reward her tireless hard work for the entire family.

　　First, for a whole month, I am going to cook dinner every day after I come back from school. I will also do the laundry and chores on Saturdays. Mother has devoted all her time and energy to us, and she deserves some time to relax. In addition, I will arrange, for my mom and dad, a trip to Paris as a second honeymoon in the hope that they can relive their joyful memories of the time when they were first married. In fact, Mom has dreamed of visiting Paris for many years. Most important of all is that I will tell my mom how much I love her and how grateful I am for what she has done for us. Mom and dad are the greatest blessing that I have ever had.

　　I bet these surprises will be the best gifts I can give Mom.

1 寫作指導

第一段	闡述主題句：參考提示裡的文字內容，點出主題句。 由於母親節就要到了，我決定要給媽媽一些驚喜來報答她對這個家不辭辛勞的付出。
第二段	發展支持主題句的說明：條列出要給媽媽的驚喜及原因。 (驚喜 1) 首先，有一整個月的時間，我要在每天放學回家後煮晚餐，還要每週六洗衣服、做家事。媽媽貢獻了她所有的時間和精力在我們身上，這些休息時間是她應得的。 (驚喜 2) 再來，我會為爸媽計畫一趟巴黎之旅，作為他們的二度蜜月，希望他們能回味一下剛結婚時的美好回憶。事實上，媽媽已經夢想去巴黎遊玩許多年了。 (驚喜 3) 最重要的是我會告訴媽媽我有多愛她、我是多麼的感謝她為我們的付出。有這樣的媽媽和爸爸是我最大的福氣。
第三段	結論：綜合上述的驚喜，提出自己的看法。 我相信這些驚喜將會是我能送給媽媽最棒的禮物。

2 重要單字

#	單字	說明
1	**reward** [rɪˋwɔrd]	(v.) 報答；獎賞 After the entrance exam, I would like to **reward** myself with a rich meal. 大考結束之後，我要去吃大餐來好好犒賞自己一下。
2	**tireless** [ˋtaɪrlɪs]	(a.) 不疲倦的；孜孜不倦的 The scientists have made **tireless** efforts to find a cure for AIDS. 科學家們努力不倦地想找出愛滋病的治療方法。
3	**laundry** [ˋlɔndrɪ]	(n.) 需洗的衣物 Amy has the habit of doing the **laundry** every day. 愛咪習慣每天都洗衣服。
4	**chores** [tʃors]	(n.)(pl) 家庭雜務 Jill will go swimming after she has done her **chores**. 潔兒做完家事之後會去游泳。
5	**devote** [dɪˋvot]	(v.) 奉獻 Jack has **devoted** his whole life to saving stray dogs. 傑克將一生都奉獻於拯救流浪狗。 ◆ devote . . . to . . .： 　其中的 to 為介系詞，所以後面要接名詞或動名詞（V-ing）。
6	**deserve** [dɪˋzɝv]	(v.) 應受；該得 After all the hard work, Tracy **deserves** a holiday. 崔西這樣努力工作，是應該好好放個假的。
7	**honeymoon** [ˋhʌnɪ͵mun]	(n.) 蜜月；蜜月假期 Mr. and Mrs. Jones are going to Italy for their **honeymoon**. 瓊斯夫婦要去義大利度蜜月。
8	**relive** [riˋlɪv]	(v.) 再體驗；再經歷 Whenever I listen to the song, I **relive** the happy moments with my grandparents. 只要聽到這首歌，我就會回想起和祖父母相處時的快樂時光。

3 重要句子及片語

1 **As Mother's Day is just around the corner, I have decided to give my mother some surprises in order to reward her tireless hard work for the entire family.**

由於母親節就要到了，我決定要給媽媽一些驚喜來報答她對這個家不辭辛勞的付出。

1) decide 可以替換成「determine」或「make up one's mind」。
2)「in order to + 原形動詞」意思是指「為了……」。

2 **First, for a whole month, I am going to cook dinner every day after I come back from school.**

首先呢，我整整一個月每天下課之後都要開伙。

「first」，用在條列事物時，可以替換成「first of all」或「to begin with」。
在寫作時我們常會用條列的方式，「第一、第二、第三……最後」等。
◆ 第二，可用 second。
◆ 第三，可用 third。
◆ 最後，則可用「Last」或「Last but not least」。
這些字通常放在句首，後面要加逗號。

3 **I will also do the laundry and chores on Saturdays.**

我週末時間也會洗洗衣服或做做家事。

1)「do（=wash）the laundry」（洗衣服）：laundry 常和 do 連用。
2)「do the chores」（家事）：chores 這個字常和 do 連用。
3)「on Saturdays」=「every Saturday」：
我們要說「每週……」時，除了可用「every + 星期」，也可用「on + 星期」（此時星期要加 s）。

4 **In addition, I will arrange, for my mom and dad, a trip to Paris as a second honeymoon in the hope that they can relive their joyful memories of the time when they were first married.**

此外我也會安排我爸媽去巴黎度假，當做是二度蜜月，希望他們會想起當初結婚時的甜蜜回憶。

1) in addition「此外」；這是作文中常用的轉折語。
可以替換成：
‧besides ‧what's more ‧furthermore ‧moreover
3)「in the hope that + 子句」（希望）：
指希望得到或擁有一樣東西，而且是在極可能的情況之下得到。

5 **In fact, Mom has dreamed of visiting Paris for many years.**
事實上，老媽想去巴黎玩已經想好幾年了。

「dream of」（夢想；嚮往）：因 of 為介系詞，故後面要用動名詞（V-ing）。

「dream of」可以指睡眠時「夢見」，也可以指「渴望」。

6 **Most important of all is that I will tell my mom how much I love her and how grateful I am for what she has done for us.**
而最重要的是，我會跟我媽說我是多麼地愛她，而且非常感謝她為我們所做的一切。

1)「be grateful to sb.（感謝某人）」；「be grateful to sth.（感謝某事）」：grateful 後面要接感謝的人時，要加介系詞 to，「to + sb.」常會省略；再接感謝的事物，且事物前要加介系詞 for。

2)「How grateful I am for what she has done for us.」這是一句感嘆句。

用法是「How + 形容詞 + 主詞 + 動詞」。

在 how 的感嘆句裡，若上下文明確時，有時會省略後面的主詞和動詞。

例如：

· How beautiful the baby is!（好漂亮的小嬰兒呀！）
　 = How beautiful!

4 Exercise

A 句子填空

1. 由於母親節就要到了，我決定要給媽媽一些驚喜來報答她對這個家不辭辛勞的付出。

   As Mother's Day is just around the _____, I have d_____ to give my mother some surprises in order to r_____ her t_____ hard work for the e_____ family.

2. 首先，有一整個月的時間，我要在每天放學回家後煮晚餐。

   First, for a _____ month, I _____ going to cook dinner every day after I come back from school.

3. 我還要在每週六洗衣服、做家事。

   I will also do the l_____ and c_____ on _____.

4. 媽媽貢獻她所有的時間和精力在我們身上，這些休息的時間是她應得的。

   Mother has d_____ all her time and energy _____ us, and she d_____ some time to relax.

5. 此外我也會安排我爸媽去巴黎度假，當做是二度蜜月，希望他們會想起當初結婚時的甜蜜回憶。

   In addition, I will a_____, for my mom and dad, a t_____ to Paris as a second honeymoon in the _____ that they can r_____ their joyful memories of the time when they were first married.

6. 事實上，老媽想去巴黎玩已經想好幾年了。

   1) In fact, Mom has dreamed _____ visiting Paris for many years.

   2) As a _____ of fact, for many years _____ has been Mom's dream to visit Paris.

B 中譯英練習

1. 我最尊敬的人是我的母親。

2. 在親戚們的眼中,她是個勤勞的媽媽也是個能幹的職業婦女。

3. 說到廚藝,街坊鄰居沒人能與媽媽匹敵。

4. 我常請教她課業的問題,她總是很有耐心地教我。

5. 她也很關心我的學校生活。

6. 有這麼好的媽媽令我感到很驕傲,我應該好好向她學習。

7. 他是一個好爸爸、好丈夫,也是個很有責任感的人。

8. 在工作上,他不僅全力以赴,而且也受同事的歡迎。

9. 下班後,他會做些家事。

10. 我父親看起來很嚴肅,但其實他是個很親切的人。

C 作文範例架構練習

說明	1. 依提示在「答案卷」上寫一篇英文作文。 2. 文長約 150 單詞（words）左右。
提示	母親節就要到了。為了感謝媽媽的辛勞，你精心策畫了一個驚喜要送給她。請寫一篇英文作文，描述你打算送給媽媽的驚喜，並說明為何要給媽媽這個特別的驚喜。

★ Brainstorming（可根據以下的句子，來幫助你完成文章）

1. Does your mother have any dreams that haven't come true yet? What are they?
2. Describe those surprises that can be bought with money and those surprises that cannot be bought with money.
3. What does your mother like to do in her spare time?
4. Express your gratitude to your mom.
5. What kind of activity do your mother and you like to do together?

6 電腦

說明	1. 依提示在「答案卷」上寫一篇英文作文。 2. 文長約 150 單詞（words）左右。
提示	電腦在當今社會的方便性及快速普及，使得我們的生活產生了巨大改變。尤其在網際網路的推波助瀾下，它已經不是一台冷冰冰的機器，而成為每個人生活中不可或缺的一部分。以「Computers」為題，寫一篇英文作文。文分兩段，第一段描述電腦的優點或缺點；第二段以自身為例，說明你對電腦的看法。

英文範文

Computers

Computers are so useful and widespread that they are becoming more and more important to almost everyone. First, computers enable us to file documents more systematically and easily. Second, they have changed the world into a global village, in which we are all neighbors. Moreover, in a few seconds on the Internet, we can gain access to the latest information on what's happening all over the world. Indeed, computers have changed our lives for the better. Of course a computer can be foolishly used to waste time. It is up to us to make sure that we use the computer wisely.

As a high school student, I have a computer of my own. I often use it to create reports and PowerPoint projects. In my leisure time, I like to surf the Internet or play computer games to relieve my mental and physical stress. Furthermore, I use the Internet to communicate easily with people in different parts of the world. Above all, with the Internet, I am able to know what's happening at home and abroad without having to be there in person. All I have to do is just click my mouse. In many ways, my computer improves the quality of my life.

1 寫作指導

第一段	第一句點出電腦的優點，接著舉出支持的論點。 ✓ **主題句** 電腦是如此的實用及普及，以致於它幾乎對每個人都愈來愈重要。 ✓ **次要句** 列舉出電腦的優點： 1) 首先，電腦使我們整理文件時更有系統、更容易。 2) 第二，它把這個世界變成地球村，在其中的我們都成為鄰居。 3) 此外，藉由網際網路，我們可以在幾秒鐘內輕易取得世界各地的最新訊息。 ✓ **結　論** 電腦的確使我們的生活更美好。當然，電腦也會讓我們虛度光陰。使用電腦的決定權在我們身上，我們必須善用電腦。
第二段	舉例說明我對電腦的看法。 身為一個高中生，我有一台屬於自己的電腦。 ◆ 我常用電腦來打報告及製作 PowerPoint。 ◆ 有空的時候，我喜歡上網或玩電腦遊戲來放鬆一下身心。 ◆ 除此之外，我可以利用網際網路輕易地和世界各地的人交談。 ◆ 最重要的是，因為網際網路，我可以不用親自到現場就得知海內外發生的事。我所需要做的只是按一按滑鼠。
結論	在很多方面，電腦提高了我的生活品質。

2 重要單字

1	**widespread** ['waɪd͵sprɛd]	(a.) 普遍的；廣泛的 The president's opinion on that issue has received **widespread** support. 總統對那項議題的看法，獲得了廣大的支持。
2	**enable** [ɪn'ebl̩]	(v.) 使能夠；使成為可能 The Internet **enables** you to know what's happening at home and abroad without going out of your home. 網路能讓你不出門便知天下事。
3	**file** [faɪl]	(v.) 歸檔 Dina **filed** those reports in chronological order. 蒂娜按時間前後將這些報告歸檔。
4	**access** ['æksɛs]	(n.) 途徑；進入的權利 The store supervisor has complete **access** to the store files. 店長有完全的權限可以進入店的所有檔案。
5	**surf** [sɝf]	(v.) 上網瀏覽 Tom spends a lot of time **surfing** the Internet every day. 湯姆每天都會花很多時間瀏覽網頁。

3 重要句子及片語

1 **Computers are so useful and widespread that they are becoming more and more important to us.**
電腦好用又普遍，對人們來說愈來愈重要了。

1) 「so + 形容詞 + that + 子句」（如此……，以致於……）：
   so 為副詞，後面要接形容詞或副詞。另一個類似的用法是「such + a/an +（形容詞）+ 名詞 + that + 子句」，such 為形容詞，後面要接名詞。
2) 「比較級 + and + 比較級」，來表示「愈來愈……」。如，「hotter and hotter」（愈來愈熱）；若是多音節的字，則要用「more and more + 原級形容詞」來表示，例如「more and more interesting」（愈來愈有趣）。

2 **Computers enable us to file documents more systematically and easily.**
電腦使我們能夠更有系統且便利地歸檔文件。

enable 的用法是通常先接「人」再接「to + 原形動詞」，即「enable sb. to 原形動詞」。

3 **They have changed the world into a global village, in which we are all neighbors.**
它們使這個世界變成一個地球村，人們彼此變得天涯若比鄰。

句中的 which 指的 global village；原句為「They have changed the world into a global village. We are all neighbors in the global village.」這個複合句裡用了非限定形容詞子句（in which we are . . .）。非限定形容詞子句可以從句子裡刪除，而不改變句子的基本意思。非限定形容詞子句不是用來確認「人物、地方、事物」的身分，而是對「人物、地方、事物」提供額外的說明資訊。這句複合句的基本意思是「They have changed the world into a global village.」，非限定形容詞「in which we are all neighbors」從句子裡刪除後，不會改變句子的基本意思。

4 **In a few seconds on the Internet, we can gain access to the latest information on what's happening all over the world.**
在網路上，用幾秒鐘的時間就可以獲得全世界最新的消息。

1) access 這個字通常和 have 或 gain 連用，即「have access to」或「gain access to」，意思是指「輕易取得」。

	2)「in a few seconds」（在幾秒鐘內）也可用「within a few seconds」。在這個句子裡為了強調輕易取得的「快速」，所以把「in a few seconds」放在句首，否則「in a few seconds」也可以放在句尾。 3)「最新消息」要用「latest information」，而不是用 newest information。latest 是指時間上的晚（最新的、最近的），newest 則是指某物是最新的，如 the newest Prada bag（最新的 Prada 包）。另外一個也容易搞混的字是 last，last 指的是順序上的晚。
5	**Indeed, computers have changed our lives for the better.** 的確，電腦改善了人們的生活。 「change + sth. + for the better」（使⋯⋯更完善）
6	**It is up to us to make sure that we use the computer wisely.** 要確保能否善用電腦，取決於我們自己。 「It's up to + sb.」意思是「取決於某人」或「由某人決定的」。
7	**Above all, with the Internet, I am able to know what's happening at home and abroad without having to be there in person.** 最重要的是，透過電腦能不出門便知天下事。 1)「可以」、「能夠」除了用 can 以外，還可用「be able to」。在寫作時用字要多元，才不會顯得單調。 2)「at home and abroad」（海內外）就是指「全世界」，也可以用： 　・all over the world 　・in every corner of the planet 3) without 為介系詞，故後面的動詞要用動名詞（V-ing）或名詞；without 可以放句首也可以放句尾。 4)「in person」（親自）
8	**All I have to do is just click my mouse.** 我唯一需要做的，就是按我的滑鼠。 1) 原句為「All that I have to do is just（to）click my mouse.」關係代名詞 that 引導一個形容詞子句修飾先行詞 all；形容詞子句是一個完整的子句（I have to do），that 只起引導子句的作用，可以省略。此句也可寫成「What I have to do is just click my mouse.」。 2) click 的意思原指「發出喀啦聲」；但因 click 這個字的發音本身就像按滑鼠時會發出的聲音，所以「按」滑鼠就用 click。

4 Exercise

A 句子填空

1. 電腦好用又普遍，對人們來說愈來愈重要了。

    Computers are so useful and w_____ that they are becoming _____ and _____ important to us.

2. 電腦使我們能夠更有系統且便利地歸檔文件。

    1) First, computers e_____ us to _____ documents more s_____ and easily.

    2) First of all, computers help us a_____ documents more s_____ and easily.

3. 再者，電腦使這個世界變成一個地球村，人們彼此變得天涯若比鄰。

    Second, computers have c_____ the world _____ a global village, in _____ we are all neighbors.

4. 在網路上，用幾秒鐘的時間就可以獲得全世界最新的消息。

    1) Moreover, in a few seconds on the Internet, we can g_____ a_____ t_____ the l_____ information on what's happening all over the world.

    2) Furthermore, _____ a few seconds on the Internet, we are i_____ of what is happening all over the world.

5. 的確，電腦改善了人們的生活。

    Indeed, computers have c_____ our lives for the _____.

6. 要確保能否善用電腦，取決於我們自己。

    It is u_____ _____ us to make sure that we use the computer w_____.

7. 有空的時候，我喜歡上網或玩電腦遊戲來放鬆一下身心。

   1) I also like to _____ the Internet or play computer games in my leisure time to r_____ my _____ and physical stress.

   2) In my leisure time, I r_____ my _____ and physical stress by _____ the Internet or _____ computer games.

8. 除此之外，我可以利用網際網路很輕易地和世界各地的人交談。

   1) Furthermore, I use the Internet to c_____ e_____ with people in different parts of the world.

9. 最重要的是，透過電腦能不出門便知天下事。

   Above _____, with the Internet, I _____ able to know what's happening at _____ and _____ without _____ to be there in _____.

10. 我唯一需要做的，就是按我的滑鼠。

    All I h_____ to do is just _____ my mouse.

B 中譯英練習

1. 一些學生沉溺於網路世界，看些沒有意義的網站，以致於荒廢了功課。

2. 有些色情或暴力的網站會對學生產生不良的影響。（色情的：pornographic）

3. 長時間使用電腦使人容易得近視眼。

4. 電腦使我獲益良多，因為它不僅提供我資訊也提供我知識。

5. 電腦對我們愈來愈重要，也真的很方便，但我們應該避免太依賴它。

6. 很多人直接或間接地被電腦控制著。

7. 就像銅板有兩面，電腦有優點也有缺點，端看你如何使用它。

8. 如果我們謹慎使用電腦，我們就不會成為電腦的受害者。（成為……的受害者：fall victim to . . .）

9. 我必須善用電腦而不是被它牽著鼻子走。

10. 我必須承認電腦已佔據了我太多的時間。

C 作文範例架構練習

說明	1. 依提示在「答案卷」上寫一篇英文作文。 2. 文長約 150 單詞（**words**）左右。
提示	電腦在當今社會的方便性及快速普及，使得我們的生活產生了巨大改變。尤其在網際網路的推波助瀾下，它已經不是一台冷冰冰的機器，而成為每個人生活中不可或缺的一部分。以「Computers」為題，寫一篇英文作文。文分兩段，第一段描述電腦的優點或缺點；第二段以自身為例，說明你對電腦的看法。

★ Brainstorming（可根據以下的句子，來幫助你完成文章）

1. What are the merits and demerits of computers?
2. Do you think its merits outweigh the demerits? Why or why not?
3. How do you use computers in your daily life?
4. How many hours a day do you spend on computers?
5. Do you think computers are wiser than human brains?
6. Are you controlled by computers?
7. Do computers have any influence on you? What are the influences?
8. Do you think our life has changed for the better because of computers? Why or why not?

7 座右銘

說明	1. 依提示在「答案卷」上寫一篇英文作文。 2. 文長約 150 單詞（words）左右。
提示	一句座右銘或影響深遠的話如同良師益友班指引著我們。想想看影響你最深的一句座右銘或話語是什麼？請寫一篇 150 個單字左右的英文作文，文分兩段，第一段以「The words that have the greatest influence on me are . . .」為起始句並加以發展；第二段則以「I have a personal experience to prove it.」為主題句闡述你的難忘經驗。

英文範文

　　The proverb that has the greatest influence on me is "Where there is a will, there is a way." Whenever I encounter problems or feel down, these words always encourage me and inspire me as well. They keep urging me to move on and make one more try. Most importantly, they help me through the tough times in my life.

　　I have a personal experience to prove it. Once I took part in a piano contest. Unfortunately, I was kicked out in the preliminary. I felt frustrated and started to lose my confidence in playing the piano. However, the saying "Where there is a will, there is a way." occurred to me. Then I decided that I would not give up and I would practice harder and compete again in the contest the following year. In the end, I won second prize, performing better than I had expected. Since then, that proverb has become my motto and my philosophy of life.

1 寫作指導

主旨	影響我最深的一句話是「有志者，事竟成」。
第一段	在開頭點出主題句，之後說明當遇到困難或心情低落時，這句話如何影響、幫助我。 ✓ **主題句**　　影響我最深的一句話是「有志者，事竟成」。 ✓ **次要句**　　說明這句諺語如何影響我 每當我遇到困難或心情低落時，這句話總能鼓勵我，同時也帶給我啟發。它不斷激勵我勇往直前、再試一次。最重要的是，它幫我度過生命中艱難的時期。 ✓ **結　論**　　電腦的確使我們的生活更美好。當然，電腦也會讓我們虛度光陰。使用電腦的決定權在我們身上，我們必須善用電腦。
第二段	利用例子來證明這句諺語對我的影響很大。 ✓ **主題句**　　我有一個親身經驗可證明這句話對我的影響。 ✓ **次要句**　　描述自己的親身經驗 有一次我參加鋼琴比賽。很不幸地，我在初賽時就被淘汰。我覺得好挫折，且開始喪失彈鋼琴的自信。然而，我想到「有志者，事竟成」這句諺語，因此我下定決心不放棄，要更努力練琴，並且隔年要再試一次。最後，我贏得了第二名，表現得比我預期得還要棒。
結論	從那時開始，這句諺語就變成了我的座右銘，同時也是我的人生哲學。

2 重要單字

1	**encounter** [ɪnˋkaʊntɚ]	(v.) 遇到（困難） Brian **encountered** some difficulties in reaching his old schoolmates. 布萊恩在找老同學時碰到了一些困難。
2	**encourage** [ɪnˋkɝɪdʒ]	(v.) 鼓勵 My mother **encourages** me to study abroad after I graduate from college. 媽媽鼓勵我畢業後出國留學。
3	**inspire** [ɪnˋspaɪr]	(v.) 啟發；靈感 The melodious music **inspired** the composer. 這首動人的音樂讓編曲人有了靈感。
4	**urge** [ɝdʒ]	(v.) 激勵；極力主張；力勸 My mother always **urges** me to never say impossible. 我媽要不我可以講「不可能」這三個字。
5	**tough** [tʌf]	(a.) 棘手的 Andy is going through a **tough** time at the moment. 安迪當時過得很辛苦。
6	**motto** [ˋmɑto]	(n.) 座右銘；格言 Judy's **motto** is "nothing ventured, nothing gained." 裘蒂的座右銘是「不入虎穴，焉得虎子」。

3 重要句子及片語

1 **Whenever I encounter problems or feel down, these words always encourage me and inspire me as well.**
每當我遇到困難或是心情沮喪時,這句話總能激勵我、啟發我。
1)「whenever」(每當)為連接詞。可放在句首或句中。
2)「feel down」(沮喪)
3)「as well」(也;同樣地:就是 also 或 too 的意思。)

2 **They keep urging me to move on and make one more try.**
它驅策我勇往直前,繼續努力下去。
1)「keep」(繼續不斷)的後面需接動名詞(V-ing)或名詞。
2)「move on」可以用在具體或抽象的意思上,具體的意思是「前進」、「往前走」,抽象的意思是「勇往直前」。
3) try 在這裡當名詞用,為「嘗試」的意思。
「再試一次」有以下用法:
· make one more try
· have one more try
· give it another try

3 **Most importantly, they help me through the tough times in my life.**
最重要的是,它幫助我度過生命中的艱難時刻。
「help through」(使度過、幫忙完成)的用法是「help + sb. + through + sth.」。
· It was Tim who helped Anna through the divorce.
是提姆幫助安娜走過離婚那段時間的。

4 **Once I took part in a piano contest.**
有一次我參加鋼琴比賽。
1) once 有名詞、連接詞及副詞等詞性,在這裡是副詞「曾經」的意思。
2)「take part in . . .」(參加),後面接要接參加的事件。可以替換成「participate in」。

5	**I felt frustrated and started to lose my confidence in playing the piano.** 我覺得好挫折，且開始喪失彈鋼琴的自信。 1) start 後面可接不定詞（to 原形動詞）或動名詞（V-ing）。 2) confidence (n.) 和 confident (adj.) 的習慣用法要記好： 　・have confidence in sth. 　・be confident of sth.
6	**However, the saying "Where there is a will, there is a way" occurred to me.** 然而，我想起了「有志者，事竟成」這句話。 「sth. + occur to + sb.」（某人想到某事）：這個用法要用事物或者 it 當主詞。在這個句子裡，主詞是「the saying "Where there is a will, there is a way"」。相同用法的字還有 strike。
7	**Then I decided that I would not give up and I would practice harder and compete again in the contest the following year.** 於是我決定不放棄，我要勤加練習，明年再來比賽一次。 1) decide「下定決心」；可以替換成「make up one's mind」或是「determine」。 2) following (adj.)「接著的」意思，所以「the following year」就是指「隔年」。
8	**In the end, I won second prize, performing better than I had expected.** 最後，我贏得了第二名，表現得比我預期中得還要好。 1)「第 X 名」英文通常會說「xxx prize」或「xxx place」，例如第一名為「first prize」或「first place」。 2)「performing better than . . .」這裡為分詞構句，這是附帶狀況的分詞構句，通常可以將它改為由對等連接詞 and 所引導的對等子句。原句為「I won second prize, and I performed better than I had expected.」。

4 Exercise

A 句子填空

1. 每當我遇到困難或是心情沮喪時，這句話總能激勵我、啟發我。

   1) Whenever I e_____ problems or feel d_____, these words always e_____ me and i_____ me as well.

   2) Whenever I e_____ problems or feel d_____, these words always give me e_____ and i_____ as well.

2. 它驅策我勇往直前，繼續努力下去。

   They keep u_____ me to m_____ on and m_____ one more t_____.

3. 最重要的是，它幫助我渡過生命中的艱難時刻。

   Most importantly, they h_____ me _____ the t_____ times in my life.

4. 有一次我參加鋼琴比賽。

   1) _____ I t_____ _____ _____ a piano contest.

   2) I _____ in a piano contest _____.

5. 很不幸地，我在初賽時就被淘汰。

   Unfortunately, I was kicked out in the _____.

6. 我覺得好挫折，且開始喪失彈鋼琴的自信。

   I felt f_____ and started to lose my _____ _____ playing the piano.

7. 然而，我想起了「有志者，事竟成」這句話。

   However, the s_____ "Where there is a will, there is a way" _____ _____ _____.

8. 於是我決定不放棄，我要勤加練習，明年再來比賽一次。

Then I decided that I would not g_____ _____ and I would practice h_____ and c_____ again in the contest the _____ year.

9. 最後，我贏得了第二名，表現得比我預期中得還要好。

In the end, I _____ _____ _____, p_____ better than I _____ expected.

10. 從那時開始，這句諺語就變成了我的座右銘，同時也是我的人生哲學。

Since then, that p_____ has become my _____ and my _____ of life.

B 常見諺語補充

1. As you _____, so shall you _____.（一分耕耘，一分收穫。）

2. Look before you _____.（三思而後行。）

3. _____ makes _____.（熟能生巧。）

4. Where there is a _____, there is a _____.（有志者，事竟成。）

5. _____ speak louder than _____.（行動勝於空談，事實勝於雄辯。）

6. It never rains without _____.（禍不單行。）

7. A _____ in time saves _____.（及時行事，事半功倍。）

8. More _____, less _____.（欲速則不達。）

9. _____ is better than _____.（笑是最好的藥。）

10. _____ waters run _____.（靜水流深；大智若愚。）

C 中譯英練習

1. 我們學校的一些老師傾向用我們的成績好壞來評斷我們。
   （依據：in terms of . . .）

2. 有些朋友可以與我們同甘共苦。（同甘共苦：through thick and thin）

3. 但一些酒肉朋友只會在你順利時出現。（酒肉朋友：fair-weather friends）

4. 我們應該謹慎選擇朋友。那些願意與我們共度難關的人才是我們真正的朋友。記住這句諺語：「患難之交才是真正的朋友」。

5. 每當 Peter 感到沮喪時，他就會打籃球。

6. 俗話說：「天才是九十九分的努力再加上一分的天份。」

7. 很多人期待豐碩的成果，卻往往忽略了背後的努力。

8. 每當我遇到困難時，我就想起媽媽曾經對我說的話，「成功只屬於努力的人」。

9. 那番話不斷地給我鼓舞，也激勵我勇往直前去做我應該做的事。

D 作文範例架構練習

說明	1. 依提示在「答案卷」上寫一篇英文作文。 2. 文長約 150 單詞（words）左右。
提示	一句座右銘或影響深遠的話如同良師益友班指引著我們。想想看影響你最深的一句座右銘或話語是什麼？請寫一篇 150 個單字左右的英文作文，文分兩段，第一段以「The words that have the greatest influence on me are . . .」為起始句並加以發展；第二段則以「I have a personal experience to prove it.」為主題句闡述你的難忘經驗。

★ Brainstorming（可根據以下的句子，來幫助你完成文章）

1. What saying influences you the most?
2. Explain the meaning of the saying.
3. How has the saying influenced you?
4. How has the saying made you different?
5. Do you have any personal experience that illustrates its influence on you?

8 給讀者的信

說明	1. 依提示在「答案卷」上寫一篇英文作文。 2. 文長約 150 單詞（words）左右。
提示	妳（Vivian）是 Student Post 裡 Reader's Corner 的主筆，妳的工作主要是回覆讀者的來函或留言。今天妳收到一封 Mike 的來信，信中說他是個嚴肅的人，對於任何事情都很認真地對待，以至於和朋友相處時不會輕易展現笑容，更不用說幽默感了。最近因為好友的一句無心之言，讓他一直放在心上久久不能釋懷，甚至一度想和這位朋友斷絕來往。現在妳要寫一封信給 Mike，告訴他該怎麼做，同時還要告訴他幽默的重要以及可能為他帶來的改變。

英文範文

March 30, 2017

Dear Mike,

  Thank you so much for your email. I know you feel pretty upset about what your friend said. Try to forgive and forget, just let bygones be bygones, and be friends again. Your friend might just have been trying to make a joke, so don't take it seriously. You wouldn't want to be disturbed by those words for the rest of your life, would you?

  On the other hand, it is important to have a good sense of humor that can serve as a kind of lubricant between people. Being humorous is not merely a matter of cracking jokes; more importantly, it is about one's ability to take a joke. Besides, if you are humorous, you can keep not only yourself but also those around you in high spirits, and you will tend to walk on the sunny side of the street. If you manage to maintain your sense of humor, you will be able to dissolve the tensions in your life and feel at ease with the imperfect world we all live in.

  I wish you luck and hope everything is going well with you.

Sincerely,

Vivian

1 寫作指導

主旨	信中應記載事項（參考提示文字的背景說明） 1) 告訴 Mike 該怎麼做 2) 幽默的重要 3) 可能為他帶來的改變
信件開頭	✓ **收信人** Mike ✓ **謝謝對方** 謝謝您的來信。
切入主題	◆ 告訴 Mike 該怎麼做：我明白你對好友說的話一定覺得相當心煩。試著去原諒並遺忘過去的種種不快，以重修舊好吧。你的朋友或許只是在開玩笑，所以別那麼在意。你可不希望下半輩子都被這一番話弄得心神不寧，是吧？ ◆ 幽默的重要：另一方面，具備良好的幽默感是很重要的，幽默是人與人之間的潤滑劑。幽默並非只是開玩笑而已，最重要的是，要能禁得起別人開的玩笑。 ◆ 可能為他帶來的改變：此外，如果你很幽默，你便能使自己及週遭的人都保持好心情，而且也會以樂觀的態度來看待事物。如果你試著維持幽默感，你將能化解生活上的緊張情況，且能在我們這不盡完美的世界中怡然自得。
信件結尾	**祝福對方** 祝你好運，希望你一切安好。

2 重要單字

1	**upset** [ʌpˋsɛt]	(a.) 心煩的 George was pretty **upset** to hear that his one-week vacation was cancelled. 聽到一星期的假期被取消，讓喬治很生氣。
2	**disturb** [dɪsˋtɝb]	(v.) 使心神不寧 The biggest problem that **disturbed** me in senior high school was pimples all over my face. 我高中時最大的困擾，就是我那時候滿臉痘花。
3	**merely** [ˋmɪrlɪ]	(adv.) 僅僅 The medicine **merely** relieves itching; however, it does not cure the skin problem. 這種藥只能夠止癢，沒有治療皮膚病的藥效。
4	**crack** [kræk]	(v.) 說（笑話） James is always **cracking** jokes and sometimes makes fun of himself. 詹姆士很愛說笑話，有時也會消遣一下自己。
5	**dissolve** [dɪˋzɑlv]	(v.) 化解 The tension in the meeting room just **dissolved** when the boss came in. 老闆走進來之後，會議室的緊張氣氛就消失了。

403

3 重要句子及片語

1	**Try to forgive and forget, just let bygones be bygones, and be friends again.** 要學習寬恕與遺忘，過去的就讓它過去，重修舊好吧。 這個句子有幾個常用的說法，要記下來。 ・forgive and forget 不念舊惡 ・Let bygones be bygones. 既往不咎。 ・bygones (n.) 往事；往昔恩怨
2	**Your friend might just have been trying to make a joke, so don't take it seriously.** 你的朋友可能只是想開個玩笑罷了，所以別那麼在意。 1) joke 通常和 make、tell 或 crack 連用來指「開玩笑」： 　・make a joke 　・tell a joke 　・crack a joke 2)「take sth. seriously」指「當真」，這個片語的用法是把所認真看待的「某事」放在 take 和 seriously 中間。
3	**On the other hand, it is important to have a good sense of humor that can serve as a kind of lubricant between people.** 另一方面，具備良好的幽默感是很重要的，幽默是人與人之間的潤滑劑。 1)「on the other hand」（另一方面） 2)「It is important to + 原形動詞」（很重要的是……）： 　在這個句型裡，真正的主詞是「to + 原形動詞」，而 It 是虛主詞。因為「to + 原形動詞」這個主詞太長（亦即 To have a good sense of humor that can serve as a kind of lubricant between people is important.），因此我們常借用 it 來當虛主詞。 3)「a sense of humor」（幽默感）

4	**Being humorous is not merely a matter of cracking jokes; more importantly, it is about one's ability to take a joke.** 幽默感並非只是說說笑話而已，更重要的是，那是一種禁得起玩笑的能力。 1) 以不定詞或動名詞作主詞時，一般視為單數，要用單數動詞。所以這個句子裡用動名詞（Being）當主詞，故要用單數動詞（is）。 2)「take a joke」（禁得起別人開的玩笑）
5	**If you are humorous, you can keep not only yourself but also those around you in high spirits, and you will tend to walk on the sunny side of the street.** 此外，你要是能具有幽默感，你便能使自己及週遭的人都保持好心情，而且也會以樂觀的態度來看待事物。 1)「tend to」（有……的傾向），後面常接原形動詞。 2)「walk on the sunny side of the street」指「以樂觀的態度來看待事物」，可以替換成「look on the bright side of things」。
6	**If you manage to maintain your sense of humor, you will be able to dissolve the tensions in your life and feel at ease with the imperfect world we all live in.** 你只要盡量保持你的幽默感，就能夠化解生活中的緊張關係，並且對我們所居住的這個不完美的世界，感到安心自在。 1)「manage to」（試著；設法做到）：後面常接原形動詞。 2)「at ease」（安心；自在） 3)「we all live in」為形容詞子句，省略了關係代名詞 which/that。原句為「you will be able to dissolve the tensions in your life and feel at ease with the imperfect world. We all live in an imperfect world.」。

4 Exercise

A 句子填空

1. 要學習寬恕與遺忘，過去的就讓它過去，重修舊好吧。

   Try to _____ and _____, just let _____ be _____, and be friends again.

2. 你的朋友可能只是想開個玩笑罷了，所以別那麼在意。

   Your friend might just have been trying to _____ a joke, so don't _____ it _____.

3. 你可不希望下半輩子都被這一番話弄得心神不寧，是吧？

   You wouldn't want to be d_____ by those words for the _____ of your life, _____ you?

4. 另一方面，具備良好的幽默感是很重要的，幽默是人與人之間的潤滑劑。

   On the other _____, it is important to have a good _____ of _____ that can serve _____ a kind of _____ between people.

5. 幽默感並非只是說說笑話而已，更重要的是，那是一種禁得起玩笑的能力。

   Being humorous is not merely a matter of _____ jokes; more importantly, it is about one's ability to _____ a joke.

6. 此外，你要是能具有幽默感，你便能使自己及週遭的人都保持好心情，而且也會以樂觀的態度來看待事物。

   1) Besides, if you are _____, you can keep not only yourself but also those around you in high _____, and you will t_____ to walk on the s_____ side of the street.

   2) In addition, if you have a sense of _____, you will make not only yourself but also those around you h_____, and you will t_____ to look on the b_____ side of things.

B 中譯英練習

1. 如果每個人都有幽默感，我們的社會將會更和諧。

2. 一個具有幽默感的人會帶給他人歡樂。

3. 樂觀的人總是看事情的光明面，且能透徹的觀察人生。

4. 別把人生看得太嚴肅。

5. 當你笑，全世界也跟著你一起笑。當你哭，你就獨自哭。

6. 我們要試著去看人生中有趣的一面，而不是活在單調而黑暗的世界。
   （單調：monotony；黑暗：gloom）

7. 做一個樂觀的人，在你周圍的人也會樂於和你做朋友。

8. 有一句英文俗語是：「笑是最好的藥物。」

9. 如果我們能笑自己的錯誤和恐懼，我們就能擺脫許多煩惱了。

C 作文範例架構練習

說明	1. 依提示在「答案卷」上寫一篇英文作文。 2. 文長約 150 單詞（words）左右。
提示	妳（Vivian）是 Student Post 裡 Reader's Corner 的主筆，妳的工作主要是回覆讀者的來函或留言。今天妳收到一封 Mike 的來信，信中說他是個嚴肅的人，對於任何事情都很認真地對待，以至於和朋友相處時不會輕易展現笑容，更不用說幽默感了。最近因為好友的一句無心之言，讓他一直放在心上久久不能釋懷，甚至一度想和這位朋友斷絕來往。現在妳要寫一封信給 Mike，告訴他該怎麼做，同時還要告訴他幽默的重要以及可能為他帶來的改變。

★ Brainstorming（可根據以下的句子，來幫助你完成文章）

1. 信中應記載事項：
   1）告訴 Mike 該怎麼做
   2）幽默的重要
   3）可能為他帶來的改變

2. What will you do if your good friend says something that makes you uncomfortable?

3. Why is it important to be humorous?

4. What would the world be like if there were more humorous people?

5. What characteristics do humorous people often have?

6. What will a person be like if he or she lacks a sense of humor?

9 導盲犬

說明	1. 依提示在「答案卷」上寫一篇英文作文。 2. 文長約 150 單詞（words）左右。
提示	請根據以下三張連環圖畫的內容，以「On my way to school this morning.」為起始句，將圖中主角所經歷的事件作一合理的闡述。

英文範文

On my way to school this morning, I noticed a blind man with his guide dog crossing the street and a car driving fast toward them. Without thinking, I rushed forward and pushed the man and the dog aside. They were safe and sound, but I was hit hard and badly injured. Apparently, the driver was speeding and didn't follow the traffic lights. As a result, the car ran into me.

I don't remember what happened after the car hit me and how I got to the hospital. When I woke up, I was lying in the hospital with a fractured leg and slight concussion. Despite my serious injuries, I was still happy to have saved the blind man and his guide dog. It's my belief that giving is more blessed than receiving.

1 寫作指導

主旨	瀏覽圖片，可以歸納出人、事、時、地等相關的故事情節。 **Who:** I, a blind man, a driver, a guide dog **When:** this morning **Where:** on the street; in a hospital **What:** A car was driving toward a blind man and a guide dog. What happened to me? **Why:** Why was I lying in the hospital? **How:** How did I feel?
第一段	利用中文寫作的「起、承、轉、合」作為段落發展的順序。 （起）今天早上在上學的途中，我注意到有一個盲人牽著導盲犬過馬路，而在此同時有一輛轎車高速朝著他們駛去。 （承）我不假思索，立刻衝上前把這位盲人和導盲犬推到一旁。 （轉）他們安然無恙，但我被車猛烈地撞上、身受重傷。 （合）顯然這位司機超速、又不遵守交通號誌。因此，車子就撞上我了。
第二段	利用中文寫作的「起、承、轉、合」作為段落發展的順序。 （起）被車撞後，我不記得發生了什麼事，也不記得我是如何到醫院的。 （承）當我醒來後，我躺在醫院裡，腳骨折且還有輕微的腦震盪。 （轉）儘管傷勢不輕，救了那位盲人和他的導盲犬還是讓我感到開心。 （合）我相信施比受更有福。

2 重要單字

1	**rush** [rʌʃ]	(v.) 衝；趕緊 William **rushed** to the office after getting the call from the manager. 威廉收到經理的來電之後就趕往辦公室了。
2	**speeding** [ˋspidɪŋ]	(n.) 超速行車 Mandy got a ticket for **speeding**. 曼蒂被開了一張超速的紅單。
3	**follow** [ˋfɑlo]	(v.) 遵守 Carefully **follow** the instructions on the bottle when you use it. 按照瓶子上的指示小心操作使用。
4	**despite** [dɪˋspaɪt]	(prep.) 儘管；任憑 Lisa went to school **despite** her illness. 莉莎雖然生病了，但她還是去上學。

3 重要句子及片語

1 **On my way to school this morning, I noticed a blind man with his guide dog crossing the street and a car driving fast toward them.**
今天早上我在上學的途中，看到了一位盲人牽著一隻導盲犬正在過街時，有一輛車子朝他們很快地開過來。

1) 「on one's way to . . .」（在某人去……的途中）。但如果要說「在我回家途中」要用「on my way home」，home 之前不加 to。
2) 「導盲犬」的英文是「guide dog」或「seeing eye dog」。

2 **They were safe and sound, but I was hit hard and badly injured.**
他們安然無恙，但我卻被撞到，而且傷得很嚴重。

1) 「safe and sound」（安然無恙）
2) hard 的形容詞和副詞同形，在這裡為副詞，指「重重地」、「猛烈地」
3) 「badly」（嚴重地）可替換成「severely」或「seriously」。

3 **It's my belief that giving is more blessed than receiving.**
我相信，施比受更有福囉。

「Giving is more blessed than receiving.」（施比受更有福。），這是英文的常用說法，要牢記。

4 Exercise

A 句子填空

1. 今天早上我在上學的途中，看到了一位盲人牽著一隻導盲犬正在過街時，有一輛車子朝他們很快地開過來。

On _____ way _____ school this morning, I noticed a blind man with his _____ dog c_____ the street and a car driving fast toward them.

2. 我不假思索，立刻衝上前把這位盲人和導盲犬推到一旁。

W_____ thinking, I r_____ forward and pushed the man and the dog a_____.

3. 他們安然無恙，但我卻被撞到，而且傷得很嚴重。

They were safe and _____, but I was hit h_____ and _____ i_____.

4. 很顯然地，這位司機超速，又沒有遵守交通號誌。

Apparently, the driver was _____ and didn't f_____ the t_____ lights.

5. 因此，車子就撞上我了。

As a _____, the car ran _____ me.

6. 在被車撞後，我不記得發生了什麼事，也不記得我是如何到達醫院的。

I don't remember what h_____ after the car _____ me and how I _____ to the hospital.

7. 我相信施比受更有福。

It's my belief that _____ is more b_____ than _____.

B 中譯英練習

1. Jack 因任意穿越馬路而被罰。（任意穿越馬路：jaywalk）

2. 農曆年將近，警察已經開始嚴加取締那些酒醉駕車的人。
   （取締：crack down on）

3. 台灣高鐵縮短了台北到高雄時間。（台灣高鐵：Taiwan High Speed Rail）

4. 就方便和效率而言，台灣高鐵使得我們的生活更完美。
   （就……而言：in terms of . . . ; as far as sth. is concerned）

5. 交通安全是攸關生死的事。

6. 行人亂穿越馬路，不走天橋、地下道或斑馬線，很可能會成為交通事故的受害者。

7. 交通當局應嚴加取締違規事件，特別是酒醉駕車、無照駕駛及超速。

8. 交通安全，人人有責。

C 作文範例架構練習

說明	1. 依提示在「答案卷」上寫一篇英文作文。 2. 文長約 150 單詞（words）左右。
提示	請根據以下三張連環圖畫的內容，以「On my way to school this morning.」為起始句，將圖中主角所經歷的事件作一合理的闡述。

★ Brainstorming（把圖中所看到及你想到東西先寫下來，以幫助自己寫出段落）

Picture 1 | on the street
A blind man and a guide dog were crossing the street.
A car was driving fast toward them.

Picture 2 | I saved the man and the guide dog.
hit by the car
hurt

Picture 3 | in the hospital
seriously injured
broken leg
glad to save them

10 流浪狗

說明	1. 依提示在「答案卷」上寫一篇英文作文。 2. 文長約 150 單詞（words）左右。
提示	在台灣，相信大家對流浪狗在街道上徘徊的景象一點都不陌生。流浪狗的問題可以說是人們對於生命不尊重的一種殘酷現實。請寫一篇英文作文，文分兩段，第一段請以你的觀點，說明妳認為造成當前流浪狗問題的原因為何；第二段請從「尊重彼此、關懷生命」的角度，提出可能改進此一社會問題的想法或法案。

英文範文

  In Taiwan, almost everyone is familiar with the sight of stray dogs wandering around the streets and licking leftovers. It is the irresponsible attitude of some of the pet owners that leads to the problem of homeless animals. Some pet owners treat their pets as a kind of fashion which they can show off in front of others, and when the fashion changes, they abandon their pets. What's worse, some pets are abused because they are treated as toys not living creatures.

  There are several things that can be done about this problem of homeless dogs. First of all, the government should set up more animal shelters to accommodate the existing stray dogs. In addition, we should appeal to the public to face the problem, promote the concept of respecting other life forms, and understand the interrelationship of all living things. Most importantly, we need to educate the pet owners to be responsible and take good care of their dogs. In this way, the problem of homeless animals can be resolved.

1 寫作指導

第一段	闡述主題句：參考提示裡的文字內容，點出主題句。 在台灣，大家對流浪狗在街道上徘徊、舔剩飯剩菜的景象一點都不陌生。這是飼主對寵物不負責任的態度造成流浪狗的問題。 ✓ **發展支持主題句的說明** 　　一些飼主把他們的寵物視為流行的事物，可以在別人面前炫耀一番，而當這個流行退去時，他們就把寵物給丟棄。更糟糕的是，有些寵物被飼主嚴重地虐待，因為他們把寵物視為玩具、而非有生命的生物。
第二段	有好幾個方法可以解決流浪狗的問題。 ✓ **支持主題句的說明：條列可以解決流浪狗問題的方法** 　　首先，政府應當興建更多流浪動物之家，來收容現有的流浪狗。 　　此外，我們必須呼籲大眾正視流浪狗的問題，提倡尊重各重生命的觀念，及了解所有生物的相互關係。 　　最重要的是，我們要教育飼主對狗狗負責任、且好好照顧牠們。 ✓ **結論** 　　如此一來，流浪狗的問題就可以解決了。

2 重要單字

#	單字	說明
1	**wander** [ˈwɑndɚ]	(v.) 漫遊；閒逛 Zoe and her friends spent the whole day wandering around the downtown area. 柔依和她朋友花了一整天在市區裡逛街。
2	**irresponsible** [ˌɪrɪˈspɑnsəbl̩]	(a.) 不負責任的 It is irresponsible to abandon pets. 棄養寵物是很不負責任的行為。
3	**treat** [trit]	(v.) 對待；看待 It is wrong to treat animals as if they were not living things. 不把動物當成生命來對待，是錯誤的。
4	**abandon** [əˈbændən]	(v.) 丟棄；拋棄 The old man's car was found abandoned next to Deer Lake. 那位老人的車子被發現棄置在鹿湖旁。
5	**abuse** [əˈbjuz]	(v.) 虐待 Several of the children in my class have been physically abused. 我班上有幾個小孩遭到身體虐待。
6	**accommodate** [əˈkɑməˌdet]	(v.) 提供膳宿 International students are accommodated on campus. 國際學生被安排住宿在校園裡。
7	**promote** [prəˈmot]	(v.) 提倡；促進；發揚 For a long time, the president of our company has promoted the concept of maintaining a balance between work and play. 許久一段時間以來，我們公司的總裁就提倡工作和休閒要並重。

3 重要句子及片語

1 **In Taiwan, almost everyone is familiar with the sight of stray dogs wandering around the streets and licking leftovers.**

在台灣，大家對流浪狗在街道上徘徊、舔剩飯剩菜的景象一點都不陌生。

1) 「stray dogs」（流浪狗）可以替換成「homeless dogs」。

2) 這個句子裡使用了附帶狀態的分詞構句，用來附加說明主要子句，通常可以將它改為由對等連接詞 and 所引導的對等子句。因此這一句可寫成「In Taiwan, almost everyone is familiar with the sight of stray dogs, and they (the stray dogs) wander around the streets and lick leftovers.」

2 **It is the irresponsible attitude of some of the pet owners that leads to the problem of homeless animals.**

是飼主對寵物不負責任的態度造成了流浪狗的問題。

1) 「It is + N. + that + V.」：這是加強語氣的用法，強調名詞的部分（即 the irresponsible attitude of some of the pet owners）。

2) that 後面的動詞要和 it is 後面的名詞一致，這裡 it is 後面的名詞是單數 attitude，that 後面的動詞要用單數 leads。

3) 此句也可寫成「The irresponsible attitude of some of the pet owners leads to the problem of homeless animals.」這個句型是強調用法，如「It is you that are to blame.」強調 you，that 指代先行詞 you，也可以用 who 指代先行詞 you（It is you who are to blame.）

4) 「lead to」（造成）可以替換成「result in」。

3 **Some pet owners treat their pets as a kind of fashion which they can show off in front of others, and when the fashion changes, they abandon their pets.**

一些飼主把他們的寵物視為流行的事物，可以在別人面前炫耀一番，而當這個流行退去時，他們就把寵物給丟棄。

1) 這句也可以改寫成：Some pet owners treat their pets as a kind of fashion. They enjoy showing off their fashionable dogs in front of others.

2) 「show off」（炫耀）

4	**First of all, the government should set up more animal shelters to accommodate the existing stray dogs.** 首先,政府應當興建更多流浪動物之家,來收容現有的流浪狗。 1) set up 就是 build,「建立」的意思。 2)「animal shelter」(流浪動物之家)
5	**In addition, we should appeal to the public to face the problem, promote the concept of respecting other life forms, and understand the interrelationship of all living things.** 此外,我們必須呼籲大眾正視流浪狗的問題,提倡尊重各種生命的觀念,並了解所有生物的相互關係。 1)「appeal to sb. + to + 原形動詞」(呼籲某人做⋯⋯),後面通常先接呼籲的「人」,再接呼籲的「事」,若此事為動詞則要用「to + 原形動詞」的形式,若為名詞則要用「for + 名詞」。可以替換成 call on。 2) face 在這裡為及物動詞「正視」的意思。
6	**In this way, the problem of homeless animals can be resolved.** 如此一來,流浪狗的問題就可以解決了。 中文的「如此一來」、「藉此」,英文可以用「in this way」、「by doing so」或「thus」,通常放在句首,且後面要接逗號。

4　Exercise

A 句子填空

1 在台灣，大家對流浪狗在街道上徘徊、舔剩飯剩菜的景象一點都不陌生。

　1) In Taiwan, almost everyone is familiar _____ the _____ of stray dogs w_____ around the streets and _____ leftovers.

　2) In Taiwan, the s_____ of stray dogs w_____ around the streets and _____ leftovers is familiar _____ everyone.

2 這是飼主對寵物不負責任的態度造成了流浪狗的問題。

It is the _____ attitude of some of the pet owners that _____ to the problem of _____ animals.

3 一些飼主把他們的寵物視為流行的事物，可以在別人面前炫耀一番，而當這個流行退去時，他們就把寵物給丟棄。

Some pet owners t_____ their pets as a kind of fashion which they can s_____ _____ in front of others, and when the fashion _____, they a_____ their pets.

4 更糟糕的是，有些寵物被飼主嚴重地虐待，因為他們把寵物視為玩具而非有生命的生物。

What's worse, some pets are a_____ because they are treated as _____ not _____ c_____.

5 首先，政府應當興建更多流浪動物之家，來收容現有的流浪狗。

First of all, the government should s_____ _____ more animal _____ to a_____ the e_____ stray dogs.

6 此外，我們必須呼籲大眾正視流浪狗的問題，提倡尊重各種生命的觀念，並了解所有生物的相互關係。

In addition, we should a_____ to the public to f_____ the problem, p_____ the concept of r_____ other life forms, and understand the i_____ of all living things.

B 中譯英練習

題組 A

1. 有一天在回家的路上,我遇到一個外國人向我問路。

2. 由於我太緊張了,導致我的腦筋一片空白。

3. 我用一些簡單的英文單字及肢體語言告訴他如何抵達目的地。

4. 由於這個經驗,我克服了在學習英語上的一些心理障礙。

題組 B

5. 如果我是個英語老師,我會盡量使課程活潑。

6. 我會設法讓學生對英文產生興趣。

7. 我會對學生強調要在短時間內精通英文是不可能的,而且學英文並不容易。

8. 我會告訴學生,要精通英文(English proficiency),關鍵(key)是要大量閱讀和收聽英文。

C 作文範例架構練習

說明	1. 依提示在「答案卷」上寫一篇英文作文。 2. 文長約 150 單詞（**words**）左右。
提示	在台灣，相信大家對流浪狗在街道上徘徊的景象一點都不陌生。流浪狗的問題可以說是人們對於生命不尊重的一種殘酷現實。請寫一篇英文作文，文分兩段，第一段請以你的觀點，說明妳認為造成當前流浪狗問題的原因為何；第二段請從「尊重彼此、關懷生命」的角度，提出可能改進此一社會問題的想法或法案。

★ Brainstorming（可根據以下的句子，來幫助你完成文章）

1. Why is the problem of stray dogs serious in Taiwan?

2. What are some of the attitudes of the dog owners toward their animals?

3. Why are the animals abandoned?

4. In order to resolve the problem of homeless dogs, what should the pet owners do and what concepts should be promoted?

5. How should we respect other life forms?

ANSWER KEY

PART 1-5

Quiz 1 ········· PAGE 60

1. My friends and I took a trip to Japan last month.
2. It rained heavily in Japan at that time.
3. Jimmy is a senior high school student.
4. We feel excited in our English class.
5. She took the medicine four times a day.
6. Andrew loves bread very much.
7. Kenny bought Lynn a ring.
8. Cliff also sent Barbie a postcard.
9. We considered Levy a powerful leader.
10. The news made us sad.

Quiz 2 ········· PAGE 61

1. My best friend is my classmate.（句型 4）
2. Her name is Karen.（句型 4）
3. Karen likes to exercise.（句型 2）
4. She is also the prettiest woman in my class.（句型 4）
5. One day she came to my house.（句型 1）

6. My brother saw her. （句型 2）

7. He was very interested in her. （句型 4）

8. My brother asked me who my friend was. （句型 3）

9. I didn't want to tell him her name. （句型 2+3）

10. My brother directly asked my friend her name. （句型 3）

11. Immediately, he invited her to attend the school party. （句型 5+2）

12. I was very angry. （句型 4）

Quiz 3 .... PAGE 74

1. Both Ashley and May like to collect stamps.

2. Not only Trent but also his friends enjoyed the movie.

3. Grandmother can't read the newspaper without wearing glasses.
   (*or* Grandmother can't read the newspaper without glasses.)

4. His umbrella is different from mine. (*or* His umbrella is different from my umbrella.)

5. The coffee is too hot (for me) to drink.

6. Joy goes to school by bicycle.

7. Joseph is such a nice person that he has many friends.

8. Jenny used to go to school by bicycle when she was a junior high school student.

9. Alexander has trouble (in) doing his English homework.

10. The book is neither interesting nor instructive.

Quiz 4 .... PAGE 84

1. The sun always sets in the west.

2. Jimmy walks to school every day.

3. Katherine is playing the violin now.

4. Walter went to the USA last year.

5. Larry will go to the baseball game tomorrow.
   (*or* Larry is going to (go to) the baseball game tomorrow.)

6. Maria has lived in Taiwan since she was ten.

7. I have been to Japan many times.

8. They swam in the river last Friday.

9. We ate some seafood last night.

10. We will visit/are going to visit our friends in Taipei next Sunday.

Quiz 5 ·· PAGE 85

1. is 2. am 3. have been working 4. was

5. was working（在過去的特定時間中強調動作的進行）/ worked（陳述過去情況）

6. quit（過去式，quit 三態同型） 7. had witnessed 8. was

9. am working/work 10. have been waiting 11. will have 12. don't know

13. am going to become/will become 14. will have made

15. will be traveling/will travel 16. will live

Quiz 6 ·· PAGE 91

A

1. Angus never breaks his promise.

2. Luke didn't come to Taipei last week.

3. Max won't stay in Taipei for two weeks.

4. Josephine cannot speak Chinese.

5. They have little snow in winter.

B

1. Frank isn't/is not a junior high school student.

2. He doesn't/does not walk to school every day.

3. He wasn't/was not chased by a dog on his way to school this morning.

4. He hasn't/has not studied English for three years.

5. He won't/will not be on vacation in Australia with his family next summer.

Quiz 7 .... PAGE 96

A

1. Can Sharon play the piano well?

2. Will she be a pianist in the future?

3. Did they eat at the restaurant last night?

4. Does she walk to school every day?

5. Is my umbrella different from yours?

B

1. Anna keeps an English diary every day, doesn't she?

2. They didn't play basketball yesterday, did they?

3. Don't you like to play basketball? (*or* Do you not like to play basketball?)

4. Didn't they have a good time? (*or* Did they not have a good time?)

5. What won't you do this summer? (*or* What will you not do this summer?)

Quiz 8 .... PAGE 101

1. When did Roger come to Greece?

2. How long will he stay in Greece?

3. How did Sean and his friends go to the Taipei Zoo last Saturday?

4. What time does he usually go to bed?

5. Where did you go last Sunday?

6. Who is that tall boy?

7. Did they go swimming in the river yesterday?

8. Will tomorrow be a fine day?

9. Does William walk to school every day?

10. Can that little boy sing the song?

Quiz 9 .... PAGE 106

1. Where is John?
2. Do you know where John is?
3. The problem is how we are going to arrest him.
4. Tell me where you went last night.
5. Tell me why you didn't do your homework.
6. Do you know how long Lydia will stay in Singapore?
7. Tell me what I should do.
8. I don't know how I can help you.
9. Do you know what Stella likes to do after school?
10. Tell me how you usually go to school.

Quiz 10 .... PAGE 109

1. Tell me where the nearest bank is.
2. Tell me why you were late yesterday.
3. Tell me where you went last Monday.
4. Could you tell me what you usually do in your free time?
5. Tell me why Carrie didn't show up last Sunday.
6. Do you know why Audrey doesn't like Dennis?
7. Do you know how long Jeffery will stay in South Korea?
8. I don't know what I can do to make it better.
9. Do you know whether she will attend Kim's recital (or not) the day after tomorrow?
    (*or* Do you know if she will attend Kim's recital the day after tomorrow?)
10. Tell me whether your parents are satisfied with what you have done (or not).
    (*or* Tell me if your parents are satisfied with what you have done.)

Quiz 11 .... PAGE 116

1. Flora was invited to the seminar by <u>me</u>.

2. My money was <u>stolen</u>.

3. The cake was made by <u>him</u>.

4. The card was written by <u>us</u>.

5. The house was painted by <u>them</u>.

6. The report was <u>written</u> by Mia.

7. My car was <u>fixed</u> by that old man.

8. The roof <u>was repaired</u> last night.

9. The house <u>was built</u> ten years ago.

10. The book <u>was written</u> by my teacher.

Quiz 12 .... PAGE 121

1. The card was put in a drawer by Eileen.

2. The song was sung by Lillian with her beautiful voice.

3. A Christmas card was sent to Steve by her.

4. The novel was written by Lynn's teacher.

5. Jim will be asked for a dance by Juliet.

6. We have been invited to the ball by Nina.

7. Two thousand people were killed by that tsunami wave.

8. The work will have been finished by Monday.

9. Both English and French are spoken by many people in Canada.

10. It is thought that she wants a necklace as her valentine.

Quiz 13 .... PAGE 127

A

1. Please pass me the handout.

2. Please stop making that noise.

3. Don't talk with your mouth full.

4. Let Jacob play volleyball with you.

5. Don't let Glen go fishing alone.

6. Let's not go hiking.

B

1. Get up, and you will see the shooting stars.

2. Get up, or you will miss the fascinating performance.

3. Get started, and you will finish the work ahead of time.

4. Get started, or you cannot finish your work on time.

Quiz 14 ·········· PAGE 129

1. Be quiet, will you?

2. Behave well, will you?

3. Let's talk in English, shall we?

4. Let's not play badminton, OK (/all right)?

5. Don't shout, will you?

Quiz 15 ·········· PAGE 133

1. Be kind to others.

2. Don't be so innocent as to believe his words.

3. Be quiet at the temple.

4. Don't (/Never) smoke in the hospital.

5. Let Janice wash her car once a week.

6. Let us (/Let's) take care of the orphans.

7. Let Steve build a snowman in front of his house.

8. Don't let Arthur (/Let Arthur not) go scuba diving alone.

9. Don't let the baby (/Let the baby not) be so noisy in the theater.

10. Don't let them (/Let them not) go to the Taipei Zoo this weekend.

Quiz 16 .... PAGE 142

A

1. Morris is fat.
2. Sandra is more beautiful than Winnie.
3. Wayne learns faster than Oswald.
4. Tess studies hardest of all the students in her class.
5. He learns most slowly of the three.
6. The red album is older than the black one.
7. This is the latest news from BBC.

B

1. happier   happiest
2. thinner   thinnest
3. better   best

Quiz 17 .... PAGE 147

1. Andrew is as noisy as Donald in English class.
2. Kenneth plays the violin as beautifully as Christina.
3. My father drives not so carelessly as her father.
   (*or* Her father drives not so carefully as my father.)
4. They sang the happy birthday song as loudly as possible.
5. The new book is not so boring as the old book.
   (*or* The old book is not so exciting as the new book.)
6. Leah is taller than Alfred. (Alfred is shorter than Leah.)
7. The red shirt is much cheaper (costs less) than the black one.
   (*or* The black shirt is much more expensive (costs much more) than the red one.)
8. Duncan is the fattest (of the three).
   (*or* Greg is the thinnest (of the three).)
9. English is the most difficult (of the three subjects).)
   (*or* Chinese is the easiest (of the three subjects).)
10. Amanda becomes more and more attractive.

Quiz 18 ········· PAGE 154

A

1. Judy plans to go to the USA and Canada next month.
2. It is nice and warm today, and the birds are chirping.
3. This is not chicken but turkey.
4. The chicken soup is very delicious but too greasy.
5. I am freezing, yet I don't want to put on a thick coat.
6. You must work harder, or you will be fired.
7. Lionel doesn't like cats, nor does Eva.
8. I have neither time nor money for the show.
9. She caught a cold, so she didn't go to school.
10. We must set off early, for it will take three hours to get to the peak.

B

Leonard and Lucy went to Spain <u>and</u> France last summer. They brought their passports, visas, baggage, some traveler's checks<u>, and</u> a camera with them. The scenery was fantastic<u>, so</u> they took a lot of pictures. They also bought some postcards <u>and</u> sent them to their friends and relatives. It was an unforgettable experience<u>, and</u> they will never forget the trip.

Quiz 19 ········· PAGE 167

1. While Evelyn is having breakfast, her husband is still sleeping.
2. Vernon will give you the answer as long as he figures it out.
   (As long as Vernon figures it out, he will give you the answer.)
3. Viola has lived in Italy since she was a little girl.
4. Because the traffic was heavy, Cliff didn't make it to the meeting on time.
   (*or* Cliff didn't make it to the meeting on time because the traffic was heavy.)
5. It was raining hard, so I didn't walk my dog.
6. Barry studied so hard that he passed the exam.
7. It was such a horrible experience that I would never forget.
8. If it rains tomorrow, we won't go on a picnic at the beach.

9. Although Harold is 25 years old, he looks like a middle-aged man.
(*or* Harold looks like a middle-aged man although he is 25 years old.)

10. Before Gilbert hands in the answer sheet, he always checks the answers carefully.
(*or* Gilbert always checks the answers carefully before he hands in the answer sheet.)

Quiz 20 .... PAGE 171

1. That the exhibition has opened makes me happy.

2. It surprises me that they have been to the exhibition.

3. It is clear that people from all over the world enjoy the exhibition.

4. I believe that the fair is entertaining.

5. We are talking about what we should buy at the exhibition.

6. The problem is where to park our car.

7. The thought that we go on foot sounds crazy.

8. Whether we will go shopping or not depends on the weather.

9. I think that the book is helpful.

10. The latest news is that the criminal is still at large.（at large：逍遙法外；在逃。）

Quiz 21 .... PAGE 177

A

1. I am afraid that I can't talk to you now.

2. I told you that Stanley couldn't make it to work today.

3. What we want is your money.

4. Sonia asked Jason if he could do her a favor.

5. I thought that I had made myself understood.

B

1. It depends on the weather whether we will go hiking tomorrow (or not).

2. It is certain that Romeo loves Juliet.

3. I believe (that) the students will benefit a lot from this activity.

10

4. Ask Laura if she can come.

5. It was true that Pamela didn't catch the train this morning.

Quiz 22 ·· PAGE 182

A

1. who/that   **2.** which/that   **3.** whose

4. whom/that   **5.** which/that

B

1. The man who/that is singing the happy birthday song will join the cocktail party.

2. This is the book which/that I borrowed from the school library.

3. He is a writer whose daughter is a friend of mine.

4. They have a cat whose name is Kitty.

5. This is the girl whom/that we met in the bookstore last week.

Quiz 23 ·· PAGE 191

A

1. Judy, who is John's sister, is my good friend.

2. The woman who/that wears a pair of glasses is a teacher.

3. The picture shows a little girl and her pet that are playing in the park.

4. The Olympic Games will take place in Athens, which is the capital of Greece.

5. This is the only program that arouses my interest.

B

1. The movie (which/that) we saw yesterday was very interesting.

2. Anthony, who will go to Australia next summer, is my high school classmate.

3. This is the house (which/that) he lives in. (*or* This is the house in which he lives.) (*or* This is the house where he lives.)

4. The story (which/that) he told me last month seems very exciting.

5. This is the most delicious food (that) I have ever tasted.

11

Quiz 24 .... PAGE 198

1. Rowing in the river, we saw a flock of ducks swimming.
   = While rowing in the river, we saw a flock of ducks swimming.

2. The sun having set, the swallows flew south.

3. (Being) Invited to a barbecue, we had to bring some eating utensils.

4. Having been told many times, Nigel begins to behave well.

5. Sunbathing on the beach, Jim saw a big wave coming.
   = While sunbathing on the beach, Jim saw a big wave coming.

6. Watching TV, Beryl heard a dog barking.
   = While watching TV, Beryl heard a dog barking.

7. Taking a walk, Florence came across her old friend.
   = When taking a walk, Florence came across her old friend.

8. Living far away from the downtown, Frank seldom goes there.

9. Not knowing how to answer the question, I kept silent.

10. Knowing that you wanted to see the movie, she bought a ticket for you.

Quiz 25 .... PAGE 203

A

1. Having read the book, Lois knew how to answer the questions.

2. (If) Not getting up at six, you will miss the flight.

3. (Even though) The shirt being very expensive, I thought it worth buying.

4. (When) The sun rising, the sea sparkles in the sunlight.

5. After saying goodbye to Judith, we went home.

B

1. Being soaked to the skin, Susie still enjoyed the performance very much.

2. After kissing the baby on the forehead, Samantha said good night.

3. Entering the house, Rosalie found that she had forgotten to turn off the light.

4. Having failed the entrance exam, he decided to study harder.

5. Being very exhausted, Virginia lay on the bed.

Quiz 26 ······PAGE 215

1. 2 → 4 → 1 → 3

Quiz 27 ······PAGE 223

1. A, D **2.** A, C

Quiz 28 ······PAGE 235

（參考答案）

My best friend, Fanny, is good at playing the piano. Although it was her first concert tonight, there were many people coming. People enjoyed her music so much that Fanny received bouquets of flowers from them. I think Fanny will become a great pianist in the future.

Quiz 29 ······PAGE 284

1. Tips on preparing for an exam.

2. Some people are afraid of exams.

3. In fact, exams are not as scary as you imagine.

4. There are several steps that can help you prepare for your exam.

5. First, make a study plan which will enable you to review all the materials before the exam.

6. Next, get enough sleep the night before the exam.

7. Staying up studying will only increase your stress and anxiety.

8. On the day of the exam, remember to have breakfast and wear comfortable clothes.

9. Remember to leave home as early as possible to avoid possible traffic jams.

10. Finally, do your best to answer all the questions.

11. If the exam result is not good enough, study harder next time.

Quiz 30 .... PAGE 285

1. My parents bought me a radio when I was 12. Ever since then, it has become my best friend and brought me a lot of happiness. Sometimes I make phone calls to radio stations to answer their interesting questions. Most important of all, it has made my life more fruitful and colorful.

2. Last month I took part in a speech contest for the first time. I was nervous and excited. On that day, I was deeply impressed by the other contestants. I did not win any prizes as I had expected to, but I learned an important lesson: Success comes from hard work.

3. One week ago, my sister and I found a stray dog on the street. It looked so cute and innocent that we decided to take it home. After we got home, Mom told us that keeping a dog was not an easy job. Luckily, Dad said that he could help take care of it. Now, the dog has become a member of our family.

4. Since the beginning of this year, I have been doing volunteer work at a local hospital. I spend one afternoon every week in the hospital helping people. I am busier than before, but I have learned to make the best use of my time. I have also learned to appreciate life and not to take anything for granted.

Quiz 31 .... PAGE 336

1

1. I think it's a good idea to practice English with foreigners.（單數名詞 good idea，前面接冠詞 a；外國人不只一位，所以用複數 foreigners。）

2. When we talk to them in English, we have to forget our own language. （to ＋原形動詞）

3. If you are afraid of talking（介系詞 of ＋ V-ing）to foreigners, you can try to practice English with your classmates and friends that have excellent English. （兩個名詞皆為複數）

4. You can share the happiness of learning English.（happiness 為不可數名詞）

5. The most important thing is to read and listen to English extensively. （is 搭配單數主詞）

2

1. I read an article . . .（沒有 readed 的形式）

2. I asked my father whether he could take some time off . . .（過去式用 asked）

3. Father was a very busy businessman, so I tried to persuade him . . .

4. I was so happy, and I was sure we would have a good time together.
（→此題錯誤皆與時態有關）

3

1. My brother and I encouraged them to go out . . .

2. At first, mother . . . （at first 為連接副詞，不可連接兩個句子）

3. After they left, . . .

4. I hoped they had an unforgettable anniversary.（→此題錯誤多與人稱名詞有關）

Quiz 32 ·· PAGE 337

（參考答案）

1. People always say, "Don't judge a person by his or her appearance." It is a sad fact that appearance is usually the first thing that people will notice. However, appearance should never be the most important thing in choosing a friend. A true friend should not pay attention to your physical beauty but the beauty of your heart. In fact, after a period of time, you will not think about what your friends look like. Instead, you just value the friendship. Therefore, it is wise to make friends with those who can really appreciate who you are, not what you look like.

2. Monday morning I felt sick after waking up. I couldn't speak because of a sore throat. My body temperature was higher than normal. Mother told me to take the day off from school, and then she took me to see a doctor. The doctor said it was only a slight cold and prescribed some medicine. Mother's anxious look made me feel she worried too much. After we returned home, Mom asked me to stay in bed and take the medicine every four hours. She took my temperature every hour to make sure it hadn't gone up again. In the evening, I started feeling better, and Mother finally felt relieved. This day off made me realize that a mother is the greatest blessing a child could have.

3. Many people make New Year's resolutions when saying goodbye to the past year. I am no exception. In the past, I would set LOTS OF goals. As time went by, I forgot my goals and never put them into practice. However, at the end of last year, I promised myself to make only ONE short-term goal. Then I made a monthly plan to review my progress. I have found that if the goal is clear and specific, it will be easier to stay focused and do all I can to achieve it. Now, I am happy to say that I am getting closer to realizing this year's resolution.

PART 6 Exercises

◆ 1 我的嗜好 .... PAGE 345

A

1. 1) is; hobby   2) hobbies; listening   3) hobbies; listening; most/best
2. plays; essential; role/part
3. cultivates; enriches
4. 1) imagine; what; would; without
   2) is; what; would; there; were
5. 1) outlet; relieve; pressures   2) outlet; pressures
6. 1) depending; mood; in   2) on; mood; various
7. 1) would; without   2) were

B

1. We must make the best of our leisure/free/spare time and arrange/plan it well/properly.
2. I am a quiet/an introverted person who enjoys indoor activities, such as collecting stamps or watching movies.
3. Surfing the net/Internet is my favorite pastime.
4. Watching foreign movies/films can help broaden/widen/expand my horizons and knowledge of the world.
5. I am every inch/bit a movie fan, so I like watching movies in/during my spare/leisure/free time.
6. I am an active/extroverted person, so I enjoy outdoor activities, such as going hiking or playing basketball.
7. Playing basketball helps to strengthen/build up my body.

◆ 2 難忘的經驗 .... PAGE 353

A

1. Preparing; for; what
2. honest; least; things; choice/option/alternative; oriented

3. 1) denied; what   2) what; is

4. 1) had; failed/flunked; determined
   2) had; flunked/failed; mind

5. stayed/sat; row; cram

6. time; so; drowsy; doze; as

7. 1) didn't; hand   2) submit; did

8. flunked/failed; make-up

B

1. We are weighed down with a considerable number of/a lot of/numerous tests and exams.

2. Because of the pressure of passing the entrance exam, we are forced to give up some extracurricular activities.

3. After school, I have to go to a cram school in order to catch up with my classmates.

4. My biggest problem in senior high school is that I have pimples all over my face.

5. I have seen numerous doctors, but it has not been cured.

6. I always try to strike a/find the proper balance between studying and playing.

7. When I play, I try not to think about my schoolwork.

8. When I study, I concentrate on what I am reading.

9. Good grades give me a sense of achievement/fulfilment.

10. As a saying goes, "never put off until tomorrow what you can do today." I am trying to cultivate/form/develop the habit of reviewing every day what I have learned in class that day.

◆ 3 寫 Email ·················· PAGE 362

A

1. 1) It; hear   2) nice; hear

2. 1) taken; back   2) delay; replying

3. 1) approaching; pile   2) to; over; pile

4. invitation; pay

5. planned; take; trip

6. 1) which; longed　2) located; looking

7. 1) fly; charm; experience　2) head; called; charm; experience

8. least; sure

9. forward; seeing

B

1. The college entrance exam will soon be over, and I will be free at last.

2. I will spend a week doing nothing, just enjoying some books that I want to read.

3. I will go to the bookstores in my neighborhood and visit some of my friends.

4. I plan a trip to Kenting National Park with my friends to spend a few days relaxing there.

5. I am going to stay in Kenting for at least a week, to enjoy the bright sunshine and vast ocean.

6. I want to learn how to surf and scuba dive.

7. I am going to take a part-time job to earn some pocket money.

8. In the meantime, I will continue to improve my English.

◆ 4 昨天是情人節 ·································· PAGE 371

A

1. 1) significant; for　2) significant; exception

2. 1) spending; put; overtime　2) celebrate; instead; overtime

3. 1) matter; why; willing　2) which; willing　3) work　4) reason; willing

4. 1) exhausted; dozed　2) worn; dozed

5. Charming; showed; blue; invited

6. candlelit/candlelight; swanky; celebrate

7. 1) woke; up　2) awakened; sound

8. 1) dawned; on; had; pile　2) realized; had; pile

B

1. I can amuse myself by reading comic books.

2. My family and I often dine out in the all-you-can-eat buffet restaurant. It is also a great place for me to get together with my friends and catch up on the latest news.

3. Kevin won the lottery, so he was going to treat us to a big meal.

4. I like dinnertime because over a leisurely dinner we can chat about what has happened around us.

5. Ian not only is handsome but also plays the guitar well, so he is an idol for many girls.

6. Once Ian skipped the class and went out with his friends to play pool. After his father found out the truth, Ian was severely disciplined.

◆ 5 母親節要到了 .... PAGE 380

A

1. corner; decided/determined; reward; tireless; entire

2. whole; am

3. laundry; chores; Saturdays

4. devoted; to; deserves

5. arrange; trip; hope; relive

6. 1) of   2) matter; it

B

1. The person I respect (the) most is my mother.
   (*or* My mother is the person that I respect (the) most.)
   (*or* Of all the people I know, my mother is the one I respect the most.)

2. In the eyes of our relatives, she is not only a diligent mother but also a competent career woman.

3. When it comes to cooking, Mother has no equal/rival/match in our neighborhood.

4. I often ask her questions about my studies, and she always teaches me patiently.

5. She also shows great concern for my school life.

6. I am very proud of having such a good mother, and I should learn from her.

7. He is a good father who is also a loving husband, and he takes his responsibilities very seriously.

8. He not only puts his heart and soul into his work but also is very popular among his colleagues.

9. He does some chores after work.

10. My father is stern in appearance but kind at heart.

◆ 6 電腦 ......PAGE 388

A

1. widespread; more; more
2. 1) enable; file; systematically   2) arrange; systematically
3. changed; into; which
4. 1) gain; access; to; latest   2) in/within; informed
5. changed; better
6. up; to; wisely
7. 1) surf; relieve; mental   2) relieve; mental; surfing; playing
8. communicate; easily
9. all; am; home; abroad; having; person
10. have; click

B

1. Some students indulge themselves in the cyberspace, surfing meaningless websites and neglecting their studies.
2. Some pornographic or violent websites have/exert a bad influence on students.
3. Using computers over a long period of time can make people prone to near-sightedness.
4. I benefit enormously from the computer, because it provides me with information as well as knowledge.
5. Although computers are becoming more and more important to us and they are indeed convenient, we should avoid becoming too dependent on them.
6. Many people are directly or indirectly controlled by computers.
7. It is just like two sides of the same coin. Depending on how you use them, computers have merits and demerits.
8. If we use computers wisely, we won't fall victim to computers.
9. I should use computers wisely so as not to be controlled by them.
10. I have to admit that computers take up too much of my time.

◆7 座右銘 ......PAGE 397

A

1. 1) encounter; down; encourage; inspire
   2) encounter; down; encouragement; inspiration
2. urging; move; make; try
3. help; through; tough
4. 1) Once; took; part; in   2) participated; once
5. preliminary
6. frustrated; confidence; in
7. saying; occurred; to; me
8. give; up; harder; compete; following
9. won/got; second; prize; performing; had
10. proverb; motto; philosophy

B

1. sow, reap   2. leap   3. Practice, perfect   4. will, way
5. Actions, words   6. pouring   7. stitch, nine   8. haste, speed
9. Laughter, medicine   10. Still, deep

C

1. Some teachers in our school tend to judge us in terms of our academic performances.
2. Some friends can help us through thick and thin.
3. However, some fair-weather friends only show up when things are going well with you.
4. We should be careful in choosing our friends. Those who are willing to help us when we are in trouble are our real friends. Remember the saying, "Friends in need are friends indeed."
5. Whenever Peter feels down, he plays basketball.
6. As the saying goes, "genius is one percent inspiration and ninety-nine percent perspiration."
7. Many people look forward to a fruitful harvest, but they often neglect the hard work/perspiration behind it.

8. Whenever I encounter/am faced with problems, I think of what my mother once said to me, "Success only belongs to those who work hard."

9. My mother's words are a constant inspiration and also urge me to move on and do what I need to do.

◆ 8 給讀者的信 ································· PAGE 406

A

1. forgive; forget; bygones; bygones

2. make/tell/crack; take; seriously

3. disturbed; rest; would

4. hand; sense; humor; as; lubricant

5. cracking/making/telling; take

6. 1) humorous; spirits; tend; sunny   2) humor; happy; tend; bright

B

1. If everyone has a sense of humor, our society will be more harmonious.

2. People with a sense of humor often bring happiness to others.

3. An optimistic person always walks on the sunny side of the street and observes life with a positive perspective.

4. Don't take life too seriously.

5. Smile, and the world smiles with you. Cry, and you cry alone.

6. We need to try to see the funny side of life instead of living in a world of monotony and gloom.

7. Be an optimist, and people around you will be happy to befriend you.

8. As an English saying goes, "Laughter is the best medicine."

9. If we can laugh at our mistakes and fears, we can get rid of many annoyances.

◆ 9 導盲犬 ...... PAGE 413

A

1. my; to; guide; crossing 2. Without; rushed; aside
3. sound; hard; badly/seriously/severely; injured 4. speeding; follow; traffic
5. result; into 6. happened; hit; got 7. giving; blessed; receiving

B

1. Jack was fined because he jaywalked across the street.
2. Because Lunar New Year is approaching, the police have cracked down on those who drink and drive.
3. Taiwan High Speed Rail has decreased the time it takes to travel between Taipei and Kaohsiung.
4. In terms of convenience and efficiency/As far as convenience and efficiency are concerned, Taiwan High Speed Rail has changed our life for the better.
5. Traffic safety is a matter of life and death.
6. Pedestrians who cross the street anywhere they want and don't walk on the overpass, underpass, or zebra crossing are more likely to fall victim to traffic accidents.
7. The traffic authorities should crack down on traffic violations, in particular, drunk driving, driving without a license, and speeding.
8. Traffic safety is everyone's business/responsibility.

◆ 10 流浪狗 ...... PAGE 421

A

1. 1) with; sight; wandering; licking 2) sight; wandering; licking; to
2. irresponsible; leads; homeless/stray
3. treat; show; off; changes; abandon
4. abused; toys; living; creatures
5. set; up; shelters; accommodate; existing
6. appeal; face; promote; respecting; interrelationship

B

題組 A

1. One day on my way home, I came across/ran into/met a foreigner who asked me directions.

2. I was so nervous that my mind became a complete blank.

3. I used some simple English words and body language to tell him how to get to his destination.

4. Owing to/Because of/Thanks to that experience, I have overcome some psychological obstacles in learning English.

題組 B

5. If I were an English teacher, I would try to keep the class as lively as possible.

6. I would try to arouse my students ?interest in learning English.

7. I would emphasize to my students that it is impossible to master English in a short period of time and it is not easy to learn English.

8. I would tell my students that the key to achieving English proficiency is extensive reading and listening.